Praise for the novels
of Catherine Anderson

"Catherine Anderson has a gift for imbuing her characters with dignity, compassion, courage, and strength that inspire readers." —*Romantic Times*

Coming Up Roses

"An extraordinary novel. Poignant, moving, rich in character, and deeply emotional. A keeper." —*Romantic Times*

Lucky Penny

"Anderson returns to her historical roots with a stirring, beautifully rendered story of the power of family, love, and trust. Her knack for creating real stories turns her books into 'keepers' and her readers into the kind of fans who will eagerly await her next book."

—*Romantic Times* (4½ Stars)

Comanche Magic

"Catherine Anderson is an extraordinary talent. She has a voice that is gritty and tender, realistic and romantic, and always unique." —Elizabeth Lowell

Here to Stay

"Another wonderful, very emotional story of the Harrigan family." —*Romantic Times*

Indigo Blue

"A marvelous, moving, poignant, and sensual love story. . . . Ms. Anderson holds her readers spellbound."

—*Romantic Times*

Early Dawn

"Never stinting on the harsh reality inherent in the setting, the author tempers the roughness with a powerful love story and remarkable characters. She draws out every emotion and leaves readers with a true understanding of life and love." —*Romantic Times*

continued ...

Comanche Heart

"Riveting, passionate, and powerful . . . everything a romance should be."
—Amanda Quick

"Highly sensual and very compelling . . . a truly spectacular read."
—Linda Lael Miller

"I thoroughly enjoyed [it]."
—Karen Robards

Star Bright

"Catherine Anderson brilliantly grabbed my attention right away with a brainy tale of intrigue . . . an emotionally moving and romantic treat that you're sure to enjoy."
—Night Owl Romance (Top Pick)

Morning Light

"This is a story not to be missed. *Morning Light* delivers on all levels, and is a fantastic read that will touch readers at the very core of their being."
—The Romance Readers Connection

Sun Kissed

"This smart, wholesome tale should appeal to any fan of traditional romance."
—*Publishers Weekly*

"Another heartwarming chapter in the Coulter family saga is on tap in the always wonderful Anderson's newest release. . . . Anderson is at her best when it comes to telling stories that are deeply emotional and heartfelt."
—*Romantic Times* (4½ Stars)

Summer Breeze

"Anderson understands the inner workings of the human soul so deeply that she's able to put intense emotion within a stunning romance in such a way that you'll believe in miracles. Add to this her beautiful writing style, memorable characters, and a timeless story and you have an unmatched reading adventure."
—*Romantic Times* (4½ Stars)

"The kind of book that will snare you so completely, you'll not want to put it down. It engages the intellect and emotions; it'll make you care. It will also make you smile . . . a lot. And that's a guarantee."
—Romance Reviews Today

My Sunshine

"With the author's signature nurturing warmth and emotional depth, this beautifully written romance is a richly rewarding experience for any reader."   —*Booklist*

Bright Eyes

"Offbeat family members and genuine familial love give a special lift to this marvelous story. An Anderson book is a guaranteed great read!"

—*Romantic Times* (4½ Stars, Top Pick)

Blue Skies

"Readers may need to wipe away tears . . . since few will be able to resist the power of this beautifully emotional, wonderfully romantic love story."   —*Booklist*

"A keeper and a very strong contender for best contemporary romance of the year."   —Romance Reviews Today

Only by Your Touch

"Ben Longtree is a marvelous hero whose extraordinary gifts bring a unique and special magic to this warmhearted novel. No one can tug your heartstrings better than Catherine Anderson."   —*Romantic Times* (4½ Stars, Top Pick)

Always in My Heart

"Emotionally involving, family centered, and relationship oriented, this story is a rewarding read." —*Library Journal*

"A superbly written contemporary romance, which features just the kind of emotionally nourishing, comfortably compassionate . . . love story this author is known for creating."   —*Booklist*

Sweet Nothings

"Pure reading magic."   —*Booklist*

Phantom Waltz

"Anderson departs from traditional romantic stereotypes in this poignant, contemporary tale of a love that transcends all boundaries . . . romantic through and through."

—*Publishers Weekly*

Catherine Anderson

CHEYENNE AMBER

A SIGNET BOOK

SIGNET
Published by the Penguin Group
Penguin Group (USA) Inc., 375 Hudson Street,
New York, New York 10014, USA

USA | Canada | UK | Ireland | Australia | New Zealand | India | South Africa | China

Penguin Books Ltd., Registered Offices: 80 Strand, London WC2R 0RL, England
For more information about the Penguin Group visit penguin.com.

Published by Signet, an imprint of New American Library, a division of Penguin
Group (USA) Inc. Previously published in a HarperPaperbacks edition. Published by arrangement with the author.

First Signet Printing, May 2013

10 9 8 7 6 5 4 3 2 1

Ⓟ REGISTERED TRADEMARK — MARCA REGISTRADA

ISBN 978-0-451-23983-9

Printed in the United States of America

In memory of Mary Catherine Christean Atwater, great-great-granddaughter of Mary and Tom Clark of Leland, Oregon, both deceased, and survived by her mother, Robyn, her father, Kent, her big brother, Dustin Christean, and other family members too numerous to list. With our tears, we will write her name in the red clay at the top of the mountain where tall pines stretch their boughs over the graves of our ancestors and beckon to each of us at journey's end. Until then, each of us will remember the lesson Mary Catherine taught us: It isn't how long we live that counts, but how many hearts we touch.

Special thanks to Amber Walden, my great-niece and goddaughter, and Mary Catherine's cousin. For obvious reasons, I originally intended to dedicate Cheyenne Amber *to her. In remembrance, she stepped aside. This dedication is a token of Amber's love as well as mine.*

Dear Readers:

Cheyenne Amber was originally published in 1994, and has been unavailable for many years. So I was very excited by New American Library's decision to reissue this work with a fabulous, brand-new cover! Because this book is a historical, I will add that while some events in the story really happened, I may have taken license with the dates on which they occurred. There actually was a cattle stampede through the streets of Denver, and the residents of the town believed they were under attack by the Cheyenne. The intoxicated pigs that Laura sees in Denver are another colorful tidbit of history that I borrowed to make the description of old-time Denver more vivid. As for the Cheyenne people, I did extensive research, so what you read about their customs, modes of communication, and way of life are accurate.

Over the years, countless readers have said that *Cheyenne Amber* ranks among their favorite stories that I've written because it offers suspense, laughter, happy tears, and a beautiful romance. I recently reread the story myself, and even though I dimly remember writing it, I was able to enjoy every page as if it were a book created by someone else. That is such a rare treat for any author! And I must say that I really *did* enjoy the read. Deke and Laura are so completely different that they play off each other beautifully in every scene. It was so much fun to watch them come to know each other on deeper levels and also come to appreciate each other's finer qualities. Toward the end I thought,

Isn't this exactly what true love should be about—peeling away each other's layers to find a beautiful gift? That is precisely what Deke and Laura do, and for their efforts they are rewarded with a deep and abiding love.

Cheyenne Amber is truly a journey of the heart, and I hope you enjoy reading it as much as I did!

All best,
Catherine

Prologue

Colorado, 1864

IF HE DIDN'T GET A DECENT POKER HAND SOON, he would be a dead man.

His body streaming sweat, Tristan Cheney felt like a kettle of boiling water capped with a tight lid. He took another hearty swig of whiskey, then plunked the ceramic jug back onto the dirt beside him. Then, as unobtrusively as possible, he wiped his forehead with his sleeve. No matter how blank a gambler kept his expression, perspiration was always a dead giveaway.

Smoke curled like a ribbon from the feeble flames, and the men who were gathered in a tight circle near the fire leaned closer to see. Tristan curled his lip. Lowlifes. Back in Boston, he wouldn't have acknowledged their kind with so much as a nod, let alone rubbed elbows with them. That had been before he married Laura, of course. Now, because of her, everything had gone to hell, and he was forced to keep company with lice-infested degenerates, the worst of the lot their leader, Francisco Gonzales. For the life of him, Tristan couldn't fathom how such a wellborn, educated man could sink so low.

Unlike his companions, who were still studying their cards, Tristan already had his own memorized. A simple task, that. All he had was a pair of deuces, for Christ's sake.

The night wind whispered in the leaves of the nearby

cottonwoods, a soothing lullaby that seemed to be making the other poker players drowsy. Burk Johnson, a thin gringo with more freckles than good sense, kept yawning, picking his nose, and sniffing. Juan Luna's eyelids were drooping, and he occasionally fondled his crotch as if the stimulation was all that kept him awake. Even Francisco Gonzales, who had won most of the poker hands and should have been eager to continue the play, looked weary and kept stretching his neck. At any time now, they would all decide to settle their debts and head for their bedrolls. The problem was, Tristan didn't have the money in his clip to back his bets, and Gonzales wasn't the kind to take an IOU.

All Tristan needed to save his ass were a few decent hands. Just a few, dammit. He had been betting on high hopes for most of the evening, praying he would get a run of luck. Maybe this would teach him not to sit in on a poker game when he was drinking. Whiskey and gambling could be a lethal combination when a man was low on money. He had anted in for the first round of cards thinking he'd play only one hand. Then he had lost and stayed in for one more round, hoping to recoup. One thing led to another, and here he was.

Please, God, get me out of this, and I'll never do it again. I swear I won't. Tristan took another bracing gulp of whiskey. What in hell should he do? He wasn't going to bail himself out of this mess on the strength of two deuces, that was for sure. He flexed his fingers around his cards and fixed a thoughtful gaze on Gonzales. In the past, Tristan had dickered his way out of similar trouble. Never when he had lost so much money, of course, but even Gonzales could be persuaded to be reasonable if given enough incentive.

Mouth dry, tongue thick, Tristan said, "Do you recall seeing my wife, Francisco?"

Nudging back his sombrero, Gonzales fixed Tristan with dark, questioning eyes, his swarthy face cast into eerie shadow by the flickering flames. "I recall seeing her, yes. Why do you ask, city man?"

Tristan forced the tension from his shoulders. The blackness of the night seemed to press in on him from all sides, and he felt swallowed by it. "She's a remarkably lovely woman, my wife. Don't you agree?"

Gonzales fanned his cards and studied them, his speculative smile flashing teeth stained brown by tobacco. "*Sí*, city man, remarkably lovely." The gurgling sound from the nearby stream filled the quiet between his words and emphasized his hesitation. "But what has she to do with our game, eh?"

Tristan stretched his mouth into a grin. "I was just thinking. I'll bet it's been a while since you've had it with a real lady."

"A pregnant one, you mean?"

Johnson came out of his drowsy stupor long enough to guffaw at the joke. Tristan shot him a glare and said, "By the time we find the mustangs and get back to my place with a herd, she'll have dropped the brat."

Gonzales's smile broadened. "And you will be a very happy man?"

Tristan leaned slightly forward. "No, you don't understand. You could be a very happy man. Think of it. A woman like Laura? Hair and eyes the color of whiskey. Being a Mex, you probably haven't had it with a blonde."

A spark of interest crept in Gonzales's expression. "Are you offering to let me diddle your wife, city man?"

"I was thinking more along the line of lending her to you for a time."

"Lending her to me?" the Mexican repeated.

Heartened by the sudden heat in Gonzales's gaze, Tristan shrugged. "I'm running a little short on funds. An honorable man covers his bets. All I've got of value is my woman. But what a woman. Skin the color of cream, and nipples so sweet and pink, you'll think you've latched onto cherry blossoms."

Gonzales rested his wrist on his knee, the faces of his cards pressed against his grimy denim pant leg. Eyes glinting, he turned his smile on the others. After a moment, he looked back at Tristan and said, "I've sucked my share of pink tits, amigo."

"She's a lady, Gonzales, a genuine lady. In the past, I'll bet you've watched women like her from afar, wanting but unable to take."

Gonzales chuckled. "Wanting and not taking, that is not my way, city man. Surely you know me better than that by now. It is true enough that your wife is very lovely. Before I ever met you, I had heard tales about her from the miners who saw her when you passed through Denver. Not many women have hair and eyes that color."

Tristan nearly whooped with relief. "Then we have a deal?"

For a moment, Gonzales seemed to consider the offer. "I am not so sure. Why should I settle for temporary possession? After I grew bored with her, a beauty such as she would bring a very fine price down Mexico way. As you say, women with her coloring are rare among my people."

Tristan sensed a sudden change in the other men. Those near the fire moved away from him. Those in the darkness behind him abandoned their bedrolls. Fear crawled up his spine. Believing himself to be among friends, he hadn't bothered to strap on his gun belt after washing up for supper.

His taunting smile still in place, Gonzales casually drew his Colt revolver from its holster and blew a breath of air into the muzzle. "Amigo, you insult me. I am too much the gentleman to borrow my friend's wife." He perused the gleaming, nickel-plated barrel, then shrugged his broad shoulders. "Every time I tasted those sweet, pink nipples and ran my hands over her creamy skin, I would think of you and feel very guilty. You understand?"

Tristan understood, all too well. He tried to speak, but his throat felt frozen shut.

"Like you, I, too, am an honorable man," Gonzales continued silkily. "The only way I could ever bring myself to enjoy your woman would be if she were widowed." He looked directly into Tristan's eyes. "And since you are very much alive, that is a problem, yes?"

Frantically searching for a path of escape, Tristan darted

his gaze left and right, but the shadowy forms of Gonzales's men stood all around him.

The Mexican went on speaking, his voice deceptively syrupy. "Being such a decent fellow, I would be filled with regret if, to get you out of the way, I had to kill you without a reason." His smile turned feral. "How accommodating of you to have given me one. It is very bad of you to sit in for poker when you haven't enough money with which to play. In this country, that is a shooting offense."

With that, Gonzales aimed his revolver and pulled the trigger.

Chapter 1

DIGGING A WELL WAS DARK BUSINESS. AS SHE emptied her shovel, Laura Cheney squinted to see. Feeling with one hand, she discovered that the damp earth in the bucket was mounded high. For what seemed the thousandth time, she set aside the shovel and started up the ladder.

One step. Two. She concentrated on counting and tried to ignore the leaden sensation in her feet. With every movement, the muddy folds of her skirt and petticoat clung to her legs, then pulled free with muted little sucking sounds. Three, four. Perspiration popped out on her face. Five, six. Dirt fell into her eyes. She swiped at her cheek, not remembering until too late that her hands were muddy. So thick and heavy, she swore she could taste it, the smell of mold and dampness nearly gagged her.

Pausing to catch her breath, Laura gazed at the sphere of light above her. Seven more rungs. A cramp knifed down her left thigh, and her leg began to jerk. She bent to knead the knotted muscle. As she shifted her position, the ladder teetered. She gasped and threw her weight against the rungs.

"Blast you to hell, Tristan Cheney. This was supposed to be your job."

Inside the well, the sound of her voice was amplified. The words, ugly and discordant, rolled back at her. The first thing she knew, she'd be taking the Lord's name in vain and smoking a corncob pipe like old Missus Peabody on the wagon train.

Heaving a sigh, she curled her hands around the rung and forced her feet back into motion. As she hauled herself upward, a water blister on her palm tore to the quick. Clenching her teeth, she kept climbing. There was a well to dig, a garden to water, and a baby to care for. Time was precious. The morning sun would reach its zenith in only a couple of hours.

As her head cleared the rim of the well, sunlight momentarily blinded her. She blinked to see and then nearly lost her balance as she focused and found herself nose to nose with a short-horned lizard. A rotund little creature with winged ridges above his beady little eyes, he sat spraddle-legged at the edge of the well. With his belly and wattled throat puffed up for battle, he put Laura in mind of a little armored gladiator. Beneath his triangular chin, she could see his pulse hammering, and by that she knew how badly she had startled him.

Too exhausted to feel charitable, she said, "Shoo!"

As slowly as cold molasses dripping from a spoon, the thorny-skinned lizard lifted one foot. After what appeared to be great deliberation, he finally managed to move another. Laura had been told that his species was one of the slowest on the continent, and watching him now, she could well believe it. At the moment, she felt like a close runner-up for the title and doubted she could defeat him in a foot race. At least he had been blessed with an ability to blend in with his surroundings.

"Shoo," she whispered again, and watched as the lizard made a lackadaisical retreat.

Badly in need of a brief rest, Laura folded her arms on the ladder and rested her chin on her wrists. The morning breeze caressed her cheeks. She gazed at the azure Colorado sky that stretched as far as she could see in all directions. The expanse made her feel minuscule, and a wave of homesickness washed over her. Oh, how she sometimes yearned for the comfortable embrace of city buildings and the wonderful smell of salt air.

No point in wishing, she reminded herself. As her husband, Tristan, so often pointed out, they were both stuck here. There was nothing left for either of them back home in Boston.

Colorado really wasn't so bad. Intimidating but lovely, the sort of landscape she had once admired in paintings. Not far from their squat log cabin, the green plains broke into hilly shrubland. Oak formed dense thickets of glossy jade interspersed by occasional clusters of dull-leafed mahogany in the rocky washes. As a backdrop, thickly forested, velvet green mountains tiered like the seats in an amphitheater to the craggy peaks of the Rockies.

To Laura, though, the most beautiful part of the landscape was the wild roses that lent the hillside splashes of color. Ranging in hue from lavender pink to vivid red, the delicate petals gave testimony that it wasn't only the hardy that could survive in this rugged country. From the flowers developed rose hips, which she could use to make perfume and medicinal tea. Thus far she hadn't made it up there to gather any, but now that she'd had the baby, she hoped to do so soon. All practical reasons aside, a bouquet of dried roses and sprigs of goldenrod would lend a bit of cheer to the otherwise drab cabin. To make a home here, that was her aim. A place so pleasant that Tristan would forget Boston and all that he had been forced to leave behind. In that lay Laura's only hope for her marriage. If she worked hard enough to be all Tristan wanted her to be, perhaps he would make an effort to change as well.

Her throat dry with thirst, she worked her mouth for moisture, swallowed, and took another deep breath before she finished climbing from the well. Her legs threatened to fold under her as she scrambled to her feet. Frustrated by the weakness she hadn't been able to shake since giving birth to her son, she lifted her skirt and one leg of her bloomers to tug up a sagging garter. To her dismay, she found a rent in the knee of her black stocking. She bent closer to estimate the damage and decided she could probably mend it.

As she straightened, a bout of dizziness hit her. She

pressed the back of her wrist against her forehead and stood there for a moment until the swimming sensation left. According to Tristan, Indian women squatted by bushes to give birth, strapped their newborns onto their backs, and then raced to catch up to their tribes. Laura wondered how on earth they managed.

She stooped to haul up on the rope and empty the bucket, pleased to note the pile of removed dirt had doubled in size with only two hours of work. A slow process, but at least she was getting it done. Tristan couldn't help but be pleased when he came home. No matter that digging the well deeper should have been his responsibility. She had predicted that the hole would go dry when he had stopped working on it last fall. *Dammit, Laura, I'll dig it deeper when the time comes. Right now I have bigger fish to fry.*

That was Tristan's biggest problem; he *always* had bigger fish to fry, and she was left to do his work. She shifted her gaze to the wilted plants in the vegetable garden, which might be all that stood between Tristan's family and starvation next winter. And where was he? Off chasing mustangs. Somehow the thought of surviving until spring on horse meat didn't appeal. Not that she believed he would bring home a herd. That was another problem with Tristan's dreams; big aspirations didn't put much food on the table.

After tossing the empty bucket back into the hole, Laura planted her hands on her hips and arched her back to get the kinks out. The snug band of her skirt pinched her waist, and she ran a finger under the cloth to get some breathing room. Perhaps meager pickings at the dinner table were a blessing in disguise. Carrying a child had not only straightened her curves but had added a few where she shouldn't have any.

Glancing toward the cabin, Laura decided she should probably go check on Jonathan. His sudden restfulness worried her. What if he wasn't feeling better but was just too exhausted to cry? Her knowledge of babies could fit in a thimble. What if he had a terrible disease of some kind?

Pshaw! Leave it to her to borrow trouble. He didn't have

a fever, and he was still nursing at regular intervals. Maybe all newborn babies were fretful for the first few days. He probably just had a little stomach upset of some kind. At least she prayed that was it. If not, the nearest physician was in Denver, and Laura wasn't certain she could find her way there.

After scraping her black high-topped shoes clean on a clump of grass, she smoothed a tendril of amber-colored hair from her eyes and headed for the cabin. As she crossed the dusty dooryard, she heard the faint tattoo of a horse's hooves. Her emotions a tangle of dread and relief, she turned and cupped a hand over her eyes, expecting to see her long-overdue husband.

As she focused on the approaching rider, her smile vanished. It wasn't Tristan. Even at a distance, she could see that the man wore a wide-brimmed hat, some sort of sombrero if she guessed right, and a black poncho, the fringed folds trailing behind him in the wind.

Retreating a step closer to the house, she stared with trepidation at the stranger. In the ten months she and Tristan had lived here, they had had company just once, and only then because some disreputable friends of his had stopped by to invite him along on the mustang roundup. Except for her baby, Laura hadn't seen a living soul since.

Spurred into action by the rider's fast approach, she launched herself into a run. In this country, uninvited visitors usually meant trouble. Earlier she had left the door to the cabin ajar so she could listen for the baby while she worked. Now she was grateful that she had. Winter dampness had warped the planks and stiffened the leather hinges, making the door stick sometimes.

She lunged through the entrance and whirled to slam the door closed. A weapon of some kind, she thought wildly. Blast Tristan's hide for taking both guns. No matter that she didn't know how to handle a firearm. A man looking for trouble would think twice before nettling a woman who toted a rifle.

She dashed to the table and grabbed up the knife she

had been using that morning to peel potatoes. Stuffing it into the deep pocket of her satin skirt, she whirled to scan the room. Her gaze settled on the handmade broom that leaned in one corner. If she stayed in the shadows and aimed the handle as she might the barrel of a gun, would the man, blinded by sunlight, be able to tell the difference? It was a chance she had to take.

Atremble with fright, she moved Jonathan's makeshift cradle to a protected corner of the room. Then she grabbed up the broom and approached the glassless window, taking care to stand off to one side and back from the spill of sunlight.

As the stranger drew up on the reins and brought his bay to a halt in the yard, Laura decided she had more in common with the little short-horned lizard than she liked to admit. In some situations, all anyone had for protection was bluff and bluster. "State your business!"

At the sound of her voice, Jonathan whimpered and squirmed, but didn't awaken. Laura was grateful for that. The less to distract her, the better.

Throwing the folds of his poncho over one shoulder and nudging back his sombrero, the man narrowed his dark gaze on the window. Dressed in a mismatch of denim jeans, black shirt, conchae-studded gun belt, and beaded leather vest, he looked mean and dangerous. His face was a swarthy brown; his jaw bristled with whiskers that caught the greasy strands of his wind-tossed black hair. On the horizon behind him, gloomy thunderheads wreathed the craggy peaks of the Rockies. "Are you Señora Cheney?"

At the question, she heard Jonathan stir again. She tightened her grip on the broom. How had this man come to know her name? Regarding him more closely, she thought he resembled one of the men who had gone with Tristan to search for mustangs, but she couldn't be certain. She had seen the group of riders only from a distance. "Y-Yes, I'm Mrs. Cheney."

"I bring news of your husband. Very sad news, I'm afraid."

He started to get off his horse, and Laura yelled, "Stay put, mister. If you get down, I shall blow your brains out."

He froze with one leg poised above the saddle. Then, very slowly, he resumed his seat. Squinting to see her, he flashed a tobacco-stained smile. "With which end of that broom do you plan to kill me, señora?"

"I . . ." There was nothing she could think of to say. Feeling more foolish than she ever had, she dropped the pitiful excuse for a weapon. In one corner of her mind, she registered that the man was well-spoken for a Mexican saddle tramp, but humiliation and fear nudged the thought aside.

"Señora, I won't harm you or the child. If you will think back, you will remember seeing me out by the barn the day your husband left to go on the roundup. He was a friend of mine."

Was? Laura locked her knees and squeezed her eyes closed. Oh, dear God. Not that.

Saddle leather creaked, and she lifted her lashes to see the stranger dismounting. The longer she looked at him, the more familiar he seemed. She supposed he must be telling the truth about being a friend of Tristan's. Not that it was much of a recommendation. Tristan's only acquaintances were seedy individuals he had met in the saloons of Denver.

As the man walked toward the cabin, spurs chinked at the heels of his dusty boots. Feeling numb, she drew the knife from her pocket, hid it within the folds of her flounced skirt, and moved to unbar the door. There was little point in trying to keep him out, after all, not with two large and unshuttered windows to foil her. Her only recourse was to be gracious and pray he would leave as quickly as he had come.

As the door swung inward, the Mexican's shadow fell across her. Wary of his getting too close, she stepped back. A husky man of lofty stature, he dwarfed the tiny room and everything in it when he entered. She clenched her hand around the smooth wooden handle of the knife.

"You neglected to give me your name," she said pointedly.

He gestured with his hands. "Francisco, señora, Francisco Gonzales. As I said, I was a friend of your husband's."

"And wh-what is this news you say you have of him?"

He took off his sombrero. "It is very sad news, Señora Cheney. Perhaps you should sit down."

"I shall hear it standing, thank you."

What looked to be regret clouded his brown eyes. "Your husband . . ." Turning the brim of his hat in his hands, he bent his head. "I am very sorry, Señora Cheney, but your husband has had a very bad accident. While chasing a herd of mustang with me and my *compañeros*, he was thrown from his horse and . . ." His dark gaze sought hers. "It is so very difficult a thing for me to say. Your husband was trampled to death."

Laura flinched. Slowly, dazedly, she went back over the words, trying to assimilate what they meant. Not just trampled, but trampled to death.

She swayed slightly as the enormity of that sank in. The knife slipped from her frozen fingers and thudded to the floor. From out of nowhere, it seemed to her, a warm, gentle hand cupped her elbow. Dizzy and disoriented, she blinked and tried to focus. Tristan wasn't going to come home.

"Wh-Where—is his body? You don't—he isn't with you."

"We buried him in the mountains, señora. It was such a very long way to bring him back here, you understand. The weather has turned so warm. . . ."

Nausea surged up Laura's throat. Tristan, dead. A corpse that couldn't be transported any distance because it was summer. *Oh, God. Oh, God.* This couldn't be happening.

He tightened his grip on her arm and steered her toward the three-legged table that Tristan had built last winter. "Why don't you sit down? I'll dip you some water, eh?"

Weakly Laura sank onto one of the stumps she had rolled inside to serve as chairs. Bracing her elbows on her knees, she cupped her face in her hands. "I can't believe it. Dead? He was so young! There has to be a mistake."

She heard the man's spurs dragging in the dirt as he moved toward the water bucket. "Yes, very young. But there is no mistake. These things happen. This can be hard, cruel country."

Hard and cruel, yes. A hell on earth. Not a place for fainthearts, to be sure. Laura dragged in a great, shuddering breath. When the Mexican turned to her, she extended a shaking hand for the dipper of water he offered her. After taking a sip, she whispered, "He isn't coming back."

She felt idiotic for stating the obvious. If Tristan was dead, he certainly couldn't come home. Never again. But knowing that and accepting it were two different things.

Slopping water over the edge, she set the dipper on the table. "How could he do this to me? What in God's name shall I do?"

The questions hovered between them, cold and stark, slicing through the sham that had been her marriage. Like a fist in her middle, it struck Laura how self-centered her reaction was. No grief? What kind of person was she? Despite everything that Tristan had done, she would never have wished him dead. But she felt no real pain. Just a terrible sense of abandonment.

Laura was no stranger to the feeling. It was a fate she had experienced at Tristan's hands more times than she cared to count, the only difference being that this time his desertion of her was not only ill timed but final. A purely irrational surge of anger jolted through her. How fitting that he should get himself killed right when she needed him the very most. How characteristic of him that was. Men. They were all alike, and only a fool depended on one.

Then the absurdity of her rage hit her, and she gave a hysterical laugh. This was one time she couldn't, in good conscience, blame Tristan for letting her down. It wasn't as if he had deliberately died, after all.

"Señora Cheney, are you all right?"

Laura stifled her laughter and straightened her shoulders. Was she all right? The question seemed to echo. Wetness coursed down her cheeks, and she realized it was tears. Laughing and crying at the same time? She cupped a hand over her eyes and struggled to regain her composure.

"I'm fine," she managed in a high-pitched voice. "I'm perfectly fine." The words no sooner passed her lips than she started to laugh again.

"Perhaps there is someone I can bring to stay with you for a few days? I think you are more shaken than you realize."

Laura pressed a hand over her mouth. Through quivering fingers, she said, "There isn't anyone."

The admission sobered her, and she stared blankly at the empty lard tin on the table that she had saved to use as a vase for dried roses and goldenrod. Flowers? In a lard tin? Another wild urge to laugh hit her. If only her father could see her now. She could almost picture the satisfied gleam in his eyes and hear his refined voice saying, "I warned you." As indeed he had. Just as predicted, she was hundreds and hundreds of miles from home, her baby was sick, and there was no one, absolutely no one, for her to turn to. To make matters worse, she had the sum total of three cents in the money jar. Three measly cents. That wasn't even enough to wire her father that Tristan was dead. It wasn't even enough to buy the paper to write a letter, not in Denver, where everything cost so dearly.

What in God's name was she going to do? The question had become a litany. Drawing her hand from her mouth, Laura swallowed and blinked again. It seemed to her that the cabin had gone into a drunken rotation.

"There must be someone," the stranger insisted. "A neighbor who comes by each day to check on you, a hired man, someone. Surely your husband didn't leave you here alone with no one to help you if something went wrong?"

The change in the stranger's voice was barely perceptible, but Laura, ever cautious around men, noticed it. The fog of hysteria fell away from her like a discarded cape. She forced herself to look into the man's eyes. She didn't like what she saw there. Careful, Laura. Shifting her gaze to the knife where it lay forgotten on the floor, she said, "Neighbors?" A thrill of fear fluttered into her throat. "The neighbors. Of course! I don't know where my head went. Yes, of course, we have neighbors."

That much wasn't a lie; she did have neighbors. The only problem was that pregnancy and inclement weather had kept her housebound throughout the winter, and Tristan had never taken her to visit them. During Tristan's absence these last three weeks, she had watched the cloudless horizon morning and evening for chimney smoke but had never seen any. That meant the other homesteads were some distance away, and no telling where.

"I nearly forgot the neighbors," she said shakily. "Ever since Tristan left, they've been stopping by every day."

"In the mornings, the evenings? When can you expect them?"

Laura's nape prickled. "They, um, they come at different times, whenever it's convenient for them. I haven't seen them yet today. They could show up at any time." She settled her hands over her waist, feeling as though she might be sick. "There's really nothing to worry about. I shall be fine."

"What is their name?" he pressed.

Drawing a complete blank, Laura stared up at him. Their name? Behind him on the canned-goods shelf sat a tin of Field's Oysters, one of Tristan's favorite extravagances, which he had indulged in regardless of whether or not he could afford it. "Fields, their last name is Fields. Henry and Olivia." She hadn't a clue where the first names had come from. "And three sons, all nearly grown."

He nodded and glanced over his shoulder at the shelf. His eyes took on a knowing gleam when he looked back down at her.

Jonathan started to cry, and Laura pushed numbly to her feet. Hurrying over to the crate, she lifted her baby into her arms. When she turned back, the Mexican was still standing there, his thoughtful gaze fixed on her. Not on her face as it should have been, but lower. Much lower. Unnerved by the way he was looking at her, Laura quickly averted her face.

Trying to pretend she wasn't alarmed, she began to jostle the infant. "He's not feeling well. A t-tummy ailment, I think. He cries and cries." Horribly aware that she was speaking too quickly and that her voice sounded shrill, she finished with, "Nothing I do seems to ease him."

"Probably colic." He studied the baby for a moment, then fixed his attention solely on her again. "He is a young one, eh? I would guess him to be only a few days old. It is little wonder you are so pale."

He flicked a glance at her soiled hemline, then returned his gaze to her breasts. Laura knew that her white blouse, which she usually wore under a stiffly boned satin bodice, had become too tight since her pregnancy, but she resisted the urge to shift Jonathan in her arms to hide herself. Like animals, some men launched an attack at any sign of fear.

"It looks as though you've been having a hard time of it," he mused. "A woman should not be working outdoors so soon after childbirth."

Since the Mexican's attention had been lingering mostly on her torso, Laura marveled that he had even noticed her pallor or the condition of her clothing. "I've managed nicely, thank you."

"Have you?" His words hung in the air, more statement than question. "When we left here to track horses, I had no idea you were in the family way. What kind of—" He broke off and assumed an expression of contriteness. "Pardon me. I intend no slander against your husband, you understand. It just seems a bit irresponsible of him to have left you so close to your time."

"I'm sure he did what he felt he had to."

"Still, if I'd known, I would have insisted he stay behind. I assume the neighbor woman attended you during the birth?"

Laura moistened her lips. "The neighbor woman, yes."

"How did you summon her when your time came?"

"With chimney smoke," she replied quickly. Jonathan stiffened in the crook of her arm and let out a shrill scream. He was probably hungry. Laura moved him to her shoulder and bounced him, praying he would temporarily forgo mealtime and drift back to sleep. "You mentioned something called colic?"

His gaze sharpened. "You have never heard of colic?"

Raising her voice to be heard above the baby, Laura asked, "Is it serious?"

A slow grin spread across his swarthy face. "No, señora, not serious. A digestive disorder of some sort, common to newborns. You have not been around many infants, I take it?"

"None," she admitted. Concern for Jonathan outweighing her fear of the man, she pressed, "Is there a remedy?"

As if to stress his discomfort, Jonathan bowed his back and screamed more loudly. Not knowing what else to do, Laura returned him to the crook of her arm and gave him her knuckle to suck. He nuzzled her hand with hungry eagerness and instantly quieted, his little mouth making audible supping sounds. The Mexican's lips quirked and he lifted laughing eyes to hers.

"I think he seeks something more substantial than your knuckle, señora."

Laura didn't need to be told what her son wanted. She felt a scalding flush creep up her neck. "The colic you spoke of. Is there anything to be done for him?" she repeated.

"Most little ones simply outgrow it, I think. If there is a remedy, I don't know of it. I have no children of my own, you understand, only nieces and nephews, but as I recall, most of them screamed with the colic."

Laura bent close to whisper to her son.

Her visitor placed his sombrero back on his head. "Perhaps the neighbor woman can tell you of a remedy, yes?"

Alerted by the note of amusement in his voice, Laura glanced up. Before she could read the Mexican's shadowed expression, he turned away. "I have your husband's things. I will bring them in, and then I must be on my way."

As far as Laura was concerned, his departure wouldn't come any too soon. He suspected she was lying about the neighbors, that much was clear, which meant he also suspected she had no means of summoning help.

While he was outside, Laura retrieved the knife and slipped it into the deep pocket of her skirt. A moment later, he returned, carrying Tristan's gun belt and black felt hat. The hat, once Tristan's pride and joy, was now smashed and covered with dirt. Seeing the hat brought home to Laura the reality of her husband's death as nothing else had. As the Mexican laid it and the gun on the table, her heart twisted. *Tristan.* Though theirs had never been a match made in heaven, Laura had always hoped. Foolish, foolish. But hope had been the only solace she had in her marriage.

Tears stung her eyes, and a searing sensation crept up the back of her throat. Tristan's last rotten hand of cards had finally been dealt to him, and this time there was no chance of his recouping the losses.

Forcing her mind back to the moment, Laura met the Mexican's gaze. "My husband had a cartridge belt and watch. Plus his rifle and money clip."

Gonzales lifted his hands. "These were all he had on him, señora. Perhaps the watch and money fell from his pockets and were trampled into the dirt? As for extra bullets, I may have overlooked them in his saddlebags."

"And his horse?"

"Dead, señora. Trampled, just as your husband was. It was not pretty."

She wanted to ask what had happened to Tristan's rifle, but she stifled the urge. Lies, all lies. Even if she hadn't heard it in the man's voice, she would have known. He brought her only a smashed hat and a rusty, antiquated gun? Every valuable possession of her husband's was mysteriously missing, including the expensive rifle he'd won in a poker game.

Mustering her composure, Laura said, "Well, thank you for coming so far to bring me what was left." She wondered why he had bothered. Surely not out of the goodness of his heart. "I'll save the hat and gun as keepsakes for Jonathan. Someday he'll appreciate having things of his father's."

He stroked his chin. "The money clip, you were hoping it was here?"

Laura tensed. The question was idiotic. The humble cabin was testimony in itself to her dire financial straits.

"If you're in need, I would be happy to loan you some money, señora. It is the least I can do."

A prickly, tight sensation crawled up Laura's neck. "Thank you for offering, but that won't be necessary."

"You are sure?" His gaze held hers. "I will not miss a few dollars, and I am always very happy to help a pretty lady."

In exchange for what? Tightening her arms around the baby, she said, "Thank you, but no."

"If you are concerned about repaying me, I am certain we can work out some sort of arrangement," he offered. His gaze darted to her hips. "There are many ways to satisfy a loan, yes?"

Laura's gorge rose. In a couple of weeks, when her milk dried up from lack of nourishment and her son wailed with hunger, she might regret being such a puritan. But she wasn't that desperate yet. "No. A loan isn't necessary."

He shrugged again. "Then I will be going, eh? Unless, of course, there is something I can do for you before I leave?"

"No, nothing," Laura replied. "You've already been more than kind."

He gave a slight bow, touched his hat, and turned toward the door. Laura stood frozen to the spot until she heard the sound of his horse's hooves fading away into the distance. Maybe she was sensing danger where there was none, but she had a horrible feeling she hadn't seen the last of him.

Cuddling her son close, Laura sat on one of the logs to nurse him. She curled her hand over Jonathan's silken cap of dark hair and watched the dark blue of his eyes as his lashes drifted halfway closed in contentment.

Her son . . . Jonathan Christopher Cheney. She shoved her fears of being alone and thoughts of Tristan aside, cherishing this stolen moment of peace, short-lived though it might be. She curled his tiny fingers over one of her own and gazed at them through tears. Then she touched a fingertip to the dimple that flashed in his silken cheek. Her son, the one worthwhile accomplishment in her life. Oh, how she loved him.

*   *   *

Two hours later, Francisco Gonzales reached the draw where he had left his men. As he swung down from his horse, he drew his jug of whiskey from his saddlebag, uncorked it, and took a long swallow.

"Well?" Johnson called from where he was lying in the shade of a cottonwood. "She alone, or ain't she?"

Francisco wiped his mouth with his sleeve and flashed a confident grin. "Completely alone, my friend, with only an empty, rusted gun, a broom, and gumption with which to defend herself." Recalling the woman's bravado, he smiled. "She's far more beautiful than she appeared at a distance. I will be none too anxious to sell her once we reach Mexico."

Johnson staggered to his feet. As he walked toward Francisco, he ran his hand down the greasy fly of his jeans. He jiggled one leg as if to reposition his considerable pride. "Hot damn! If yer as randy as me, we ain't gonna leave out fer Mexico fer at least a week." He glanced sideways at Parker Banks and winked. "I'll hump that sweet little piece of baggage till she begs me fer mercy."

Parker snorted. "Way I remember it, you aren't that long on staying power. If you don't lay off the jug, I'll be surprised if you can even get it up."

"Not with a package like her!" Johnson came back. "Just stand aside, boys, and watch how it's done."

Parker laughed. "When the day comes I gotta learn how to diddle by watching the likes of you, I'll be laid out in a coffin. Besides, who says you get a go at her first?"

Johnson threw a questioning look at the Mexican. Francisco inclined his head. "A privilege of leadership, my friend. When I have grown weary of her, the rest of you may draw straws."

Chapter 2

THE WELL WAS DRY, THE MEAT SUPPLIES LOW, she had three cents to her name, and her husband was dead.

Determined not to feel panicked by the endless expanse of rolling hills that stretched north from the house, Laura fixed her attention on what she was doing and emptied yet another bucket of dirt from the well onto the growing mound. When she tossed the container back into the hole, the metal made a hollow thunk when it hit bottom. No splash. Not even a muddy plop.

What if she dug and dug, and she never hit another water table? She sank her teeth into her bottom lip. She couldn't waste time on what-ifs. There was too much work to be done, and only her to do it.

Hugging her waist, she turned to gaze with dry eyes at her vegetable garden next to the cabin. It was approaching noon, and the plants had to be watered. It wouldn't be easy hauling buckets up from the stream, but she would manage. This evening when the sun went down, she'd dig on the well some more. Pray God she wouldn't have to dig far.

Jonathan was still asleep when she reentered the cabin. At least something was going right. It would worry her sick to leave him here if he were screaming, which she'd have to do if he woke up. The vegetables were too important to let them perish.

As she approached the table to fetch the water pail, Laura's gaze fell on Tristan's gun belt. She glanced over her shoulder at the doorway and recalled the speculative leer on the Mexican's face that morning. Gnawing her lower lip, she ran tremulous fingers over the rusty gun butt. It almost looked as though someone had dunked and soiled the gun to corrode it. She had no idea how to use the revolver but felt certain it couldn't be that difficult. A simple matter of pointing it and pulling the trigger, surely. Regardless, the mere sight of it on her hip would discourage most men.

Decision made, she lifted the belt. It felt heavy as she pulled it around her hips and fastened the buckle. A little strap anchored the gun in its holster. She experimented at unhooking it and then practiced her draw. The trigger felt cold when she curled her finger around it. As cold as death. She shoved the thought away. As wary as she was of guns, she thanked heaven for this one. Once she cleaned it and bought some ammunition, it would not only give her and Jonathan some means of protection, but might provide them with meat when she became proficient at shooting it.

Ammunition would cost money, and she was going to need supplies as well. With reluctance, she looked at the straw-filled flour sacks she had stitched together to serve as a mattress for the crudely framed bed. Though Tristan had sold nearly every valuable Laura had brought with her into their marriage, she had managed to keep one hidden from him—her late mother's watch. Of quality gold and inset with rubies, the heirloom should bring a good price from a jeweler. As much as she hated to part with it, practicality dictated. She could use the proceeds to wire her father of Tristan's death. With the remainder, she would stock up on supplies and ammunition.

In a few days when her vegetables had grown enough to survive a full day without water, she would go to Denver. She knew the general direction and would allow herself plenty of daylight to travel by, just in case she missed the town and had to double back. A short trip like that shouldn't hurt Jonathan. As a precaution, she would take both the mare and the mule so she would have a spare mount if one of the sorry beasts went lame.

Dread filled Laura at the thought. Born and raised in Boston, where honing her sense of direction had never been necessary, she wasn't absolutely certain of the way. What if she missed Denver and had to wander around the endless grassland? Neither of her mounts was up to that. She had only one flask in which to carry water. If she got lost, she and Jonathan might die out there, if not from hunger and thirst, then at the hands of hostile Indians. Not long ago, a young man had ridden into Denver with several arrows in his back.

Memories rushed at Laura. While journeying west with the wagon train, she had witnessed Indian brutality first-hand. One hot afternoon, two women had wandered away from the wagons in search of a bathing spot and encountered Indians. Just beyond range of the white men's rifles, the savages, who had greatly outnumbered the people in the wagon train, had made a show of raping and torturing their female captives. Laura still had dreams about the incident and woke up to the sounds of those women's screams.

She returned the gun to its holster and curled her hands into fists. She would find Denver because she had to. To fret, days in advance, about all the things that might go wrong would accomplish nothing.

Despite her resolve, other worries niggled their way into her mind. Would her father reply to her telegraph message this time? Surely he would. Not even Sterling Van Hauessen could continue to hold a grudge once he learned that Tristan was dead. And if he did wire her back? What then? Even if he forgave her for marrying against his wishes and sent her the money to go home, Jonathan wouldn't be old enough to make the trip until spring. Somehow, she would have to survive the coming winter on her own.

You asked for this. Remember, Laura? Two months into the marriage, you swore you'd leave Tristan one day, and that once you did, you'd never depend on another man again. Well, now it has happened. You got your wish.

Somehow she never imagined her freedom coming at a time like this, when she was stranded in the middle of nowhere with three cents to her name. As unreliable and temperamental as Tristan had been, at least he had brought home meat sometimes, and on rare occasion he had even won a few hands of poker to replenish their cash. Now she couldn't even count on that.

Swinging the bucket loosely in one hand, she left the house and walked toward the stream. Three round trips later, her legs would scarcely hold her up, and she still had ten rows of vegetables yet to water. Weary beyond words, she leaned a shoulder against the cabin. Her back ached, and her breath came in shallow little pants. She rested only long enough to slow her breathing, then set off again.

Large boulders and river rock lined the banks of the stream. Tristan had never cleared a footpath, so she picked her way, stepping over looming stones when she could, circling them when she couldn't. In her exhaustion, she no longer noticed her surroundings and scarcely heard the soothing whisper of the breeze in the cottonwoods. Her sense of awareness had become centered on one thing: making her feet move. It didn't matter that her stomach was cramping or that the muscles in her legs were quivering and aching. All she could allow herself to think about was the vegetable garden, because it was the only thing that would keep her and her baby alive next winter.

With that thought looming in her mind, Laura chose her footholds and started over another boulder. As she stepped onto the rock, the sole of her high-button shoe lost purchase. Waving her arms, she tried frantically to keep her balance. As she scrambled for another foothold, her legs shot out from under her and she pitched sideways into a crevice between the stones.

The next instant pain exploded in her temple, and everything went utterly black. The last sound that registered in her mind was the clanking of the empty bucket as it hit the rocks.

"Where the hell is the bitch?"

Francisco picked up the screaming infant and started to

jostle him. He studied the dim cabin, recalling how protective the Cheney woman had been of her son. She wouldn't have wandered far. Yet his men couldn't find her.

"Did you check down by the creek?" he asked Parker.

"We spotted some tracks leading that way, but they petered out at the rocks. Johnson checked all along the banks. He didn't find a sign of her."

Francisco offered the newborn a grimy knuckle to suck. "Son of a bitch. Where could she have gone?" He stepped to the unshuttered window to peruse the sky. It was well over an hour past noon. Strike and flee, that was his motto. He couldn't remain here much longer, not without running a risk. "Did someone comb the hillside behind the house? She might have tried to hide."

Even as he said the words, Francisco doubted them. A woman who stood her ground with only a broom as a weapon wasn't likely to abandon her baby when she saw a group of riders approaching.

"No sign of her up on the hill, either." Parker swept off his hat to scratch his grizzled blond hair. "Strange. It's like she vanished."

Francisco thinned his lips. "A woman doesn't just vanish."

A thoughtful frown pleated his brow. Maybe he had misread the Cheney woman. What if she hadn't been lying to him about her neighbors? The thought made his guts knot. After hearing of her husband's death, she could have left the sleeping infant here while she went to beg assistance from her friends.

"Is her horse gone?"

"Nope," Parker assured him. "Both it and the mule are in the shed. Poorest excuse for a horse I've ever seen, and the mule isn't much better."

Francisco gazed thoughtfully at the can of oysters on the shelf. He could have sworn . . . Shaking his head, he came back to the moment. If the horse wasn't gone, it didn't seem likely that the Cheney woman could be at the neighbors'. There were no other spreads within easy walking distance, and he didn't think she would have wanted to leave her baby alone too long.

Think being the key word, however, he couldn't gamble that he was right. If she had gone to the neighbors, she might return at any moment. A lone, unarmed woman was one thing. But a woman with a man and three grown sons to back her up was quite another. In a skirmish, Francisco preferred to pick the spot so he and his men had an advantage. There was a wooded hillside behind this cabin and a thick line of trees along the creek, all of which would provide too much cover. He had no guarantee that one of the farmers might not survive a shoot-out to describe him. Francisco had many names to bandy about, but only one face, and he guarded it closely when he was up to no good. Thus far, that practice had always kept him a step ahead of the law.

Johnson stepped inside the low-ceilinged cabin. After glancing around, he spat tobacco juice on the dirt floor. "She ain't nowhere round close, that's fer sure. What we gonna do now, boss? Wait fer her, or what?"

"We cannot afford to wait." Francisco considered the situation for a moment. "If we take the baby, she will find a way to come after us."

Johnson gave him a blank look. "Yeah? So what're ya gettin' at?"

Francisco jostled the baby again. "Sometimes, amigo, you are so stupid, I wonder if you have brains or straw between those dirty ears of yours." He shifted the infant to his shoulder. "Use your head, yes?"

"But, Gonzales! If she gets help and follows us, we stand to get our asses shot off. Folks don't take kindly to baby stealers."

"We are over twenty strong," Francisco reminded him, "all of us quick with guns. The law in Denver has its hands full right now with the Indians. If she goes for help, the sheriff won't be able to spare her but one or two men, if that many. We can pick the spot for a confrontation. Are you saying you're afraid of a couple of dirt diggers, amigo?"

Johnson fidgeted. "Hell no, I ain't afraid. But I thought the plan was to get the bitch, diddle her for a week or so, and then take her down to Mexico so we could sell her."

Francisco smiled slowly. "If she comes after us with a small volunteer posse, what is to stop us from doing just that? We will trade the baby to the Indians, just as we planned, and leave a very good trail for them to follow while we're at it."

Understanding finally dawned on the thin gringo's face. "And we'll snatch her?"

A cold glint came into Francisco's eyes. "That or kill her. She has seen my face, my friend, and that, I cannot let pass."

"She can't prove nothing. What's to say you took her kid?"

"She will have her suspicions. I prefer not to risk seeing her in a courtroom one day, called as a witness to identify me."

"How are we going to feed the brat without her along?"

Francisco curled a gentle hand over the newborn's silken head. "He won't be the first infant to survive for a couple of days on broth and a sugar tit."

Laura slowly opened her eyes and tried to focus, uncertain where she was. Pain. In her head, along her back, at her hip. She felt as if someone had bludgeoned her. As though she were lying in a box, walls of gray rose all around her. She stared at the rectangle of sky above her. The sun slanted at her, angry yellow in a nimbus of blinding white. Cottonwood leaves danced in flickering splendor against azure, the silvered limbs of the trees dipping and swaying gracefully. She could hear the creek gurgling near her somewhere.

With a muffled groan, she tried to turn her head. A hard surface butted her temple. She slid her gaze sideways. A rock. Slowly, her sense of reality returned. Lots of rocks. She was surrounded by them. How on earth?

Memory flooded back. She had been hauling water. Her shoe had slipped on a boulder. She had started to fall.

"Oh, dear God! Jonathan!"

Clenching her teeth against the agony of movement,

Laura clawed at the rocks and scrambled to her feet. When she straightened, blood rushed to her head, and pain exploded in varying shades of black within her skull. She staggered and grabbed on to a boulder for support. How long had she lain here? Minutes, hours? From the position of the sun, she suspected the latter.

She made her way out of the rocks. Her baby. He might have choked. Or smothered in his blankets. Her sweet, helpless little baby!

When she reached the house, Laura nearly fell into the room in her haste. She was halfway across the packed dirt floor before the condition of the interior registered. The place had been ransacked, the camelback trunks emptied, the shelves swept clean. The burlap bags on the bed vomited straw.

"Jonathan!" She raced to the little crate that had served as his bed. When she saw it was empty, she clamped a hand over her mouth to stifle a scream. Gone? Whirling, she panned the room. Through parted fingers, she cried, "Jonathan?"

For a moment, she thought a bear must have come into the cabin, but then she saw that the damage had been wreaked methodically and that certain items were missing. Her hand mirror, the blanket from the bed, the can of oysters on the shelf. And her baby.

She steeled herself against a cold, crawling fear. Who in God's name would steal a child? Jagged little whimpers began coming up her throat. She gulped to stifle them and ran outside. Once in the yard, she started to run in one direction, then wheeled to go in another.

"Jonathan!" she screamed on the crest of a tearing sob. "Jonathan, where are you . . . ?"

Only silence and the whisper of the afternoon breeze floated back to her. Her breath coming in shallow pants, she turned in a circle. Her gaze fell to the churned-up earth. Horses had been here. A number of them. Hugging her waist, she staggered about the yard. Boot prints. The cuts of spurs. A picture of the Mexican's leering face flashed before her.

"Oh, God. Oh, God, help me."

Laura knew from experience that God helped only those who helped themselves. She made a conscious effort to pace her breathing and walked the yard in ever-widening circles. At last she spotted what she was searching for, hoof-prints heading away from the cabin. She lifted her gaze in that direction. North, they had taken Jonathan north. Or was it northeast? Hoping to use the sun as a reference point, she anxiously searched the sky, silently damning herself for her own ignorance. The sun changed direction with the seasons. Didn't it? This wasn't Boston, for God's sake. There were no street signs. Why hadn't she demanded that Tristan teach her how to find her way out here?

In all her life, Laura had never felt so inadequate. Curling her hands into fists, she tried to sort fact from hysteria. Some men on horseback had been here. They had stolen her baby. She had to do something. But what? Chase them? Her mare was in as sorry a shape as she was.

The mare! Terrified that she might find an empty stall, Laura raced to the lean-to barn. Her relief was so great when she saw the mare and mule that she nearly fell to her knees. Without the animals, she had no means of making it to Denver. But of course they were here. A swaybacked horse and an ancient mule? They weren't worth stealing. The only thing on the whole place worth taking had been Jonathan. And, of course, her mother's watch. Wheeling, she ran back to the cabin.

She paused inside the door to get her breath. Calm down. You have to think. Moving toward the bed, she saw that the stuffing of each burlap sack had been searched, which meant her mother's watch had probably been found. On the off chance that it hadn't, she sifted through the straw. Her one means of getting supplies for the coming winter was gone.

This can't be happening. I'm having a nightmare. That's all. Only, it wasn't a nightmare. Her gaze caught on the crock where she kept her savings. She checked inside and discovered that her three pennies had been overlooked by the thieves, not that the sum would help her much. Woodenly she stumbled to Jonathan's crate. Only one of his flannel blankets had been left. She reached to touch the softness. Her baby. She could almost feel the warmth of him clasped in her arms.

Nearly strangling on a sob, she clenched her fingers in the blanket. Pressing it to her face, she inhaled the sweet scent. As she tried to sort her thoughts, only one thing came clear. She had to get her son back, and to accomplish that, she was going to need help.

Chapter 3

DUSK WAS FALLING QUICKLY THREE HOURS later when Laura hesitated on the uneven boardwalk. She gazed across Blake Street at the flank of keystone arches that fronted the Elephant Corral, a popular Denver saloon. A pole banner sporting a tusked elephant jutted from above the second-story windows, beyond which Laura assumed were rooms where a lonely man could rent a bed and the company of a sporting woman for the night. Tristan had returned home from Denver more than once smelling of perfume.

Down on the banks of Cherry Creek to her right, several well-armed soldiers from the First Colorado hooted with laughter at the antics of four pigs that had been caught rooting in some discarded brandy cherries. Laura couldn't decide who was acting silliest, the swine or the men, and it was certainly debatable who was the more intoxicated. To her right, a group of rifle-toting male civilians stood on a corner, passing a liquor flask.

Trying to gather enough courage to cross the street, Laura hunched her shoulders and hugged her jacket close against the nippy night wind that whistled along the avenue between the rows of buildings. Carried by the breeze, a white piece of paper skipped along a wagon wheel rut. She glimpsed large block print that read PURGE COLORADO OF MURDERING SAVAGES.

Trouble with the Indians. As if she needed another complication. Grit blew in her eyes, and she blinked away tears, not at all certain they were caused by the sting. Why now, of all times? She needed help.

Desperately. But with a Cheyenne uprising threatening the town, the sheriff doubted she could find a single, God-fearing man, including him, who would leave his family or the citizens of Denver right now to help her.

Everyone she had approached thus far had been sympathetic. It was a terrible thing, her child being kidnapped. At any other time they would muster volunteers but at present, every able-bodied man was needed here. Surely she could understand.

Laura understood, all right. From the sheriff on down, every man she spoke with had implied the same thing. She had one hope of assistance, and that from a fellow who was anything but God-fearing. She stared at the saloon, wishing this nightmare away. But wishes were for fools and children, not grown women who knew better. She had to go in there, and the longer she stood here prevaricating, the more difficult it would be.

According to the sheriff, Deke Sheridan, the best tracker in the territory, had just ridden in from a cattle drive and could probably be found at the Elephant Corral, his preferred drinking establishment. "He's not the kind of gent I'd normally recommend to a lady," the lawman had apologized. "Raised by the Cheyenne, you know, and right now that doesn't make him too popular. From what I've heard, he feels a lot of loyalty to the Indians, and some folks wonder whose side he'll take in a fracas. His being so fast with a gun makes people uneasy about turning their backs on him. Not quite civilized, if you know what I mean."

A chill had run up Laura's spine upon hearing that. "Not quite civilized?" she repeated.

The sheriff shrugged. "He's the best we've got to offer. Look on the bright side, Mrs. Cheney. There's not a man in this whole territory who can hold a candle to him when it comes to sniffing out a trail. And given his Cheyenne background, he's one of the few white men I know who can ride around out there right now without fear of losing his scalp."

Recalling the conversation, Laura shivered again. Raised by Indians and not quite civilized? What about her scalp? Or wasn't that a consideration? The sheriff said a family named Huntgate had been massacred by Cheyennes only three days ago southeast of Denver. Their mutilated bodies had been displayed over at the post office in an attempt to shock people into taking retaliatory action. Now she was being advised to seek the aid of a man rumored to be more loyal to the Cheyenne than the whites?

"Mind you, when he's here in town, it seems to me trouble finds him instead of the other way around," the sheriff had assured her. "Could be that folks are doing him a disservice with the ugly talk. Feelings are running kind of high around here against anyone associated with the Cheyenne."

Somehow Laura didn't find that very comforting.

A drunk staggered from the saloon into the street. The sound of rowdy voices and laughter trailed out behind him from the dimly lit saloon. She dug her fingernails into the velvet nap of her jacket. It looked to her as if half the able-bodied men in Denver were busy getting drunk and disorderly. If the Cheyennes did attack, they'd certainly have easy pickings.

"Hey there, honeybee! What you doin' out here all alone?"

The deep voice startled Laura, and she whirled to confront two men who had somehow approached from the left without her hearing them. As they drew near, the stench of whiskey and sour sweat blasted her in the face. Before she could move, the smaller of the two grabbed her arm.

"Well, now, aren't you a pretty little surprise."

Frightened, Laura tried to break free. "Unhand me, sirrah!"

"Hey. No need to be unfriendly," the taller one said. "If there's trouble later tonight, you'll be mighty glad of our acquaintance." He patted the gun on his hip. "You can bet them Huntgate females learned firsthand why white women prefer death to capture by Indians. Thanks to fellows like me and Gerald, you gals here in Denver don't have to worry."

At the moment, the biggest threat to Laura's peace of mind didn't come from savages. With a violent twist of her body, she wrenched away and stumbled off the boardwalk into the street. As she retreated toward the saloon, she straightened her jacket and tried not to look intimidated. When she had put enough distance between herself and the men to feel safe, she turned her back on them and ran.

The sound of male laughter and catcalls coming from inside the saloon grew louder as she gained the opposite boardwalk, but Laura didn't allow herself time to worry about it. As dangerous as he might be, Deke Sheridan was the only hope she had.

As she pushed open the door of the Elephant Corral, three intoxicated men spilled out over the threshold. She executed a quick sidestep. With a ribald laugh, one of the men clamped an arm around her waist and spun her in a clumsy dance step. Before Laura could extricate herself from his rib-crushing hold, he twirled her into the arms of a companion. Already light-headed from recent childbirth and the blow to her temple, she was as intent on warding off dizziness as she was their groping hands.

"She's as drunk as we are!" one man noted with a laugh.

Laura twisted her face aside to evade wet lips, feeling as though she might be sick. To her surprise and great relief, the man holding her relaxed his arms. She staggered free and grasped the doorframe for balance. Before another of the men had an opportunity to grab her, she escaped inside.

A saloon . . . Laura had envisioned such places. Paintings of naked women. Half-dressed dance girls slinking about and singing ballads. Men slavering over them. Gambling and drunkenness and all manner of wickedness.

The Elephant Corral was nothing like she had pictured. There was a lewd portrait of a hurdy-gurdy girl hanging above the bar, but that was the only similarity. The dancing girls inside were provocatively but fully clothed, and, for the moment at least, no one was singing or seemed to be frothing at the mouth. To her right, two miners had their upper bodies angled over a tabletop to compete at arm wrestling, and they were surrounded by spectators placing bets. As for gaming tables, she could see the dim outlines of them in the far corners of the room, all encircled by patrons, but the clouds of cigar smoke and an oily kerosene haze nearly obscured them.

Feeling horribly out of place, she peered through the lantern-lit gloom and searched for a man who looked uncivilized, no easy task for a woman from Boston who was accustomed to seeing gentlemen turned out in frock coats, matching trousers, and brocade satin vests. Big and dark, the sheriff had said when describing Sheridan. She searched for a burly giant with a matted black beard and an Indian feather stuck in his hair. Someone unkempt and lice-infested, the sort whose bear-hide jacket probably had fleas.

When she finally spotted a feather, it wasn't attached to greasy hair as she anticipated, but neatly tucked into a hatband of cobalt trade beads that encircled the crown of a dusty John B. Stetson. She froze and studied the owner of the tan-colored hat carefully. He stood at the bar, one foot propped on the boot rail, his manner suggesting he was oblivious to the hoots and catcalls coming from the arm-wrestling table behind him. Definitely tall and dark, she decided, but the word *uncivilized* did him an injustice. Lean yet well muscled, with a subtle air of tension about him, he would be better described as dangerous.

He wore tight denim jeans and a blue chambray shirt, the usual garb for a cowboy, but there the comparison ended. Tucked behind his ears, his mahogany hair hung in a thick, gleaming curtain to his shoulders. Instead of the usual leather belt, he wore an Indian-patterned, scarlet sash at his waist and a gun belt slung low over one hip, the holster anchored with buckskin thongs at his thigh. The sleeves had been torn from his shirt, leaving the armholes ragged to reveal sun-burnished and powerfully roped arms.

Though she studied him in profile, she could see that his

collar hung open to reveal a bronzed chest with two medallions nestled in the deep cleavage of muscle, one a crudely fashioned disk with a heathen symbol of some sort etched upon its face, the other a sunburst of bear claws. On his feet, he wore knee-high moccasins that sported layers of long fringe from calf to ankle.

The way her luck had been running, there was no question in Laura's mind that he was Deke Sheridan. An absurd blend of savage and white man, he had Indian written all over him, and was obviously proud of it. Feeling paralyzed, she stood there gaping at him, too intimidated to go closer, yet knowing she must. Uncivilized? He probably ate bloody raw meat for breakfast.

As she took a hesitant step toward him, she noticed a large, rust-colored dog curled at his feet. Its massive head at rest on broad paws, the beast looked as unfriendly as its master. Clamped between its wicked-looking teeth was a deer foreleg, hide and sinew dangling at the severed knee joint. Laura's stomach lurched, and she missed a step. Another man standing at the bar turned and spied her. Ignoring his come-hither grin, she walked straight by him.

"Mr. Sheridan?" At her approach, the dog dropped the deer leg and snarled, its loose jowls glistening with drool. Laura ignored the warning, convinced the animal wouldn't be allowed in a public place if it were truly vicious. "Pardon me. Are you Mr. Sheridan?"

With a bottle of Mon'gehela whiskey partway to his lips, the owner of the tan Stetson turned to regard her with a gaze as clear as ice shards, barely tinted with blue. Laura didn't know if it was the cast of his sun-darkened skin striking a contrast or if his irises actually lacked pigment. Spiked at the corners with weathered lines and fringed with luxurious sable lashes, his eyes looked as though they had once been a brilliant blue and the sun had bleached them to an unnerving tarnished silver. She knew it was probably her imagination, but she felt stripped by his steady regard, not in a physical way, but emotionally, as if he gazed into her instead of at her. The dog snarled again.

"Who's askin'?" he demanded in a silky voice.

Too rattled to think straight, she replied, "I am, obviously."

Never taking his eyes from her, he put the whiskey bottle to his mouth again, took a long swallow, then wiped his lips with the back of his hand. The lower contours of his face shadowed by a day's growth of beard, his was an arresting countenance, the cheekbones high, the cord of tendon pronounced along his squared jaw. Sharply cut and blatantly masculine, his features had the appearance of chiseled walnut. The high bridge of his nose sported a knot where an old break hadn't mended correctly.

"You got a name," he finally asked, "or do I just call you 'obviously'?"

Laura decided he must be drunk. "I'm Mrs. Laura Cheney."

His gaze flicked downward. "Hello, Mrs. Laura Cheney." With a notable lack of enthusiasm, he added, "Pleased to meet ya."

Laura knew she was a sight. She hadn't taken time to bathe or change her clothing before setting out for Denver. Her skirt was caked with dry mud, her hands were filthy, and God only knew what her hair was doing. Naturally curly, it had an irritating way of defying a braid at the best of times, and this wasn't one of her better moments.

"Well, are you or aren't you?" she pressed.

"Ain't I what?"

She clenched her teeth for a moment to keep from saying something she might regret. "Are you Mr. Deke Sheridan?"

"Drop the 'mister,' honey, and I'm your man."

Laura shifted her weight, and at the movement, the dog's growls rose an octave. She forced her fists to uncurl. Sheridan thumped the snarling animal with the soft toe of his moccasin. "Shut up, *Okema*. The lady'll think we ain't sociable."

He said the word *lady* as though it didn't sit well on his tongue, and the hostility in his gaze when he looked back at her was unmistakable. Laura pressed her lips together, uncertain how to proceed. Then she blurted, "Mr. Sheridan, I need your help."

"What kinda help?" He raised one dark eyebrow. "My gun ain't for hire, if that's what you're after. You'll have to save your own ass from the murderin' Cheyenne."

Even though she hadn't expected this to be easy, Laura was starting to feel panicky. Apparently Deke Sheridan had taken an instant dislike to her. "My son has been kidnapped. Early this afternoon sometime. Some horrible men ransacked our cabin and took him. I need to hire a good tracker, and the sheriff recommended you. He says you're the best in the territory."

His mouth twisted into what she surmised was a smile. "Tell him thanks for the brag, but I ain't interested."

With that, he turned back to the bar as if to dismiss her. Laura reached out to touch his arm. When she did, the dog sprang at her, teeth bared. In the nick of time, Sheridan managed to catch the animal by its ruff. "Goddammit, Chief. Sit your worthless ass down before I give it a swift kick."

Thanking the Almighty for Deke Sheridan's quick reflexes, Laura grabbed the edge of the counter. She stared down at the wild-eyed dog, not at all certain she trusted its owner to keep a firm grip. The animal's snarls had drawn curious stares from some of the other customers. "He's vicious," she said weakly.

"Nah, just a little cantankerous around the edges." Still bent at the waist, he slanted her a glare from under the brim of his Stetson. "What d'ya expect when you start to make a move toward me?"

Laura heard the faint tinkling of piano keys. Before she could reply, the tinkling became an earsplitting rendition of Julia Ward Howe's "Glory, Hallelujah," to which several male voices picked up the chorus, more than half of them off-key. She raised her volume to compensate. "I only meant to tap your arm and get your attention."

"Well? Now you got it."

She stared down at him, wishing the brim of his hat didn't make it so difficult to read his expression. "Mr. Sheridan, please, you're my only hope. Won't you help me find my son?"

Pressing a hand to the dog's back, he forced it to lie back down, his touch firm but not unduly rough. Judging from the way the dog hung its head, Laura suspected that Sheridan wasn't always so gentle. Her sympathy went out to the animal, vicious though it was. She knew how it felt to be bullied.

"I mean it, you ornery cur. Bite the lady, and you'll be toothless come mornin'." His expression still threatening, Sheridan straightened. "Mrs.—what'd you say your name was—Clancy?"

"Cheney."

He touched a finger to the brim of his hat and nudged it back. "Look, I'm real sorry about your kid. But I got too many irons of my own in the fire to tend anyone else's. Come sunup, I gotta hit the trail again. A lot of rustlin' goin' on lately. I can't afford to leave my cows out there to graze and have half of 'em get stole. I'm movin' 'em to high country for the summer. You understand? Nothin' personal. I just can't help you."

Somehow Laura couldn't believe it was nothing personal. Every time Sheridan looked at her, his eyes seemed colder.

"You tried Isaac Holmes or Pete Brassfield?" he asked. "They're both fine trackers, and one of 'em might not be as busy as me."

"I'll pay you," Laura tried. Before seeing the sheriff, she had visited the Methodist church. The pastor there had given her the nine dollars and ten cents she needed to send a ten-word dispatch to Boston. Pray God her father would answer her wire and send her some funds. "Any amount you name. I can get money, lots of it."

He gave her clothing another once-over. "I don't doubt it. But money ain't the issue. I'm a cattleman with a ranch to run. It ain't like I'm the only man in Denver good at trackin'."

"Please. No one else will help me. They're all afraid that

the Cheyennes might—" She broke off and moistened her lips. "There's a threat of Indian attack."

"So I've heard."

"All the other men feel they're needed here to defend the town."

"Except for me?" There was no mistaking the bitter edge to his voice. He raised his hands, the conversation clearly at an end as far as he was concerned. "I ain't available, lady. I can't make it much plainer. Find yourself another man."

Laura balled her hands into fists and watched as he took another swig of his whiskey. "My child's life is at stake."

"I got cattle to move, I told you. Go ask Holmes or Brassfield."

Laura had taken all the kicks in the teeth that she intended to for one day. Men! Every last one of them was bent on keeping women in their place, subservient, pregnant, and helpless. Yet where were they when emergencies cropped up? Off somewhere frying bigger fish. Rage reached a flash point inside her so quickly that she didn't take time to consider her next move; she simply acted. With no memory of having drawn it from the holster, she somehow had Tristan's gun in her hand. The piano music and singing stopped short.

"To blazes with your miserable cows. My son could be dying while you sit there nursing that stupid bottle, and I can't waste precious time hunting up another man. Unless you want your hide aerated, you'll come with me peacefully."

Deke had never heard the word *aerated*, but when he saw the Cheney woman's gun from the corner of his eye, it wasn't difficult for him to get her gist. In his thirty-one years he had found himself at the wrong end of a pistol more times than he cared to count, and his usual reaction was to slap leather. His speed had saved his life more than once. But this was the first time a white-faced, trembling female had ever pulled a gun on him. Taken aback, he was a split second slower on the draw than normal, and in that second, he managed to control his reflexes. In the next heartbeat, he was damned glad of it. The silly little fool didn't even have the hammer cocked.

Even if she pulled the trigger, which he seriously doubted she would, the weapon would fail to fire.

Acutely conscious of the pall of silence that had fallen over the saloon, Deke slowly turned his right hip in to the bar, placed a moccasin across Chief's back to keep him down, and then rested an elbow on the counter. His relaxed stance belied the anger that welled inside him. He might have shot her. Didn't she realize that? If he had, both of them could have lost their lives, she with a slug in her chest, he at the end of a rope.

Riled up against the Cheyenne the way they were, Deke knew the men in this town would string him up and ask questions later if he killed a white woman. Especially one like her. Despite the sorry condition of her clothing, she had the unmistakable look of a lady, an impression that became magnified every time she opened her mouth. He'd never heard such an eastern twang.

Where the hell was her husband, anyway? She needed a good paddling for doing something so stupid. Deke narrowed his eyes, wishing he could do the honors. He'd be crazy to lay a hand on her. But, by God, that didn't mean he couldn't teach her a lesson she'd never forget.

She obviously couldn't tell a gun's ass from its nose. He nodded at the weapon she held in one shaking hand. "It might do a better job of aeratin' my hide if you cocked it."

Under any other circumstances, the horrified expression that swept across her face might have made him laugh.

"Cocked?" She held the gun as she might have a rattle-snake, her right arm extended straight out from her body, her white-knuckled hand choking the butt.

"That tit stickin' up on top," he directed helpfully. "You gotta pull it back for the firin' mechanism to work."

Bringing up her other hand to help hold the weapon, she crooked a small thumb over the hammer. Her arms shook with the effort she expended to draw it back. Even from where he stood, Deke could see the mechanism was badly rusted and in sore need of oiling. None too worried that she'd get the gun cocked until well into next week sometime, he made no move to interfere.

With all his attention fixed on her and what she might try next, Deke finally saw past the smears of mud to note the amber color of her eyes, accentuated by hair almost exactly the same shade. The first comparison he drew was to the color of an expensive brandy that went down smooth and warmed a man clear through. The second was to rotgut whiskey, the kind he used to drink when he couldn't afford better, quick to intoxicate and hell on slick runners when he woke up the next morning.

While Laura Cheney continued to wrestle with the corroded gun, he took in details about her that he had ignored earlier, mainly because he never gave a white woman a second look unless she earned her living on her back. A burgundy satin skirt caked with mud clung to her hips and slender legs. A matching velvet jacket that showed little wear finished the outfit. He was no expert on women's duds, but he recognized elegance when he saw it, even if it was badly soiled and a size too small for its wearer.

Laura Cheney had either gained weight recently or she had stolen another woman's clothing. Since she was sure as hell no thief and, in his estimation, couldn't afford to lose an ounce of the feminine softness that padded her fragile figure, he could only suppose she had been painfully thin in the not-so-distant past.

When she finally managed to get the stubborn hammer cocked, Deke took a deliberately slow swallow of whiskey, regarding her along the length of the bottle. He heard everyone else in the saloon scatter for cover. Deke didn't bother. He was willing to bet Laura Cheney had never fired a revolver in her life, and that she wouldn't start now. For one, he doubted a weapon so corroded with rust and dirt would fire right even in experienced hands. Secondly, the look in her eyes told him she didn't have what it took to kill a man.

Trembling so violently that he feared she might drop the gun, she aimed the wavering muzzle in his general direction. "I mean it, Mr. Sheridan. Come with me, or I shall shoot."

Deke, warming to the game more by the second, managed not to laugh. "If you aim to hit me, you'd best hold your hands steady."

In a gallant attempt to do just that, she locked her elbows and closed one eye to sight in. Deke wondered how in hell she thought she could miss when she stood less than three feet away. He plucked the weapon from her grip, pointed it at the floor, and pulled the trigger. Nothing happened.

"Most guns shoot better when they're loaded, too."

Except for the streaks of mud and those arresting amber eyes, her face went absolutely colorless. Then the fight drained out of her, and she bent her head. As Deke laid her gun on the bar, he noticed that she was swaying slightly, as if all that kept her on her feet was sheer grit. With her head at a different angle, he spotted some dried blood at her hairline. His cocky grin faded, and he started to feel a little ashamed.

Now that they knew no bullets were likely to fly, the other brave souls inside the saloon began to emerge from their hiding places like roaches from mopboards. One man hooted and yelled, "Hey, baby. I got a loaded pistol, primed and cocked. You wanna put it to some good use?"

At the gibe, Laura Cheney looked up, her amber eyes unfocused and bewildered. Deke doubted she understood what the bastard meant and figured that was just as well. She took a faltering step backward. Then another. He watched as she spun and fled from the saloon.

Silence. He glanced neither left nor right, the taste of well-executed vengeance bitter at the back of his throat. Vengeance for what? That was the question. When he turned back to the bar and took another swig of whiskey, the liquor no longer had a bite. He stared past the shelves of bottles opposite him at his reflection in the mirrored wall. His washed-out blue eyes stared back at him. Blue, not brown. With hatred for the Cheyenne running so high in town and spilling over onto him, he sometimes forgot who he actually was, Deke Sheridan, not *Shakeka S'ski-si-coh'*, Flint Eyes.

Even so, he owed the Laura Cheneys of this world nothing. Under any other circumstances, she would have walked two blocks out of her way to avoid him on the street. He could spot her sort from a mile away, noses always in the air, afraid of him and trying to hide it, too good to breathe the same air he did. To hell with every damned one of them. It took some nerve for one of her kind to come seeking him out when her luck ran sour.

He upended the whiskey bottle and took several big gulps. The blast of fire that hit his guts reminded him that even Mon'gehela could make a man sick if he guzzled too much of it. He set the liquor aside. Down the bar from him lay a neatly folded newspaper. Determined to put the Cheney woman's face out of his mind, he grabbed the paper and spread it open. Using a blunt fingertip to keep his place, he worked his way through the groups of letters, mouthing syllables, imagining the sounds until he got each word figured out. A slow process, reading, but he was self-taught and damned proud he knew his letters.

The first thing he read was an advertisement for Dr. Tumblety's Pimple Banisher, only one dollar per bottle, one of its many attributes being that it could make old faces look young and beautiful. Deke wondered if it would help skin that had gone tough as saddle leather from too much sun.

Next he scanned the lurid details of the Huntgate massacre. Governor Evans was calling upon "patriotic citizens" to volunteer for militia companies. Another article claimed that since the massacre, some of the women in Denver and outlying towns had started carrying small bottles of white powder. Strychnine . . . so they could avoid fates worse than death in the event of Indian attack. He pictured Amanda Carrington, one of the snootiest bitches in town, walking to Sunday services with a bottle of strychnine tucked between her breasts. He grinned at the thought and wondered what it would take to scare her into snorting a little of it.

His smile faded as his thoughts doubled back to Laura Cheney. Did she carry a bottle of strychnine? She had been terrified of him from the get-go; he had read that much in her expression. And he wasn't even a true Cheyenne. It amazed him that she had actually risked drawing a gun on him. If she had been told about his tracking skills, she must have heard about his reputation with a gun. That meant she was desperate enough to try almost anything.

What if she was right, and Holmes or Brassfield wouldn't help her because of the Indian threat? If she had been fool enough to risk her life by confronting him with an unloaded gun, she might get it into her mind to search for her child by herself. If she did, she'd better have herself a bottle of that white powder handy. Cheyenne tempers were hot. If, in that mood, they came across a lone white woman, God only knew what they might do.

"It ain't my problem." Deke glanced down at his dog. "Right, *Okema*?"

Chief, whose name translated to *Okema* in Cheyenne, ceased gnawing on his bone. He offered no comment, yea or nay, not that Deke had drunk enough whiskey to expect one. Yet.

He patted his breast pocket in search of his tobacco pouch, then forgot what he was doing as he once again pictured Laura Cheney's pale face.

Damn it to hell. Earlier when he had come into the Elephant Corral, his plan had been to wash the trail dust from his throat with several slugs of whiskey, take a long, hot bath, and then partake of an accommodating woman and a good night's sleep, in that exact order. Come morning, he had to get his saddle-weary ass back on a horse again. He deserved one night of leisure. The last thing he needed was a frantic, amber-haired woman with more courage than sense to throw a hitch in his get-along.

And wasn't that the problem? When it came to white women, there wasn't a whole lot Deke found to admire. But, then, it wasn't often he ran across one who dared to draw a gun on him. Of all the things he had been taught to value as a kid, courage ranked high on the list. He had to hand it to Laura Cheney. She might not be the smartest thing to ever come down the pike, but she had guts.

He shoved away from the bar, picked up the fool woman's gun, and glared at his dog. "Don't say one goddamn word, you mangy, good-for-nothing cur. She spells trouble. I know it, and you know it. But what else can we do?"

With a woebegone expression, Chief secured the deer leg between his teeth and lumbered to his feet. Sometimes, particularly when halfway finished with a jug of Mon'gehela, Deke could swear the animal understood him. Together, they left the saloon. Once on the boardwalk, Deke scanned the street.

"I wonder where in hell she went."

At the question, Chief lowered his nose closer to the ground and took off toward Front Street. Deke fell in behind him.

"If you're followin' the trail of that little shepherd you was shinin' up to earlier, I'll kick your butt, you randy old coot. There ain't no way you're gettin' some if I don't."

Chief stayed with the scent. At Front, he hung right. When he reached Wazee, he cut left. Deke saw a livery stable up ahead. "Son of a bitch," he muttered. "If she ain't plannin' to leave town, why does she need her horse?"

To Deke's surprise, Chief didn't stop in front of the stable, but circled around behind it. Once the dog gained the yard out back, he dropped to his belly and went back to gnawing on his deer leg. Deke approached a little more cautiously. Good night vision and sharply honed senses made it easy for him to pick out Laura Cheney from the shadows. Head bent, body sagging, she stood with one arm draped over the swayback of her horse. He had never seen anyone look quite so down at the mouth.

Chapter 4

"I AIN'T NEVER IN ALL MY LIFE SEEN A SORRIER-lookin' pair."

The deep voice coming from the shadows made Laura jump. Holding on to her old mare's saddle horn for extra support, she turned slightly and peered through the moonless gloom.

"From where I'm standin', I can't tell if the horse is holdin' you up, or the other way around."

Laura recognized that silky voice. Since she couldn't see its owner, she felt at a distinct disadvantage. Listening for footfalls, she tensed to run. Her heart skipped when his looming figure stepped out from the shadows less than five feet away.

"If you followed me to have more fun at my expense, Mr. Sheridan, I've concluded your entertainment for the evening. Please go back to your bottle and leave me alone."

He never broke stride. As everything else about him did, his soundless walk unnerved her. She saw that he held Tristan's gun in his left hand. She didn't believe for a minute that he had come after her to return it. The nearer he drew, the larger he seemed. Much taller than he had back at the saloon, much broader at the shoulder. She remembered how quickly he could move. If he meant to cause her grief, she was in big trouble.

Exhaustion made her limbs feel heavy. Her every instinct urged her to flee, but, God help her, she didn't think she could. When he drew to a stop, he stood close enough to touch her, and it seemed to Laura that the darkening air was filled with man. Tall, dark, braided with muscle, he intimidated her with every breath he took. Her frightened gaze shifted to the heathenish medallions that decorated his chest, representative of a people as brutal as the land from which they came, rapists, mutilators, murderers of women and children. She leaned more heavily against the horse, accepting with numb resignation that whatever he had in mind, she was too spent to fight him.

"Where in hell's your husband?" he asked. "At a time like this, he oughta be here."

The question came so suddenly that it made Laura jump. Terrified to admit how completely alone she actually was, she said, "My husband is otherwise occupied."

Sheridan looked none too pleased to hear that. "Well, since he ain't here to say it, I will. Never aim a gun when you don't plan to shoot. And until you get practiced up, it'd be smart to choose targets that won't shoot back. You came just that close to gettin' your cute little ass shot off."

"Excuse me, but as I recall, I asked for your help, not advice."

"Yeah? Well, advice ain't the only thing you didn't ask for that I've a good mind to give you."

Already on edge, Laura grew truly alarmed at the subtle threat in his voice. She straightened and slipped her hand into her pocket, her numb fingers groping for the hilt of her kitchen knife. "Since you obviously have no intention of helping me, why don't you be on your way, Mr. Sheridan?"

He shifted his weight to one foot, the change of position throwing one lean hip outward. After following the path of her hand down to her pocket, he riveted her with those silver eyes. "Sweetheart, there's two things you maybe oughta learn, and the quicker the better. The first is that you can't stir a hornet's nest without gettin' buzzed by a bee. The second is that you're bound to regret it if you do what you're thinkin' about doin'."

When she spoke, her voice sounded thin even to her.

"How can you possibly venture a guess as to what I intend to do?"

His firm mouth slanted into a slow grin. "I got ten dollars that says you have a knife in your pocket." The gleam in his eyes turned feral. "And I got fifty that says I'll take it away from you, slicker than greased owl shit, if you pull it on me. I think you'd best leave it right where it is. You've bellied up to trouble one too many times tonight as it is."

"I'm not afraid of you."

"I ain't sayin' you should be. I'm just sayin' I'm liable to get outa sorts if you pull a knife on me."

Laura kept a firm grip on the knife handle. "You don't care to be threatened. Neither do I. You expressed an intent to harm me, and I've made ready to defend myself. Shall we leave it at that?"

Moving a bit closer, he pressed a leathery fingertip to the underside of her chin and lifted her face slightly, the touch so light, it was more a caress. The raw power that emanated from his body forestalled Laura from doing anything that might set him off. She imagined that hand curling around her throat as Tristan's had so often done.

"Honey, I don't threaten. If I had meant to harm you, it'd be a done deed. Pullin' a stunt like that could've got you killed. You don't march into a saloon, walk up to a strange man guzzlin' whiskey, and pull a gun on him. Most times, he swaps lead first and asks questions later."

With that, he nosed Tristan's gun into the holster on her hip. Then he stepped back, giving her a bit more room to breathe. Laura could feel him looking her over. After doing so at his leisure, he turned slightly away and regarded her pack mule.

"Where'd you get these critters, from a slaughter pen?"

Laura forced her chin back down. "What business—" She heard male voices drifting to them from the street. Drunks. Even if she screamed, she doubted anyone would come help her. Closing her eyes, she swallowed. "Mr. Sheridan, please. Why have you followed me?"

He didn't answer. The prolonged silence finally forced

her eyes open. He stood there gazing down at her, his expression unreadable in the shadows. After a long, drawn-out moment, he said, "Damned if I know."

The response so confused her that she could only stare. Before she could gather her thoughts, he asked, "How much?"

For a moment, she thought he was propositioning her. She'd heard smoother deliveries, but never from a more frightening prospect. "For what?"

"How much you willin' to pay for a tracker?"

She couldn't think what to say. A stinging sensation washed over her eyes. "You mean you've decided to help me find my son?"

"No help to it. It's all you can do to stay on your feet. You been ailin' or somethin'? No man in his right mind would take you on a hard ride."

Laura ran her cottony tongue over her lips. "H-How much do you generally charge for tracking?"

"Don't."

"You don't charge?"

"Don't track. Like I said, I run cattle."

"I shall pay any price you name." Her pulse quickened. "You won't mind waiting until we return here to get the money, will you? I mean . . ." She gestured with her hands. "I can get it, no question of that. But it may take a few days to get it wired from Boston. That's where I'm from, Boston."

"Never would've guessed." He pinned her with those unnerving quicksilver eyes again. "You sayin' you don't got the money now?"

She envisioned him growing angry and walking away. "My father's wealthy, very wealthy, and—"

"Hallelujah for him." He shook his head. "If you don't beat all. Come into a saloon, offer a man any amount of money he names, then draw a gun on him to butter the bread. And come to find out, you got a run-down excuse for a horse, a pack mule that's nothin' but hide stretched over bone, and no money."

"My baby's life is at stake. How can money even be a concern?"

"Baby?" he repeated incredulously. "I hope that's the mama in you talkin'. How old is this kid?"

"Three days," she whispered.

"What?"

"Three days," she said more loudly.

"Three days old?" When she made no reply, he said, "Christ!," the sound more hiss than word. "How in hell did you lose a newborn baby, lady? When they're that young, most mamas is joined to them at the hip."

"I didn't lose him. He was stolen."

"And where in hell was you while he was gettin' stole?"

Tears sprang to her eyes. "How dare you insinuate I neglected my baby."

"I ain't insinuatin' nothin' of the sort. It's just—" He swiped his mouth with the back of his wrist. At the sudden movement, she flinched, then felt silly when she realized he had no intention of striking her. By the set of his shoulders, she could see his frustration was mounting by the second. He took a deep breath and exhaled slowly. "All right. Let's back up and start over. I didn't spit that out the way I meant. It just took me off guard, him bein' so young. A newborn baby puts a whole new shine on things."

His shadowy form seemed to swim, and she realized she was looking at him through tears. "What difference does it make how old he is?"

"A big one. It ain't like I can throw him a piece of jerky and say he's fed. Jesus, lady, a baby? I figured he was old enough to walk, that he had wandered off from you or somethin', and then got stole. Three days old? With babies fresh out of the oven like that, most mamas is still countin' fingers and toes, not sashayin' off and leavin' 'em. This ain't Boston, you know."

Laura had never wanted to smack someone so badly. "I *didn't* leave him!"

"You must've. Otherwise, you wouldn't be here. A group of men who'd steal a baby would take one look at that hair of yours and snatch you, too. Hell, an Indian brave would trade twenty of his best horses to get his hands on a woman like you, and, trust me, honey, that's low bid. So don't stand there tellin' me you was there, and that your baby got took and you didn't."

A sob snagged in Laura's throat. She struggled to get her voice. "Our well went dry. I had no choice but to leave Jonathan alone inside the cabin while I dug it deeper. At noon when the sun started to get hot, I went down to the creek to haul up water for the vegetable garden. I fell in the rocks and hit my head. I was unconscious when those men stole my baby, not sashaying off somewhere. How dare you accuse me of such a thing!"

"Where in hell was your husband while all this was goin' on? Did he get stole, too?" He paused for a moment, as if expecting a reply. "He should be the one combin' Denver for a tracker. This is a dangerous town. Especially the saloons. You got any idea what kind of men go in those places?"

Rigid with outrage, Laura cried, "I think I have an inkling."

The insult seemed to bounce right off him. "Answer my question. Where's your husband? After I kick his no-account ass, I'll do my business with him." He shook his head. "Three days out of childbed and diggin' a goddamned well? The son of a bitch oughta be lynched."

"He's dead!"

At the admission, he fell silent. Trembling with hurt and anger, Laura turned toward the horse and pressed her face against its neck. In that moment, all the resentment that had built within her over the last several weeks became focused on him. "Just go away. I don't need or want your miserable help. Just go away."

She heard no footsteps, but given the eerily silent way he moved, that didn't mean much. The quiet stretched into a minute. Then two.

"If this ain't a hell of a mess, I don't know what is."

Barely able to speak, she managed a shaky "Yes, well, it's my mess."

The faint sound of his moccasin scuffing dirt came to her. Then he sighed. "If you was diggin' a well and haulin' water, I reckon it's understandable, you leavin' the kid alone."

Laura made a fist in the horse's mane. At this point she no longer cared what he might do to her. What difference did it make? Her sweet, precious baby. He had only her to rescue him, and she hadn't even left Denver yet. The way it appeared, she might not. "I don't need an ignorant ass who says 'ain't' with every other breath and constantly uses the wrong verb tense to tell me my actions were understandable, thank you."

To her surprise, he didn't take up the gauntlet. "I never meant to— It just struck me as curious, that's all, you not bein' there with your baby."

"You made it perfectly clear what you thought. 'This ain't Boston'! I wish it were. At least decent human beings live there. 'Sashaying off'! What did you think? That I was busy powdering my nose when it happened?"

"Now that you explained, it's clear as rain you wasn't." She heard him make an unintelligible sound under his breath. "It ain't often I apologize."

"Don't inconvenience yourself on my account."

"For what it's worth, I'm sorry."

Laura couldn't bring herself to look at him, not with tears streaming down her cheeks. "I'm a good mother."

"I never said you wasn't."

"I may not be good at very much else, but I love my baby and I'm doing the best job I can."

"You bein' here and not in bed where you belong proves that."

In his voice, she heard a note of dismissal. Accepted or not, he had apologized, and now he was ready to move on. Her stung feelings wouldn't let her put it behind her quite that easily. She still itched with the urge to slap him, maybe because his accusation had struck a chord. She wasn't a good mother, not because she didn't try, but because she didn't know how to be.

From the corner of her eye, she saw him move toward her mule. "It's gonna be one hell of a trip, you know. You're in no condition to hare off on a long ride, we won't be able to stop very often, and you'll be eatin' my drag dust most of the time."

She jerked erect, not quite certain she had heard him right. Brushing impatiently at the tears on her cheeks, she said, "You mean—are you going to help me, after all?"

"Honey, I left a half-drunk bottle of Mon'gehela sittin' on the bar at the Elephant Corral. I didn't part company with it to stand out here in the dark with you and swap insults."

She thought she glimpsed a flash of white teeth and suspected that he had smiled. He pulled a wad of cloth from one of her packs and stared at it. Before he shoved it back, Laura recognized her spare set of bloomers, which she had brought along to use as rags for her childbirth flux.

Giving her mule a kindly pat, which from his large hand was more of a slap, he turned to regard her. "No two ways around it, you gotta get another horse and pack animal."

"I haven't the funds to buy them."

He circled to the other saddlebag. "This where you put your rations?" He unstrapped leather, jerked up the flap, dived a hand into the bag, and swore. "There ain't enough grub in here to last a day."

"I brought what I could."

"We'll have to get more. Exactly how much money do you got?"

Her mouth felt as dry as dust. "Only three cents."

She heard him give a humorless laugh. "Can I pick 'em? A woman straight out of childbed with a dead husband, a lost baby, and three cents. One of these days, I'm gonna have the good sense to run the other way when I stumble into a mess like this." Pulling the mule along behind him, he strode toward her. "Can you stand on your own if I take that horse?"

"Where?"

"Around front to trade her off."

"I thought I made it clear that—"

"I know, Boston. You ain't got the funds."

"Then what—" Laura caught herself from falling as he seized the mare's reins and drew the animal into a walk. "Wait a minute. Where are you—? What are you doing with my horse?"

"Your rich daddy's gonna wire you money, right? You can settle with me when it comes."

He never missed a step, and she had no choice but to follow him as he led her animals around the side of the livery. The red dog ambled out from the shadows to fall in with them, the deer leg still clamped between its jaws. "Any idea at all who took your kid?"

Feeling oddly separated from reality, Laura related the events of the day and her reasons for suspecting the Mexican, Francisco Gonzales.

As Sheridan drew the animals to a stop in front of the stable doors, he asked, "You think he did it because he's Mex or because he's no-account?"

"Pardon?" She peered at him over the bony back of her mule.

"From what you say, you was out cold down by the crick when it happened. You can't have seen much of nothin', so you're only speculatin'. I can speculate with the best of 'em, so I got no quarrel with that. My question is, do you got any call to suspect the Mex, other than his skin color?"

"Are you implying that I'm prejudiced, Mr. Sheridan?"

"You got another reason for actin' like I got bugs?"

Laura drew up her shoulders. "I am not a prejudiced person, and I have not behaved as though you have bugs! The thought never crossed my mind."

He looked unconvinced.

"Besides," she added quickly, "you're not really—" She broke off and searched for a tactful way to put it. "You're, um, not . . ."

"Cheyenne?" he supplied.

"Exactly."

"Exactly wrong. I was raised by the People, most times I think like one of 'em, and for the most part, I look like one. I scare the snot right out of you, and if you say I don't, you're a liar."

Laura took refuge in silence.

He gazed down the street for a moment, then returned his attention to her. "Back to the Mex. Let me put it another way. Did he do or say somethin' to make you think he'd swipe a baby?"

"His character was questionable, to say the least."

"How'd you make that call?"

"He was filthy."

"Just because a man don't wash don't make him a baby thief."

"He looked at me in a highly improper way."

"You can't hang a man for lookin'."

"He stared."

"At what?"

Laura's face flamed. "At places no decent man would."

He shook his head. "Boston, I know you're broke, so pardon me for makin' note of it. But you've outgrown your clothes some."

She tried to read his shadowed face. "What has that to do with it?"

"You're stressin' your seams in some interesting places."

Shocked momentarily speechless by the observation, Laura couldn't gather her wits to retort before he led her animals inside the stable. She followed more slowly. Within minutes, her tracker had procured her a new mount and mule, charging both to his credit because he didn't have the necessary cash on him. The sum he now owed on her behalf made her feel panicky. What if her father refused, as he had so many other times, to wire her money?

With a speed born of long practice, he transferred her saddlery onto the newly acquired animals. After tightening the belly cinch on the bay gelding, he turned toward her.

Before she guessed what he meant to do, he seized her by the waist and lifted her onto the saddle. Though she tried to hide it, she winced. In the livery's dim lantern light, she saw his silver eyes sharpen.

"You sure you can handle ridin'?"

"I'm certain of it." She tried to find a more comfortable position, conscious all the while of his gaze on her. "About the Mexican. I didn't form an impression on looks alone. He made a highly improper suggestion."

"Like what?"

"He . . ." Laura tugged on her jacket tails and took the proffered reins. "He offered to lend me money and suggested I repay it in an indecent way."

She thought she saw a twinkle of amusement in his eyes. "Where I come from, men do that kind of anglin' with tradin' pitch."

"What?"

"Tradin' pitch. For startin' fires. It comes mighty dear to a Cheyenne woman's lodge when the winters get long and wet." He checked the length of her left stirrup, then moved to check the right. "When I was young, I spent half my time lookin' for boles veined with pitch."

"Are you saying that Cheyenne women have so few morals that they . . ." The thought was so scandalous, she couldn't put it into words. "For pitch?"

"Most would rather freeze their asses off." He curled a warm hand around her calf to lift her foot into the stirrup. After a measuring glance, he did some readjusting. "But there's always the exceptions to be found if a man keeps liftin' lodge flaps. Mighty nice exceptions."

Laura gaped at him. He glanced up and flashed her a grin rife with mischief. "Can't hang a man for tryin', Boston. To my way of thinkin', there's a big difference between admirin' a filly and foreleggin' her."

"Forelegging?"

"Throwin' a loop and bringin' her down by the front feet," he explained. "It's not pretty, and likely as not, the filly gets her neck broke. But she's caught. Don't look to me like the Mex tossed you any loops."

Laura felt heat flag each of her cheeks. "That he made such a suggestion was indicative of a badly flawed character."

"Depends on how you look at it, I reckon. So if it's all the same to you, I'll hold off on a verdict till I size the poor sap up for myself."

With that, he grabbed the new mule's lead rope, seized her gelding's harness, and led the procession from the livery.

Their next stop was at the general store, where Deke Sheridan pounded on the locked door so hard, he shook the window glass. When the proprietor finally answered the wall-rattling summons, he snarled a greeting. Sheridan and his dog snarled back, and the intimidated shopkeeper allowed them entry. With painful slowness, Laura swung down from the horse and followed her tracker into the shop, more than a little horrified by the goods he was so quickly gathering into a pile next to the counter scales.

"Mr. Sheridan," she said softly. "Mr. Sheridan?"

He didn't have a shirtsleeve to tug, so Laura had no choice but to walk at his heels and lightly tap his arm. Because the red dog flanked her, she touched Deke Sheridan with even more trepidation than she might have otherwise, which was saying something. Evidently the animal had deemed her harmless, for he didn't growl or offer to leap at her. When at last frustration prodded her into abandoning good manners, she raised her voice and said, "Mr. Sheridan, we must have a talk."

He hefted a box of rifle cartridges as if to check its weight and shot her a questioning glance. "So talk."

"Not in here," she whispered fiercely. "Outside."

He tossed down the box and gestured that he would follow her. Once they gained the boardwalk, Laura hunched her shoulders against the cool wind and searched for words. The dog padded past her to lie in the dirt at the edge of the boardwalk. "You mustn't be buying things left and right."

"I don't take off into hard country without supplies, Boston. That's suicide."

Laura squeezed her eyes closed. "I might not be able to pay you back for all that stuff."

"I thought you said—"

"I stretched the truth a bit."

"How much is a bit?"

She lifted her lashes. "I'm estranged from my father."

He nudged his hat back and surveyed her from beneath arched brows. "Can you talk English, Boston? More than one new word a day taxes my thinker." At her blank look, he clarified, "What in hell does 'estranged' mean?"

"He has disowned me."

"You sayin' he don't lay claim to you no more?"

Laura flinched. "Sort of."

"Shit."

"It's not as bad as it sounds. Now that my husband's dead, he'll probably forgive me. There's every chance he'll send me money. Really, there is. It's just that . . ." She waved her hands toward the store. "I don't want to get you into a financial bind if it should happen that he doesn't."

He planted his hands on his hips. "Let me get this straight. You've got three cents, and it's iffy that you can get more? I just dropped over a hundred dollars at the livery, I'm lookin' at spendin' another seventy or so here, and I'm hirin' on as your tracker. You ever heard of gettin' in so far over your head, you can't touch bottom, Boston?"

"My name's Laura, and I never intended to spend any money, if you'll recall. I told you I couldn't afford a horse and mule."

"You told me your daddy had money up his ass, that's what you told me."

Laura wrung her hands. "I know you have every right to be angry."

"Damn straight."

"I should never have implied that I could definitely get the money. But please, try to understand that it's my baby out there. I'd lie, steal . . ." Her gaze locked with his, and a horrible tightness clenched her stomach. "I'll do anything to get him back, Mr. Sheridan. Anything."

His mouth twisted. "We talkin' tradin' pitch again?"

The boards beneath Laura's feet seemed to lose substance. In her peripheral vision, the ground and surrounding buildings seemed to swell and recede. She had to force her next words up a paralyzed throat. "What am I supposed to do? Say, oh, well? I haven't got the means, so I'll just sit here and let them keep my baby?"

"You could let a man know what he's bitin' off before he's got a mouthful." He hooked a thumb over his shoulder toward a saloon across the street. "See them windows on the second story? Up there, a man can rent himself a woman for ten dollars. For fifteen, he can stay all night. No offense meant, honey. You're pretty enough to get most men's juices flowin'. But there ain't a piece of ass on earth that's worth a hundred and seventy dollars."

His dog thumped down on the boardwalk at his feet and, as if to second the vote, let out a mournful whine around the deer leg between its teeth.

"Do I look like a man who can afford to throw away that much money?"

Laura closed her eyes. "No. And it was never my intention that you should."

An image of Jonathan flashed inside her mind, so small, so soft and warm, so helpless. It was all she could do to keep her emotions in check. A horrible urge to laugh struck her. She had just offered herself to him. Offered herself, like so much baggage. And he was turning her down, flat. To add insult to injury, he had referred to her as a piece of ass. As though she were a thing and not a person. Not even a very tempting thing, from the sound of it. Humiliation brought tears to her eyes. To stoop that low, and then be turned down. And by the likes of him? She felt filthy—the sort of filth that might never wash away.

Struggling for her voice, she said, "Just explain matters to the proprietor and put everything back. I shall take care of the livery stable owner. Surely he'll be reasonable." She swallowed and forced herself to meet his gaze. "Please accept my apologies for inconveniencing you as I have."

Laura turned to step off the boardwalk. Sheridan seized her arm. "What're you plannin' now?"

Uncomfortably aware of the leashed strength in his grip, she glanced down at his hand. "I'm going to return the horse and mule. Don't worry. I'll be certain your account is credited."

"And then what?"

Surprised that she was able, Laura pulled her arm free. "I must find my baby."

He jerked his hat off and raked a hand through his long hair. In the time that had passed since he found her behind the livery, the moon had come up, and in the silvery shafts of light, his darkness and odd dress made him look all the more Indian. "Alone, you mean?"

Her voice quavery with emotion, Laura said, "As you've so eloquently pointed out, Mr. Sheridan, I haven't the funds to hire help." She stepped to the gelding and lifted her foot into the stirrup. Before pulling herself up, she looked back at him. "I really am sorry. I know it may not count for much, but I'm not given to lying very often."

"Wait a minute."

She hesitated, her hand clenched on the saddle horn. He came off the boardwalk with one long stride, then stopped near her to gaze at his feet. He slapped his thigh with his hat before looking up at her.

"You can't take off out there alone," he finally said. "Under the best of circumstances, you could get hurt or lost. And right now, with the Cheyenne in a dither . . ." His voice trailed away. Even by the dim light of the moon, she could see the corded tendon along his jaw bunch and relax with every clench of his teeth. "If they came across a whiskey-haired woman right now, there's no tellin' what they'd do. The only guarantee is, you'd wish you was dead by the time they finished doin' it."

"I appreciate the warning, but I'm well aware of the dangers. They don't factor into this very neatly."

"Meanin'?"

"Meaning I must find my baby, the devil take the consequences."

He caught her arm before she mounted the horse. "I'll take the job."

Laura froze and looked back at him. "Pardon?"

"Let's go in and get the supplies."

She glanced toward the store. "But—what about money?"

"I'll stake us."

"But what if I'm unable to pay you back?"

"We'll work somethin' out."

"Like what?"

His white teeth flashed in another slow grin. "Havin' second thoughts, Boston?"

Laura felt that awful, sick sensation again. But the way she saw it, she had no options. "My name is Laura, and no, I haven't room for second thoughts where my baby's life is concerned."

"Good. Then we've got a deal. Let's go get the supplies."

Chapter 5

BEFORE LEAVING TOWN, LAURA'S NEW TRACKER had to fetch his horse, packhorse, and gear. Then he had to make arrangements with his foreman to continue the cattle roundups and drives during his absence. While he did the latter, she waited outside yet another rowdy saloon with their horses. Oddly enough, none of the drunks going in and out of the building offered to pester her. One look at Deke Sheridan's mount seemed enough to discourage them.

Like its owner, the magnificent black stallion had an Indian look. Though its saddle was ordinary enough, the blanket beneath sported a gaudy Cheyenne pattern in the weave. The animal's harness was decorated as well, on the strap behind its left ear with a feather similar to the one Sheridan wore on his hat, and on the throat strap with a medallion, a cluster of animal teeth, and a string of cobalt beads. Distasteful-looking ornaments, she decided, very like the ones suspended on rawhide strips around her tracker's neck. But distasteful or no, they branded the horse as Deke Sheridan's, which for the moment seemed to be working in her favor. Apparently no one wanted to pester the man's traveling companion and risk his retribution.

Thus reassured, Laura no longer felt a need to have Tristan's rusty gun on her hip. The weapon was heavy and, because she couldn't tie the holster to her thigh, tended to flop about every time she moved. Glad to be rid of it, she unbuckled the gun belt and stowed it in one of her saddle-bags.

Laura noticed that although she didn't suffer the attention she had before, men stared at her as they passed. She drew herself erect in the saddle, ignoring the discomfort in her nether regions. What were they thinking when they gaped at her that way? She didn't like the possibilities that came to mind. That she was Sheridan's woman, perhaps? Her reputation would be in shreds the instant she rode out of town with him. People would whisper, scandalized that she had kept company with him. Not a Cheyenne, but as close to it as he could get. Everyone knew how those savages treated white women.

Laura's mind stumbled on that thought. She tightened her grip on the saddle horn. What in God's name was she about to do? She peered through the darkness toward the edge of town. Within minutes, she'd be out there in that vastness with a man who admitted to being more Cheyenne than white. What if this was all a ghastly trick? What if he had no intention of helping her but was luring her out of town to get her alone? Memories of the two women on the wagon train flashed inside her head. Their screams, the evil laughter of the braves who raped and mutilated them.

The buildings along the boardwalk went into a slow rotation. Laura rubbed her throbbing temple, afraid she might faint. Her thoughts trailed to Jonathan. He was all that mattered. No matter what happened out there in the wilderness with Sheridan, at least she would know she had tried.

A sudden shout made Laura turn. In the moonlit darkness, she could barely discern the shape of a man running up the street from the edge of town.

"They're attacking!" he screamed. "Sweet Jesus, they're coming this way, hundreds of them. In a flat-out run!"

A woman somewhere along the street wailed in terror. Within seconds several other female voices took up the lament. Men spilled from doorways, jerking on their boots and jackets, loading rifles as they ran. A child began to screech. Laura stared in befuddlement. Who was coming?

She tried to see, but beyond the town there was only moonlight and shadow.

"Off the streets! Run to the shelters!" "Every available man, go to the armory!" "Son of a bitch, I don't got a gun!"

The frenzied voices pelted Laura from all sides. Gritting her teeth against the pain it caused, she twisted in the saddle to see better. A man in trousers and a long-sleeved white undershirt came running up to her. As he jerked up his suspenders, he yelled, "You deaf? Get to a shelter!"

Laura gaped at the women who seemed to have come from nowhere to cut frantic paths up the street. Most dragged children in their wake. One young mother carrying a baby tripped on the hem of her skirt and crashed to her knees. Her terrified sob caught at Laura's heart. Bathed by light from the windows, another woman sped along the boardwalk, struggling as she ran to shove a cork into the mouth of a small bottle. Her hands shook so violently, the white granules within spilled out and powdered the front of her bodice.

Suddenly Laura heard a distant thundering sound. Hooves. Hundreds of them, pounding the earth, the sound coming toward town.

"Run, honey!" a matronly woman called to her. "Run for your life."

Growing truly alarmed, Laura started to slide off the horse, only to be stopped by a hand on her knee. She looked around. Deke Sheridan stood beside her gelding. Even in the dim light, she could see the distant expression in his silvery eyes as he scanned the horizon. He cocked an ear to listen.

"Wh-Who's coming?" she asked.

"Cheyenne," he replied. "Or so the damned fools think."

At the word *Cheyenne*, Laura jerked. He tightened his grip on her leg. "Cheyenne? Oh, dear God. We must hide!"

"Most of the buildings here is wood. If it's Cheyenne comin' this way, they'll torch everything in their path."

Another woman ran by, waving a small bottle so her female friend might see it. "Did you bring yours? We'll need enough for the children!"

Laura saw Deke stiffen. Then, before she guessed his intent, he darted into the street and caught the woman by her arm. In a voice braided with urgency, he said, "Don't go givin' any of that to your kids, lady. You understand? Not until the last second."

The woman fell back. Her scream was weak but eloquent. If the devil himself had grabbed her, he couldn't have elicited a more horrified reaction. As though the touch of her were suddenly contaminating, Deke let go of her.

"It ain't the Cheyenne comin'," he called after her. "You hear me? Give that to your children, and you'll regret it."

Harkening to the terrified shouts resounding around her, Laura slid off the horse and broke into a run, her one thought to escape with the others. Sheridan snaked out an arm, caught her at the waist, and lifted her half off her feet. She spun into a steely embrace that crushed her to his broad chest. Though she struggled, she couldn't extricate herself from his hold.

"Trust me. It ain't Cheyenne comin'."

He drew her back toward the horse. Her feet didn't connect solidly with the ground until he deposited her where he wanted her, between him and the animal's front shoulder. Only then did he release her. Gaze fixed on the end of town, he swept off his hat and looped the bonnet string over the saddle horn. "There ain't a Cheyenne alive stupid enough to attack a town this size with that much warning."

Since that made sense, Laura turned to look and saw a black cloud, which she could only assume was dust, rising toward the moon. "What is it, then?"

"Damned if I know." A faint mewling sound filtered toward them. Upon hearing it, he started to laugh. "Jesus Christ, it's cows! The damned fools is runnin' from a herd of cows."

Laura giggled, albeit a little hysterically. Behind her, she could hear the townspeople still trying to muster a defense. Men were being called to volunteer; women shrieked; someone yelled, "Rifles! This way for rifles!"

The stampeding herd of cattle lost its momentum at the edge of town, and only a few lead runners spilled onto the street. The bawling noise grew increasingly louder. It took several minutes before Laura heard its origin acknowledged by the men who had taken up positions along the boardwalk.

"It's cows, Horton!"

"Cows?" was the incredulous response. "You kidding?"

"Hell, no, I'm not kidding. Can't you hear them?"

"All this over cows? Where's the damned fool who raised the alarm?"

Deke's white-toothed grin seemed iridescent in the darkness. Weak with relief, Laura clamped a hand over her mouth to stifle her giggles. His gaze dropped to hers, and his smile broadened. Retrieving his hat, he put it back on and chuckled. The warm sound was Laura's undoing, and her laughter escaped.

"You think it's funny, you Indian-loving bastard?"

The angry, masculine voice made Laura whirl. A man carrying a rifle came striding up the street. Though she felt certain it wasn't his intention, Deke stepped sideways as if to shield her when he turned to confront the stranger. His shoulder partially obstructed her view.

"No offense meant. I ain't laughin' at you, mister, but with you."

"Who the hell do you hear laughing? Women and children terrorized! Running for their lives! You have a twisted sense of humor." The man spotted Laura. "And you! Picking mighty shady companions, aren't you, ma'am?"

"That's the Cheney woman," another man called as he emerged from shadows. "Her kid got snatched. She's hiring Sheridan to find her baby."

The first man snorted upon hearing that, his gaze never leaving Laura. "You leave town with him, ma'am, and you're crazy."

Laura felt Deke stiffen.

"He may be white on the outside, but he's Cheyenne in every way that counts! A murdering, raping bastard, just like the rest of them." He shot a look at Deke. "Tell her, Sheridan. Tell her the truth, or I will."

"Sounds to me like you're the one all warmed up."

Laura no longer found anything about this humorous.

"He lived with them," the man cried. "Lived with them, ate with them, slept with them, made love with them. And while he was one of them, the bastard murdered with them. Ask him if he didn't!"

Laura couldn't have spoken if she tried. She glanced up at the stony profile of Deke's face.

"Go on, deny it if you will!" The man shifted his grip on his rifle, the new angle of the butt threatening. "Tell her you never lifted any scalps! That you never had your turn on a white woman who was pleading for mercy from animals that didn't know the meaning of the word. Tell her!"

Deke stood there in rigid silence.

The man stepped closer, his body atremble with suppressed rage. "He did it, Mrs. Cheney. He'll turn on you, just the same. If you leave with him, you'll mark my words; don't think you won't."

Laura felt the muscles at the backs of her legs quivering.

The man spat in the dirt at Deke's feet. "I realize you got a baby to find, but going off with him isn't the way. Stay here, where you're safe. Give us a few days. We'll help you. I promise you that."

A few days? Laura thought of Jonathan out there somewhere in the possession of that Mexican. Her breasts ached, a reminder of the life-giving link between mother and child. Within a few days, her baby might perish for lack of nourishment. She had to go now. Tonight.

Never taking his gaze off the raging man, Deke said, "Boston?"

The question that laced the word needed no explanation. Laura stared up at him. The feather in his hatband peaked over the crown of his Stetson, a testimony etched in silhouette against the dim light coming from the saloon.

"You goin' or stayin'? Make up your mind."

"Going," she whispered.

"Louder," he shot back. "Say it so the man can hear you."

Laura swallowed to get her voice. Even so, it came out with a tremulous ring of indecision. "I shall go with Mr. Sheridan."

"You're a fool, then!"

Laura couldn't argue that. The way she saw it, Sheridan would have denied those horrible accusations if there hadn't been some truth to them.

Less than an hour into the ride, Laura's senses were bombarded on every side by one form of discomfort or another. Her body was bruised from the nasty fall she had taken that day. Her head ached from the blow to her temple. The lower half of her torso, still tender from childbirth, panged with the constant and jarring rhythm of her horse's gait. And she was exhausted. She slumped, hoping that the change of posture would give her relief. She curled a leg around the saddle horn with the same aim in mind. Nothing helped.

It seemed that it was taking much longer to reach the mountains than it should. They rode and rode, but it didn't appear that the Rockies were any closer. Sheridan wanted to see the horse tracks around her cabin for himself. From there, he hoped to pick up the kidnappers' trail. The plan made sense to Laura. But how long was it going to take to get back there? Two more hours, maybe three? She already felt as though they had been riding forever.

When Deke drew his black to a stop, Laura finally noted his absence beside her, twisted in the saddle to glance back, and nearly lost her seat. He nudged up the brim of his hat to regard her. "You okay?"

"I'm fine."

He studied her for a tense moment that made her wonder what he had in mind. A chill ran up her spine as she looked behind him. The dim glow of Denver's lights had vanished. She was completely alone with him now.

"Wh-Why are you stopping?"

He fixed his attention on the horizon. "You're gettin'

weary. In case you start noddin' off, it might be best if I take the lead from here."

At his words, another kind of dread filled Laura, for she had known this moment was inevitable. She turned to peer at the looming mountains and tried to pick out peaks that looked familiar, her reason being that she felt certain she could find the cabin if she aimed for landmarks she saw every day.

She indicated a blob of misshapen black on the horizon. "That way."

He drew his stallion abreast of her gelding. "That way? Can you name me a direction?"

Tension mounting, she surveyed the line of mountains again. "Westish?"

"Westish," he repeated blankly.

"Sort of west," she clarified.

"We can't go sort of, Boston. Sort of could take us to hell and gone the wrong way."

She nibbled her bottom lip. "It worked fine coming."

"What worked coming?"

The impatience in his voice made her horribly uneasy. When Tristan had used that tone, a cuffing hadn't been long in coming. "The sort-of method," she explained in what she hoped was a confident tone. "I picked out where I thought Denver was and went that way. Sort of northeast, I think. If it was good enough to get me there, it should work to get me home again."

Even by the dim light of the moon, the stunned expression that crossed his dark face was visible. Laura shifted sideways in the saddle to put a bit more distance between them.

"Let me get this straight. Are you sayin' you don't know which direction your cabin is?"

"I—I have a fair idea."

"Then would you mind tellin' me with no *ish* stuck on the end? West, southwest, which is it?"

She regarded the mountains again. "Well, you see, Mr. Sheridan, it's not quite that simple. I don't know *specifically* which direction I'm going." She jabbed a finger. "Just that I believe it's that way."

"You believe?" A long silence elapsed. Then he said, "Jesus Christ," his tone making it inapparent whether he was cursing or praying. Laura wrapped the reins she held around one hand, drawing them tighter and tighter. "Are you sayin' that I'm ridin' around out here at night, takin' my lead from a woman who ain't got no idea in hell where we are?"

Laura thought that summed it up pretty well, but the look on his face made her afraid to say so. Evidently her silence was answer enough. He swore again and jerked off his hat.

"I found Denver, didn't I?" she hastened to remind him.

"How? I'm surprised you ain't still wanderin' around out there. Westish? Jesus Christ. Tell me I ain't hearin' this."

Despite her fear that he might cuff her, one of Laura's biggest failings had always been her mouth, and she couldn't stifle the words that sprang to her tongue. "You ain't hearing this."

Returning his hat to his head, he gave her a look that spoke volumes. Already regretting her comeback, she braced herself for a blow, which had always been Tristan's reaction to her sassy mouth. Laura truly had tried to overcome that flaw—getting cuffed was no fun, after all—but she had never quite cured herself of the habit. Long on nerve and short on reticence, that was her, and always at the worst possible moments.

Hoping to defuse the situation, she drew up her shoulders. "In my own defense, Mr. Sheridan, I must say that I think going westish will work just fine if you'll give it half a chance."

He pinched the bridge of his nose. After a moment, he lowered his hand and blinked as if he thought the scenery might change.

"How lost can I possibly get? That's the question to ask yourself."

"Pretty damned lost."

"You can only ride so far without running into mountains," she retorted, "and when that happens, I shall know we've gone too far."

"Jesus Christ."

The increased sharpness of his tone made her all the more wary. She edged her gelding away from his black. The dog plopped down on the dirt between their horses, content to gnaw on its deer leg while they conversed. Judging from the set of Sheridan's shoulders, Laura feared his irritation might soon erupt in anger. Growing more frightened by the moment, she searched for something to say that might calm him. "It's not as bad as it sounds. I did the same thing going to Denver. When I ran into the telegraph lines, I realized I had gone too far and turned back. It was rather elementary, actually. I simply followed the poles straight into town."

"Jesus Christ."

Her nerves snapped. "I do wish you'd stop saying that!"

"What would you like me to say?"

"Anything but taking our Lord's name in vain."

He narrowed an eye at her. "Shit."

In for a penny, in for a pound. Meekness never had been her forte. She raised her chin a notch and let fly. "I must say that you're not being very tolerant, Mr. Sheridan. It's certainly nothing to swear over. I shall find the cabin. Just give me a chance."

"You can't hardly stay in the saddle now," he came back. "I can't go draggin' you all over the goddamned country tryin' to find where you live."

"It seems to me you're the one who's becoming frazzled." She rubbed at a streak of flaking mud on her cheek. "I'm sure I look far worse than I feel. Out of necessity, most women are quite adept at preserving their resources."

"Is that so?"

"Absolutely. You might be well served to follow my example."

He fixed her with a smoldering gaze. "Is that right?"

Gathering courage, Laura nodded. "You shall not see me expending unnecessary energy on temper, I assure you."

He curled his hands around the saddle horn and pushed

forward in the stirrups. As he resumed his seat, he took a deep breath and muttered something unintelligible.

Laura moistened her lips. "I realize it must be slightly disconcerting to you that I don't know my directions."

He muttered again.

"But I was raised in a city, you know. There were street signs if I needed to find my way, which wasn't a frequent occurrence. I usually rode in the carriage, and the driver took me where I wanted to go. West, north, south, it's really not a question that crops up in Boston."

"Jesus Christ."

"You are being unnecessarily ugly. I'm doing the best I can."

He nudged his hat back to gape at her. "You got any idea how far we could ride to hit them mountains?"

Laura stared at the peaks. "They don't appear to be much farther than a hop, skip, and jump."

"That's because the air in this country fools the eye, sorta like a magnifyin' glass does. Somethin' can look like it's right over yonder, and you can ride for hours to reach it."

She recalled her earlier impression that it was taking an uncommonly long time to make any progress. "Oh, my."

"Oh, my? Honey, that don't say it by half. If you miss your place and we ride clear to them mountains, what're we gonna follow once we hit 'em? There ain't no telegraph lines this far west. You plannin' to sniff your way back and forth until we trip over our noses into your yard?"

His voice was bordering on a yell, and every word made Laura start. When he finally grew quiet, she said in a thin voice, "There's the creek. It runs past the cabin. Once we find it, we shall simply follow its course."

"Your crick got a sign on it or somethin' that says it's your crick? There's a hell of a lot of cricks in this country."

Tears sprang to her eyes. Furious with herself, she blinked them away. Unfortunately, it wasn't quite so easy to control the quaver in her voice. "I'll find it, I said. It's my son out there, remember?"

At that, he fell silent. After a long moment, he said, "I

reckon we all got our ignorances. For me, it's talkin'. For you, it's goin'." He took another deep breath in a visible attempt to calm down. "Okay. You say it's westish." He studied the horizon. "How about the crick? It got a name?"

Laura felt more tears welling. "Tristan never mentioned one."

"It don't sound like your husband did much that was useful."

Laura seconded that, but it seemed wrong to speak ill of the dead. Gazing out across the miles of open country, she began to feel panicky. She threw Sheridan a frantic look. "If you're right, and I'm unable to find the cabin—" Her voice cracked with the intensity of her emotion. "What on earth shall we do if I can't take you to it?"

For the first time since discovering how inept she actually was at finding her way, he didn't look quite so angry. For a moment, she even thought she detected a glimmer of sympathy in his eyes. But then she decided it must be moonlight. "I'll find it, Boston."

"Do you truly believe you can? I thought you said we were lost."

He heaved a weary-sounding sigh. "I ain't never got lost in my whole life." At her dubious look, he drew his brows together in a scowl. "Lost is not knowin' where the hell I'm at. I know where I am. I just ain't sure where I'm goin'."

"Oh." She rubbed a hand over her eyes. "It doesn't seem to me that there's a measurable difference."

"That's because you ain't sure where you're at, you ain't sure where you're goin', and you don't got the—" He broke off and cleared his throat. "You don't got the know-how to figure out either one."

Laura had the feeling that he had nearly said she didn't have the brains. Given the circumstances, she didn't suppose she blamed him.

He swung off his horse, circled the dog, and strode toward her. Grasping her waist, he lifted her down to stand beside him. "Don't look so gloomy. It may take more doin' than I reckoned on, but I'll find where you live. If there's one thing I'm a fair hand at, it's findin' my way."

He led her to a spot of dirt that was free of rocks and bathed by the light of the moon. Crouching, he smoothed the surface with his palm, then picked up a twig. Glancing up at her, he said, "Come on down here, girl, and do what you do best."

So tired she felt numb, she dashed at a tear on her cheek. "At this point, I'm not sure I do anything well. Even a stupid dog can find its way home."

He shot a look at Chief. His eyes held a definite twinkle when he glanced back at her. "You run at the lip real good, Boston. It's one of the first things I noticed about you. You can talk up one side of a man and down the other so fast, he don't know what hit him." He patted the dirt. "So get down here and start talkin'. Tell me how it looks around your spread."

Hope ribboned through Laura. "You mean you can find it if I tell you what it's like there?" She sank to her knees. "From my door, I can see the most beautiful peaks. All craggy, like big jags of granite."

She met his gaze to find him studying her with an odd expression on his face. Her voice trailed away. "What?" she asked.

"Nothin'. I was just makin' a picture of it in my mind." He smoothed the dirt again. "How many peaks? And how're they shaped?"

Laura did a fair job of describing the landscape while he tried to duplicate it in the dirt. "No, not like that." She grabbed the stick and sketched the peaks herself. "From my dooryard, that's exactly how they look."

He studied the drawing for a moment. "Lookin' at them mountains from this angle . . ." He pointed with a finger to illustrate. "In the mornin', lookin' at them that way and standin' in your dooryard, where does the sun come up?"

Laura closed her eyes, concentrated, and raised her right hand, positioning it as precisely as she could to indicate where the sun rose in the sky. When she lifted her lashes, he nodded, then pushed to his feet and helped her to stand. "You did good, Boston. Real good. I think I can find it. Or at least get you close enough to know where you're at."

Relief made her legs feel weak. "Do you, really? Thank God. Which direction is it?"

"Westish."

Chapter 6

THE MORNING WIND WHISTLED DOWN A ROCKY wash and raised dust funnels in an erratic path across the dooryard. Particles of dirt blew into Laura's eyes. She blinked rapidly to clear away the tears. If she displayed weakness of any kind, Deke Sheridan might change his mind about taking her with him on such a long trek.

Feeble sunlight slanted into her face. In her distorted vision, her newly hired tracker was a large blur of blue chambray, denim, and bronze skin. His manner surly and uncommunicative, as it had been most of the night, he paced the yard to examine the tracks left behind by the kidnappers and their horses. Chief, his constant shadow, plopped down nearby to gnaw on his deer leg. The dog had carried the gory possession all the way from Denver, a feat that seemed rather phenomenal to Laura. But, then, nothing about Deke Sheridan or his pet was ordinary.

Returning her attention to the man, she wondered for at least the dozenth time what had compelled him to help her. More than once she had seen his lips thin with distaste when he looked at her. What was it about her that he found so objectionable? Though she didn't count herself the highly admirable sort, especially out here where her ignorance manifested itself at every turn, she didn't normally inspire active dislike, either.

Unbidden, the dire predictions made last night by the man in Denver returned to torment her. She couldn't discount Deke Sheridan's failure to deny the accusations made against him. He had stood there in stony silence, not even reacting when the other man had spat at his feet. Sheridan might be many things, but she couldn't believe him a coward. He must have had reason for not retaliating, the most obvious that the charges were true.

Observing him now, it wasn't difficult to believe he hated all white people. At first glance, he looked pure Indian with his dark hair and skin. Only his silvery eyes betrayed him. Everything else about him seemed unnervingly savage, from the impossibly silent manner he moved to the expert way he studied the tracks, tracing them lightly with his fingertips as if in tactile communication with the earth itself.

She hugged her waist. If the man intended to harm her, he had already had opportunities. His only reason for waiting would be to lure her farther from Denver. If her body was found, the townspeople might lay the blame at Sheridan's door. They had last seen her in his company, after all.

Stop it! Just stop it! If she continually tried to second-guess this man, she would drive herself mad. His reasons for coming with her didn't matter. All she cared about was that he help find her baby. If he turned on her later, she would face it then. At least she was trying to do something, which was better than waiting in Denver for help that would come too late.

His gaze fixed on a trail of footprints, Sheridan straightened and walked toward the creek. Numb from what had seemed to her an endless horseback ride, Laura couldn't muster the energy to go after him. Her legs felt permanently bowed, her backside bruised, her insides ached relentlessly, and to make matters worse, her chest hurt with every breath she drew. She wanted nothing more than to sink to the ground and curl up in a miserable ball. Only thoughts of Jonathan kept her standing.

When Sheridan drew near the stream, he slowed to pick his way through the rocks, his half-crouched stance suggesting that he was still following a trail. In beds of stone, how could he possibly tell where someone had walked? Halfway down the bank, he hunkered near a cluster of large boulders, bent forward to study something, and then slowly stood, her water bucket clasped in one hand. Incredulity washed over her as she realized it had been her own footprints from yesterday that he had been following. En route back to the yard, he jerked off his hat and slapped it against a thigh, his every step exhibiting a distinct play of muscle beneath the tight denim of his jeans. It would definitely not be wise to make an enemy of this man.

While somehow managing to keep a grasp on the Stetson, he measured off a scant inch with thumb and forefinger. "You came just that close to seein' what hell is like."

The statement swam in her mind for a moment. "Pardon?"

He gestured at the stream. "A man followed your tracks clear down to the rocks. He walked within four feet of where you was layin'. If he had been as good at trackin' as a Cheyenne, he would've found you." Flat and unreadable, his eyes met hers. "Looks to me like he combed the bank on both sides for a goodly distance each way."

A crawling sensation washed over Laura's skin.

Indicating the other footprints in the yard, he added, "It's plain the sons of bitches searched for you, and searched hard. If them boulders hadn't hid you from sight—" He broke off and turned to gaze at the mountains. "My guess is they was comancheros or renegades."

The information hit Laura with the impact of a fist. "H-How can you possibly de-determine that?"

Setting his hat back on, he knelt on one knee and jabbed a blunt finger at the dirt. "Them there cuts was left by a Spanish spur, what us cowpokes call a Californee spur. Ain't many white boys who wear 'em."

Laura couldn't help but notice that, despite their uncommon size and breadth, his work-hardened, badly scarred hands were oddly graceful, the tips of his nails remarkably clean and half-mooned with white. Hands so callused they were probably impervious to the winter cold or the bite of barbed wire. Hands that, knotted into fists, could probably concuss a full-grown bull, and most likely had.

Indicating another mark, he said, "That was left by an Anglo spur. There was unshod horses in the group, too, which leads me to think Indians traveled with 'em. Mix gringos, Mexicans, and Indians together, and you usually come up with comancheros or renegades."

Pressing a hand to her lower back, Laura bent stiffly to look. "I see little difference in those two footprints."

He touched the first track. "See how much deeper the spur cuts is on this one? And here, in front of the heel, see that little line goin' across?"

"Yes."

"A Mex wears his spur loose with a chain under the instep of his boot. That's what made the line. An Anglo wears a tight spur leather." He took measure with the tip of his little finger. "The rowels is bigger on a Californee spur, too, and leave a deeper cut."

After comparing the two prints more closely, Laura began to note the dissimilarities. Finally convinced, she straightened. Struggling to stay calm and keep her thoughts focused, she said, "You guess them to be comancheros or renegades? I didn't realize there was a difference."

His lips drew back over gleaming white teeth. "There ain't. Not so's you could tell, anyhow. You take the dirtiest, cruelest white men you can find, toss in a few Indians and Mexicans who can give 'em lessons in meanness, and you got comancheros or renegades. They got loyalty to nothin' and nobody, and what one don't think of, another one will. You can be damned glad they didn't find you down in them rocks. By the time you came around, the party would've done commenced, with you providin' the fun."

While passing through Denver, Laura had seen men such as he described, the sort who seemed to thrive on being cruel.

"Men like those took my baby?" As though it had become a turbulent body of water, the earth seemed to churn and swell into rolling waves under her feet. "They have my Jonathan?"

She heard the bucket clank. Strong hands curled over her upper arms. "Don't go faintin' on me."

Laura felt the chambray of his shirt pressing against her face, the disgusting necklace of bear claws pricking her cheek. She flattened her palms against vibrant warmth and dimly realized her fingertips had found purchase on his chest, that the lean, hard length of his body was holding hers erect. She knew she should pull away. His sort needed little if any encouragement to take liberties, especially with a white woman. But, God help her, she didn't have the strength.

She had imagined he might smell vile, as those in his profession often did, a rank blend of cow manure and rancid sweat. But instead, masculine though it was, the smell of him was inexplicably soothing, a blend of earthen scents like those she sometimes caught on the Colorado wind.

The sheer strength of him made her all the more aware of her own frailty. The muted but steady thrumming of his heart set a cadence that made her own sound thready and frantic. His grip on her arms was such that her shoulders were lifted and compressed, the heels of her shoes raised slightly off the ground.

Villain or protector? She was too exhausted to speculate. This moment presented her with challenge enough. Tristan was dead, and she was alone, so horribly alone. Jonathan's fate rested entirely on her shoulders, and right now, her shoulders didn't feel very broad. To rescue him, she was faced with a grueling journey on horseback. No matter how desperately she yearned to be strong, she wasn't certain her body could endure the punishment.

"My baby . . . Oh, God, oh, God. I want my baby. Why has this happened? Whatever shall I do?"

He slid one of those heavy, pawlike hands down from her shoulder to rub her back. Laura couldn't resist the sturdiness of him. Even though he clearly disliked her, even though she knew him to be potentially dangerous, he was the only comfort she had. She dug her fingers into the rock-hard muscle of his chest. If he thought she was weak, she no longer cared. Pride was something she had possessed yesterday.

"I don't think they'll hurt that baby," he said gruffly. "I can damned near promise you that. He's money in their pockets."

His words offered Laura a feeble ray of hope. Though she tried to stifle the sob that welled from within her, it erupted, dry and crackly. "D-Do you really think not?"

"My guess is that their main reason for comin' here was to take you. Across the Rio, a woman with your colorin' would bring a mighty dear price. When they couldn't find you, they must've settled for the kid."

"But why? To sell him in Mexico? He'll never survive that long a trip. And even if he could, what decent person would buy someone else's baby?"

"Looks to me like they're headin' northwest into high country, probably to try tradin' him to Indians."

"Indians?" The word rushed from Laura on an expelled breath of horror. "You think they might trade my baby to Indians?"

She found the strength to move slightly away from him. "Not Indians," she whispered, remembering the unspeakable things that had been done to the Huntgate family, and that only a few short days ago. "Why would Indians want a white baby?" The terrible possibilities were chilling. "To— to torture and mutilate him? Dear God in heaven, they're animals. Why would they want a white baby unless they meant to kill him?"

His hand ceased its kneading motion on her back, and she felt his body stiffen. Too late, she registered exactly what she had said. And to whom she had said it.

"I— Mr. Sheridan, I didn't mean—" She staggered and nearly lost her footing when he set her away from him.

"Somethin' you should know about them *animals*," he said, emphasizing the last word with exaggerated clarity.

"Some Indian women is barren. Or sometimes their little ones just don't live. Either way, all they know is that their arms is empty. I was only four years old when my folks was massacred by Kiowa. Two weeks later, the Cheyenne stole me from 'em in a raid. Never once was I treated bad, not by either tribe. If your Jonathan gets traded to Indians, he'll be loved by some squaw like he was her own. That's a damned sight more than I can say about any fancy white lady who got stuck with a redskin baby, you included."

Even shaded by his hat, his quicksilver gaze glittered. A muscle twitched along his jaw as he knelt on one knee to reexamine a boot track. The wind caught his mahogany hair and drew it across his burnished face. A few strands caught in his lashes, but he seemed not to notice. His anger electrified the air, and his suddenly curt manner said more plainly than words that, in his opinion, if anyone was an animal, she was.

Laura could think of nothing she might say to mend her fences. She stood there in a helpless quandary, knowing she had to do something. She needed Deke Sheridan desperately. What in heaven's name would she do if he rode off and left her?

"Mr. Sheridan, I—"

"I think enough's been said," he interrupted, his speech clipped. "You got your way of thinkin', I got mine, and there ain't no mixin' the two."

"But I don't want you believing that I dislike Indians on general principles."

"Don't you?"

"No, I—"

With a sudden upward jerk of his chin, he cut her short and swung a scathing glance to the front of her jacket. "I think you could put this time to better use than just standing there. Don't you, Mrs. Cheney? Looks to me like your cream's risin'."

Laura hadn't a clue what he meant. He plucked at his shirt to draw her gaze. When she looked down and saw two dark splotches on the chambray, she wanted to die. She pressed a hand to her chest, horribly aware of the dampness under her palm.

Blood surged to her cheeks, turning her skin so hot it burned. Her lips parted, but no sound came forth. Without a word, she stumbled toward the cabin, her one thought to escape the searing contempt in his silvery eyes.

Already wanting to kick himself, Deke watched Laura flee to the house. House? He'd seen some hovels in his day, but never one so poorly built. Cheney must have been drunk when he fitted those saddle-and-rider corners.

He glanced down at the wet spots on his shirt. If Laura had noticed them on her own, she would have been humiliated enough. Highfalutin city gals didn't own up to having breasts, let alone mother's milk.

He rubbed between his eyebrows. Jesus, what was the matter with him? She was three days out of childbed, so weak she could scarcely stand up, nearly hysterical with fear for her baby, and he was taking shots at her.

So she hated Indians and considered them to be little more than animals? Given the recent hostilities between the whites and Cheyennes, who could really blame her for thinking that? She had no way of knowing that her own people had been just as vicious, or that they had been the first to behave like animals. It wasn't something white folks were likely to brag about.

Deke took a deep breath and slowly expelled it. He wanted to roll a cigarette and drown himself in a jug of whiskey. Maybe in several jugs of whiskey. So he could forget the past, forget Laura Cheney and his promise to help find her baby, forget every damned thing, most especially himself and what he had become. That last was the kicker. When he turned his gaze inward, he was no longer certain he even recognized himself.

He had been living up to his bad reputation for so many years, it had become second nature; that was the problem. Deke Sheridan, bad and fightin' mean, easy to rile, fast with a gun, and always ornery drunk fifteen minutes after he hit town. A mask he had worn these last fourteen years, nothing more, his way of giving back as good as he got and to hide his hurt because the white world, where he had once believed he could belong, had shunned him.

A man will go the way he walks.

That wise Cheyenne saying, one of his adoptive mother's favorites, whispered softly to him from the past. He saw himself at about ten, puffing out his chest and bullying the smaller boys. His mother had placed a gentle hand on his shoulder and said, *"Flint Eyes, a man will go the way he walks. Fix your gaze far ahead of you and see where it is that you go."* Now Deke realized that saying had a far deeper meaning than any he had ever interpreted. He had walked the way of his reputation, pretending to be exactly what people expected him to be, and now his feet had been on the path for so long that they knew no other way.

Damn him to hell for his mouth. A decent man would go after Laura Cheney and apologize. Deke guessed he wasn't decent. Either that or his yellow was showing. The truth was, the woman scared him spitless.

Every time he glanced into those big amber eyes of hers and saw the pain reflected there, every time she amazed him by pushing herself just one step farther when he knew another woman might have already collapsed, he tasted fear on the back of his tongue. Not just because she was beautiful, although that was definitely a part of it. What really got to him were his feelings of protectiveness toward her. Sentiments like that toward a woman like Laura Cheney bordered on madness. He was nothing, a crude and uneducated, half-savage cowboy she wouldn't even speak to under other circumstances.

Face it, Deke. You were fool enough once to let a city woman get you astraddle a buck-and-rail fence, and then the little bitch kicked your feet out from under you. Hatin' Laura Cheney and makin' damned sure she hates you is the only way you know of to protect your balls.

Pushing to his feet, Deke aimed a kick at the bucket and sent it clanking and rattling over the uneven dirt. So he didn't like himself much for the way he had treated her.

What the hell difference did it make? No one else liked him much, either, and he should be accustomed to it by now.

It was probably just as well. If Laura Cheney didn't set out on this journey despising him, she undoubtedly would by the time it was over. In the end, this entire mess would boil down to choices, damned difficult choices, and he would be the only one capable of making them.

A suffocating sensation crept up the back of his throat. No matter what he had told Laura to ease her fears, the heartbreaking truth was that her child's chances of survival were mighty slim. Three days old, and taken from his mama by a ragtag bunch of misfits? Jesus. How long could an infant survive rough handling and a grueling journey on horseback with only possibly broth and sugar water as nourishment?

Not long, if Deke guessed right. Not long at all. Three days, on the outside. Maybe less. Under ideal circumstances, Deke would have made every effort to catch the kidnappers quickly, before the baby suffered the ravages of starvation and before the Indians got possession of him. But the circumstances weren't ideal, and Deke could think of no way around them. The other men already had a day's head start, and traveling with a city woman, fresh out of childbed, was bound to slow Deke down even more.

Considering Laura's background and the fact that she had probably never known much hardship, she had surprised him at every turn so far, not complaining even once during the long ride from Denver. She was clearly prepared to push herself harder than she probably should to reach her son.

The question was, could he allow it? The answer was no. Not to save a child who might be beyond saving.

"We're going to do what?" Laura asked a few minutes later. Her previous embarrassment was completely eclipsed by this turn of events. Surely she hadn't heard him correctly. "Mr. Sheridan, we can't lay over here until noon! We will lose nearly six hours of daylight."

Standing only a few feet away, her tracker gave an insolent shrug. "I'm tuckered."

He was tuckered? Laura was so exhausted that she could scarcely think. She clenched her teeth. Her baby was in peril, and he planned to take a nap? She wouldn't stand for it.

Struggling to keep her voice calm, she said, "You can't be serious. Think what might happen to my child during the delay."

"He's money in their pockets, I told you. They'll take good care of him. As for us losin' time, travelin' with a kid is bound to make 'em haze. We can afford to stop more often."

"Haze?"

"It's a cowpoke word for pushin' slow. If you round up some weak strays, you haze 'em back to the herd." He arched a dark eyebrow. "You and me don't even talk the same language half the time, do we, Boston?"

Laura chose to ignore that. "If the kidnappers will be traveling at a slower pace, I'd prefer to press our advantage."

He stroked his chin. "I can understand you bein' anxious, but trackin' takes a toll. I need to rest up before we start."

Laura could see that her present tack was getting her nowhere. "Mr. Sheridan, correct me if I'm wrong, but isn't it customary for the employer to decide when it's appropriate for an employee to rest?"

"Yep."

"Well, then? I really must insist that we leave immediately. I realize you must be weary. I'm feeling the strain myself. But surely you're not that exhausted."

He shrugged again.

"I am *not* going to lose six hours of daylight!"

Jabbing a thumb over his shoulder, he said, "I reckon you can go ahead without me."

"You know perfectly well I would become hopelessly lost."

"You're tellin' me? Honey, you couldn't find your ass with both hands if you had directions printed on both cheeks."

Laura stood there for a moment with her mouth hanging open. He was the most filthy-mouthed, outrageous, infuriating, disgusting, *impossible* individual on God's sweet earth. With great effort, she managed to ignore what he had said. "In view of the fact that I intend to pay you a great deal of money for your services," she reasoned, "it seems only right that I should decide when we stop."

"Nope."

"What do you mean, 'nope'?"

Ignoring her question, he sauntered across the yard to where he had laid his saddle. A quick glance told Laura that he had unsaddled her horse as well. While her attention was on her gelding, Sheridan stretched out on the dirt, tipped his hat down over his eyes, and pillowed his head on his riding gear. When Laura saw what he had done, she grew so furious, she could scarcely contain herself.

"Mr. Sheridan!"

He didn't so much as twitch.

"Don't you dare go to sleep!" She ate up the distance between them with shaky strides. "Look at me!"

No response.

"When I pay a man to do a job, the least he should do is acknowledge me when I address him!"

He shoved his hat back. "You keep bringin' up money. The way I recollect, you paid me what the little boy shot at."

"What the little boy—" She broke off. "Can you clarify that, Mr. Sheridan?" At his blank expression, she added, "Clarify means explain, say more clearly, expound upon."

"Expound?" He looked disgusted. "Most little boys shoot at nothin', which is what you paid me, nothin'. That plain enough for you?"

Laura had never met anyone with such a knack for making her angry. So angry that she momentarily lost sight of how dangerous he might prove to be should she provoke him. "You are being deliberately obtuse. It's not as if you don't understand the principles of credit. I know you have an account at both the livery and general store. You charged over a hundred and seventy dollars last night."

"Don't remind me. Thinkin' about it gives me heart-burn."

She chose to ignore that comment as well. "Our arrangement is no different. I am retaining your services on credit."

"No, you ain't. To get credit, you got to have income, and all you got is outgo. Come to think of it, you ain't even got that unless my outgo counts. I make it a standin' rule never to take an IOU from anybody who ain't a good risk. I get real ugly when I don't get paid."

"My father—"

"Leave your daddy out of this."

"He happens to be a very important factor, my collateral, so to speak."

"He's a long shot is what he is."

"He's a very wealthy man."

"Boston, understand somethin'. You could promise me a million dollars, and it wouldn't count for shit." He gestured at the churned dirt in her dooryard. "If I go chasin' after twenty comancheros, I face a real good chance of gettin' gut-shot. It's a little hard to collect what somebody owes you when you're layin' tits up out in the middle of nowhere."

Never in all her life had Laura met anyone to equal this man. The sudden rush of anger had made her feel faint. Pressing her wrist to her forehead, she cried, "If that's truly how you feel, then why did you agree to take this job?"

"I thought we went over that last night," he said with a chuckle. "Tradin' pitch, remember? Now, there's somethin' I can collect on."

She dropped her arm to glare at him. "You are despicable."

"Despicable. Now, there's a word."

"Disgusting, is that plain enough for you?"

"If you think I'm so despicable, why'd you agree to take my services out in trade?"

"I was desperate! And only the worst kind of cad would take advantage of that."

"Then I reckon I'm a—what was that you said?"

"A cad."

"That's me. A cad. Right now, a real tired cad, and I'm gonna take a nap."

"After which, I suppose you intend to ravish me. God forbid that you should risk getting gut-shot before getting your miserable due."

He tipped his hat back down over his eyes. "Boston, you could wear a man out with that tongue of yours. As for me ..." He lifted the Stetson again and grinned. "Ravish? You got a fancy word for every damned thing, don't you?"

Laura's hand itched to slap him. "Well? Is that or is that not your intention?"

The hat dropped back down over his face. "It'd take a mean-hearted man to ravish a woman whose south end is in as sorry shape as yours is. You walk like you're still sittin' on a horse." He repositioned his shoulders against the saddle to get more comfortable. "Why don't you just lay down and take a little nap? If you're still bent on me ravishin' you later, I'll see if I can muster it up. I ain't a man who likes to disappoint a lady."

For a moment, Laura was struck absolutely speechless by his audacity. "Me? Me, bent on it? Of all the arrogant, concei—"

"A real charmer, ain't I?" He gave a low chuckle. "Just lay down, Boston. We got a lot of miles to cover."

At a loss for anything else to say, Laura whirled and walked toward a tree a safe distance away—if any distance from a man of his caliber could be considered safe. "I shan't be able to sleep a wink! Not a blessed wink. I hope you enjoy your rest while I sit here staring at you!" Gingerly she lowered herself to the ground and braced her back against the cottonwood trunk. "And for your information, the proper grammatical usage is lie, not lay. I lay my bedding upon the ground, and then I lie on it."

"Do it however the hell you want. Just take a god-damned nap."

Deke heard nothing more out of his new boss. He could usually sense when someone was staring at him, and he didn't have that feeling. After a few minutes, he inched the brim of his hat up. She was still sitting with her back braced against the tree trunk, but her head had lolled to one side, and judging by the way her spine was curling, it wouldn't be long before she toppled. Out like a snuffed candle.

Grabbing his bedroll, he pushed silently to his feet and walked toward her. Sunlight filtered through the canopy of cottonwood leaves and dappled her pale face with flickering shadows. Her eyelids were stained blue with exhaustion. Deke shook out his bedroll, then bent to move her. She murmured in her sleep as he lifted her onto the pallet. He drew his wool blanket over her, surprised when she murmured again and turned her cheek against the back of his knuckles.

He jerked his hand away. *Damn her to hell.* He wasn't about to let her get under his skin. Only a fool got himself tangled up in barbed wire twice. And he wasn't playing the fool again, not for her or anyone else.

Chapter 7

LAURA AWOKE TO PAIN, NOT IN ANY SPECIFIC place, just an all-over ache that started in the top of her head and radiated to her toes. Startled by the realization that she had not only slept, but that Deke Sheridan had covered her with a blanket, she jerked to a sitting position, terrified he might have left her. When she saw his horse grazing nearby, she went limp with relief.

She regretted sitting up so suddenly. The tenderness across her lower back had become excruciating. When she turned her head, a complementary pain exploded behind her eyes. She squinted to block out the glaring sunlight. Her skin felt hot and dry, yet she wanted to shiver. Sick, she was horribly sick.

No! her heart protested. I can't be ill. Jonathan needs me! Mustering all her determination, she pushed to her feet and battled away a nauseating dizziness. Deke Sheridan was hunkered near the horses repacking his saddlebags. She noticed that his hair looked slightly damp, as if he might have bathed, that his jaw no longer sported whiskers, and that he wore what appeared to be a fresh shirt, another blue chambray with ragged armholes.

With his every movement, the braided muscle in his upper arms bunched and rippled under his glistening bronze skin. For a moment, Laura stood there and stared at him. Had she truly laced him up one side and down the other, or had she dreamed it? She had to curb her tongue with him.

If she didn't, he might use one of those massive fists to shut her up. No Tristan he, with fine-boned hands and more temper than strength. If Deke Sheridan decided to physically retaliate, she would find herself in big trouble.

She bent to roll up his bedding, then found it nearly impossible to straighten. She wondered if perhaps she had strained some muscles in her back yesterday while digging on the well. The long winter and her pregnancy had made her unaccustomed to such heavy outdoor work.

Yes, she assured herself, that was it. As for feeling hot and shivery, she'd been lying in the sun and covered with a wool blanket. She probably had become too warm, and now she was exposed to the cool breeze blowing down off the mountains. She wasn't ill. She couldn't allow herself to be. That was all there was to it.

She turned and walked toward Deke Sheridan on unsteady legs. At her approach, he glanced over his shoulder, his startling, washed-out blue eyes intent on her face. That look made Laura miss a step, and she sincerely wished she could throw the bedding to him rather than move closer.

Hopefully he had meant what he said about his lack of interest because of her condition. Not that she would bet her last three cents on it. From the stories she had heard, Cheyenne braves enjoyed inflicting pain on the white women they raped, the more viciously the better, and after they finished, they played torturous games with knives until their victims expired. Sickened at the thought, Laura drew up her shoulders. Deke Sheridan had no intention of raping her. If that was his plan, what was stopping him? Nothing, unless he meant to wait until they were well away from here.

"Looks like that little bit of sleep put some color back in your cheeks."

Gathering her courage, she handed him the bedroll. "I'm ready to ride."

As he pushed to his feet, he gave her an assessing look. Laura gazed back, acutely aware of how he towered over her. Trading pitch? Just the thought made her heart skitter. Yet even now, in the light of day, she could think of no alternatives to the decisions she had reached last night. Jonathan was all that counted.

"Is your back painin' you?" he asked.

Dismayed that she had been so obvious, Laura drew her hand from her tailbone. "It's bothering me a little. I pulled some muscles yesterday while digging on the well. It's nothing I can't work out by moving around a bit."

He continued to study her. "You sure that's it? You ain't feelin' poorly, are you?"

"No. What gave you that idea?"

A speculative gleam came into his eyes. Laura straightened her shoulders, afraid that he might guess how awful she actually felt. He wouldn't allow her to accompany him if he thought she might be sick, and if she couldn't go along, there would be little point in his going. Jonathan might be able to get by on nothing but gruel and broth until he reached an Indian camp or was rescued, but he couldn't survive a return journey on the same inadequate diet.

Ignoring the pain that knifed behind her eyes when she looked at the sun, Laura managed a bright smile. "We couldn't ask for more perfect weather. Not a cloud in the sky!"

He followed her gaze. "Enjoy it. Once we reach them mountains, it'll rain buckets at least once a day."

Praying her trembling legs wouldn't betray her, she strode toward her gelding to get him saddled up. As she reached for the bridle, Deke Sheridan's large hand closed over her wrist. Startled by his nearness, she jerked around. To her eyes, he seemed a yard wide across the shoulders. She couldn't help but recall the strength of his arms when he had caught her around the waist last night.

"I'll take care of the horses," he said firmly.

"I want to do my share."

"And I'll decide what that is."

"I'll just tend to the pack animals, then."

"No, you won't. You just gave birth. A woman shouldn't be liftin' so soon after. Like I said earlier, we got a lot of miles to cover, and you ain't gonna make it unless you take it easy."

Laura thought of all the times Tristan had thrown Indian women up to her, touting their strength and endurance. "I'm surprised to hear you say that, Mr. Sheridan. I've been told that squaws give birth on the march."

A hooded look came into his eyes as he prized the bridle from her fingers. He said nothing to refute the statement, but his closed expression hinted that he found it absurd. For just an instant, Laura felt vindicated. Contrary to Tristan's opinion, perhaps she wasn't such a weakling after all.

Deke Sheridan's next words relieved her of that notion. "Honey, no offense meant, but with you bein' city bred, you wouldn't measure up to a Cheyenne woman if you stood on a stump in thick-soled boots. What they can do and what you can do is two different things."

A lot of miles. Those words became a litany in Laura's feverish mind during the endless hours on horseback that followed. Keeping her gaze fixed on Deke Sheridan's broad back, she reminded herself constantly how fortunate she was. Because Jonathan's continued good health meant a profit for the comancheros, they would take great pains to keep him well. In the shadow of that, her own discomfort and the risks she was taking seemed unimportant.

For most of the afternoon, except for brief rest periods, Sheridan pressed their horses and pack animals relentlessly to climb ever higher into the foothills through a discontinuous band of dense thickets: skunkbrush and serviceberry, bitter brush and wild rose, oak and mountain mahogany. Rufous-sided towhees sang from the shrubs where they were nesting, harmonizing beautifully with the melodious trills of indigo buntings and Virginia warblers. Striking a discordant note, noisy bands of shrub jays squawked with displeasure when the horses got too close.

In her memory, Laura had never seen such an abundance of small animals. Chipmunks and golden-mantled squirrels poked up their heads from ground holes. Startled by the loud ringing of hooves striking rock, rabbits bounded everywhere in frantic, zigzag paths. Deer mice, dwarf shrews, and yellow-bellied marmots scurried for cover in the thickets.

To her surprise, Deke Sheridan's dog ignored the darting mammals and plodded ceaselessly along in his master's wake, the bloody deer leg ever present in his mouth. To keep her mind off her worries, which increased with every passing mile, Laura spent a great deal of time watching the dog and making silent wagers. When he stopped to scratch, surely he would lay the deer leg down. He didn't, and she owed herself a dime. When they stopped for a quick meal of jerky and water, she bet herself that the dog would abandon the deer leg while he ate. Instead, he placed it safely between his front paws while he devoured the pieces of jerky his master gave him.

"That animal is abnormal," she finally commented. "He's been carrying that deer leg all the way from Denver. Surely his jaws are tired by now."

"Years back, he was chained to a tree and starved near to death. He ain't never forgot it. He always packs himself a bone of some kind. I reckon it makes him feel safe."

"The poor thing. Perhaps one of us should carry it for him."

"Yeah? I'll let you be the one to take it away from him. I tried once, and he damned near bit off my arm."

As she absorbed that information, Laura observed the trotting dog. Chained to a tree? That suggested someone had deliberately starved the poor thing. Little wonder Chief had snarled so viciously at her last night. She was a stranger, an unknown element in a world where he had once known cruelty. Laura was wary of strangers herself, and though she didn't snarl, she supposed she did her fair share of bristling to ward off men.

Much to her dismay, she saw a mountain lion in the distance once. The sighting alarmed her and she couldn't help but wish she were armed with something more than a paring knife. Her tracker was a human arsenal on horseback, a gun belt around his hips, a huge knife and scabbard on the red sash at his waist; and as if those weapons weren't enough, a rifle and small axe rode securely in leather boots at the back of his saddle.

He seemed constantly at the ready to use those weapons, aware in an almost uncanny way of every movement around them and reacting to it before Laura even sensed the motion. More than once, she saw him reach for his gun, then draw back his hand at the last moment. With a building sense of dread, she realized he was worried that they might be ambushed, by comancheros or Indians; she wasn't sure which.

Because he stopped so frequently to check the tracks they were following, Laura became accustomed to sitting on her horse, numb with exhaustion yet nervous, waiting while he walked a circle around her, the thought never far from her mind that she still wasn't certain she could trust this man. It was for that reason that she was so acutely aware of his every movement when he drew up yet again, dismounted, and walked to the opposite side of his stallion. He flexed his shoulders slightly, to work out the cricks, she surmised, and then gazed off into the distance. Laura followed his look, wondering what he saw.

She was still searching the grassy hillside before them when she heard an odd sound. Glancing down, she located its source on the ground in front of Deke Sheridan's spread feet. For a moment, she stared at the growing puddle, quite certain her eyes were deceiving her.

"Mr. Sheridan!"

Startled by her cry, he jerked. The next instant, his gun flashed above his horse's back, his free hand poised to fan the hammer. The muscles in his dark face taut with tension, he spun around, clearly prepared to blow a hole in anything that moved.

"What?"

Already regretting her outburst, Laura gulped. But the damage had been done, and there was naught to do now but continue as brazenly as she had begun. If there was one lesson she had learned over the last two years, it was never to let a man know she was afraid of him. "Were you voiding?" she asked a little shrilly.

He turned that ice blue gaze on her, only suddenly it no longer seemed cold. Searing might have better described it. Laura was still conscious of the fact that he had his gun ready to fire, and for a horrible moment, she feared he might shoot her.

"Was I what?"

There were times when Laura wondered whether her life might have proved less stressful had she been born without a mouth. The pitch of her voice now markedly thin, she managed to repeat herself. "Were you voiding?"

The incredulous expression that came over his face made her hands convulse on the reins. He stared at her for a moment so fraught with tension, she could scarcely breathe. Then he glanced down. From the movement of his shoulders, she guessed he was shoving his gun back in its holster and jerking at his pants.

"So-oo-n of a-aa-a bitch!"

She jumped at the snarled curse. A shuffling sound drew her attention to the ground, and she saw that he was rubbing one moccasin in the dirt. A decidedly *wet* moccasin.

In a high-pitched voice, clearly intended to emulate hers, he said, "Mr. Sheridan! Were you voiding? Je-sus Christ." His head snapped up, and he leveled her with a glare. "Hell, no, I wasn't *voiding*. You screech like that again, and I swear, I'll give you an ass warmin' you'll never forget. I damned near shot the dog."

Laura gulped again. Hoping to calm him down, she said, "Mr. Sheridan, surely there is no need to get so testy."

"Testy! You scare me out of a year's growth, and you think I'm testy? Testy don't say it by half. For two cents, I'd jerk you off that horse and paddle your little behind. If it wasn't for the sorry shape it's already in, I damned sure would!"

"I—I'm sorry. I was simply— It just took me aback."

"Aback?" he bit out.

Laura's muscles felt so brittle, she feared they might snap. "Well, truly, Mr. Sheridan, it is a bit beyond the pale for you to—you know—right out here in front of God, me, and anyone else who cares to look."

"Beyond the pale?"

Judging by the way he kept repeating everything she said, Laura was beginning to think that, in addition to a year's growth, she had scared the good sense out of him as well, if indeed he had any. "Yes," she said weakly. "Beyond the pale. Those with a modicum of couth don't do such things."

"What I got is a wet foot," he shot back. "Couth? What in hell is that? As for doin' it in front of you, you couldn't see a thing."

None too certain he wouldn't carry through on his threat to jerk her off her horse, Laura strove to keep her expression carefully blank and forced herself to meet his gaze. "That much is true, I suppose, if one discounts decent proximity."

"Decent what?"

"Mr. Sheridan," she said, striving rather desperately for a soothing tone, "I've already apologized. What more can I say?"

"God only knows. That's one thing you ain't never short on, honey, and that's words."

"I didn't intend to startle you."

He swiped the back of his hand under his nose. "Well, you sure as hell did. Out here ain't no place to screech at a man when he ain't expectin' it."

"I'm sorry. As I said, you took me aback, and I . . ." She waved a hand. "Please carry on, Mr. Sheridan, in whatever fashion you wish. Far be it from me to criticize. It just seems to me that it would be little enough trouble for you to walk out into the bushes when you have a need to commune with nature."

"Boston, there ain't a bush for a mile that hits above my knees. You really want me to walk out there and commune? A fine fix you'd be in if I wandered off clear to hell and gone and somethin' happened!"

He had a point. Two, actually. She would certainly be in a fine fix if he wandered too far afield, and when she searched for a suitable bush close at hand, she couldn't see one. They happened to be in a grassy area that sported few woody plants. "Perhaps you might have waited for a more opportune moment."

"Next time I'll stop by a crick, that's for sure," he said as he walked back around his horse. "Leastways then I can wash my goddamned foot."

After swinging up into the saddle, he swept his hand over his face, giving his eyes a rub on the descent, then wiping his mouth with the back of his wrist. Laura averted her gaze, afraid he might yet decide to vent his anger. Voiding, not five feet from her? She simply couldn't credit it. The man had no manners whatsoever.

Without so much as a word to her, he dug his heels in and sent his horse into a jarring trot up the path. Already accustomed to keeping the pace, Laura's gelding fell in behind, snapping her teeth together with every step. She clung to the saddle, determined to follow without complaint at whatever speed Sheridan set.

A little farther north as the slopes became steeper, she noticed that the oaks became strangely absent, giving way to mountain mahogany that interrupted sparse stands of ponderosa pine.

As if he noticed her appraisal of the landscape, Sheridan, his mouth still tight with irritation, finally slowed the pace of his horse and indicated the terrain with a sweeping gesture. "We've come north of Denver. There ain't no oak up this way." Inclining his head, he said, "That's ninebrush. And that's hawthorn. Take a good look and file it away in your memory. If it ever happens that you gotta take these foothills on by yourself and you're travelin' south, you'll know to head east for Denver when you start seein' thickets of oak."

Laura tightened her grip on the reins, wondering a little frantically if he planned to abandon her. She could think of only one thing that might be more frightening than being in

these hills with Deke Sheridan, and that was being here
without him. "I'd never find my way out of here," she said
shakily.

"Hell, Boston, goin' east, how lost can ya get? Telegraph
lines, remember?"

Laura wished his horse would get a bee up its nose and
throw him clear into next week. "Fortunately, as long as I'm
with you, I don't have a worry. Correct, Mr. Sheridan?"

"In this country, you ain't got no way of knowin' what the
next minute might bring."

With that, he nudged his stallion back to its former pace,
coaxing the string of packhorses to fall in behind. Laura cast
a frantic look around at the different species of flora and
tried to imprint their images on her mind. No oak north of
Denver. It seemed a simple enough thing to remember, but
for her, it wasn't, not at all.

She dug her heels into her gelding's flanks. "Mr. Sheridan? You don't have it in mind to leave me out here alone
for some reason, do you?"

As if the question startled him, he wheeled his horse
around to regard her. The late-afternoon sun slanted under
the brim of his hat, bathing the right side of his dark face.
His eyes caught the light like prisms. Her gaze dropped to
the heathen medallion and the sunburst of bear claws on his
chest, and she felt idiotic for having pressed him. He had no
loyalty to her, and like other men, if the mood struck him to
take off, he probably wouldn't think twice about the woman
he left behind.

There was no mistaking the indignation in his expression. Laura had dealt with this reaction before, more times
than she cared to count. When she had questioned his intent toward her, Tristan had always taken offense as if it
were an insult to his masculinity that she should doubt him.
In the beginning, Laura had been fooled by that stiff-necked
pride.

"I took this job, didn't I?" he bit out.

Laura wanted to scream at him not to answer her question with a question. That, too, had been one of Tristan's

tricks, always putting her on the defensive. Why couldn't men give simple yes or no answers?

"I ain't a man to take on responsibility and then shuck it."

Laura surmised he meant *shirk* and bit the inside of her lip to keep from correcting him. Not that his choice of words made a whit of difference. What mattered was whether or not she could trust him. Bitter experience told her not to. But considering his present frame of mind, she wasn't fool enough to indicate that.

"I meant no offense, Mr. Sheridan. It's just that the thought of being alone out here frightens me."

He gave her a purely scathing appraisal with eyes that made her feel stripped. "Well, you can stop frettin'. Even when it's as plain as the nose on my face that I've made a mistake, I don't light out."

"A mistake? How so?"

"Look at you, and answer me that yourself. I let you rest till damned near noon, and six hours later, you're so played out, you're shakin'. Even your voice is shakin'." He gestured with a broad hand. "Hell, honey, we could be on a Sunday ride for all the ground we've covered."

"I am not played out," Laura protested. "If my voice is shaking, it is only because the thought of being left alone out here unnerves me. I'm not at all sure I could find my way, and I haven't any means of protecting myself."

"Not played out? I'd hate to see what tuckered is. I'll tell you right now, false pride don't take a body far in this country. Even the thin air turns against you. You'd best tell me when your steam runs out. I ain't a mind reader, and I'll keep goin' till you have the good sense to tell me different."

He turned his horse back onto the trail. "As for the other, I ain't gonna leave you, no matter how temptin' you make the thought. If something happens to me, you'll have my weapons, and until you learn to follow your nose, let Chief lead you."

Laura threw the dog a dubious glance. "He'd know to take me to Denver?"

"Nope. But he's got sense enough to sniff out people,

and he's a fair judge of character. If you was lost, I don't reckon you'd be too choosey."

Laura conceded the point and reined her gelding in behind his black again. "No, I don't suppose I would." Not too choosey at all, she added silently. The fact that she was in these mountains with a man like Deke Sheridan was testimony to that.

The steady ascent frequently pitted horses and riders against steep terrain. Laura clung grimly to the saddle, ignoring the pain in her back and chest as she leaned close to her gelding's neck. There were moments when she so pitied her mount that she might have followed Mr. Sheridan's example and walked had she not been so weak. The one time guilt drove her to try, he ordered her back on the horse, claiming her weight, unlike his own, was so slight that the animal would scarcely notice it.

The Rockies . . . Even as awful as she felt, Laura was awestruck by their beauty. Seeing them from a distance was nothing compared to actually being high in the foothills. Sometimes she felt close enough to reach out and touch the craggy peaks, which seemed to stretch forever against a pale blue sky. She marveled that anyone had ever found a route through them.

Deke Sheridan seemed so at home here in the high country that she was finally driven to ask, "Did you spend a lot of time up here as a boy?"

"Not much," he called back over his shoulder. "The Cheyenne is a plains Indian. But they came into the mountains sometimes."

Laura frowned slightly. "To hunt?"

"Nope. There was always plenty of game in the lowlands."

"To escape the summer heat, then?"

He took a moment to answer. When he finally did, the last traces of irritation had dissipated from his voice, a great relief to Laura, for it was frightening to have him angry with her. "Mostly to do the unexpected. Ain't nothin' like bein' where you shouldn't to avoid trouble."

Her frown deepened. "Trouble? Enemies, you mean?"

"You sound surprised. The Cheyenne do have enemies, and the braves ain't so different from white men when it comes to worryin' over their women and children. When trouble is on their heels, they ain't too proud to hide for a spell so it can pass 'em by."

"Could it be Cheyennes that the comancheros are going to meet?"

"Could be. Especially right now, what with all the hostilities. I ain't seen no writin' yet to tell me what kind of Indians are up this way."

"Writing?"

"What you'd call marks, I reckon. To us that can read Indian sign, it's writin'. Cowpokes call it an Injun post office. When I spot some, I'll show you."

"Why do they leave writing?"

"To say where they're headin'. Indians break off into groups—bands is what you folks call 'em. Sort of like in your white towns, the groups of people live together, the only difference bein' that their towns move to follow the wild game. In your world, just 'cause you live in one town don't mean you ain't white like the folks in the next town. It's the same for Indian tribes—a village here, and a village there. They leave writin' so others in their tribe can find 'em if there's a need."

Despite her exhaustion, Laura was alert enough to notice how he referred to the "white world" as if he didn't belong in it. He clearly considered himself to be a Cheyenne, and given her vulnerability, that wasn't particularly reassuring.

"So your people have a means of communication, then, rather like our telegraph wires?"

"Except you gotta go lookin' for the messages."

"Aren't they afraid their enemies will read the messages?"

"Depends on the enemy. If they're warrin' with other Indians, they don't leave sign but send out riders to take word to other bands. If they're hidin' from whites, they got

no call to bother. Most white men is too damned ignorant
to read the marks Indians leave for each other."

He drew up his horse and leaned sharply sideways to
study the tracks they were following. After a moment, he
straightened, apparently deep in thought. "Boston, I know
you're gonna pitch one hell of a fit, but my gut's tellin' me
we should make camp for the night. I don't like the looks of
this trail we're followin'."

Laura nudged her horse closer and, following his example, bent to look at the tracks. She couldn't see anything
troubling about them. "What is it you don't like? It looks to
me as if we still have a clear trail to follow."

He took off his Stetson, looped the bonnet strings over
his saddle horn, and turned his face into the breeze. A far-
away expression came into his eyes, and he seemed to be
listening to things she couldn't hear. With his dark hair
hanging loose to his shoulders and his burnished skin kissed
by fading sunlight, he looked unnervingly savage, his powerfully muscled body coiled tight with tension. She glanced
nervously over her shoulder.

"Mr. Sheridan," she whispered, "what is it?"

"Nothin' if you don't suspicion engraved invites."

"Pardon?"

His expression cleared, and he focused on her face. "An
invite, Boston. That's what this trail we're followin' is."

"You're complaining? It's a trail a child could follow. We
ought to be thankful."

He smiled slightly. "Men don't leave tracks this clear unless they're hankerin' to get found."

A chill ran up Laura's spine. "A trap, you mean? But
why?"

She immediately regretted having asked that. The smile
left his mouth, and he ran his gaze slowly over her person.
"You're a beautiful woman. Whiskey hair and whiskey eyes,
and skin the color of cream. Maybe back in Boston, you
ain't nothin' grand, but out here, honey, you're a sight for a
hungry man's eyes. I'd say you've got yourself some admir-
ers that ain't willin' to accept defeat."

Unsettled, Laura looked away. "What shall we do?"

"I can tell you what we ain't gonna do, and that's walk into an ambush. I didn't take this on so's I could serve you up to 'em like a pigeon on a platter. We gotta get off this trail."

She swung back to regard him. "I have to go after my baby, Mr. Sheridan, regardless of the risk to myself. We can't abandon these tracks!"

He pushed up in the stirrups to stretch his legs. With a flex of his shoulders, he resumed his seat. "Did I say anything about abandonin' the tracks? I said we gotta get off the path. What we'll do is ride left flank and crisscross to make sure we ain't losin' the scent. It ain't the easiest way, but it's damned sure the safest."

"Why make camp so soon? Can't we commence riding flank right now?"

He shot her another appraising glance. "You're spent, and the most we got left is an hour before we gotta start lookin' for a safe spot to lay over."

"I can easily go for another hour."

His mouth quirked at the corners. "If it'll make it easier to accept, Boston, it'll be gettin' dusk in a few minutes, and to ride flank, I need good light. So far, for the biggest part, we been ridin' already broke trail. When we get off the beaten path, we'll have to blaze our own way."

All Laura could think about was reaching Jonathan. "Perhaps we might stick to the beaten path another hour, then?"

"And accept a comanchero invite? There ain't nothin' to say they ain't waitin' right over the next hill. Probably not, but there you got it." His ice blue gaze delved deeply into hers. "You don't wanna find out. Trust me on that."

Though Laura's sense of urgency made her yearn to press forward, common sense prevailed. It would be foolhardy to risk walking into a trap. If captured by comancheros, she wouldn't be much use to her son. Her only choice was to do as he suggested and trust him.

Trust him? Those words swam through Laura's mind repeatedly over the next two hours as daylight gave way to darkness and the only light came from a smokeless little fire no larger than Deke Sheridan's Stetson. So enemies could approach from only one direction, he had chosen a boxed-in draw as their resting spot for the night, a steep hill to their backs and both flanks.

A tiny stream not much wider than the length of her foot ribboned through the draw to provide them and their horses with water. Laura was ensconced on a blanket beneath a canopy of mahogany branches while Deke rubbed down their horses with handfuls of grass and then proceeded to do all the other necessary chores.

Her protests about not helping him didn't exactly fall on deaf ears, but his surly responses left no room for argument. She was to rest, and that was all he wanted her to do. Though she longed to prove she could carry her share of the load, Laura was afraid to ignore his orders. She had riled him a number of times today already.

Sitting idle gave her too much time to contemplate the coming night. As she watched Deke move about the camp, her thoughts turned to the inevitable moment when they would retire. When he crouched to lay a fire, her gaze became fixed on the play of muscle across his back and the way it stretched the chambray of his shirt taut. Even with the chill of night descending, he hadn't donned a jacket, and she wondered if he ever felt cold. To her, the wind had a bite, and it would undoubtedly get worse at this altitude as the night wore on.

Her gaze slid downward from his upper back to his waist. The man was built in a classic wedge, narrow of hip, broad at the shoulder. When the fire leaped to life under his expert coaxing, he twisted slightly to avoid the flames, seemingly relaxed in the crouched position, his thighs flexing under the faded denim to maintain his balance. A study of grace ... and wildness. Without the Stetson to cover it, his dark hair lifted in the breeze, then settled in a mahogany curtain around his shoulders.

Before it grew fully dark, Laura gathered a supply of

clean rags from her saddlebags and made her way into the thick brush to seek privacy. Coward that she was, every unfamiliar noise made her start. She couldn't help but remember the mountain lion she had seen earlier that day. To complicate matters, her breasts were excruciatingly tender, which made expressing her milk a trial. Making short work of it, she hurried back to camp and Deke Sheridan's unnerving company. As frightening as he was, she found him preferable to ravening beasts.

After washing off his left moccasin, his reasons for which Laura didn't care to recall, and oiling his weapons, he prepared a simple meal of bacon, gravy, and skillet biscuits. Laura greatly enjoyed the coffee, but her stomach rebelled at the introduction of food. A little at a time, she pushed the bread and bits of bacon off the edge of her tin plate for Chief, hoping her tracker wouldn't notice who was actually eating her supper.

They were only a half day's ride from her cabin, not nearly far enough for him to discount the possibility of turning back. She couldn't let him know she wasn't feeling well. Her baby was out there, and she was going after him if she had to crawl the entire way.

"Ain't my cookin' fancy enough for you?" he asked when the meal was finished.

For fear he might guess the truth, Laura avoided meeting his piercing gaze. "My appetite is just a bit off. Weary, I suppose."

He picked up her plate, his movements abrupt with irritation. "Well, I'll warn you now. This is as good as it gets, Boston. Eat what's put afore you, or do without."

Before bedding down for the night, he walked some distance from their camp to a tall pine tree and tossed a rope over one of the limbs to suspend their food bags some ten feet above the ground. Laura watched him with mounting curiosity.

"Why did you hang our food in a tree?" she asked when he returned to the fire.

"Bears," was his curt reply.

Chapter 8

LAURA INCHED CLOSER TO THE FLAMES AND glanced uneasily over her shoulder. The shadowy world beyond the feeble glow of their little fire suddenly seemed ominous, and every sway of a tree limb made her pulse quicken. "Mr. Sheridan, did I understand you to say bears?" She gave a nervous little laugh. "That is not to say I was unaware they were in this country, you understand. But surely they don't venture near humans."

"They can smell food from miles away, and they ain't shy when it comes to fillin' their bellies. If they come callin', I don't want to lose any of our supplies."

"Are you saying that bears might visit our camp?"

He glanced up from the dying fire. "No call to worry. You ain't on their menu of good things to eat, Boston." With the toe of his moccasin, he banked and spread the hot coals, extinguishing the last of the feeble flames.

"Shouldn't we keep the fire going?"

The red glow of the embers illuminated his face, revealing his slight smile. "A fire this size wouldn't scare off a mouse, honey, let alone a bear. But left to burn all night, it might draw two-legged critters. I'm more leery of the latter."

With that, he went for their bedrolls. Laura waited to shake out hers until Deke chose his spot. She laid out her own bedding on the opposite side of the fire pit, preferring to keep a safe distance.

The night wind quickly burned out the glowing coals. As Laura's eyes grew accustomed to the darkness, the moonlight seemed brighter, but not enough for her to distinguish one shadowy shape from another. While journeying west, she had always slept inside the wagon. Not that a barrier of canvas had been much protection, but at least it had been something.

It seemed to her that she no sooner got comfortable—or as close to it as possible—than a scream echoed eerily down the draw. She huddled deeper beneath her wool blanket. "Mr. Sheridan," she whispered, "did you hear that?"

"Yep."

Laura wondered why he just lay there. "I think a woman screamed."

In a deep voice laced with amusement, he replied, "That was a cougar, Boston. They sound like a woman sometimes."

Laura stared wide-eyed at the shifting shapes in the darkness. "A cougar? As in a mountain lion?"

"Some folks call 'em that."

"It sounded awfully close, didn't it?"

"Sound carries up here, especially at night. No call to worry. Cougars don't usually attack humans unless they're starvin'."

The only word in that sentence that Laura truly assimilated was *usually*. Oh, Lord. Her precious little baby was somewhere in these mountains tonight. So tiny and so defenseless. Tears filled her eyes, and she shivered. Was he warm? Had those horrible men thought to feed him? Would they grow impatient if he cried? And, most importantly of all, were they keeping close watch to protect him from predators?

Her concerns for Jonathan led in an unbroken circle back to herself, for without his mother to feed him, Jonathan was doomed. Her body stiff with tension, she strained her ears for unfamiliar sounds. She tried to reassure herself. Chief lay only a few feet away, and so did Deke Sheridan. The pair had probably slept outdoors like this a thousand times, and since neither of them appeared uneasy, she shouldn't be, either.

Deke watched Laura stare at shadows, first one, and then another, her face as pale as milk. Training of a lifetime had given him good night vision, but she obviously didn't have the same advantage. He knew she was fashioning bears and cougars out of stumps and bushes. Recalling his childhood, he also knew that those imagined shapes could seem to move if you stared long enough.

At first Deke believed she would wear herself out and eventually fall asleep. Not so. If anything, she became more and more fidgety, rolling onto one side to stare one way, then switching sides to stare the other. She was clearly too nervous to sleep. If she had been any other city woman, he might have been highly amused, but given Laura's physical condition, he didn't feel like laughing. She needed her rest. Tomorrow would be a long day, and she was already on the brink of collapse, whether she admitted to it or not.

When he saw her shiver with cold, the decision was made for him. All he needed was for her to take sick. With a sigh, he pushed to his feet. Grabbing his rifle and bedding, he moved around the fire pit toward her. At his approach, he heard her sharp intake of breath.

"What is it? Is something out there?"

"Nothin' that ain't s'posed to be."

"Then why are you walking around in the dark?"

Convinced she would deny being afraid and spring from her bed if she guessed what he meant to do, Deke didn't immediately answer. Laying his rifle within easy reach, he snapped his blankets and brought them floating down over her. As he unbuckled his gun belt and laid it carefully on the ground, he said, "I reckon you're just so temptin', Boston, I can't resist you." Before she could react, he stretched out at her back and slipped under the covers with her. "Why should a man freeze his ass off when he can spoon with a pretty woman and keep warm?"

"Spoon?" she echoed.

Steeling himself for her reaction, Deke pressed close to

her slender backside. "Don't tell me you ain't never spooned?" He bent his knees and pressed them against the backs of hers. "What does folks in Boston do for excitement?"

She leaped at the contact of their bodies. "Mr. Sheridan!"

"There, you see? Slick as two spoons in a drawer." After a moment, when she gave no sign of relaxing, he added, "Honey, I'm so played out tonight I couldn't rise to the occasion if you stripped off naked to do a shake and jiggle. Believe me, you're safe as can be."

As he fit himself more snugly against her, he felt her body go rigid. For an instant, he questioned the wisdom of joining her. After all, his aim had been to make her feel secure, not threatened, and he could accomplish that by simply making his bed next to hers. But then he felt her shiver again, and his doubts fled. It was colder than a witch's tit in these mountains after the sun went down.

Laura held her breath and squeezed her eyes closed. *A shake and jiggle?* Oh, God, oh, God. How had she ever come to be in this situation? If, by any stretch of the imagination, their bodies fit together like two pieces of silver, hers was of the teaspoon variety, and his was the size of a soupspoon. The heels of her shoes hit the fronts of his moccasins well above his ankles. Even through the layers of her skirt and petticoat, she could feel the searing heat of his hard thighs pressed against the backs of her legs.

Letting her air out in a shaky rush, she said, "Mr. Sheridan, I truly don't think this is a champion idea."

He looped a warm and heavy arm over her waist. "At least this way you don't gotta be scared of bears and cougars. I'm so damned ornery, they'd take one look and run the other way."

Ornery; now, there was a point to ponder. Suddenly things like bears and mountain lions were the least of her worries. "I shan't sleep a wink. This is highly improper."

"The neighbors out here ain't much for tongue waggin'."

He settled a hand on her midriff. Laura stared at the moon-silvered shapes that had seemed so frightening only a moment ago. Which presented more of a threat, a hungry cougar or Deke Sheridan? The size of his hand alone was intimidating, the heel resting directly above her navel, the side of his forefinger, from first knuckle to tip, pressing against the underside of her right breast. To make matters worse, the breadth of his shoulders exceeded hers by a goodly margin, and his body felt like a heavy blanket of vibrant muscle all around her.

Played out? He was accustomed to hard riding, and for far longer stints than what he had endured today. He was lying through his teeth! He could probably work his way through a whole chorus line of shaking and jiggling dance-hall girls and never work up a sweat.

Tension constricted her throat, and she found it difficult to breathe. Even a gentle invasion so soon after childbirth would surely kill her, and she doubted Deke Sheridan knew how to be gentle.

His fingers flexed around her ribs, and she braced herself for an assault. "Relax, Boston. You're strung so tight, I could pluck notes."

Thankful she had two free hands, she grasped his wrist with one, and two of his leathery fingers with the other. To her horror, she felt his forearm tense against her. Then his thumb began to make light sweeps over the cloth of her dress, the forays harmless, yet terrifying. She had no illusions. He could easily subdue her and caress her in that fashion wherever he chose.

"Relax, honey." He gave a theatrical yawn. "I ain't exaggeratin' a bit. I'm flat tuckered. Ain't you?"

Her heart bumping against her ribs, Laura abandoned his fingers to grab his thumb. "Mr. Sheridan?"

His husky reply was once again laced with laughter. "Ma'am?"

She bit down hard on her lower lip. After a miserable moment of indecision, she murmured, "About our bargain."

"Bargain?"

Loath to bring it up, she murmured, "You know . . . the trading pitch?"

"Ah, that bargain. What about it?"

She dragged in a bracing breath. "It's just ... well ... I think it's only fair to inform you that I'm suffering from a decided lack of enthusiasm."

"A decided lack of enthusiasm?"

"It's n-nothing personal, you understand."

She felt his breath stir the wispy curls at the nape of her neck. A slight shift of his hand on her midriff nearly made her heart stop. "Mr. Sheridan, please."

Keeping his palm securely anchored on her ribs, he shoved up on his other arm and leaned over her. In the darkness, he was a black, hulking shape that emanated male strength. Laura wasn't certain what to expect. She only knew that her pitiful little paring knife, which had served so well to discourage men in the past, would provide her with scant protection. Deke Sheridan probably picked his teeth with a blade that size.

Memories rushed at Laura of all the times on the wagon train when Tristan had gotten in over his head playing poker and offered other men a night with his wife as compensation for debts he couldn't pay. She would never forget the sound of canvas being swept aside, of heavy breathing, as those drunken visitors climbed clumsily into her wagon, determined to get their money's worth out of her. *No* wasn't a word they had been willing to accept until she had emphasized the message with the prick of her knife, and even then, she had been roughly handled during the struggles more times than she could count.

"Please, don't hurt me," she managed in a thin voice.

Though she couldn't be sure, she thought she heard him sigh. "You know what I do at times like this, Boston? I say 'what the hell' and just let whatever's gonna happen happen. When you're outflanked, it's the only thing you can do."

"Outflanked?" she squeaked.

This time there was no doubt; he did sigh. He tried to move his hand, and Laura's grip turned so frenzied, she embedded her nails into his flesh.

"Why do I got the feelin' this could go on all night, with neither one of us gettin' a wink of sleep?"

"If you're unhappy with the accommodations, why don't you move back into your own bed?"

"Because we're layin' under it, and because you're scared and freezin' cold, that's why."

"I am not scared. And I'll grow warm after a while."

"Damned right, 'cause I ain't movin'." He flexed his fingers. "Honey, I'll have to amputate that thumb come mornin' for lack of circulation. You reckon you could lighten your hold a hair?"

"If I do, you'll touch me someplace."

"I'm touchin' you now, and you ain't dyin' from it."

"You're only touching my ribs."

"And you think the reason is that puny little grip of yours?" So quickly it startled her, he flicked his wrist, turned his hand, and captured both of hers in a steely grip. "If I have it in mind to touch that breast, I don't reckon anything you can do is gonna stop me."

Angling a thigh over her hip, he rolled her onto her back beneath him and pinned her legs. With the same horrifying ease, he drew her wrists above her head and held them there, firmly anchored to the ground. So terrified she could scarcely think, Laura stared up at the dark shadows of his face. Moonlight glanced off the stubborn thrust of his jaw and shimmered like diamonds in his eyes.

"Just that easy," he informed her silkily.

To Laura, the next seconds seemed endless. Even in the dim light, she saw his white teeth flash in a smile—a feral, taunting smile that chilled her blood. Transferring her wrists into his right hand so he could elevate himself with the same arm, he used his free hand to toy with the top button of her jacket.

"So what d'ya think?" he demanded.

What did she think? She was inches away from being raped—that was what she thought.

With deft fingers, he slipped one of her jacket buttons from its loop. "You ain't holdin' my hand no more, right?" His teeth flashed at her in another smile. "Fact is, I'd say you're as helpless as a snubbed, hobbled, and tail-twitched mare."

Horrible images crawled into Laura's mind. Though she had never witnessed the breeding of horses, Tristan had once told her how mares were rendered helpless and immobile so a stallion could mount them easily.

"I am not a mare, Mr. Sheridan."

"No, and I ain't a stallion that needs help gettin' the job done. So what's stoppin' me?"

The tendons along Laura's throat felt paralyzed. "N-Nothing, I suppose."

"You suppose?" He unfastened another button. "Honey, I've wrestled calves bigger than you and had 'em trussed in three seconds. There ain't no *suppose* to it." Inserting his finger through a button loop, he tugged lightly on her jacket. "Anything I want, and it's mine to take. You sure as hell can't stop me."

Her body straining to be free, Laura angled her face away from his and gulped down a sob. "Just do it, then. I won't beg, if that's what you're after."

"What I'm after is a good night's sleep."

To her utter amazement, she felt him refasten the button he had just slipped from its loop. She swung a startled gaze to his.

"I'm just makin' a point, Boston," he added, his smile no longer seeming quite so feral. As he refastened her other button, he bent his head and planted a light kiss on the tip of her nose. "My point bein' that there ain't no sense in you layin' awake all night, scared to death, with your fingernails dug into my hand. If I wanted to rape you, I wouldn't bother with bein' sneaky about it. Hell, it ain't like you can holler to the neighbors for help, now, is it?"

Laura gaped at him.

He drew back to regard her, his eyes glinting with mischief. "You want me to go through it all again?"

"No. I get your point. I think."

He pressed his loosely curled knuckles under her chin to lift her face slightly. "You think?"

"I understand," she amended quickly. "You could force yourself on me if you wanted, but you don't."

"Not quite," he said with weary resignation.

One of them was crazy, and she didn't believe it was she. "Then what is the point?"

"I could, and I want to, but I won't. That's the point." Having made that proclamation, he released her captured wrists and drew his leg off of hers. "I ain't tried to rape me a woman in so damned long, I think I've forgot how, anyway. And just as well, to my way of thinkin'. A lot of effort and not much pleasure, if I recollect it right."

As he resettled himself beside her, Laura lay there in frozen silence. With terrifying ease, he had just pinned her beneath him, unfastened her jacket, and kissed the end of her nose, all to prove he could force himself on her anytime he wished? She wanted to slug him. No, she wanted to kill him. But first she thought she might be violently sick.

"You reprobate!"

"What happened to cad?"

"A cad doesn't describe—" Laura ground her teeth, determined not to give him the satisfaction of knowing just how badly he had frightened her. "You're a degenerate! A scoundrel of the worst sort! I hope you enjoyed bullying a helpless woman."

"Not a bit."

Even through her anger, she heard the sincerity in his voice.

"I tried tellin' you I wouldn't hurt you. But you got your mind made up about what kind of man I am, and you didn't believe me."

Laura couldn't deny the truth of that. She hadn't believed him. "And I do now?"

"Yep. Leastways you will once you calm down and think about it."

His hand curled back over her ribs, the sturdy grasp of his long fingers warm, his leathery palm heavy. She instinctively clasped his wrist, but her grip was less frenzied now, and terror no longer closed off her breath. Incredulously she realized that his barbaric tactics had worked. Now, beyond a shadow of a doubt, she knew just how easily he could have his way with her. The fact that he was making no move to do so could only mean he had no such intention.

As her heartbeat slowly returned to normal and her breathing grew less labored, Laura went back over all that he had said, and one comment loomed foremost in her mind.

"Then you did rape women when you were with the Cheyenne?"

"Tried," he corrected. "There's a mountain of difference atwixt doin' and tryin', though if you'd asked me at the time, I ain't sure I could've told you what it was."

"Tried?" Laura circled that. She couldn't imagine Deke Sheridan coming out the loser in a physical contest with a female. "Can you elaborate on that, Mr. Sheridan?"

"Elaborate?"

"Explain."

"Nope."

"'Nope'? And whyever not?"

"'Cause I don't like talkin' about it, for one. It's a long story, for two. And for three, you gotta get some sleep. If you don't, you're gonna take sick, and if you take sick, you won't be no use to that boy of yours once we find him." He traced another circle with his thumb, but now the caress that burned through the cloth of her dress felt curiously soothing instead of threatening. "Just trust me on it, Boston. I ain't a man to—" He broke off and fell quiet for a moment. "That hand of mine ain't goin' nowhere. If that's what I had in mind, it'd be a done deed."

She closed her eyes on that. "You make me feel like a sausage wrapped in a biscuit."

"Well, leastways you know I ain't fixin' to take a bite."

Surprisingly, Laura believed he truly meant that. Silence settled over them again. A few feet away, she could hear Chief's raspy breathing. The wind whispered in the pine boughs above them and blew wispy clouds across the moon. She gazed at the stars that hung over the craggy peaks of the Rockies. So long a time seemed to pass, and Deke lay so still, that she finally decided he must be asleep. Mustering all her courage, she forced her grip on his wrist to relax.

"There's a smart girl," he murmured near her ear. "And ain't it just amazin' how that hand stays put with no help from you?"

The teasing note in his voice was unmistakable, and Laura grinned in spite of herself. "You are an absolutely despicable wretch."

"If you're tryin' to insult me, Boston, stick to English. All them fancy names you keep comin' up with is wasted on me."

Laura was too drowsy to think of other words, and she was no longer absolutely certain the description even fit. When she compared the way Deke had touched her to the way other men had, she noted two marked dissimilarities, one being that Deke was by far the strongest, the other that he had been far gentler. Not even his grip on her wrists had hurt, and never once had he punished her with his greater weight.

Laura closed her eyes again, this time because she felt so indescribably weary. As cold as the ground beneath her was, at least she was toasty warm where his body pressed against her. The radiant heat of him soothed the relentless ache across her lower back. She wished the same were true of her right breast. The velvet of her jacket was damp, and the cold of the earth had turned the cloth icy. Relinquishing her hold on Deke's wrist, she slipped her cupped hand around herself to ward off the chill. Unfortunately, her hand was nearly as cold and offered little protection.

Later, perhaps, she might roll over and warm her front against him, she promised herself. After he fell asleep, of course.

Somewhere nearby in the darkness, a limb snapped. Laura registered the sound, but felt no apprehension. For an animal to harm her, it would have to go through Deke Sheridan to reach her, and that realization made her feel inexplicably safe.

Her thoughts drifted to her baby, and she once again

wondered where he was, if he had been fed, if he was warm. She could almost feel the silken cap of his hair against her fingers, almost smell the sweet baby scent of his skin, almost see the dimple that flashed in his cheek when he drew up his little mouth to suckle. Tears burned in the back of her throat. She fell asleep praying that God would keep him safe until she found him.

Resting his head beside Laura's on the rolled wool blanket, Deke found his nose tantalizingly close to her hair. He inched closer. No perfume or toilet water. Just a clean woman scent. He couldn't remember the last time he had held a decent female in his arms—maybe because he didn't really want to remember.

He could feel the underside of her right breast with his fingertips. Under the pad of his thumb, he could also feel the light, fluttery rhythm of her heart. Unlike a sturdy Cheyenne woman, she felt small and fragile. Pinning her beneath him had taken so little effort, it had surprised even him.

The protective feeling he had felt that morning welled within him again. This time he couldn't shove it away. A little gal like Laura Cheney needed looking after, and he was the only man around to apply for the job.

A tired smile touched his mouth. A reprobate? He had flat come up in the world since meeting her.

Left to his own devices, Deke relaxed his hand on her midriff, resisting the urge to follow the delicate ladder of her ribs up to softer places. It wasn't easy. He'd been on the trail for weeks and hadn't eased himself on a woman in all that time. He had healthy appetites, and abstinence wore on him. Even if that hadn't been the case, though, he would have been tempted by Laura Cheney, in part because she was such a pretty little thing, but mostly because he admired her pluck, whether he wanted to or not.

A decided lack of enthusiasm? Another grin settled on his mouth. She couldn't even say no without tonguing the subject to death.

As she drifted more deeply into sleep, he felt the change

that came over her body. She lost her inhibitions and leaned more heavily against him. Then her breathing altered, the pace becoming slow and measured. Next, she wriggled her bottom more snugly into the cradle of his thighs to seek his warmth.

For Deke, the contact was sweet torture. He hugged his arm more closely around her, then lay perfectly still and forced his mind to other things. His cattle. The problems he'd been having with rustlers. The profit he had made on the last drive to Denver. Soon his eyelids grew heavy. He curled his shoulders around hers and pressed his face against her sweet-smelling hair. Adrift in a hazy state somewhere between dreams and reality, Deke was only vaguely conscious of Laura's slender fingers grasping his wrist. Assuming that she felt threatened by his touch even in her sleep, he offered no resistance when she moved his hand. His palm settled on damp velvet. Very cold damp velvet. His fingers instinctively conformed to the feminine shape, and his thumb had already embarked on a foray to trace its crest when awareness slammed into his brain.

His eyes shot open. A raspy intake of breath that might have become a snore caught crosswise in his throat. In a purely involuntary reaction, the muscles in his arm jerked. For a moment he lay there, incredulous and perilously close to laughter. If she woke up, she would never believe she had started this.

Not thrilled at the thought of what her reaction might be, he had every intention of moving his hand, but when he began to draw back, she hugged his forearm, shivered, and twisted slightly at the waist to settle her breast more comfortably in his palm. When she grew still once more, the backs of his knuckles were trapped between her and the blanket, and he felt the relentless chill that crept up from the earth.

Deke relaxed and let his hand remain where she had placed it. Soon the heat from his flesh warmed the softness it covered. A handful of pure trouble, that was what he had, and he'd damned well better remember it. There was something about her that was working its way under his skin like a goddamned chigger.

With a little luck, maybe he'd find her baby tomorrow and could deliver her back to Denver the following day. He prayed that would be the case, not just for his sake, but because he didn't think he could bear having to tell her that the child might be, and most probably was, dead.

Three days, on the outside. That was how long he guessed a baby that age could survive without breast milk. Luck— he needed a nonstop run of good luck. So far, it seemed to him he'd had nothing but bad. There were twenty-four hours left of that three days, and within his mind as he drifted to sleep, he thought he could hear a clock ticking away the precious minutes.

When Laura next opened her eyes, the first feeble streaks of dawn bathed the little clearing with pinkish light. For a moment she stared at the pine needles before her nose, uncertain where she was. Then the moldy scent of the forest registered on her sleep-numbed senses, and she remembered the previous day.

As awareness returned to her, measure by measure, she identified the heat at her back as Deke Sheridan's broad chest. His heavy, muscular arm rested in the cradle above her hip, his roped forearm angled across her ribs. Tender with fullness, her right breast, which she had tried so desperately to keep him from touching last night, was cupped in his leathery palm, his long fingers curled warmly and possessively around her. She could tell by the limp weight of his touch that he was fast asleep.

Laura was shocked that he had dared to take such a liberty and that she had allowed it; her first instinct was to jerk away. She quickly stifled the urge. If he woke up, she had no idea what his reaction might be, and she didn't care to find out. With great care, she tried to ease his hand away, hoping to disengage herself, he none the wiser. Gingerly she captured his fingers. Then, inch by inch, she slid his palm down toward her midriff.

He murmured in his sleep and, with a flick of his wrist, freed his hand to return it with unerring accuracy to its former resting place. Laura's breath snagged in her throat when his thumb brushed across the peak of her nipple. Then his fingertips joined in the play, light and searching, as if he were slowly coming to awareness and trying to identify what he held in his hand.

She knew the exact instant he woke up. His breath caught midway up his throat, his body went stiff, and his arm turned steely in its strength around her. But most telling of all was the altered pressure of his fingertips, one moment a tentative searching, the next a well-practiced stroke of thumb and forefinger that sent a shock of sensation deep into her belly.

"Please don't," she whispered raggedly.

He jerked away and pushed up. Though she squeezed her eyes closed in humiliation, Laura could feel him staring down at her. Well aware that most men wouldn't let such an opportunity pass, she fully expected him to make a nasty comment of some sort that would probably embarrass her all the more. An insinuation that she had been enjoying his touch, no doubt.

Instead, she heard him rise to his feet, put his gun belt back on, and walk off. After a moment, she gathered the courage to crack open one eye and saw that he was down at the stream refilling their coffee can. En route back to camp, he gathered twigs and small limbs in his free hand.

"I'll have coffee ready in a few," he called in a sleepy voice as he kindled a morning fire. "I don't know about you, but I could use some."

Laura pushed to a sitting position. That was it? A comment about coffee? She waited for him to send her a lascivious look, but he didn't even glance in her direction. As he snapped the limbs he'd gathered into smaller, more manageable pieces, her gaze was drawn to his large hands. The power in his grip was undeniable. Yet all she had experienced at his touch last night was gentleness.

An odd tightness rose in Laura's throat, and she quickly

turned away, rubbing one wrist and testing it for soreness. She didn't find a single place where the grip of his fingers had left a bruise.

Feeling even more ill than she had last night, Laura went to her saddlebags to get some fresh flux cloths before she went for her morning walk. To her dismay, her supply of rags, torn from the spare set of bloomers she had brought along, had diminished to one thin strip, not nearly enough for her needs. Sitting back on her heels, she contemplated her predicament. Because their journey thus far had afforded her little privacy, she had been burying the soiled rags instead of tucking them away somewhere so she could rinse them later for reuse. Now she wanted to kick herself.

"Somethin' wrong?"

Laura jumped at the question and turned startled eyes toward Deke. "Wrong?"

Those all-seeing eyes of his shifted to her open saddlebags. When he looked back at her, his expression was speculative. "You needin' somethin'?"

Laura moistened her lips. The only spare cloth she had left was the one blanket of Jonathan's that the comancheros had neglected to steal. She couldn't help but feel that the blanket was her only remaining link to her baby, and she couldn't bear to part with it. "You wouldn't happen to have any"—she averted her face, praying he wouldn't guess why she was asking—"spare rags, would you?"

She sensed rather than heard him move toward his own gear. In her peripheral vision, she saw him crouch and rifle quickly through his clothing. His hand reappeared holding a shirt.

"Actually, Mr. Sheridan, I wanted something I might rip up."

He walked toward her, holding out the garment. "It's old. Take it."

Laura couldn't bear to meet his gaze as she accepted his shirt. Just thinking of what she meant to use it for brought heat to her cheeks. "Thank you. When this is over, I shall buy you another."

With that, she pushed up and wheeled away. As she sought a private spot in the thick brush to tend her personal business, she couldn't help but wonder if he knew what she was about. The thought so humiliated her that she decided there was no way she would risk his seeing her rinse out the soiled rags at the creek. Perhaps his next choice of a campsite might provide her with more privacy along a stream. With shaking hands, she found a weak seam in his shirt and set to work, ripping the cloth into strips she might use. She neatly folded the extra swatches and hid them in her pockets so she might slip them into her saddlebags later.

The morning air was chilly, and Laura shivered as she unfastened her jacket and opened her bodice. The cool temperature turned out to be only the start of her troubles. Her breasts were tender to the touch, and at the end of the ordeal, she had managed to express very little milk. Convinced the long, jarring horseback ride the day before was responsible, she tore a length of muslin from the bottom flounce of her petticoat and fashioned a makeshift supporter for her bosom. At this rate, she would run out of underthings before this journey was over.

On the way back to camp, Laura felt oddly disoriented and dizzy. She stopped once to lean against a sapling. Pressing the inside of her wrist against her forehead, she checked herself for fever. As far as she could tell, she wasn't too warm.

Deke had breakfast on the fire when she returned. Laura set herself to the task of rolling up their bedding. As she bent to grab the last blanket, a stitch in her back made her gasp. Deke glanced up from turning the bacon. "You okay?"

Laura brushed a tendril of hair out of her eyes. "Fine," she lied. "I'm just not accustomed to all this riding and then sleeping on the ground."

As she carried their bedding over to where their saddlebags lay, Deke's worried gaze followed her. Her face was frighteningly pale, to his way of thinking, and he didn't like the stiff way she walked. He had a gut feeling all wasn't well.

He smiled slightly at the frown that pleated her forehead

when she opened her saddlebags and saw the collection of women's sage he had gathered. She lifted one of the absorbent leaves to examine it, her face a study of perplexity. Fully prepared for her to glance his way, Deke averted his face in the nick of time. He was quickly learning that she was a funny little thing and bashful as hell about bodily functions, especially her own. With luck, she would realize what the leaves could be used for and save him having to explain it to her.

"Can you take over watching the bacon?" he asked.

She strapped her saddlebags closed and walked unsteadily toward the fire. Looking down at her pinched face, Deke once again felt cause for concern. Her color had turned unnaturally bright along her cheeks, from embarrassment, no doubt, which told him she had indeed guessed what the sage was for. But despite the high color on her cheeks, the rest of her face was chalk white. A feverish sparkle glazed her usually liquid eyes, making them look more like amber glass this morning than pools of whiskey.

As she assumed the role of cook, Deke ordered Chief to stay with Laura, collected his rifle, and took off into the brush, careful to take a different direction than she had until he was safely out of her sight. Then he cut back to find her tracks, which he followed unerringly to a tiny clearing. A quick glance around revealed nothing. Then he spied a patch of disturbed dirt. With the toe of his moccasin, he unearthed the evidence she had so carefully buried. His stomach dropped when he saw the crimson-soaked rags.

"Son of a bitch!"

He clenched his teeth against a wave of anger, which was quickly followed by concern. The crazy little fool. What was she trying to do, kill herself?

Chapter 9

STILL FEELING A BIT DIZZY, LAURA SET HER-
self to the task of finishing breakfast, glad for an opportunity, however small, to help with camp chores. As she
stepped around the fire, Chief growled, and she threw him
a glare.

"After feeding you all my dinner last night, and you're
guarding that stinking bone from me?" She clucked her
tongue. "Shame on you."

Jowls frothy with slobber, the dog snarled again as Laura
moved around him. She shook her head and decided to ignore him. Dumb animal, anyway. As if she would take that
horrid deer leg away from him. She bent over to reposition
the pan of bacon, then turned the thick slabs of meat. As
she started to straighten, Chief capped his earlier growls
with a chest-deep rumble that raised the hair on her neck.
She wasn't anyplace close to his bone now, she realized.

The oddest sensation crawled up Laura's back, a feeling
that eyes were pinned on her. Her heart skipped a beat as
she slowly turned around. At her movement, Chief surged
up from his resting place.

Not ten feet away stood three Mexicans, though to tag
them ethnically as Mexican was, in Laura's opinion, an insult to their nationality. She doubted these three deserved
the honor of comparison. Their stench drifted to her, so
strong it nearly took her breath.

"Señora," one said with a polite tip of his filthy hat. His

yellow, decayed teeth flashed in a grin that creased his swarthy face. "We smelled your coffee. We were hoping that maybe you could find it in your heart to share a leetle?"

Laura gaped. Never had she seen men so grimy or so wicked-looking. They stared back at her with shifty, blood-shot eyes. All three wore garments of Spanish accent, their fringed leather vests and pants bradded with tarnished conchae. She saw that they had removed their spurs, probably to sneak up on her. Their horses were ground-tied at the opening of the draw, a goodly distance away.

At a loss for words and wanting to kick herself for ignoring Chief's warnings, she inched toward the dog, which was still snarling and crouched to leap. She noted that one of the Mexicans held his right hand near his gun and that he watched the canine warily. Praying she wouldn't be bitten herself, Laura rested a trembling hand atop the animal's massive head. Chief would be shot before he ever had a chance to move; of that, she had no doubt. She didn't want Deke Sheridan to come back and find his pet dead; she owed him that much, at least.

"Easy, Chief," Laura said thinly.

"He is not a very friendly dog," the man to her right said softly. "Please keep him under control, señora. It would be a shame if we had to shoot him. Would it not?"

Laura threw a glance in the direction Deke had gone.

"Yeah, a real shame," a dangerously low voice said from somewhere behind her.

She turned to see her tracker step out from a stand of brush. He moved forward with a deceptive laziness belied only by the quick shift of his eyes from one stranger to another. In his left arm, he cradled his Henry rifle, his hand curled loosely over the butt. His right arm hung relaxed at his side, his fingers slightly curled. Clearly he was ready to go for his Colt. Laura thanked God she had moved next to Chief, safely out of the line of fire.

"If you was to shoot my dog, I reckon I'd have to shoot you," he informed the Mexican softly. "I've learned over the years that bein' too quick at pullin' the trigger puts me to a lot of extra work. Grave-diggin', you know. I'd be right obliged if you'd save me the trouble."

The man who had threatened the dog drew his hand away from his gun and flashed a smile that made Laura's skin go cold. "We seek no trouble, señor. Not if we can steer clear of it."

Deke came to a stop abreast of Laura. Silence settled, the only sounds those of the small fire, the sizzling bacon, and the can of boiling coffee. Never glancing her way, he said, "Laura, honey, take Chief and go for a little walk." He hesitated a moment, then called to the dog, *"Okema! Ni-ne-e-meh' equiwa!"*

Chief ceased his snarling and moved closer to Laura. She curled her fingers in the dog's loose ruff and tugged him along behind her, surprised that he abandoned his deer leg and followed her without a fuss. At the edge of the clearing, she glanced back at Deke, loath to leave him. For one, she felt bad about deserting him to face such unfair odds alone, and secondly, she couldn't help but wonder what might happen to her if something happened to him. Not very noble of her, she knew, but there it was.

As though Deke sensed her hesitation, he said softly, "Go, Boston. Chief'll find the way back for you."

Laura ducked into the brush, shielding her face with one arm, holding the dog with her other hand. Her first instinct was to run as far as her legs would carry her. If the eager way Chief lunged against her grasp was any indication, he seconded that motion. However, as the sound of the men's voices faded, Laura's suspicious nature dragged her footsteps to a halt. She would be a fool to trust Deke Sheridan too far, and thanks to Tristan's many betrayals, she was certainly no fool.

Ignoring Chief's whines of protest, she retraced her steps to find a hiding place, dropped to her knees, and parted the brush to peer toward camp. Chief promptly clamped his jaws over her arm and tugged her off balance.

"Stop it!" Laura cried softly, and batted at his massive head. He ignored her and continued to pull, not sinking in his teeth enough to hurt, but letting her know he meant business. Laura tried to free her arm. "Shoo! Bad dog! Go away! Shoo!"

Chief clearly didn't respond to commands given in English. He was going to rip her jacket if he didn't stop. Laura pried at his teeth.

"*Okema!* No!"

Laura wasn't certain what *Okema* meant, but she had heard Deke say it, and it got the dog's attention. With a low whine, he released her arm. Laura was so surprised, it took her a moment to recover her composure. Then she gave the animal a light pat on the head.

"Yes, well . . . *Okema.* Good dog," she whispered.

That problem settled, she parted the brush to peer toward camp. With a disgusted-sounding grunt, Chief dropped to his haunches beside her. At this distance, the men's voices barely reached her, but she could still make out most of what they said. She wondered how much of their conversation she had missed.

Right now, the Mexicans were asking Deke what he was doing up here with such a pretty riding companion. Didn't he know that was inviting trouble? Deke replied that trouble kept him shooting sharp.

At least he wasn't backing down, which had been Laura's greatest fear. She had no idea what she would do if he rode out and left her at the mercy of those three, which certainly wasn't beyond the realm of possibility. She was nothing to him, and up against three gunmen, who would blame him for cutting out? For far less reason, Tristan had left her to fend for herself more than once.

One of the Mexicans said, "Some men would pay a dear price for a woman like that."

As if that came as a novel thought, Deke assumed a ponderous expression and nudged a smoldering piece of firewood with his toe. "You think so? How dear a price?"

"Perhaps as much as a hundred."

Deke chuckled and shook his head. "She'd bring a thousand across the border, first crack. I could get two if I bided my time. To save myself havin' to make the trip, I might part with her for five hundred, but not a penny less."

Another of the Mexicans hooted with laughter. "Surely you are not serious, señor."

Deke shifted his hold slightly on his Henry. "Dead serious."

The pulse-pounding wave of anger that crashed over Laura made her miss what the strangers said next.

Deke replied, "Well, then, my friends, I reckon you'd best talk to your boss. Five hundred, no less, or I don't deal. You go tell him that."

"It is a very long ride to reach him," the Mexican to the right of the fire protested.

"We ain't travelin' none too fast," her tracker countered. "If you're that interested in the woman, you can catch back up with us."

The man standing in the middle removed his hat to run grimy fingers through his hair. After putting the hat back on, he said, "Señor, be reasonable, yes? Our leader wants the woman very badly. We have approached you with a very fine offer when we might have been less polite. Perhaps you should take your hundred dollars and count yourself lucky."

Deke braced his gun hand on his hip and met the man's gaze across the fire. "My bacon's burnin', and my coffee's boilin' dry. If you wanna swap lead, you greasy son of a bitch, then hop to it. Otherwise, go back to your leader, tell him what I said, and don't let me see your face again till he's ready to pay the money I want."

The lethal tone of Deke's voice chilled Laura. She could see that it had no less of an effect on the three Mexicans.

"You are loco, señor," the tallest stranger commented dryly. "Three guns against one? You'd be a dead man before you cleared leather, eh?"

"Maybe. Maybe not. I reckon I can take two of you. I just ain't decided which two. You wanna be first?"

"Are you truly so sure of yourself?"

"I am. And if you knew my reputation, you wouldn't be

standin' there flexin' them fingers of yours near that gun. I've killed men for less. Makes me real nervous."

The middle man nodded. "Ah, yes. It comes to me now, señor. I thought I knew your face. Deke Sheridan, are you not?"

"It ain't a face most folks forget."

The Mexicans all stiffened at this affirmation of Deke's identity. They seemed none too anxious now to draw on him.

"We will speak to our leader," the man in the middle said. "Perhaps he will agree to a leetle bit more money."

Deke said nothing as the three turned and walked back toward their horses.

"You miserable, slimy, double-dealing, worthless . . ." Laura staggered to a stop near the fire, so angry, she ran out of adjectives. Chief flopped down on the dirt near her feet and let loose with a mournful whine. Laura cast him a derisive glance and cried, "Oh, do shut up, you bothersome beast!" Then, redirecting her gaze at Deke, she fairly screeched, "How could you? And to think I was actually starting to like you!"

"Really?" Deke's eyes, twinkling with mischief, trailed with insolent slowness over her face. "That sounds promisin', Boston. How much were you startin' to like me?"

"A negligible amount, but anything would be an improvement on my first impression of you, which you've just reaffirmed." She pointed a finger in the direction the Mexicans had disappeared. "How could you offer to sell me to those horrible men, and for a measly five hundred dollars?"

His mouth quirked at the corners. "Worked, didn't it? They left."

"And what if they had agreed?"

"I reckon I would've had to shoot the bastards. The thing is, they didn't. Five hundred's a steep price for a little bitty gal like you." He gave her a speculative once-over. "Not that I'm findin' fault."

Laura's mouth dropped open. The hint of a grin she had

detected on his lips a moment ago slowly broadened into a smile that she yearned to scrub from his face.

"I've always maintained anything more'n a handful is a damned waste, anyhow. You're just right to my way of thinkin'."

Laura resisted the urge to hug her chest, and she absolutely refused to blush. "They might have taken you up on it! Even now, how can you know they won't return with the money?"

His gaze swept away from her and settled at the mouth of the draw. Pursing his lips, he seemed to consider that possibility. "Oh, they'll come back. No question of that. But not with no money."

The hair on Laura's nape prickled. "What do you mean?"

"Just what I said. They'll be back." A muscle twitched along his jaw. "They'll just hold off till their odds is a little better, that's all. No point in riskin' a bullet in their hides if they can take me later when I ain't expectin' it."

Her anger fled. "Then you had no intention of striking a bargain?"

He narrowed an eye at her. "If I meant to sell you, I'd take the hundred and be glad they offered that much. A hundred dollars is a fine price for an armload of trouble." His expression turned thoughtful. "The way I see it, I got one choice, and that's to pound leather and lose the bastards."

"Lose them?"

"There ain't no way I can take all three of 'em. Not face-to-face and swappin' lead. And now, sure as hell, they'll wait for dark and creep up on us." He shrugged as if that said it all. "I gotta get shut of the sons of bitches."

Laura moved to take the charred bacon off the flames. "I'm ready to ride."

He grasped her wrist before she could touch the skillet handle. "You'll burn yourself." He proceeded to move the hot pan with his bare hand. "As for you bein' ready, honey, you ain't goin'."

Laura froze in a half crouch, her arm still extended

toward the fire. Panic flared within her. "What do you mean, I'm not going?"

He straightened and nudged the coffee can off the coals with the toe of his moccasin. Then he began kicking dirt to extinguish the flames. "Just what I said. I can't make good time if I take you along." His silvery eyes took on a glint. "You're flowin' like a storm-swole crick. A ride like I'm gonna have to make would kill you."

Laura felt heat rising up her neck. How could he possibly know . . . ? She tugged on the tails of her jacket. "I beg your pardon, sirrah?"

"You heard me right." His gaze gave her no quarter. "How come you didn't tell me you was bleedin' so heavy?"

Laura longed to break eye contact but couldn't. "Mr. Sheridan!" she said in her most indignant tone.

"Don't get your back up with me. Not about this," he retorted evenly. "There's some things that need sayin'. You ain't in no condition to ride, never even should've climbed on a goddamned horse, and I'm mad as hell you lied to me about it."

"I didn't!"

"You sure as shit did. I asked if you was feelin' poorly, and you said you was fine. That's lyin' in my books."

"And what of my books? There are some things a lady does not, under any circumstances, discuss with a gentleman."

"You ain't got a book, not on this trip, and I ain't no gentleman."

Laura lifted her chin and glared at him. "I can keep up."

"You can't take the pace, and you know it."

"At least give me a chance!"

"Nope."

She knotted her hands. "I *hate* it when you say that word. 'Nope'! Just who do you think you are? God Almighty?"

His eyes searched hers. "We'll find your baby, or we won't. That's up to whatever God it is you pray to. But I ain't lettin' you push yourself till you do yourself serious hurt."

"So you're *leaving* me?" she cried shrilly. "That's a dandy solution! How long did it take you to concoct that plan, about three miserable seconds?"

"There's no call to be scared, Boston."

"I am not scared," she retorted in a tremulous voice.

"I'll be back."

"Oh, sure you will."

He stepped slowly around the fire. "Honey, listen to me."

Laura batted his hand away, shivered, and hugged her waist. "Don't touch me, and don't call me *honey*. If you're going to leave me, just do it. I certainly can't stop you."

"I ain't *leavin'* you. Leavin's when you don't come back, and I—"

"Those Mexicans will be back. You said so yourself. The truth of it is, you're taking the coward's way out. Leaving me alone so they can have easy pickings. And saving your own hide while you're at it."

Tears rushed to her eyes. She fully expected her accusations to enrage him, but she didn't care. At least his anger would be honest. She couldn't bear to be left behind again, pacified with lies, counting on some man who had no intention of coming through for her.

Memories rolled through her like waves, the images pounding on the sands of her mind with brutal impact. She saw herself, eight and a half months pregnant, begging Tristan not to leave her. Then she recalled how it had felt later, his promises nothing but dust, when she had gone into labor, her body afire with agony, her mind frozen with terror because she faced giving birth alone. She couldn't bear that kind of betrayal again. Not again.

"Laura . . ."

She spun away and fixed her gaze on the Rockies, hating the craggy peaks, detesting them. How many times in the last ten months had she stared at them, feeling alone and frightened? This time it wasn't Tristan leaving her behind, but for reasons beyond her, her sense of betrayal ran just as deep. Maybe deeper. Possibly because Deke Sheridan epitomized strength, and somewhere, deep in her heart, she had hoped he was different.

After leaning his rifle against a rock, he curled his large hands over her shoulders. His grasp was heavy and warm, anchoring her where she stood while he stepped close, his chest at her back, his head bent to press his cheek against her ear. She felt the rasp of his beard, and it seemed those whiskers embodied everything masculine, everything she had come to resent.

"Honey, listen to me."

Laura closed her eyes, familiar with that placating, soothing tone of voice even though she had never heard Deke Sheridan use it. Only Tristan. But Tristan had taught her well with his honeyed lies. Numbly she listened, just as Deke demanded, because, as always, she had little choice. As he outlined his plans, the words became a confusing jumble in her brain. Only one sentence rang clear, and upon hearing it, she whirled to face him.

"You're taking all the horses?" she said incredulously. "Even mine?"

Pressing a frontal advance this time, he grasped her shoulders again. "Those fellows may not be as good as the Cheyenne at trackin', but they can read sign, Boston. If I don't take all the horses, they'll know some are missin' and guess what I'm up to. I'll load your saddlebags down with stone so it looks like your gelding is carrying your weight." Releasing one of her shoulders, he took her chin in his hand and lifted her face. "You gotta trust me. What kind of man'd leave you stranded out here at the mercy of those three?"

"What kind of man wouldn't?"

He ignored that. "I'll lead them to hell and gone off our scent, then double back. If there's any way I can, I'll be here with you before dark."

Laura closed her mind to what he was saying. She had trusted before, and all trusting had ever done was make her troubles worse. She ended up waiting around, counting on someone else until it was nearly too late to help herself. Not this time. The fact that Deke Sheridan was taking her horse, blast his miserable hide, was all the affirmation she needed that he was hightailing it out of here and abandoning her.

"You're leaving me right here? Where they last saw us?" She prayed he would say no, that he'd give her some reason to hope.

"Not in the open. I'll hide you deep in the brush and wipe away our footprints as I back my way out." He smiled slightly. "All the tracks will lead north, Boston. They'll never think in a million years that I'd leave you here alone."

Because it was such a despicable thing to do. Even low-life comancheros had conscience enough to know that. But she was resigned. Deke Sheridan outweighed her by a good hundred pounds, nearly every ounce solid muscle. She couldn't enter into a physical contest with him for one of the horses and hope to win. If he had his mind set on going, he would go, and nothing she said or did would stop him. She supposed, if she were faced with the same circumstances, she'd skedaddle, too. The odds were stacked against him. Why should he risk getting shot for a woman and baby who meant nothing to him?

Determined to make one more try at appealing to his sense of honor, if he even had one, which was in doubt, Laura struggled to keep her lips from trembling and said, "If you leave me here, I'll die. One way or another. And my baby as well. You do realize that? My life is one thing. But what of my child's? Can you truly toss it away as if it means nothing?"

The question tore at Deke, and when he looked into Laura's eyes, the pain he saw there nearly changed his mind about leaving her. He wished he could get his hands around Tristan Cheney's neck and squeeze the life out of the miserable bastard. Laura's reaction to his plans told Deke far more than she probably realized, namely that being left alone to dig a well three days out of childbed had been the least of her trials.

"Honey, when they do come back, they'll ride straight by. I promise you that." He glanced at the opening of the draw. "I'll scout around before I hightail it to make sure they're not out there someplace watchin'. That's the only way they could ever know you was here. Trust me on that."

She stared up at him with that same stricken look on her face. Deke wished he knew some way to reassure her. As long as he could still put one foot in front of the other, he would come back for her, or die trying. Hell, he'd crawl back if he had to. But the wounded expression in her amber eyes told him that nothing he said would ever convince her of that. Sometimes a man's actions had to do his talking for him.

He wouldn't let himself think about her baby. That non-stop run of good luck he had prayed for last night hadn't come about, and from the way things looked, it might be all he could do just to keep Laura safe.

As quickly as he could, Deke prepared to ride. When all was ready, he gathered the supplies and blankets he had set aside for Laura and led her deep into the brush. When he found a cluster of boulders that would protect her on three sides, he spread one of the blankets out for her to sit on, then removed his gun from its holster. He had another six-shooter in his bags if he needed it, and he would rest easier knowing Laura had some means of defending herself. Slowly, so he felt certain she could follow his instructions, he showed her how to load the gun and cock it, then theorized on proper trigger pulling and aim.

"Don't shoot unless something's right on top of you," he cautioned as he slipped the weapon back into its holster. "The sound of a shot out here will carry and draw them down on you like flies to honey. You understand?"

Her gaze averted, she nodded listlessly. Deke could only wonder what had happened in her life to make her trust so little. She looked so small and fragile, so hopeless. He cast a frustrated glance around, trying to imagine how she must feel, unpracticed with a weapon, unable to find her way out of here, and soon to be without a horse.

Still, there was no help for it. Leaving her here, where she would be safe, was the best plan. There was no way Deke could hope to outrun those Mexicans, and contrary to what he had told Laura, he couldn't lead them off the scent for any period of time. With any tracking skills at all, they would figure out his game eventually and realize he intended to double back.

He had one chance. That was to leave a clear trail and then wait to ambush the bastards. It would be dangerous business. Too dangerous to allow Laura to be anywhere nearby. She would be far safer here. Deke thought about leveling with her, but quickly discarded the notion. It would be bad enough to let her fret the entire time he was gone, afraid he might not choose to return. Telling her he could end up dead, with no choice in the matter, might send her into a real panic.

"I'll leave old Chief here to keep you company. That oughta convince you I'm comin' back. Who'd leave a worthless, no-account mongrel like him behind?"

She didn't respond to the teasing question.

He strapped his gun belt around her slender hips, using the tip of his knife blade to punch a new buckle hole so he could draw in the band of leather to fit. The entire time he worked, she just stood there, her face resolute, her eyes slightly unfocused, her arms limp at her sides.

"Boston, I swear I'll be back if I gotta crawl every inch of the way. Won't you try to believe that? Why would I say it if I didn't mean it?"

No reaction. Just that empty, hollow look. As he straightened, Deke sheathed his knife and took her face between his hands, hoping to say with his eyes what he couldn't seem to get across with words. She accepted the touch passively, not betraying by so much as a twitch that she was even aware of the contact.

With a discouraged sigh, he swept off his hat and removed the hatband of cobalt trade beads. The loosened feather drifted slowly to the ground as he put his hat back on and fastened the circlet of beads around Laura's slender neck. Lifting stray tendrils of her hair free, he said, "Don't take it off. Promise me that?"

She still refused to look up at him.

"Them beads is known all through this country by the Indians," he explained. "My Cheyenne mother strung 'em for me when I killed my first—" Deke glanced around the tiny clearing, then scraped a hand across his mouth. "Anyhow, I've always wore 'em since. If any Indians come around while I'm gone, they'll recognize the beads and leave you be."

He curled a finger under her chin and forced a smile. "Hey, Boston?" No response. Deke ran his thumb across her mouth. "Hell's bells, I never thought I'd see the time when you quit talkin'. The least you could do is give me a proper send-off with some of that fancy name-callin' of yours."

She still didn't look up. Deke took a reluctant step back, knowing he had to go, but hating to leave her when she felt like this.

"I don't want you doin' nothin' but restin' the whole day," he told her. "Maybe stayin' quiet will stop the—" He broke off, not wanting to throw fuel on the fire by bringing up something *ladies* shouldn't discuss. "We got a baby to go find when I get back, remember, and the more you rest now, the more we can ride later."

Nothing. Deke had never seen anyone look so dejected. He swallowed and scuffed the heel of his moccasin in the dirt. Damn it! What had Tristan Cheney done to her?

"I'll be back," he assured her, once again striving for a teasing tone he could only hope didn't sound as forced as it felt. "I got a hundred and seventy dollars to take out in trade, remember? Only a fool'd turn his back on that sweet bargain."

At that, he saw something flicker in her eyes. A sick sensation settled in his guts. Like a goddamned burr in a dog's tail, his reputation hung on, and he couldn't seem to shake it.

Stepping back to her, he captured her small face between his hands. Digging his fingers in at the hinges of her jaws, he forced her teeth apart so he could plunder the sweet, moist recesses of her mouth.

At the first contact of their lips, Deke felt a shock that bolted into his guts, shot down his legs, and felt as though it blew out the bottoms of his feet. *Sweet Jesus.* She even tasted like whiskey, honeyed and mellow, yet searing hot.

As he took a long pull at her mouth, he nearly forgot what he was about. But tenderly seducing her wasn't his aim.

He forced his tongue deep into her mouth and did what he did best, which was act like a first-class bastard. Only this time, it didn't come easy, and he felt no satisfaction, no sense of giving back as good as he got. She tried to arch away and brought up her small hands to shove against his chest. But instead of turning her loose, as he longed to do, he used his strength to hold her fast and took what she didn't want to give.

Startled and clearly frightened, she whimpered into his mouth, her breath warm and incredibly sweet. Deke savored the flavor of her, pretty damned sure he'd never get another taste as he slid a hand up her ribs to cup her breast. At the last instant, though, he couldn't quite bring himself to do it. Not after her frantic attempts to stop him last night. He settled for claiming relatively harmless territory on her side, dangerously close to tempting softness. She jerked as though he had finished the deed—jerked and then sobbed. That sob nearly undid him.

He hated himself. Her struggles to escape him became more frenzied, but he held her a little longer—long enough to make sure she wouldn't forget what a no-good bastard he was.

Finally loosening his arms, he said, "I'll be back, Boston. Maybe you'd like to forget our bargain, but there ain't no way I am. Not till I get my money's worth out of you."

Still struggling to be free, she staggered when he released her. As she regained her balance, she shot him a glare of pure loathing and wiped the taste of him from her swollen mouth with the sleeve of her jacket. Though he had to reach deep, he managed a cocky grin.

The expression on her face was the only reward Deke figured he was ever likely to get for this bit of business. Dread, revulsion, fear of him. At least she no longer looked worried about his abandoning her. Now she was anticipating his inevitable return and looking none too happy at the prospect.

Chapter 10

FOURTEEN HOURS LATER, WEARY THOUGH HE was, Deke rode fairly tall in the saddle. Not even the fact that he'd had to leave Laura alone in the dark for far longer than he had hoped could dampen his spirits. With Chief to look after her, he felt sure she was still all right. Mad, maybe, and probably scared to death. But that mood wouldn't stick with her long.

Deke felt like whooping and singing. Not only had he managed to dispense with the three Mexicans without getting his ass shot off, but on the way back here, he had finally spotted some Indian sign. Cheyennes were camped at Cougar Flats, less than a day's ride away, and they were Deke's own band, people he knew and loved, and who loved him.

What all of that boiled down to was that Laura's baby was probably alive and well. The comancheros could have made it as far as Cougar Flats in two days, maybe in as little as one and a half. With careful handling, Jonathan could have survived that long. And seeing as how the Indians happened to be some he knew, Deke's chances of bargaining with them for the return of Laura's son were far better than with strangers.

His prayer for a run of good luck had been answered. The Great Ones had taken their own damned time in getting around to it, but who was complaining? He couldn't wait to get back to Laura and tell her the news. She'd be happy as a bug. Hey, she might even forgive him for how he had told her good-bye this morning. Even if she didn't, she was bound to come around when he put that baby back in her arms.

That thought made Deke's smile of satisfaction vanish. His resolve not to become emotionally vulnerable was growing more elusive by the moment, and unless he wanted to sit in for another round of heartache, he had better get a handle on things. Before he knew it, he'd be delivering her safely back to Denver, and he'd probably never see her again if she had her way.

The feelings he was starting to have for her were dangerous. He was who he was, and there was no changing it. Determined to put such foolishness from his mind, Deke guided the horses carefully through the thick brush. He had enough troubles without borrowing any. The comancheros might be doubling back from Cougar Flats already, and they'd be sure to have their eyes peeled for their three *compañeros*, no doubt hoping the men would have Laura in their possession. When the bastards realized that Deke had killed their friends and then disappeared with the woman they wanted so badly, they'd be as thick in these hills as fleas on a dog's back. Since Deke had no intention of getting his hide shot full of holes, or of letting the comancheros get their hands on Laura, he couldn't waste any time in transporting her to the flats where his people were camped. Not even comancheros would dare to nettle the Cheyenne.

As Deke drew near the spot where he had left Laura, his smile returned. For a fancy bit of city fluff, the girl had smarts. She hadn't built a fire. Given her fear of long-toothed critters, he was surprised. Not that he had ever doubted she had mettle, just not much sturdiness to go with it.

Pulling up near the rocks, Deke swung from the saddle. "Hey, Boston!" he called softly. "It's Deke. Don't go aeratin' my hide for me."

No answer. One hand still on his stallion's shoulder, Deke paused to listen. Chief appeared from out of the darkness and whined a greeting.

"Hey, Okema."

Deke bent to pat him, then made his way around the boulders. He saw Laura huddled on the blanket.

"Laura?" He knelt beside her. Relief washed through him when she stirred. "Hey, there, girl. You had me scared for a minute."

She pulled herself partway up and peered at him through the moonlit gloom. "Mr. Sheridan?"

Deke smiled. "If it was anyone else, you was s'posed to shoot him."

She rubbed her jacket sleeve over her eyes. "You came back."

"I said I would, didn't I?" For a woman who had been so terrified of being left alone, she sure didn't act overjoyed to see him. He remembered the manner in which he had said good-bye. Looking back, he was none too sure that had been one of his wiser moves. Now he'd be faced with the chore of convincing her he wasn't as bad as he had pretended to be. He drew away slightly and braced his arm on an upraised knee.

"And the Mexicans?" she asked groggily. "Did you lose them?"

"Yep, and I've got great news. Cheyennes are camped less than a day's ride from here. I'd bet my savings your baby's with them. And they're Cheyennes that I know personal. Somebody up there's smilin' on us."

He thought he saw tears sparkle in her eyes. "Thank God." After a long moment, she pushed more erect. "Less than a day away, you say? And you think Jonathan is with them?"

Deke wanted so badly to wipe the worry from her mind that he was a little more adamant in his reply than he might have been otherwise. "No think to it, honey. He's with them, or I'll eat my hat. And they'll treat him real fine till we get there. I promise you that."

He shifted his weight onto the other knee so she had plenty of space to sit up. Removing the cobalt beads from around her neck, he put them back on his hat, then searched the ground for his feather and stuck it into the band at a jaunty angle. Next, he transferred his gun belt from her hips back to his own. As he bent to tie the holster thongs, she gave a shaky sigh that brought his head up. "You feelin' okay?"

"I'm fine."

Deke had heard her sing that tune before. Though he couldn't put his finger on it, something about her seemed off the mark. The odd note in her voice, he decided. "You startin' to wake up?"

"I wasn't asleep."

"Then why didn't you answer when I called you?"

"You called? I'm sorry. I guess I didn't hear you." She seemed to be searching for him in the shadows. "When will we leave?"

"Are you sure you're feelin' up to it?" he asked, knowing damned well she wasn't, and that she'd lie rather than admit it.

"Of course."

Reluctantly he said, "We can go whenever you're ready, I guess." As quickly as he could, Deke explained his concerns about the comancheros doubling back. "The way I got it figured, they probably reached my people sometime today, which means they'll more than likely hit their backtrail tonight or come mornin'. Are you sure you're feelin' up to more ridin'?"

"Have I a choice?"

She had a point. "We won't push it hard," he promised.

With a nod, she replied, "I can go for another day, Mr. Sheridan. It's a simple matter of staying in the saddle, after all."

Deke wished there were other options, but there weren't. He rose before she did and reached to steady her as she struggled to her feet. Together, they gathered up the supplies he had left behind for her. Getting ready to ride was quick business with the horses all ready to go, and within minutes, they headed out, Deke in the lead, the pack animals trailing behind him.

It seemed to Deke they had been riding less than an

hour when Laura called softly to him. "Mr. Sheridan, I fear I must stop for a rest."

At the sound of her voice, his guts went tight. His Boston, asking to rest? He could scarcely believe his ears.

"I simply haven't the strength to press onward, I fear. Perhaps a short break will revive me."

Dropping the pack animal rope, he wheeled his horse and rode back to her. At his approach, she said, "I'm so sorry."

Sorry wouldn't plug bullet holes, but Deke refrained from saying so.

She pressed the inside of her wrist against her forehead. "I think I have a fever. And I'm feeling unaccountably dizzy."

Her words made his pulse skitter. "Honey, are you still—"

"No," she interrupted, clearly uncomfortable with his asking. "Resting all day helped with that."

It was small comfort to Deke. She didn't look any too good. A fever? Shit. He touched a hand to her cheek. Her skin was icy from the chill headwind that blew down off the snowcapped mountains. Still, he had been around her long enough to know she wouldn't claim to be sick unless she truly was. He stifled a frustrated sigh. With comancheros riding drag, what the hell was he going to do?

She pushed at a curly tendril of hair that had fallen over her eyes. When it immediately fell back to block her vision, she set her slender fingers to work. The braid that encircled her crown had slipped from its moorings and hung to one side, the thickly roped strands unraveling. She struggled to set it right, then sighed and let her arms drop heavily to her sides, clearly too weak to finish the task.

Deke's heart went out to her. He knew how frantic she was to reach her baby. To be defeated by her own frailty must be bitter medicine to swallow. "Well, I guess there's no help for it. We can't travel with you like this."

"No. I'm sorry."

"No point in feelin' sorry, honey. It ain't your fault if you're ailin'."

"I'm sure I'll perk up if I can just rest for a bit."

Somehow Deke doubted that, but again he refrained from saying so. It wasn't as if he hadn't known what he was biting off when he had agreed to take this job. His most immediate concern was what to do. Come dawn, nearly twenty men would be searching for them, if they weren't out there already. Even with the surrounding underbrush as a blind, he didn't dare build a fire here, and if she was truly taking sick, he'd need one to doctor her.

Somewhere to hide her . . . On the way here, he had seen an abandoned mine that tunneled its way into the side of a hill. He hadn't gone close, but with a little luck, maybe the diggings would serve.

"Can you push it for a few more minutes?" he asked. "I got a spot in mind where we might lay over."

"Certainly," she said in a stronger voice.

Deke took heart. Maybe she was right and a few minutes would restore her. Knowing her, she hadn't eaten while he was gone. He'd fix her up some bacon, with hot biscuits and gravy, and pour several cups of hot coffee down her. That'd shore her up if anything would.

Preparing to resume their ride, she leaned forward to catch the reins and, in the process, nearly pitched headfirst to the ground. Deke shot out a hand to steady her, and then, without consciously making the decision, found himself moving her from her gelding to his stallion.

As he settled her in front of him, she insisted, "I can ride the remainder of the way by myself, Mr. Sheridan. Our combined weights will be too hard on the horse."

"You let me worry about the horse," he told her gruffly as he slipped an arm around her waist. "Lean back against me, honey. Rest if you want. I won't let you fall."

As he nudged his black into a walk, he heard her give a low moan. He bent to see her face. "Boston? What is it?"

She was biting her lip and took a moment to answer.

"I'm just a bit sore, that's all. A few minutes to rest—that's all I need."

"Where do you hurt?"

"All over," she admitted. Then she quickly added, "But it's not that bad. I'll work it out. It's just that I've been lying still and soreness has set in. Muscles, probably." Her voice turned thin. "I'm sorry for being such a mollycoddle."

Deke tightened his arm around her. "I think you're doin' just fine," he told her, and he meant it. Better than fine. Most white women never would have started out on this journey. "Where are you hurtin' the worst?"

He felt the tension that crept into her slender frame. "I, um . . ." She dragged in a shaky breath. "My unmentionables, mainly."

"Your what?" He bent close again, fairly certain he had misunderstood.

"My unmentionables," she said more clearly.

Despite the gravity of the situation, he smiled slightly, tempted to wring her little neck. Her unmentionables? He could see he had his work cut out for him. "Your breasts? Where, honey?"

"Mr. Sheridan!" she said in an indignant little voice. "For shame!"

He splayed a hand low on her belly. "Here?"

She clasped his wrist. "Just because I'm feeling a tad ill doesn't mean I intend to abandon all propriety."

Deke wasn't sure what the hell propriety was, and he didn't particularly care. He kneaded her belly, and she gasped. Her obvious tenderness in that area answered one of his questions. For just an instant, panic jolted through him. Childbed fever? Then he discarded the notion. She'd be on fire with fever if that were the case, and so sick she could scarcely stand up.

Not that he intended to take this lightly. Her symptoms could be the beginning stages, and he'd be a fool not to treat them accordingly.

"You hurtin' anywhere else?" When she didn't immediately answer him, he nearly lost his patience. "In your breasts?" Another long silence. "Boston? Goddammit, answer me. This ain't no time to be bashful."

She hunched her shoulders, angled an arm over her chest as if she feared he might attempt to touch her there as well, and finally nodded her head. Deke clenched his teeth. So much for food and coffee as a cure. This might be more serious than he had first thought, and with her being so bashful . . . Jesus. It was definitely going to be one hell of a long night.

Three hours later, Deke knelt at Laura's side where he had laid her earlier and nudged her awake. Her eyes went wide as she glanced uneasily into the blackness beyond the light of the fire he had built.

"We're in an old mine," he explained as he held out a steaming tin cup to her. "I hid the horses and covered the entrance with brush so no one can see the fire. There's a couple of air shafts to bleed out the smoke. We'll be safe in here."

She drew her bleary gaze back to him, then focused on the cup. Placing a hand over her middle, she said, "I'm nauseated. I don't care for anything to drink."

Deke tried an encouraging smile. He had to get the potion down her. Without it, she would never let him touch her without putting up a fight. He had no doubt that he could overpower her. The Cheyenne had taught him more than a few tricks when it came to handling frantic females, but just the thought of doing such things to Laura, even for her own good, made him feel sick. "This here'll take care of your stomach," he promised. "And it'll help if you do got a fever."

She sat partway up and craned her neck to peer into the cup. "What is it?"

"*Ujapihgi*, medicine. Or maybe a better word's tea." He flashed her another smile and moved the cup close. "Try a sip." When she jerked back, he laughed and said, "What's the matter? You think I might poison you?"

"Is it some kind of Indian concoction?"

Deke wasn't going to lie to her. "My Cheyenne mother is a medicine woman, and she taught me to make it. Just 'cause it's an Indian remedy don't make it bad, honey."

She wrinkled her nose. "What went into it? What's it supposed to do?"

"Several things went into it," he admitted. "Some bark and roots I gathered up, and some cactus buttons I had in my bags. As for what it does, I kinda mixed remedies to save you havin' to drink too many different things. A fever remedy, for one, and it'll help ease that pain in your belly." He hesitated, then added, "There's a couple of dream medicines in it, too."

"Dream medicines?"

"To relax you."

She shot him a suspicious glance. Deke met her gaze, trying his best to look harmless.

"What kind of dream medicine?"

"Just drink it, Boston. Please?"

"No. I don't wish to be relaxed."

Deke rubbed his chin and sighed. "You gotta drink it. Pain in the gut like you got is nothin' to play around with so soon after childbirth. You could end up real sick. How can I stop that from happenin' if you won't take the medicine?"

"I don't mind plain medicine. It's the *dream* part that's worrying me."

He tried for the harmless look again. "Hey, honey, don't you trust me?"

"No."

"Not even a little?"

"No."

"Jesus Christ."

"There, you see? You respect nothing, not even the Son of God."

"He's the son of your God, not mine."

"If you don't believe in Him, why do you constantly petition for His divine intervention?"

"For his what?"

She pushed the cup back at him. "Never mind. Suffice it

to say that I shan't be consuming a relaxant. It would be foolhardy when in the company of a man of your godless persuasions."

"I ain't godless. Hell, I bet I got more gods than you. Wanna count?"

"No, thank you. It's a case of quantity versus quality, I'm sure."

Determined, Deke curled her hands around the cup. Her fragile little fingers felt hot. Then he decided it had to be the heat radiating from the cup that he felt. Gazing into her wary eyes, he considered his options. To hell with looking harmless. He wasn't any good at it.

"Boston, we got a problem. The way I'm seein' it, one way or another, you gotta drink that tea. You can save me and yourself a lot of trouble if you do it on your own."

She raised her chin in stubborn defiance. "Please don't misinterpret this as a challenge to your considerable arrogance, Mr. Sheridan, but as strong as you may be, it would be nigh unto impossible to make me swallow. In the attempt, most of your precious tea would be spilled."

Deke regarded her for several tense seconds. "I can get that tea down you and never spill a drop. It's a trick I learned from the Cheyenne. Easy for me, not too fun for you, but it works. Now, are you gonna drink it, or should I get started?"

Chapter 11

FROWNING AS IF SHE WERE CONTEMPLATING his threat and weighing her chances, Laura swayed slightly, clearly so weak that sitting up took all her concentration. "You're a miserable wretch."

"I know. I'm a miserable lot of things. But I make a fair tea. Take a sip." Deke tried for another harmless smile, for good measure. "You can trust me, honey. You got my word on it."

With a resigned expression clouding her sweet face, she finally put the cup to her lips, then grimaced at the taste. "Oh, lands, it's awful! Sweet and bitter at once."

"I know." He rocked back on his heels. "Just take it slow. The more you drink, the better it'll taste. By the bottom of the cup, you'll be askin' for more."

She took another sip and shuddered. "Somehow, I doubt that." Licking the bittersweet taste from the corner of her mouth, she lowered the cup to her lap. Her attention came to rest on the extra bark and plants that Deke had resting near the fire. "What are the reeds for?"

Deke glanced over his shoulder. He had searched high and low to find the hollow woody stalks, no easy task in the darkness. With a shrug that he hoped appeared casual, he said, "They're part of one of the remedies my mother taught me to make." That wasn't exactly a lie. Without the reeds, he couldn't get the medicine inside of her to treat the internal inflammation, which he felt certain was responsible, at least in part, for that tenderness in her abdomen. He had no intention of telling Laura that, however. A woman as bashful as she was would guard her "unmentionables" until her dying breath. He inclined his head at the cup. "Another sip."

She lifted the tin container obediently to her lips. "Mm, you're right. After the first shock, it isn't as bitter." She smiled wanly and downed another mouthful. "You know, I do believe it is settling my stomach."

Deke moved to crouch at the fire and stir the thick paste simmering over the low flames at the outer edge.

"What's that?" she inquired.

"A poultice mixture." Hoping she wouldn't notice the third container of remedy, which already sat to one side cooling, he reached to stir the pot heating at the center of the fire. "And this is . . ." He shrugged. "I reckon the best word for this stuff is tea, like I said." He gestured at the cup she held. "I can't recollect all the names of the plants that went in it. I just know 'em when I see 'em.

"When I was a boy, I had to go gatherin' with my mother, and while we was pickin', she explained what the different barks and roots was used for. Sometimes I went along with her when she was doctorin', mainly to help carry stuff. Even so, I learned a lot. I'm not as good as her, of course, but I'm a fair hand at healin'. Ain't often I lose a sick cow, anyways, and that's more'n I can say for most ranchers."

She strangled on a swallow. "You use your mother's medicine on cows?" She eyed the cup askance.

Deke chuckled. "Trust me, Boston. I ain't got you confused with a cow."

"I should hope not."

"Not a chance. Some women, maybe, but you're the farthest thing from a cow I ever seen."

A slight blush crept up her neck, and he thought he glimpsed a pleased smile on her softly curved mouth. "Really?"

"Yep. No tail."

Her eyes widened; then a dimple flashed in her cheek. "You, sirrah, are unconscionable."

"Thank you."

"It isn't a compliment. It means you are without conscience."

"Way I see it, Boston, a conscience ain't much use anyhow." He rapped the spoon on the edge of the pot. "Just makes a man feel bad. No point in that. What's done is done."

"Some people are guided by conscience and, as a consequence, refrain from doing those things they fear will make them regretful."

He gave her a slow grin. "What fun would that be?"

She made an exasperated noise. "You are clearly beyond help."

"But I'll die happy."

She drained the cup, set it aside, and sank back onto the blanket, her lashes sweeping low over her beautiful eyes. For a very long while, she lay quiet. Then she suddenly said, "How very lucky you were. Going gathering and doctoring with your mother, I mean. I never knew mine."

Deke's interest was piqued. "Not at all?"

She angled an arm over her brow, looking as though the least movement took all her strength. "She died when I was born."

His heart caught. "From childbed fever?"

It took a second for her to reply. "No, she bled to death while giving birth to me." He saw her fingers curl weakly. "The physician very nearly didn't save me. My father always . . ."

"Always what?"

Her throat worked to swallow. "I think he hates me a little because I caused her death."

Deke gave the thick mixture at the edge of the fire another stir to make sure it wasn't sticking to the bottom of the pot. White men. Though their blood ran in his veins, he doubted he'd ever understand them. "Bein' born wasn't exactly your fault, Boston. How could he hold that against you?"

She sighed. "I don't believe he sees it that way."

Sitting back on his heels, he held his palms over the flames to warm them. A lengthy silence fell. Gazing thoughtfully into the licking tongues of fire, he mentally ticked away the passing minutes. After what he judged an adequate passage of time, he pushed to his feet, wondering how much longer it might take for the tea to affect her. A smile touched his mouth as he recalled the times in his youth when he had ingested dream medicine.

Being female, Laura wasn't on a quest, of course, and her visions probably wouldn't be ones of divine edict, but she was bound to see beyond herself. When the effects wore off, she would have little recollection of this reality, but detailed memories of another. What had to be done had to be done, but there was no point in making her suffer through it when he had a means of sparing her.

As he drew closer, Deke found himself wishing she had the strength to tend herself. Damn his yellow streak. She couldn't even tidy her braid. He just hoped the tea would make her completely unaware. If it didn't, she might never forgive him for this night's work.

"How you feelin'?"

She drew her arm from her eyes. "Less nauseated."

Deke's worry intensified. He guessed that it had been twenty-five minutes or more since she had drained the cup, and the way he recalled, the tea's first effects came on far more quickly. So far, Laura seemed completely lucid. "Dizzy-headed?"

"A bit."

That was a good sign. Deke closed the remaining distance between them. "How's the belly? Still hurt?"

She took refuge behind her arm again. "You think I'm rather silly, don't you?"

He hunkered beside her. "Silly?"

"A prig."

"A what?"

"A fusser," she elaborated.

Deke bit back a smile. "Nah, I don't."

She peeked out at him from under her sleeve. "Do you realize that until coming here, I never went into public without wearing my gloves?"

He wasn't sure how that related. "Is that so?"

"I suppose you think that's absurd."

"Not if it was cold back there in Boston. Was it?"

She gave a startled giggle. "Cold? Sometimes, of course, but I wore gloves because—" She broke off and giggled again. "It wasn't appropriate to proffer my hand to a gentleman if it was bare. That's why I wore gloves."

"Ah." Deke dipped his head to see her eyes. Her pupils were becoming dilated. His mouth quirked in a grin as he came to the realization that for Laura, this was loose behavior. He should have known. Talking . . . her strong point. "I reckon you got cured of that notion quick in this country."

She sighed. "This country has cured me of more than wearing gloves."

"Really? Pretty different from Boston, hm?"

For a long moment, she didn't answer. Then a ragged sob tore up from her throat, and she burst into tears. Deke couldn't help but be startled. The tea was supposed to make her feel peaceful.

"Boston?" He drew her arm down. "Honey, what's wrong? Do you still hurt? Why are you crying?"

"Because," she said. "Poor Jonathan. Why did he get stuck with a mother like me?"

He circled that cautiously. Talk about out of the blue. "You're a good mother. You told me so, remember?"

"I lied." She passed a hand over her cheek and sniffed. "His diapers fell off. And that Mexican said he had colic. I didn't know what to do." She turned tear-filled eyes to him. "I didn't even know how to have him! It's a wonder he didn't bleed to death before I realized the cord had to be tied. And then, on top of all else, I left him alone so those men could steal him. How can you call that being a good mother?"

The muscles at the back of Deke's neck drew tight. "Tristan wasn't with you when you gave birth?"

She blinked. "With me?"

Anger, hot and suffocating, crawled up Deke's throat.

"He went to find mustangs. How else were we to ever get ahead?"

For some reason, it had never occurred to Deke that the man hadn't been there with her when she had his child. "He left you alone when your time was close? I thought . . ." He rubbed a thumb above her ear to catch a trail of tears. Her skin felt surprisingly warm, far warmer than it had earlier when they were riding. The heat from the fire, he assured himself. "Couldn't he've gone huntin' mustangs later? Jesus, was he out of his mind?"

"I'm not completely helpless," she said defensively.

"Boston, I wasn't—"

"Yes, you were! You wouldn't think it was awful if he had left a Cheyenne woman."

"I sure as hell wou—"

"Even I can have a baby without help. I may not be good at much else, but I did manage that part just fine. And you can't take that away from me."

Deke started to say something, then clamped his mouth shut.

"People can't help where they were born." A bruised look came into her eyes. "I know you think I'm a flibberti-gibbet. And I suppose, by your standards, that perhaps I am. But I've done the best I can. It's extremely unkind of you to constantly remind me of how inept you think I am."

"Inept?"

"Useless."

"I don't think you're useless."

"Then why do you call me Boston? Because you hold me in high esteem?"

Deke ran a hand over his face. "Damn. Honey, I don't think you're useless. I think you're—"

"Don't say it! It's enough just to have my baby gone and be so sick I can't go get him. I can't bear it if—"

"I think you're wonderful," he inserted.

She turned a startled gaze to him, her pupils gigantic black orbs lined with amber. "You what?"

"I think you're wonderful," he repeated, and grasped her shoulders to sit her up. "A wonderful mother. And one hell of a woman."

"You do?"

"It wasn't your fault you didn't know how to tie the cord when Jonathan was born. Hell, it ain't like babies come with instructions printed on their backsides."

"No," she agreed. "I wish they did."

"As for you lettin' him get stole, what was you s'posed to do, leave the well dry?"

"I could have taken him with me while I hauled the water. Like Indian women do, on my back somehow."

"You ain't got a cradleboard," he reminded her.

"I could have fashioned something."

"And then maybe killed him when you fell in the rocks." She caught her bottom lip between her teeth, still looking unconvinced.

"You did the best thing," he insisted. "The *only* smart thing, which was to keep him at the cabin where he was safe. It ain't your fault comancheros came along and snatched him."

"You truly think not?"

At that precise moment, she seemed about twelve years old to Deke, her mouth still quivering, her huge eyes luminous in the firelight and filled with uncertainty. He touched a finger to the tip of her small nose. "I know it, no think to it. You was doin' a fine job of bein' a mama, and when you get your baby back, you'll keep right on doin' fine. What you don't know, you'll learn. Lovin' him like you do, that's the most important thing. The rest'll just come with time."

"As if you know anything about babies."

"I know more'n most. In an Indian village, everybody helps watch after the little ones. I was changin' moss bags before I was dry behind the ears."

"Moss bags?"

"Moss is used by the Indians for diaperin'." Searching her gaze, Deke decided most of her distress had passed. A bemused smile played upon her mouth now. He cupped her chin in his hand and tipped her face toward the ceiling. She definitely had more of a fever than he first thought, he decided. "Tell me what you see up there."

She blinked and focused on the blackness above them. "Nothing."

"You just ain't lookin' close enough."

She frowned slightly. "I'm looking, but there's nothing . . ."

A wondrous expression crept across her face. "Oh, Mr. Sheridan," she whispered. "Why did you wait so long to tell me they were up there! Aren't they lovely?"

Wondering what kind of images the dream medicine had conjured for her, Deke smiled and began unbuttoning her jacket. "Do you reckon you could call me Deke?"

She dropped her chin. "What do you think you're doing?" she demanded to know as he drew her jacket back and began unfastening her badly soiled blouse.

Deke hesitated, wondering if maybe he was starting too soon. "I'm undressing you."

She seemed to consider that for a moment. Then she said, "Oh."

He grinned and went back to the buttons.

"For a moment, I thought . . ." She started to laugh and went a little limp in the spine. He grasped her arm to steady her. "You'll think I'm silly, but for a horrible moment, I thought you were removing my clothing."

Her giggle was infectious, and he chuckled. "Would I do that?"

"I certainly should hope not. It would be highly inappropriate."

He peeled both jacket and blouse down her slender arms. As he tugged the garments over her hands, she giggled again.

"Now what?"

She shook her head. "It just occurred to me that you are removing my clothing."

"I reckon I am." He unfastened the snug waistband of her skirt. "No wonder you've got a bellyache, girl. This thing's cuttin' you in two."

"I've become fat. Skinny in the wrong places, and fat in the wrong places, that's me. I suppose I should be grateful

I'm no longer an ugly bag of bones." She flashed him a purely mischievous grin that dimpled one cheek. "Now I'm simply ugly. Tristan would be so pleased." She drew her fair brows together. "Not that I ever cared if my bones jabbed him, you understand. As I saw it, jabs were no more than he deserved, and for me, his lack of interest was a blessing."

Deke grasped the hem of her chemise. He could think of a number of ways to describe her, but bony wasn't one of them. When he glanced back at her face, he saw that her smile had turned wistful.

"He never really wanted me," she confided. "It was my father's money he was after all along." She wobbled slightly as she lifted a hand to snap her fingers before his nose. "The instant my father learned of our marriage and disowned me, I went from being the love of his life to bony and repulsive. It wasn't the wedding night of every girl's dreams, I assure you."

The hurt in her eyes was unmistakable, and he momentarily forgot what he was doing. He wanted to tell her how beautiful he thought she was, but now that the tea was taking hold, he doubted she would remember. Still, the shock of what she had said prompted him to ask, "The man called you repulsive and bony on your wedding night?"

She gave a startled laugh. "Well, he certainly didn't tell me *before* our wedding night, or I wouldn't have married him, would I?"

That made sense. He guessed.

"Trust that I was not *that* stupid," she informed him. "Young and easily fooled, yes, but not entirely witless. And I certainly smartened up quickly enough, albeit after it was too late." She lifted her hands in a gesture of fatalistic acceptance. *"C'est la vie!"*

Oddly enough, Deke didn't need that translated. "That ain't how it always is," he assured her. "And Tristan Cheney was a damned fool. You're a beautiful woman, and any man in his right mind would have loved you on your wedding night the way you were meant to be loved. I sure as hell would if I got a crack at it."

"You would?"

He grinned. "You can bet your last three cents on it. There ain't a whole lot to you, but you're put together about as pretty as I've ever seen."

"Do you truly think so?"

"I truly do." He gave her a wink. "Like I said, anything more than a handful is a damned waste, anyhow. Nice, very nice."

She blinked, her expression saying more plainly than words that momentary clarity had come over her and she was wondering how the conversation had turned to something so highly inappropriate. "I beg your pardon?"

He chuckled. "Nothin'." Returning his attention to the task at hand, which was to divest her of her chemise, he said, "Lift your arms, sweetheart."

She made an effort and nearly toppled in the process. Deke caught her from falling. Then he grasped her pointed little elbow and managed, with some maneuvering, to bend her arm and work it inside the armhole, where it became trapped, her hand dangling limply at her shoulder. He moved closer, jerked the garment above her hips, and shoved his arm up the front. After some fishing, he located her wrist.

"This is like tryin' to work wet leather laces through moccasin eyelets," he muttered as he twisted her limp arm around. "Am I hurtin' you?"

She smiled. "Not at all, Mr. Sheridan. Carry on. However, I must say that I don't believe there is room in here for both of us."

Her bewildered expression struck him as funny, and he started to laugh. Since she was already in a frame of mind to giggle, she joined in. Deke wrapped his free arm around her to keep them both from toppling. When his mirth finally subsided, he still had his arm up her chemise, and hers was still bent double and stuck. He dragged his out and sat back on his heels to study the predicament.

"We gotta get it out of there. It's either that, or I have to cut the chemise off you."

She dimpled a cheek at him again. "We must get what out of where?"

"Your arm," he said, swallowing back another laugh. "It's stuck."

She looked down, regarded her twisted arm and dangling hand for a moment, and then began untying the row of tiny ribbons at the front of the chemise.

"If you could do that all along, why in hell didn't you?"

"Why in hell didn't I what?"

"Untie the goddamned thing."

She glanced down again in bewilderment. "I didn't realize you wanted me to." She flashed him another impish grin. "Besides, it's patently obvious it has laces. I should think a connoisseur of the ladies such as yourself would know his way around a chemise."

"The ladies I connoisseur with ain't usually wearin' extra wrappin'."

"My goodness. If not a chemise, what do they wear?"

"Never mind," he said with another suppressed laugh, and reached to draw the muslin down her arms. As he leaned close, he looked into her eyes and said, "You in there, Boston?"

She wrinkled her nose. "A moment ago, we both were."

He grinned. "Wiggle your arm out."

She did so, and he tugged the muslin over her other wrist, then tossed it aside. "What the hell's this?" he demanded, plucking at the strip of petticoat she had wound around herself. She studied the cloth for a moment as if she had never seen it before. "Oh, that." She lifted her gaze to his chest and let loose with another tinkling giggle. "It's a supporter," she whispered. "I don't suppose you've ever needed one."

Deke worked a finger inside the wrapping. "Shit. What're you tryin' to do to yourself, girl? It's too damned tight."

She arched her brows and leaned toward him. "Of course it's tight, you silly man. What good would it be loose?"

He clenched his teeth. There wasn't much point in beating a dead horse. Catching her chin on the edge of his hand, he directed her gaze back to the shadows above them. "It's been a spell since you looked. What d'ya see up there now?"

While she searched the blackness, he unwound the petticoat flounce from around her. As her breasts spilled free, he assured himself there were two different ways a man could look at a woman, real close or hardly at all, and his aim was the latter. Sweat broke out on his face.

"Oh, aren't they beautiful?" she whispered.

Deke didn't know what she was looking at, but he had eyes for only two things. "Yep," he said in heartfelt agreement.

"And the colors. Just look at the gorgeous colors!"

The delicate pink of wild roses, he thought.

"That blue. It's absolutely shimmery. Oh, how I wish I could do that. Don't you?"

"Do what?" he asked absently as he gently prodded her satiny flesh. Her skin was alarmingly hot. This wasn't a slight fever, after all, but a raging one. "Jesus Christ, honey, your breasts are caked."

"Fly," she said on a dreamy breath. "Straight into heaven with the angels. Or are they butterflies?"

Deke's head came up. "Butterflies," he said harshly.

Further exploration told him just how serious her condition was. He didn't believe she had abscesses yet, but it wouldn't be long before she did. Caked breasts and an internal inflammation that could very well be childbed fever. While she carried on a one-person conversation, unable to decide if her dream creatures were angels or butterflies, he sat back and braced an arm on his knee, more frightened than he had ever been in his life.

"I'd say they're butterflies," he finally replied.

"Hmm." She regarded the blackness thoughtfully. "No, I think it's angels. Oh, how I'd love to fly away with them."

"Well, you ain't," he said with a little more force than he intended. "So get it straight out of your mind. And it ain't angels; it's butterflies."

She frowned slightly, still staring upward. "Butterflies? Are you certain? They certainly— Oh, Mr. Sheridan, I do so wish we could go with them. Just for a bit."

"No," he said softly, and grasped her shoulders. "Honey, look at me." When she lowered her eyes to his, he tightened his grip on her. "I want you to stay down here with me. You understand? You gotta promise me."

Her lips parted, and her lashes fluttered. "But I—"

Deke gave her a little shake. The things seen on a man's vision walk always had meaning. Laura's being a female was no guarantee that she couldn't see things that had meaning as well. Though Deke doubted angels existed, she clearly believed they did, and if she was seeing them flying around above her, it couldn't be a good sign.

"Promise me you won't go with them," he insisted harshly.

"But they're so beautiful. I've never seen anything so beautiful."

That made two of them, for Deke had never seen anything so beautiful as Laura. Grit and beauty. The two didn't usually ride double. Maybe that was why he hadn't guessed how sick she really was. Damn her stubborn little hide. She must have been feeling poorly as early as yesterday, if not before that, yet she hadn't let on. He should never have let her climb on a horse, let alone ride for hours in rough country and sleep on the cold ground.

Now that he thought back, all the signs had been there. Her pallor. The way she constantly held a hand over the base of her spine and winced when she moved. If he had seen a Cheyenne woman behaving like that so soon after childbirth, he would have snapped to attention. But because Laura was a bit of city fluff, he had ignored the signs, believing her when she claimed she had sore muscles.

Sore muscles? Guilt tore at him. Even as recently as five minutes ago, he had been laughing. Laughing and taking his time, like a goddamned idiot. This was bad. Real bad. He had seen women in less serious condition who had died despite everything his Cheyenne mother had done to save them.

With a frightened gaze, he studied her fragile features. *Why do you call me Boston? Because you hold me in high esteem?* The truth hit him now, with the impact of a mule kick right between the eyes. The girl loved that baby so much, she would have died in the saddle trying to reach him. A bit of city fluff? All his life with the Cheyenne, he had been taught to admire courage and bravery. How could he have been so blind that he hadn't realized how deeply those two qualities were ingrained in this woman? Had he not looked? Or had he simply refused to see?

Deke couldn't bring himself to answer that.

Very gently he lowered her to the blanket and finished divesting her of her clothing with shaking hands. She chattered like a squirrel, jumping from one topic to another. Her father's repeated betrayals. Tristan, leaving her, again and again. He could scarcely concentrate on anything she said. Scared, he was so damned scared. He couldn't remember ever feeling quite so unsure of himself. He wished his mother were here. What if he forgot to do something? What if he had chosen the wrong plants? What if—

Deke cut the thoughts short. There was no room within him for doubts. His mother wasn't here, and he couldn't leave Laura long enough to go fetch her. This was up to him. He had to do it, and he had to do it right, no room for error.

Chapter 12

THE CLOUDS WERE THE PALE PINK OF WILD roses and the milky white of moonbeams, or so Deke Sheridan said. Laura thought the pink a deeper shade and the white more a silver, but since he sounded so certain, who was she to argue? It was all rather strange, actually. Though she was definitely walking on clouds, she couldn't feel them beneath her. It was like flying in a way, only, of course, she knew she wasn't. Deke Sheridan wasn't an angel or a butterfly, and he was in the clouds with her. She tried to picture him with wings—of any sort—and the image made her burst into hysterical laughter.

She quickly sobered. It was very unkind to have such cruel thoughts. He was being so gentle with her. Such nice hands. Somehow they made the hurting stop, wrapping her in radiant warmth, soothing even those throbbing places deep inside her.

Magic. Yes, that was it. He had magic in his fingertips, and everywhere he touched her, he made her glow. Sometimes she felt as though she lost all substance, that she had become a part of the rainbow-colored clouds, that if a wind came up, she might disappear like canting smoke.

But Deke Sheridan held on to her, with his hands, with his voice, cautioning her not to leave him. He sounded so frightened that Laura decided she should stay. At least for now.

*   *   *

Deke bent to rinse Laura's blouse, then held it up against the sun to be sure he had gotten it clean. Satisfied, he wrung out the water and draped the garment over a bush to dry next to her chemise, pantalets, and petticoat. The only thing left to wash was the length of petticoat flounce she had used to bind her breasts. Every time Deke looked at it, his guts knotted. A supporter? He sighed as he set himself to the task of scrubbing it clean, his mind taking inventory of his saddlebags.

He had only four shirts left since giving one to Laura yesterday morning, and that included the one he was wearing. Still, he reckoned he could get by with only three. When she grew well enough to ride—he refused to contemplate the possibility that she could die—she might need extra support of some kind during the daylong journey to Cougar Flats. Since he could use something to keep his hands busy, anyway, to prevent him from drifting off to sleep while he watched over her, he figured he might as well ply a needle and thread. Not that he was much of a hand at it. The most sewing he usually did was to restitch a seam or a button. But he figured he could fashion a halter from one of his shirts easily enough. Something better than this, anyway. He held up the petticoat flounce and shook his head. All that sewing his Cheyenne mother had forced him to do in his boyhood might finally come in handy.

If Laura had only asked, he would have helped her design some kind of supporter yesterday morning. But oh, no. Better to painfully bind her breasts than admit to a man she had any. As if he hadn't noticed? The girl was so bashful, she was a danger to herself.

As he pushed to his feet, Deke glanced toward the mine. Since the onset of Laura's fever, his biggest worry had been how much she might remember about all of this. That was so loco, he couldn't quite credit it. He had twenty comancheros to be concerned about, and that was a passel of concern. Plenty enough to keep his mind busy, anyway. If she woke up with recollections of how intimately he was caring for her, he'd have to deal with it then.

For now, he had to think of a way to keep Laura alive until she recovered. With twenty comancheros hot to find her, and he with only one rifle to fend them off, his only hope of saving her pretty little neck was to get some reinforcements. To do that, he needed to signal for help.

Risky business, that. Smoke signals, by nature, could be seen by everyone, not just the people they were meant to reach. Still, it was a chance Deke had to take. It was either that, or wait for death to come calling. For himself, he could accept that. But not for Laura. He guessed her to be no more than twenty, if that old, and she had a son to raise. Her life had scarcely begun. He wouldn't let it be cut short, not if he could help it.

The wind canted the smoke into Deke's face, and he angled an arm over his eyes, his lungs convulsing. God, how he hated wet fires. With a deep cough, he caught his breath and stepped out of the upsurge. Gazing across the foothills, he congratulated himself on picking a perfect high spot, far enough from the mine not to invite visitors, yet visible for miles.

"Be watchin'," he whispered, holding the blanket over the plume of smoke for a prolonged period of time, then following with two quick obstructions to complete the signal. "Come on, Black Stone. Send a message back to me."

For several minutes, Deke continued flapping the blanket. Then he quickly put out the fire. If Black Stone could see the smoke in Cougar Flats, so could every comanchero in these parts. A yearning for moments gone by and forever lost filled Deke's mind as he knelt by a good-sized rock. Using a smaller stone, he propped the larger rock's edge upon it, then moved back to survey his handiwork. To the casual observer, it would look as though nature had arranged the shale. To a not-so-casual observer, the message would have no meaning. Only Black Stone, his cousin and boyhood companion, would know what to look for. At least, Deke hoped he would.

So many memories. Black Stone, his spirit brother, the

one and only friend Deke had ever trusted completely, even to this day. As boys, they had cleaved together like a woman's plump breasts. Filled with themselves and pubescent masculine arrogance, they had scorned the standard way of leaving messages set forth by their Cheyenne forefathers and had devised their own secret code, exchanging vows that one would always find the other in time of need. A small rock placed beneath a stone meant the endangered one waited to the south, a small rock placed atop a larger one meant north, and so on.

Childhood nonsense. Would Black Stone even remember? So many years had passed. When Deke thought back to those times, he felt separated from it all, as if those memories were pages from a storybook and had never actually happened. Two children, racing on the wind, their laughter ringing across sun-kissed grassland. Carefree boys, the years ahead of them a promise they took for granted, brothers forever because they had chosen to be. Life had been so simple then, their world one of absolute truths that were never questioned.

Only upon reaching adulthood had they learned the most difficult truth of all, that nothing in life remained constant. Even the sun was sometimes hidden behind clouds. The boys they had once been stepped over into manhood, and from that moment on, their paths stretched before them in different directions. Brothers in spirit, yes, but never of the flesh.

Before going to his horse, Deke closed his eyes. In that moment, he shed his white identity and looked into himself for Flint Eyes, the one who had gone to warm himself at Cheyenne fires so long ago. He felt the wind kiss his skin, carrying whispers that had no meaning, yet said so much. He was small, so infinitely small, standing as tall as he could beneath the sky. He prayed that the Great Ones would see him and hear the song in his heart, that they would not turn their faces from him because he had walked a path away from them for so many years.

"Set my feet the way I should go," he whispered in Cheyenne. "See me safely back to the place where I must wait, to the woman who leans upon my strength. Lead my brother Black Stone to us, so we may have safe escort to the People and be embraced by them."

The prayer finished, Deke ran for his horse, leaped into the saddle, and dug in with his heels. He had to get the hell out of here before the comancheros came down on him like horseflies on shit. He wheeled his horse north. Away from the mine. Away from Laura. Later he would veer south and begin covering his tracks as he returned to her.

Heavy of heart because Black Stone had sent no answering smoke signals, Deke ran a dripping cloth over Laura's feverish skin. She batted helplessly at his hands when he bathed her swollen breasts.

"No, please . . . Tristan, we can't afford oysters." She drew her brows together and averted her face. "You'll lose again. Don't play poker tonight. Please? We haven't enough money." A dry sob racked her slender body. "My knife. Where is my knife? Oh, God, he's nearly in the wagon. Tristan sent him. I just know it! Without the knife, what shall I do?"

Deke set aside the wet rag and slipped a hand under her head. "Here, honey. Drink."

She averted her face again, trying to avoid the cup he pressed to her lips. "I don't—" She strangled, then obediently began to swallow as she caught her breath. "I don't want it," she protested after she drained the cup.

Deke lowered her to the blanket. "Go back to the place of dreams, little one," he whispered softly. "Go to the rainbow. I will keep you safe."

"*Quagheunnega?*" she repeated with a bewildered frown, her beautiful eyes unfocused.

Deke realized he had spoken to her in Cheyenne. "*Quagheunnega*, the rainbow. Do you see it? Go into it and drift with the colors. *Ne-pah-loh*', sleep."

The distress melted from her expression, and a smile touched her pale lips. Deke sighed and began to bathe her skin again. When he finished, he sat back and waited for the tea to establish its hold on her before he reached for the reeds. Lightly resting a hand on her feverish thigh before he began, he searched her face for any sign of awareness. The fire that raged within her was enough for her to bear without his heaping shame upon her as well.

"Laura, are you away from me?"

Her long lashes fluttered drowsily. "Away? No." She touched his arm with quivering fingertips. "You are with me. Inside the rainbow. Don't you see it?"

What Deke saw was an angel—he knew exactly how one looked because Laura had described them to him in vivid detail. Only his angel was earthbound, not because she chose to be, but because he kept a firm grasp on her and constantly called her back. "Yes, I see it," he whispered. And it wasn't a lie. Her smile was as radiant as a rainbow and warmed cold places deep within him that he hadn't known were there. "It's beautiful."

She ran the tip of her tongue over her lips. "You won't leave me, will you, Mr. Sheridan?"

"No, I ain't leavin'."

"Promise? You won't go away like Tristan?"

Sadness filled him. "No, honey. I'm here, and I won't go away."

The second day, Deke once again went to a high spot and sent up signals, then arranged stones to direct Black Stone to the mine, this time indicating he should go west.

Laura was showing signs of improvement. After all the sleepless hours, after working so feverishly to save her, was it all to go for nothing? He was only one man. He couldn't protect her from twenty killers, not for long.

Sooner or later, the comancheros would stumble upon the mine. Each afternoon when Deke ventured to a hilltop, he spied signs of their presence in the area. They obviously had a fairly good tracker with them and knew he hadn't headed back for Denver yet. They were searching feverishly for him and Laura, and as with all searches well executed, this one had only one possible conclusion.

Laura would die if he tried to move her right now on horseback. Transporting her as far as Cougar Flats on a travois probably wouldn't hurt her, but such a trip would be slow going and would make them vulnerable to attack without plenty of armed men riding guard. He had no choice but to wait at the mine for someone to come. The comancheros or Black Stone, that was the question, and only the Great Ones knew which it would be.

The next afternoon while tending Laura, Deke sensed a presence. He froze and looked toward Chief, who snoozed next to the fire. Usually the dog detected the approach of others almost as soon as Deke did. A friend, then? Chief had a lazy streak and quite often chose to ignore the approach of those he trusted. No-account mongrel.

After covering Laura and pushing silently to his feet, Deke picked up his rifle and slipped past the blind of brush he had piled in front of the mine entrance. As he emerged into sunlight, his senses sharpened, and he quickly ducked into some underbrush to scan the slope below. A man on horseback moved from the shelter of the aspens into the open, his long hair drifting in an ebony curtain around his muscular brown shoulders. Nearly hidden among the trees behind him, Deke saw other Cheyenne warriors on horseback. At a quick count, Deke guessed there were more than twenty of them, all heavily armed. No comanchero in his right mind would launch an attack against a force of Cheyenne that size. With a relieved smile, Deke stepped from his hiding place, a hand raised in greeting.

Black Stone leaned toward the fire to pour himself another cup of coffee. In the flickering light, his chiseled features gleamed like rubbed mahogany, and his eyes glittered like polished onyx, unreadable yet penetrating. Deke met his gaze steadily.

"So you return to the People only to fetch this woman's child? A child sent to us by the Great Ones to heal my wife's broken heart?"

Behind him, Deke could hear Laura's soft, even breathing. But more than that, he felt her nearness in the very pores of his skin. Whiskey and cream, more intoxicant than woman, and he had fallen under her influence as surely as a thirsting man succumbs to strong drink. She didn't know it, had no way of knowing it, but she stood at a fork. What Deke chose to say next could set her feet upon a path of joy, or one of heartache.

Deke couldn't quite believe this was happening. Of all the men to have adopted Laura's son, why Black Stone, his spirit brother? And why to replace a child Black Stone had lost? Deke could no more harden his heart to his brother's grief than to Laura's, yet he had to choose between them.

Forcing himself to think carefully before he answered, Deke turned his gaze inward by breaking eye contact with Black Stone and looking into the flames. Three months ago, Black Stone's four-month-old son had passed into the Great Beyond. Three days ago, his young wife had put Laura Cheney's starving infant to her breast, giving him the sustenance that her three-year-old firstborn could do without and her dead child no longer needed. A miracle in the eyes of the People, a white child sent by the Great Spirits to replace the much-loved Cheyenne baby whom illness had so cruelly taken.

Deke thought it more nightmare than miracle because he had come to claim that child, and in the claiming, he would cause Black Stone's grieving wife to wail and weep, no longer over the loss of only one baby, but two. To make matters worse, the resentment Deke saw in his brother's eyes when he looked upon Laura was unmistakable. Right now the Cheyenne were filled with hatred for all whites. Laura's sense of loss if she couldn't reclaim her son would mean nothing to them. The only way Black Stone would ever agree to part with the child who now brought his wife such solace was if he believed that child to be Deke's.

Deke considered the magnitude of what he was about to do and Laura's probable reaction when he explained it to her. To claim Jonathan as his son, and thus ensure the baby's return to Laura's arms, Deke would also have to claim Laura as his wife. If he took such a step, he would consider himself truly married to her, not just for the duration of their visit to the Cheyenne camp, but forever.

Laura would be beside herself if he did such a thing without at least consulting her first. But what else could he do? There was no time to play with; he had to act now or let her lose her baby. Would she understand his reasons for doing it? Did he even understand them himself?

Deke knew the answer to that was no. But some feelings ran too deep for understanding, and his for Laura fell into that category. He couldn't explain them, couldn't even bring them out and study them so he could try. He knew only that she had been abandoned to fate by men one too many times already in her young life and that he had promised her he wouldn't do the same. It would kill her if she lost that baby, and it would kill him to stand aside, watching while it happened.

Black Stone seemed to grow impatient with the silence, and after taking a mouthful of coffee, he spat it into the flames, his disgust for Laura engraved on his noble features. "Take the whiskey-haired woman back to her wooden walls. I care nothing for her tears. The child of her womb now belongs with me and my woman, forever into the horizon."

Deke swallowed and met his brother's gaze. The Cheyenne language came to his tongue far more easily than English, and he fell into the cadence as though he'd left the People only yesterday. "You, the brother of my heart, would keep my son from me?"

For a moment Black Stone's expression remained harsh. Then he seemed to realize what Deke had said and looked stricken. "Your son?"

The decision had been made, and there was no turning back for Deke now. "Of course, my son. *Ni-ne-e-meh'*, see. Not only with your eyes, Black Stone, but with your heart! My woman lies naked beneath my *aquewa*, and you doubt? You say you care nothing for her tears. I can understand that. Just as you must understand that I do."

Black Stone bent his dark head. "I see."

"I am filled with such sorrow, brother. I weep inside over the child you have lost. But I cannot cut my own child from my heart to end your grief."

"No." Black Stone straightened his shoulders. "I thought the woman was ..." He glanced toward Laura, and his mouth thinned with disgust. "You always were one to rescue birds with broken wings. I thought perhaps this woman was such a one, and that you were trying to mend her sorrows. I did not know she was one with you."

Deke felt like vomiting, was afraid he might. Laura, one with him? Wouldn't she be delighted when he told her the news. He had never lied to Black Stone. It was little comfort to know, in this instance, that the lie had become a truth the moment it passed his lips. "My wife, and your sister-in-law. Now do you have a care for her tears?"

Black Stone's expression remained like granite. "You know the song within me, just as I know yours. I will return your son to you, just as you would mine to me. But recognize this whiskey-haired woman as my sister-in-law? No, that I will not do."

Deke knew it would take Black Stone time to accept Laura. As far as that went, Deke was still reeling himself. His wife? Once this initial shock wore off, he would push Black Stone to acknowledge the marriage. But for now, with so many of his own emotions to handle, dealing with Black Stone's feelings was simply too much. It was enough that his brother had agreed to return the child. "It lays my heart upon the ground to cause your woman pain," Deke said in a gravelly voice. And it was the truth. How he wished there were another way. "I have great hope that she will find comfort in holding your firstborn son in her arms, and that her breasts will not ache for long over this second loss."

His eyes glistening with unshed tears, Black Stone nodded. "Firstborn or second, the pain is great." A slight smile finally touched his lips. "I should have seen the truth of it, yes? When the traders handed the child to me, I sensed the rightness, and when I gave the infant to my woman, it was as though her arms had never been empty. Now I know why. I loved the child so easily because he was yours."

Deke nodded. For better or worse, the lie was truth, and the truth was the most complicated of lies. He had just laid claim to a woman he doubted would ever willingly submit to him, and a child he had never seen.

Black Stone took a deep, bracing breath, pushed to his feet, and said, "Well, my brother? We have a travois to build to carry this whiskey-haired burden you have acquired."

Deke glanced at Laura. A burden? Black Stone had no idea just how great a trial she might yet prove to be. He rose and met his brother's gaze. "As you say, we have a travois to build. To carry my wife."

Black Stone shrugged, his expression conveying that only a crazy man would honor a white woman in such a way. "Think of it, my brother. By tomorrow at this hour, you'll be eating Medicine Woman's cooking."

Deke winced, for his Cheyenne mother's skill ran to herb gathering and tending the sick, not food preparation. "You and Star will invite me and my woman to supper often, yes?"

Though Black Stone's eyes still reflected the bitterness of his feelings toward Laura, he was clearly determined to put a bright face on it for Deke's sake. He laughed heartily and rubbed his broad chest. "We will invite you, but only if you treat me nice."

"Does that mean I have to lose to you at arm wrestling?"

"And also at cards and checkers."

Indians. Laura saw them, heard them, smelled them. They rode horseback all around her in the rainbow-colored clouds, their dark, painted faces indistinct, their black hair glistening in golden light. Sometimes treetops and blue sky swirled around her. At other times, she felt certain her bed was bouncing and jiggling. Crazy, so crazy. How had she come to be surrounded by fierce warriors?

Oddly, she wasn't frightened. Deke Sheridan was with her. At moments he seemed to be walking beside her. Only she was lying down, so that couldn't be. At other times, all seemed to go still and his face appeared above her, his ice blue eyes aching with concern, his hands gentle as he tipped a flask to her lips and bathed her skin with coolness. During those quiet times, Laura saw no warriors and wondered where they had gone. They always seemed to return, however. It didn't matter. Deke was there, and he had promised to stay with her. He wouldn't allow the redskins to kill her. She wasn't certain how she knew that. She only sensed that it was so. And in her swirling dreams of shimmering colors, that was enough to comfort her.

So exhausted he could scarcely hold his shoulders erect, Deke drew his stallion to a stop on the rise above Cougar Flats. Laura slept peacefully on her litter behind him. The afternoon was warm. There was no urgency to get her down to the village. As he always did when he came back to the People, he could afford to steal a few moments before he went in to face them.

He fixed his gaze on the mountain park below where conical lodges peppered the shady aspen glades and vast sweeps of green grass. Smoke canted lazily in the breeze to find the sky in trailing ribbons of gray. The myriad smells of roasted meat, coffee, stews, puddings, and even popcorn teased his nostrils. Dogs yapped. Children squealed. Laughter rang out.

Home. The word meant different things to different people, but for Deke, home was this village, wherever it happened to be. Seeing it again filled him with a bone-deep yearning for a world forever lost to him. These people, so simplistic, so in harmony with nature, were a part of him as no other ever could be. *Shakeka S'ski-si-coh'* — Flint Eyes — his Cheyenne name, which he wore with intense pride, was also his greatest heartache, for there was an inescapable truth in his people's belief that a man's eyes were the pathways to his soul.

Though Black Stone's young wife was probably anxiously awaiting his arrival, Deke's adopted brother paused on the rise beside him. Deke wondered if Black Stone was putting off the moment when he would have to tell Star she must return the white boy child to his mother.

"It is the same, yes?" Black Stone whispered in Cheyenne.

Deke's throat tightened as he met his brother's gaze. It seemed Black Stone had lingered, not to put off the inevitable, but to share in this moment of intense gladness and pain. Deke should have known. Hadn't it always been thus, he and Black Stone, thinking as one? Now Deke had betrayed him—for a woman who probably wouldn't understand or appreciate the seriousness of what he had done, or the sacrifice.

"Yes, it is the same," Deke agreed in a tight voice.

"The snow surrenders to spring and summer grass, the grass gives way to *pah-co-tai'*, the autumn, and then the snow comes again. The seasons are ever changing. You and I change. But the village, it is always"—Black Stone smiled—"the same."

"It is good to have one thing that does not change," Deke noted wryly. "Is this your way of saying the fingertips of age have traced my face?"

Black Stone grinned and glanced back to be certain Laura was resting peacefully. Then he bent his ebony head to toy absently with his pinto's reins, which he held lightly in one hand. When he looked up, his obsidian black eyes ached with sadness. "Your marriage . . . to this woman with whiskey hair. It may set your feet on a path even farther away from us."

Deke had thought of that and knew it would probably be so. Laura, the fancy-mannered lady from Boston, would never enjoy coming here for prolonged visits, and Deke would not feel comfortable leaving her behind to come without her. "Yes, a path farther away from you," he admitted.

"It is your wish? To stay away and become only a name we mention in stories told to children by our winter fires?"

Deke swallowed hard. "It isn't my wish, Black Stone. Never that. But you know how lonely my way has been."

"You could have married a Cheyenne woman."

Deke stiffened. "My heart wandered that way once, long ago. I cannot walk backward in those footprints."

"Sugar Girl, sister to the one you once loved, has become a very beautiful woman, and this is her twentieth summer. After all you sacrificed to avenge her, I always hoped that one day you would see her as a man does a woman, that you might be the one to lead her back into the sunshine and give her the right to hold her head high again."

Deke knew of another beautiful girl who walked in shadows with shattered pride as her companion, and it was her hand he wished to hold. He glanced back at Laura. "I love Sugar Girl; you know that. But not in the right way. Some other man will cross her path and find that he can't keep going his own way unless she walks beside him. It will be that man who will be able to take the sadness from her eyes, not me."

"And from where will this man come?" Black Stone asked bitterly. "None of the young warriors ever look her way when choosing wives. You know that. It will take a man who cares nothing for the chattering of women. Someone who won't care if he is called 'he who walks in old moccasins.' You are the only warrior I know who could pretend not to hear the sharp tongues, who would wear the old moccasins with pride."

Frustration welled within Deke. "I'm not the man for her, Black Stone. She accepts that. I accept it. Yet you cannot? If it is meant to be, a special man will be sent by the Great Ones. If he cares for her in the way I mean, he'll be determined enough to win her heart. You will see. But that man is not me."

Puffing air into his cheeks, Black Stone nodded, his expression one of reluctant acceptance. After a moment, his smile returned. "I hope this special man crosses the girl's path soon and takes her to his lodge. She eats more than two growing boys. I'm afraid she will soon be as large as Many Stomachs. Perhaps that is why this man you speak of won't continue to walk his own way after he crosses her path. Because he won't be able to get around her."

"Sugar Girl?" Deke chuckled at that and shifted his grip on his horse's reins. He felt more ready now to go into the village and face his memories. "Last winter when I saw her, she was as thin as a willow."

"She is still thin. Star thinks she must have great holes in the bottoms of her feet. All the food runs straight through her and out onto the ground."

"She still loves sugar and molasses?"

Black Stone's mouth quirked. "We have changed her name?"

Deke knew that was an answer in itself. Still smiling, he fixed his gaze on the lodges. "It is time, Black Stone. If I linger here much longer, my mother will be told of my coming and walk out to meet me on her shaky old legs."

Black Stone thrust out a hand to grasp Deke's arm. "You will linger one more moment? As a favor to me, the brother of your heart?"

As much as he loved Black Stone, Deke sometimes found his tenacity irritating. Once the man sank his teeth into a bone, he seldom turned loose of it without harsh words. "I will spare you a moment, my brother, but not my ear. Not if you hope to turn my heart away from this woman I now call wife. It is done. We have a son. Your warnings come too late."

"You have not yet formally made her your wife according to our ways. As it stands now, you have sipped the milk but not purchased the cow. It is not too late to change your mind. Keep the child and send this worthless woman back to her white family dishonored. No one here will think less of you for this, not over a whiskey-haired female who is dirt beneath our feet. She is as nothing to us."

The harsh words were ones Deke could not ignore. As chief of the Horse Soldiers, Black Stone commanded great respect, not only in this band but throughout the Cheyenne nation. His disgust for Laura would be contagious if he expressed it openly. The People would forever scorn her. Deke couldn't let that happen, for a woman scorned was a woman spit upon. There was even a possibility that Laura might suffer physical abuse from the other squaws when Deke wasn't near at hand to protect her.

A man could dig his own grave with lies; Deke already felt as though he were dying—a little at a time. There were no choices, though, not now. He had picked his path, and now he had to walk along it. He jerked his arm from Black Stone's grasp. "If my woman is nothing to you, I am nothing to you. Get yourself away from me. Your face is no longer one I wish to look upon."

With that, Deke jerked on his stallion's reins and headed down the slope, feeling with every step that he was wading more deeply into quicksand.

"Flint Eyes! Flint Eyes!"

The cry rang in Deke's ears a hundred times and in as many different voices. Star and Sugar Girl saw him first, and both launched themselves into his arms for a hug of greeting. Male hands clapped him on the back. Children who were old enough to recall his prolonged visit last winter jostled one another to cling to his legs. Flint Eyes. *Shakeka S'ski-si-coh'.*

Several curious youngsters gathered around the litter when Deke drew his horse to a stop near a lodge that bore a large painted bear, the sign of medicine, on its flap. Touching the black's shoulder in silent command for it to stand fast, Deke strode quickly to Laura, waving the youngsters away.

"*Scoote Nipe! Scoote Nipe!* Whiskey! Whiskey!" they cried excitedly.

One little scamp of about ten summers pulled a knife from his belt. "*Ni oui-thai-ah'*, my hair!" he proclaimed, and advanced on the litter.

"*Mat-tah'*, no!" Deke barked. "*Equiwa neewa,* the woman is my wife!"

A collective gasp rose around Deke, and he realized what he had said a little too late. A ring of shocked faces, belonging to both adults and children, stared at him in astonishment. Glancing toward the lodge, he saw his mother standing in the doorway, the brightly painted flap nudged aside by one frail arm. More snow had touched her hair since he had seen her last winter, and the months had also etched lines more deeply into her skin. A thin, bony skeleton with grizzled braids hanging over her stooped shoulders—that was what she had become.

But to Deke, she was beautiful. He looked into those warm, liquid brown eyes and felt warmth enfold him. "*Neegah*, my mother," he whispered.

"You have not forgotten me?" she asked saucily.

"Never—not even when I am dust in the wind."

She planted gnarled hands on her hips. "It seems you have walked the path of forgetfulness, you who calls me mother! Is it not the way to at least direct a mother's gaze toward your chosen one and ask for her words of wisdom?" She wagged a scolding finger. "Bring me a puppy I have never seen, Flint Eyes, and I will smile. A pony I have never seen! But a wife? And a yellow-hair, at that?"

After going for so many days without sleep, Deke had to wonder whether he could even carry Laura into the lodge. A quarrel with his mother right now was more than he could contemplate. He knew the way around her temper and took it. "She may be dying, this woman I call wife."

"Then take her off somewhere. I don't want dead offal outside my door."

Deke pretended to search for a place to dump her. "Where? Under the trees over there . . . that would be a fine place for the wife of Flint Eyes to die, yes? Or to the horse pasture? That would be a fine place. She is offal, this mother of your first grandson."

Chobeka Equiwa, Medicine Woman, narrowed her eyes on Laura's pale face. "Say this to me again? The mother of my grandson?"

Deke managed a weary nod. "My heart is heavy with shame. To bring you such a one? You are right. I cannot expect you to save her, though that is what I hoped. I am a stupid, ungrateful, disrespectful son."

Medicine Woman hobbled a bit closer to have a better

look. After giving Laura's frame a measuring glance, she snorted. "A twig! No fine, strong warrior could be borne by such a skinny thing as that." She threw up her hands. "Always, I say to you, look first at a girl's hips! And what do you choose? Not a fine, strapping female to bear you healthy sons, but a twig."

"You're right. I'll throw her away. She's an ugly thing anyway."

Medicine Woman shook her head. "And have my grandson blame me for letting his mother die? Ach! I can't believe I raised such a rock head. Get back, get back!" She placed a palsied hand on Laura's forehead. "There is fire inside her."

"I know. Why else would I bring her here to you?"

"Because you have no sense. How could you drag my daughter-in-law about when she is afire like this? Do you think I can work miracles?"

"No. It was foolish of me to think you could."

"She will surely die, being handled so roughly. Men! If I put all your brains in a bucket, I couldn't make soup."

As weary as he was, Deke had to work at hiding his smile. "I'll just haul her over to the trees and let her die there."

"You will bring the poor thing inside my lodge—that is what you will do. And then you will stay away so you can do her no more harm." She shooed away the children. "Hurry, Flint Eyes. I must tend her. There is no time to waste."

Deke scooped Laura up into his arms, taking care that the blankets didn't fall away from her nude body.

"Don't drop her, you clumsy man." Medicine Woman hovered anxiously as Deke strode to the lodge. "Such a small one, Flint Eyes! Let us hope she is stronger than she looks. What is it that ails her?"

"She had the baby only a week ago. There is fever in her belly, and her breasts became caked." As Deke lowered Laura onto his mother's bed, he quickly apprised Medicine Woman of the treatment he had administered to Laura to keep her alive this long. "She is much better than she was, my mother. Much better. I believe she is past the most dangerous time."

"Perhaps it was I who raised you after all. You have done well," she said with relief. She touched Laura's forehead again. "You are right. The fire does not rage. I would say it is about to burn out." She lifted perceptive eyes to Deke's. "But if she journeys back to wellness, my son, why does she sleep this sleep of death?"

Deke quickly explained that he had kept Laura sedated since the onset of her illness. "She is very shy," he said lamely.

Medicine Woman's gaze sharpened. "With her husband?"

The question tripped him up. He started to reply, then shut his mouth, rubbing wearily at his forehead.

"Flint Eyes, whenever you rub your head like that when I am talking to you, I know it is to keep me from seeing into you." She grabbed his wrist and drew his hand aside. "Look at your mother and explain this shyness."

Deke couldn't find any words. Lying wasn't something that came easily to him, and never to this woman. She had taught him better at the end of a switch when he was seven years old.

"Ach, Flint Eyes. What kind of trouble have you gotten yourself into this time?"

Chapter 13

LAURA AWOKE AS THOUGH FROM A LONG AND very deep sleep. For a while she simply stared at the small fire, not caring to move, her predominant feeling one of separateness. The shadows beyond the fire didn't seem real. Her body felt as though it belonged to another. Her memories of how she had come to be here were a confusing jumble, none of which made sense, and all of which eluded her when she tried to examine them.

Slowly she began to notice small things. A can of coffee and a pot of something that smelled like venison stew simmered on the coals. A rifle and bow were leaned against the leather wall opposite her. Next to the gun rested Deke Sheridan's Stetson and gun belt. Chief slept nearby, his large head pillowed on his paws, a fresh deer leg lying inches in front of his nose. Along the wall behind him were a trunk, a neat pile of parfleches, and a stack of pots and pans. Suspended above him was a clothing rod, from which hung a woman's leather dresses.

Where was she?

Laura tried to remember, but everything was a jumbled swirl of images, all confusing, Deke Sheridan's dark face and strangely light blue eyes the only constant. Pain. She remembered feeling on fire with pain, and then cold, so cold that her body jerked and her teeth clacked.

Not at all certain she had the strength, she pushed partway up. Her body trembled at the effort, and she felt momentarily dizzy, a sensation that slowly passed. She ran a hand down the front of her blouse, which felt more roomy across the bust, the cloth crisp as though it were freshly washed. Her breasts no longer felt tender.

She prodded herself gingerly and detected no sign of fullness. Her eyes closed on a rush of dread. Her milk had dried up. Her baby! How was she to feed him once she found him? She struggled more erect, and the brightness of the fire went into a slow rotation. She waited for the swimming sensation to subside, then pressed a hand against her middle. No pain. It was the oddest experience, as though she had blinked and been healed of all her hurts. Had she been unconscious? And if so, for how long? She searched her surroundings. It all seemed familiar, yet she had no recollection of having spent time here. A round room of some sort? No, a Cheyenne teepee. Oh, dear God, she was in the Indian village.

Pictures flashed in her mind—of Deke Sheridan, of an abandoned mine. Fever—she had been stricken with fever, and he had gathered plants to brew a remedy. Tea. A bitter yet sickeningly sweet concoction that had nearly gagged her. And dream medicine. It all came back to her, slowly, piece by piece. Being coerced to drink the tea, feeling strange.

And then a jumble of senseless images. . . .

Weary beyond words, Laura sank back onto the thick layer of furs that served her as a bed. Outside, she heard voices ringing out, those of men, women, children. Pots clanked. A horse galloped past. A dogfight erupted, the snarls quickly silenced by a yelp. Indians. Speaking gibberish. All around her. Fear lanced through her, but she couldn't hold on to it. She was too exhausted. Though she fought to keep them open, her eyes drifted shut, and blackness closed around her.

"Good evenin', lazybones."

Laura blinked and searched for a face to go with the voice. Slowly one came into focus. Darkly handsome, with high, sharp cheekbones, a stubborn chin, a jaw delineated with corded tendon, a full mouth, hard yet strangely sensual. Handsome? How odd that she should think of Deke Sheridan in those terms. Yet she couldn't deny the truth of it. With shorter hair and more conventional clothing, he would be devastatingly attractive.

"Mr. Sheridan?" she croaked.

He seemed amused by her formal address, and his brows lifted slightly, bold slashes above his unnervingly light eyes. "Who else?"

"I've been ill?"

His jaw ticked. "You could say that. Real ill."

"For how long?"

"Close to a week."

Laura moaned. "Oh, no . . . My baby."

"Your baby's fine. He's with my sister-in-law Star, Black Stone's wife. I saw him just a few minutes ago, and he's gonna get fat as a little butterball, the way he goes after the—" He broke off and rubbed his nose. "Anyhow, here in a couple of hours, Star'll be bringin' him over for a visit."

"A visit?" Laura echoed shrilly. "He's here? Jonathan's here? And he's all right?"

"Right as rain."

An indescribable joy filled Laura. "You're sure? You wouldn't—lie to me."

His mouth tightened. "I ain't gonna claim I never lie, Laura, 'cause I'd be lyin'." He chuckled at the joke, then shrugged. "But I try not to make a habit of it." He reached to touch her cheek. As he withdrew his hand, the tension seemed to ease from his shoulders. "You're holdin' your own. No fever."

"You've been caring for me?"

His mouth curved in a slight smile. "Hell, no. I turned you over to all them comancheros and went huntin'." He hesitated. "Actually, I tried to pawn you off on my mother once we got to the village, but you got in such a stir at seein' an Indian, she could only care for you when you was asleep."

The thought of being touched by some Indian woman

made Laura's skin crawl. "I—I hope I didn't unintentionally offend her."

"She's got a tough hide. I was the one tempted to wring your neck. Until I got rested up, anyhow."

"I kept you from resting?"

"Let's just say you gave it your best shot."

She searched his face. "You saved my life, didn't you?"

"I did what needed doin'. Whether or not you lived wasn't up to me."

"Thank you."

He looked away as if her gratitude made him uncomfortable. When he brought his gaze back to her, he said, "You ready to try them legs?"

Laura wasn't sure she had the strength. "To go where?"

"For a walk. I figured you might be wantin' to—how'd you put it that time?—commune with nature?"

"I'm surprised you remember." Thin and tremulous, her voice didn't sound like her own. But, then, her body didn't feel as though it belonged to her, either.

"I got a good memory. Hell, after bein' around you all this time, I got so many big words tucked away in my head that once I find out what they all mean, I'll talk fancier than you do."

Laura glanced uneasily at a flap she presumed served as the teepee doorway. "Aren't—aren't there Indians out there?"

"You could say that."

"H-How many?"

He pursed his lips. "I ain't counted heads, honey. A hundred and fifty, maybe more."

"Oh, mercy. I—I believe I'll just stay here. Thank you all the same."

He chuckled at that. "You can't hide in here. Besides, most of 'em already saw you when I brung you in."

"They did?"

"And only one went for your scalp." He grasped her arm to help her stand. "Come on outside. The air'll do you good, and I'll fight all of 'em off."

Laura didn't appreciate his joking about something she found so horrifying. "The one—who tried to"—she reeled to her feet—"take my scalp, you stopped him?"

"Yep."

Laura didn't trust her legs and clung to his arm. It was the oddest sensation, as if her mind were separated from reality by a thin veil of transparent cotton. The simplest thing, such as curling her fingers or making her foot move, took all her concentration.

"After your walk," he said, "it'll be time for you to eat a bite. I got some stew simmered up. My mother offered to fix it, but ..." He caught her from falling. "Well, you'll soon learn she ain't much of a cook."

Laura didn't care about eating. "You said Jonathan will be brought to me soon?"

"For a visit."

"Why for only a visit? I want him now."

"Honey, you're too weak to tend him. As soon as you're strong enough, I promise."

Honey, weak, promise ... Laura focused on the words as they came, not quite assimilating their meaning before more pelted her. She nodded, alarmed at how quivery her legs felt. Drawing back the hem of her skirt, she was surprised to see that she was even wearing her shoes. A walk, to commune with nature, after which she would eat stew. Only, her legs didn't feel as if they meant to cooperate. If this was a crazy dream—which it surely must be because one didn't awaken from a week's illness still wearing one's shoes—then she wanted to wake up. A walk through a Cheyenne village, to commune with nature, with Deke Sheridan as her escort?

"Mr. Sheridan, I'm not at all certain I can make it by myself." And if she couldn't? Maybe his intention was to assist her. The thought helped clear the cotton out of her brain. Deke Sheridan, her personal nursemaid? Wild laughter welled in her chest, but by the time it worked its way up her throat, it had turned to panic. "Perhaps I should wait a bit."

"Don't you need to go?"

"Yes, but I can't let you . . ." Laura realized what she was saying and blushed. "Mr. Sheridan, please. There are some things a lady simply doesn't talk about."

He gave a low laugh. "Fine. We won't talk about it. I'll just help you do it."

She was too weak to draw her arm from his grasp. "I beg your pardon?"

He slewed his dark head around, his eyes alert to her every expression. "Laura, trust me. We'll figure somethin' out once we find a bush."

Trust him? This had little to do with trusting and everything to do with— Dear God, she had been ill for a week? During which time he had been forced to care for her because she had refused the ministrations of his mother. She took a step forward and her leg folded. He looped a strong arm around her waist to catch her. Laura leaned into him, feeling strangely . . . *safe* was the word that came to mind, but she quickly discarded it. Deke Sheridan was the last man on earth to make any woman in her right mind feel safe.

Bearing almost all of her weight, he helped her to the teepee entrance and shoved aside the flap so they could exit. Fading sunlight slanted into Laura's eyes, momentarily blinding her. When her sight returned, she gasped. Everywhere she looked, there were Indians and teepees. Women hovered over small fires; unarmed warriors reclined on fur pallets. She shrank against Deke and clutched his shirt.

"What if they try to attack me?"

"They won't. Welcome you, maybe." He bent to see her face. "If that happens, let me do the talkin'. Okay? There's things you gotta know before that tongue of yours starts wigglin' at both ends."

"They could understand me?"

"Some of 'em."

"What things must I know? Are their customs so strange I can't even speak to them?"

"As soon as we talk, you can speak to 'em all you want."

A squaw straightened from over her fire as Laura and Deke passed her camp. The woman fixed Laura with a piercing gaze. Long, black braids. A dark face that looked like cured hide. A leather dress covered with animal teeth and beads. She held her stirring spoon as though she were thinking about thumping someone with it, namely Laura.

A dozen other dark heads turned, and Laura saw hostility in each set of black eyes. "They hate me."

"They don't. You just look funny, and they're studyin' you."

"I look funny?"

"Here, darlin', you're the odd one out."

"Are you certain that's all it is?"

"I'm certain."

A little boy of about seven came running up to them. He had the thickest head of ebony hair Laura had ever seen, and it hung well past his shoulders. Dressed only in a string and loincloth, he was shamefully naked to Laura's way of thinking. And dirty. His skin was dull with a coat of dust.

Hunching over, he gripped his bony little knees and peered up at Laura's face, his black eyes dancing with mischief. *"Scoote Nipe Equiwa!"* he cried. Then he began to stagger about as though he were drunk. *"Scoote Nipe Equiwa!"*

"What's he saying?"

"Your new name," Deke informed her with a low laugh. "Whiskey Woman. The story has it that you was once normal-haired and normal-eyed. Until a trader pried you open and poured you full of whiskey. So full it turned your eyes a funny color and came spillin' outa your scalp. The reason you're so pale is because that much whiskey'd make anybody look peaked."

Laura's legs nearly buckled. She reeled in the circle of Deke's arm, fairly certain she would fall if not for his support. The little boy giggled with delight, backed up a few paces, and began jabbering loudly, his finger pointed at Laura. *"Scoote nipe t'kar-chi*, whiskey legs! *Ni-ne-e-meh'*, look!"

Children came running from every crack, or at least it

seemed so to Laura, all of them taking up the chant, which Deke translated for her. *Whiskey legs. Look! The story told by Many Stomachs is true! See how she walks!*

Laura felt like a lone granule of sugar in a village full of ants.

Very cute ants. All of them with great, round, black eyes. Hair so ebon, it flashed blue in the sunlight. And giggles such as Laura had never heard, from deep in their bellies, ringing around her. If she had closed her eyes and not listened to the words, she might have thought they were white children.

They were certainly as curious as white children. As Deke led Laura to a narrow, aspen-lined stream that coursed crookedly through a thick copse, the imps followed along as a noisy escort. Angling left, Deke helped her to a fallen log, then gently lowered her onto it.

"There you are." He turned away and yelled, "*Weh-pe-theh*, go!"

The children shrieked and scattered. Within seconds, nary a sign of them could be seen. Shaking his head, he shifted his attention back to Laura.

She braced her hands on her knees, feeling as though she had just run five miles without pausing for rest. She was shaking and panting and sweating. It was disgusting.

"Can you hang on to the log?" he asked.

Laura blinked, uncertain what he meant for an instant, then awash in humiliation as understanding dawned. "I—yes—the log. Of course."

Deke jabbed his thumb over his shoulder. "I'm gonna go back over yonder on the other side of that brush and have me a smoke. When you're done, all you gotta do is holler."

She nodded, too embarrassed to articulate a reply.

When she'd finished, she shook as though she were palsied. Leaning forward to brace her hands on her knees again, she dragged in great drafts of air. Slowly but surely, the heart-pounding fatigue lessened, and her vision sharpened. She stared at two damp circles that had formed on her bodice. Her breasts were leaking? How could that be?

Several possibilities slammed into her brain. She shoved them all away. What mattered was that she still had milk. After a week of illness, it was a miracle. A miracle! She would hug the joy of that close and not allow herself to think of how it had come to pass.

With weak fingers, Laura unfastened her blouse and chemise only to discover she was wearing a— She stared in bewilderment, then plucked curiously at the blue chambray halter that hugged her breasts. What on earth? It was the strangest garment she had ever seen, clearly fashioned from one of Deke's shirts, original shoulder seams intact, sleeves and collar detached, the body cut away to form a scooped neckline in front and sheared off to hit just below her bosom. The soft material was neatly tucked with darts to fit snugly around her midriff and firmly support her fullness, joined by three buttons between her breasts.

She plucked at the neckline to examine the neat little stitches that bound the edge. Someone with a very skillful hand had fashioned this to her exact measurements.

Laura closed her eyes and bit her lip. *Dear God!* She pictured Deke Sheridan drawing the chambray around her, and she wanted to die. She knew as surely as she knew her own name that he must have been the father of this creation, at least in part. Even if his mother had done the sewing, she couldn't have been the one who tried the garment on Laura for a proper fit.

The images that crawled through her head were so abhorrent to her that she groaned. Pulsing fire crept up her neck and seared her cheeks. How dared he take such liberties? She'd never be able to face him again. He would smirk; she just knew it. She could only wonder that he hadn't already.

The realization that he hadn't gave her pause. He had behaved as if nothing untoward had occurred, as though he had never set eyes on her naked body, let alone touched her.

There was nothing for it. She had to take her cue from him and pretend the same. This last week never happened.

She had been ill. He had cared for her because there had been no one else. Now she must pick up the shreds of her dignity and proceed from here.

Acutely aware that Deke Sheridan lurked nearby, waiting for her to call for him, she quickly refastened her clothing. Her task completed, she eyed the stream with longing, but she was far too weak to rinse her face. What must she look like? With searching fingertips, she touched her hair and discovered it was drawn back into a smooth braid that hung loose between her shoulder blades. Deke had brushed her hair? She hadn't the faintest recollection of it, but supposed he had.

What else had he done for her while she slept? Still aware of how loosely her blouse fit her, and curious as to why, she felt under her arms and found that triangular insets of muslin had been neatly stitched into the seams to provide more room. On the heel of that, she also discovered that the more generous waistband of her skirt was due to the addition of a leather-thong button loop.

It seemed that Deke Sheridan might have done everything for her this last week, even going so far as to alter her clothing. Laura swallowed. Everything? She couldn't bear to think of it. She needed to call him. She couldn't sit here on this silly log forever, after all. But oh, God, she didn't want to face him.

Chapter 14

"LAURA, YOU OKAY?"

She stiffened and glanced up. "Yes, fine." It took her a moment to gather enough composure to add, "I'm ready to go back now if you've finished smoking."

Deke rose from the rock he was sitting on and parted the brush to step into the clearing. Laura was perched on the log, exactly as he had left her. Well, not exactly. The stricken look on her face hadn't been there before. His throat went tight as he approached her. When she glanced up at him, he saw tears shimmering in her eyes.

He had known this moment would come, and he had done everything he could to make it easier for her, even making sure she was completely dressed before she woke up. Over the last week he had rehearsed a dozen different things he might say to her—that there were some things a man just didn't think about when a woman was so ill . . . that he had been so worried, he had noticed very little else . . . that he could scarcely even remember what her naked body looked like. Now, gazing into her huge amber eyes, all those well-practiced lies fled his mind.

The truth was that everything about her had been branded upon his brain, and until the day he died, he would remember every sweet line and curve of her slender body, every imperfection, every texture.

He feared he might botch it if he tried to lie. Or, worse yet, blush to the roots of his hair. As bashful as she was, the less said, the better. The trick would be to pretend nothing had happened. That she had never been ill. That he had never intimately cared for her.

He bent to help her stand, and as his arm curled around her waist, he felt her whole body quivering. She'd never make it back to the lodge on her own steam, and he didn't expect her to try. He caught her behind the knees with his other arm and swept her up against his chest. She gave a startled squeak, then clung to his neck. The embrace warmed him and felt right. He wasn't sure when or even how, but sometime over this last week, he had come to feel she belonged to him in a way that no one else ever had. Looking down into her huge amber eyes, he thought, *Neewa*, my wife, and realized he was not only reconciled to their marriage now, but pleased that fate had thrown them together.

Deke jostled her to get a firm grip, then tucked in his chin to meet her sparkling gaze. Her color was high with embarrassment and shame. He wanted to tell her those feelings were unnecessary, but somehow he didn't think this was the moment to reveal their new relationship. Soon. He had no choice but to tell her soon, or she'd let the cat out of the bag in front of Black Stone. But now definitely wasn't a good time.

Dinner for Laura consisted of venison broth and two tiny pieces of meat, stingy portions in her opinion, but that was all Deke would allow her to have. She was so ravenous that, despite his warnings, she gulped down the meat with greedy urgency, then followed it with quick swallows of broth, all the while thinking of ways she might convince him to give her more food. To her surprise, by the time she finished the meager portions he had doled out to her, she felt pleasantly replete. And horribly exhausted. Which reminded her of how seriously ill she must have been.

Setting her empty plate and cup on the furs beside her, she leaned her back against the leather wall. Gray plumes meandered lazily up from the fire pit to find their way out of the ventilation hole above them. The smell of smoke filled her nostrils, but was not so strong as to be disagreeable. Deke sat cross-legged at the opposite side of the fire, his thoughts apparently on the flames. Chief, a vague red lump on the shadowy ground nearby, serenaded them with soft snores.

The sound made Laura sleepy, but with Deke in such close proximity and murdering savages crawling as thickly as ants just outside, she couldn't quite bring herself to lie down. Unless it lay beyond reach of the firelight, there wasn't another pallet inside the lodge, and judging by the number of furs used for her own bed, she doubted Deke had set aside any for himself. She feared he might join her for a nap if she fell asleep. Though she had no recollection of it, she suspected that he had been sleeping beside her since arriving here. And where had his mother slept? As far as that went, where was his mother, anyway? Surely this must be her home. Laura considered asking Deke where the woman had gone, but somehow the words stuck in her throat.

From outside came the voices of his people, their language a confusing collection of guttural grunts. Friends? Relatives? Acquaintances? Murdering fiends, one and all. It was nothing short of miraculous that she was actually in their midst and still in possession of her hair. In the back of her mind she knew Deke was all that stood between her and certain death, but that was a predicament she would have to confront later—when she felt stronger. For now, it was enough to deal with each moment as it came, the present one being that she was weary, yearned to see her baby, and was beginning to wonder when she would, if ever.

"Didn't you say Star—was that her name?—that she was going to bring Jonathan to me in a couple of hours?"

He glanced up. "She will. Time isn't as important here as in your world. No clocks. Pretty soon . . . in a couple of hours—that means when someone can get around to it. Besides, it ain't been an hour since I said that."

She sighed and looped her arms around her knees, determined to look at the bright side. Her baby was alive and well. She would see him soon, get to hold him. Just the thought made Laura ache with longing. That Jonathan was in the possession of some Indian woman was a fact she couldn't quite bring herself to contemplate. Smack-dab in the middle of a Cheyenne village? Whenever she thought about it, she broke out in a cold sweat. All she could do was trust in Deke Sheridan and think beyond that horror, to the moment when she would have her baby safely back in Denver, where no harm could befall him.

Before she knew it, she and Jonathan would be away from here, she assured herself, and all of this would be nothing more than an unpleasant memory. Somehow—and she didn't care what she had to promise to accomplish it—she would convince her father to send her enough money to stay in Denver at one of the hotels until Jonathan was old enough to travel. Then home to Boston, where she and her son truly belonged. The nightmare that had begun with her marriage to Tristan was almost over.

"Laura," Deke said in a husky, strangely tentative voice. "There's somethin' I got to tell you."

Laura blinked to clear away her daydreams—visions of the elegant parlor in her father's house, of rustling silk dresses and dainty porcelain teacups, of sophisticated and richly garbed visitors who engaged her in intelligent conversation. As the pictures faded, the primitive lodge and Deke Sheridan, her present companion, came back into focus. She doubted his forefinger would even fit through the handle of a teacup, and if he knew how to make intelligent conversation, she hadn't as yet witnessed the phenomenon.

Sometime during her illness, probably upon their arrival here in the village, he had doffed his Stetson and had begun wearing the hatband of cobalt trade beads as a headband, a change that made him look all the more a savage. She had also noticed that he now wore his shirt unbuttoned, probably so he could shed the garment whenever he joined his half-naked heathen acquaintances outside. Laura supposed she should be grateful that he had bothered to put the shirt back on when he reentered the lodge. Even with it hanging open, it was better than his wearing no clothing at all on his upper body.

She dragged her gaze from the diabolical-looking necklaces that decorated the bronze planes of his muscular chest and forced her mind onto what he had said—that there was something he had to tell her. "Yes? And what is that you must tell me, Mr. Sheridan?"

He took a deep breath. "You ain't gonna like it too good."

Laura had a horrible feeling he meant to confess how intimately he had cared for her during her illness, a revelation she would happily forgo. "I'd rather pretend this last week . . ." She hunched her shoulders. "I appreciate your care of me, but I'd be pleased to pretend it never happened."

He gave her an odd look. "That ain't it."

"Oh." She managed a relieved smile. "Then what?" The wary expression on his face made her heart catch. "It isn't— Jonathan's okay, isn't he? You did say he was okay."

He held up a staying hand. "He's fine. This ain't about him." Then he frowned. "Well, that ain't exactly so. In a roundabout way, everything comes back to Jonathan, I reckon."

Laura released a pent-up breath. Nothing really mattered to her as long as her baby was safe and she could see him soon. Not even if she had to wade neck-deep through a village of Cheyenne Indians to do it. "Then what, Mr. Sheridan?"

He picked up a sliver of kindling and twirled it in his long, callused fingers. "You remember that first night I saw you? And you sayin' there wasn't nothin' you wouldn't do to get your baby back? Is that still how you feel?"

Laura licked her lips. Were they back to that again? She wasn't at all sure she liked his tone or the expression in his eyes. "I, um, yes, of course I still feel that way. Jonathan's my baby, my own flesh and blood."

He touched the sliver of wood to a hot coal, then watched the tip catch fire and burn out. "Right now, hostility between your people and mine is runnin' real high."

"Yes."

"The Cheyenne got a lot of hate in their hearts for whites. I won't go into the right and wrong of it on neither side, but that's how it is."

Laura wished he would get to the point. "I'm aware of the hostilities, Mr. Sheridan. What is it you're trying to say?"

He sighed. "To throw the lasso quick, what it boils down to is that they wouldn't care if you never got your son back. You bein' white, your tears ain't nothin' to them."

"Are you saying they aren't going to return my son to me?" she asked in a voice suddenly shrill with panic.

"No. They're gonna give him back. It's just . . ."

"Just what, Mr. Sheridan? You're frightening me."

He threw her an exasperated glance. "Do you think you could call me Deke? After all we been through, and you're still sayin' 'mister,' like you don't even know me. It's irritatin' as hell."

"Deke," she amended. "I'm sorry. It's only that . . . Well, where I come from, it isn't proper for a lady to—"

"This ain't Boston—it's Colorado," he shot back.

Laura nodded and cast a nervous glance around. For the life of her, she couldn't recall what he had been saying.

He muttered something under his breath. "I'm sorry. I don't mean to be sharp. It's just that I got a load of tellin' to do, and I ain't sure how to say it. You callin' me 'Mr. Sheridan' makes it all just that much harder."

Laura could see that he was indeed agitated, which only added to her trepidation. Whatever it was he had to tell her, he clearly didn't find it easy. In her experience, he wasn't a man who usually minced words. "Whatever you have on your mind, say it straight out, Mr. Sher—I mean, Deke. That's always best."

Regarding the sliver of kindling again, he pursed his lips and blew on its glowing tip. Silence followed, a long, nerve-racking silence that made Laura want to shake him. Finally he said, "One of them Cheyenne out there, Black Stone, he's my spirit brother."

"Yes, you mentioned that. It's his wife, Star, who has my baby, isn't it?"

"That's right." He coughed nervously. "He, um . . . him and me, we kind of adopted each other, years back when we was boys. That probably sounds funny to you, but among the People, adoption carries as much sway as blood, and folks can just up and decide to be related if they got a real special fondness for each other and a good reason. Me, I didn't have no brother. Medicine Woman, she's barren, so there was only just me. And her husband, Passes Much Wind, he didn't want two wives. I wanted a brother bad, and Black Stone and me . . . well, we tied a knot atwixt us."

"Passes Much what?"

He rubbed beside his nose. "Some of the names around here might strike you a little odd. Passes Much Wind—well, he was sort of a champion at it, and the soldiers in his society, they named him that."

"I see," she murmured, only, of course, she didn't see at all. Indeed, this conversation had her head so muddled, she wanted to scream. Her baby, that was all she cared about. Couldn't he understand that?

"Anyhow, back to Black Stone, my brother. A few months ago, his baby son died."

Laura tightened her arms around her knees. Suddenly she sensed what was coming. "And he was the one who traded with the comancheros for Jonathan. That's why his wife has my child."

Deke nodded. "Just my luck." After saying that, he shook his head. "No matter. Whether it had been him or someone else, we'd still be in the same fix." He met her gaze across the licking flames. "After their baby died, Black Stone's wife grieved real hard. Him givin' her the new baby eased her pain."

Laura closed her eyes, suddenly terrified. "Since he hates white people so much, how—how on earth did you persuade him to return Jonathan to me?"

"Well, that there's the thing."

She lifted her lashes. "You did convince him?"

"Yep."

He looked none too happy about it. "Mr. Sheridan, please get to the point. My heart can't take much more."

His tone dripping sarcasm, he muttered "Mr. Sheridan" under his breath and then flexed his shoulders, one hand clamped over his neck to knead stiff muscles. "I don't reckon you ever been told how Indian folks get hitched?"

Laura frowned, totally bewildered by the shifts in this conversation. "No, I—can't say that—I, um, don't believe so. What does it matter?"

"Oh, it matters," he assured her.

"How?"

"That's what I'm tryin' to . . ." He sighed again, the sound indescribably weary. "It just does, that's all. When a man takes a fancy to a woman, he goes to her oldest brother or closest male relative and . . ." With a wave of his hand, he dismissed those particulars. "Anyhow, if he and her relative reach a happy agreement, the man sends horses and all manner of nice presents to her family. All her brothers and male cousins—every damned body who can afford it—they choose from the gifts and replace 'em with things of like value, so there's a real nice spread of stuff. And then they mount her up on a real fine horse, or wrap her in a blanket, and take her off to her new husband with all the exchanged gifts, the idea bein' that she goes into her marriage with all she needs to set up housekeepin'. The new husband, he hauls her down off the horse when she gets to his lodge and takes her inside to—well, that goes without sayin'. And that's it. They're married, right and proper, and it's a done deed."

To Laura, that was a rather startling revelation. "Just like that? No wedding ceremony or vows or anything?"

"Sometimes—most times, in fact—there's a big party to celebrate sometime afterward."

She had no idea why he was telling her this, or what he expected her to say. She searched her mind for a polite rejoinder. "How . . . quaint."

He rubbed the day's growth of whiskers on his chin.

"And what of the woman?" she couldn't resist asking. "Isn't she consulted before her brother takes all the presents?"

"A brave who wants a girl for his wife usually wraps her in his blanket a few times to test her feelin's toward him. Before he starts sendin' presents." At Laura's shocked expression, he grinned weakly. "The blanket part—that ain't like it sounds. It's a courtin' thing, nothin' more. They stand together by the central fire or wherever, with other folks all around, and they talk love talk."

Love talk? "Oh. And if she doesn't wish to talk . . . love talk?"

"Well, it depends on how set the brave is on havin' her and how much account her male relative gives to her feelin's on the matter."

"You're saying she has no choice if her relative decides she must marry?"

"Cheyenne women usually trust the men in their families to look after them and to decide what's best. It ain't often a brother's mean about choosin' a husband for a girl, and most times she accepts what he decides without no fuss."

"How barbaric." Laura shuddered. Then it occurred to her that, for all practical purposes, it wasn't much different from a woman's lot in the white world. She knew that better than anyone. "What if she has no male relative?"

"That don't happen much because there's usually parents or cousins to act as her brother, but when it does, she gets to have her own say about who she marries up with."

"That's something, at least."

"Most times, anyhow."

"Most times? You mean sometimes she doesn't have a say even if she has no relatives?"

"I'm gettin' to that. Sometimes weddin's don't go the regular way. Say a girl gets a hankerin' for some brave her brother don't show favor to. Well, girls has been known to elope. Other times—" He broke off and swallowed. "Well, let's say a brave takes a shine to a girl, and she don't to him. He might just sort of"—his voice dipped to a gruff whisper—"take her."

"Pardon me?"

"Take her," he said more loudly. "He might just sort of—you know—make off with her. Either way, elopin' or bride stealin', he waits a few days 'til her family gets over bein' mad and then . . ." He threw up his hands. "What the hell difference does it make? Once he makes off with her, proper or otherwise, she's his wife if he can make it right with her family. If a girl don't got a family, there ain't even that to worry about. A done deed. They're married."

Laura tipped her head to regard him. "What has this to do with Jonathan?"

He puffed air into his cheeks, then slowly exhaled it. "The thing is . . ." He raked his hand through his hair. "Jesus. Why I'm so nervous, I don't know. You ain't much bigger than a minute."

Laura frowned. What did her size have to do with anything?

"Just don't scream when I tell you," he cautioned. "I know you're gonna want to pitch one hell of a fit, but don't. Black Stone might hear you."

Laura's heart had begun to pound. "Mr. Sheridan?"

He groaned. "While you was asleep, Boston, things got real complicated." As though he couldn't quite bring himself to look her directly in the eye, he cast his gaze slightly downward and regarded her through a sweep of dark lashes. "Anyhow, I didn't see no way around it, and I told Black Stone you was my wife and that Jonathan was my son. So's he'd give the baby back to you."

Laura had been expecting him to say something horrible. Her body went limp with relief. "Oh, Mr. Sheridan." Emotion turned her voice shaky, and tears filled her eyes. "I don't know what to say. How shall I ever thank you?"

He looked uneasy. "I don't think you're sniffin' down the right trail here. I told Black Stone you was my *wife*."

"I know." She blinked to clear away the tears. "How absolutely chivalrous."

"Chivalrous. Is that good?"

"The finest of compliments."

An uncertain smile touched his mouth. "Then you ain't mad?"

"Mad? No! If it wouldn't be so highly inappropriate, I'd hug the breath right out of you." She brushed at the tears rolling down her face. "Thank you so much from the very bottom of my heart."

His attention sharpened. "Surely you ain't so proper you can't hug your husband? I'm all for them fancy manners of yours, honey. Believe it or not, they're kind of growin' on me. But we gotta draw a line somewhere."

Laura froze with her fingertips glued to her cheek. "I beg your pardon?" She swallowed a pocket of air that felt the size of a hen egg. "Did you say husband? That you're my . . ." She dropped her hand to her lap. "I must have misheard you."

"You heard me right. Didn't you listen to nothin' I said? About Cheyenne customs and all? While you was asleep, I married you."

Chapter 15

DEKE COULD SEE LAURA WAS STRUGGLING against a rising panic. Sitting cross-legged with his shoulders slumped to rest his arms on his knees, he was doing his level best to look harmless. But if that skittering pulse in the hollow of her throat was any sign, he wasn't pulling it off.

He supposed he should feel guilty for putting her in such a spot. But he didn't. Regrets, yes. He had plenty of them, but not over anything he had done or intended to do. What he regretted were the things that had put such fear in her eyes because it would make it so very hard for her to trust again.

And trust him, she must. He wasn't responsible for this situation; he only meant to rectify it, if he could. Why, then, should he feel bad if he got something he wanted in the bargain, namely this woman? Over the last week, Deke had come to want her, not because he had decided to, but simply because it had happened. After what he had suffered at the hands of one fancy city woman, he would be a fool to risk the same again. But Laura had staked a claim on his heart.

And now he was staking a claim on her. With no guilt, with no regrets, with no hesitation, and he would make no apology for that, not to her or himself. Raised as a Cheyenne, Deke didn't believe things happened accidentally. For every breath of breeze, for every drop of rain, for every heart that beat, there was a purpose. His people believed life was a tapestry, the weave complex, the pattern controlled by powers beyond comprehension. Deke saw the births of a man and woman as events that took place at the opposite outer edges of that tapestry, the proceeding days, weeks, months, and years a braid of textures and colors that swirled relentlessly toward a center point where their individual patterns finally blended and became more intricate. If a man was lucky, the woman he met and became interwoven with in that central swirl brought with her a brilliance that shimmered as beautifully as Laura's eyes.

He wouldn't run from what he sensed was meant to be. And he wasn't going to allow Laura to run from it, either.

"Did you say married?" she finally whispered, her eyes stricken and pleading with him to say no.

Deke steeled himself against that look. For a week he had not only kept Laura alive, but had kept her world from toppling, and now he was kicking the shims out from under her. His only consolation was that when she fell—which he would see to it she eventually did—it would be into his arms.

He reached to rub his nose and discovered his hand was shaking. Jesus. This was a fine state of affairs. It was up to him to get this over with as quickly and painlessly as possible before Star came with the baby.

"Yep, married, that's what I said."

The minute Deke spoke, he wanted to slug himself. Cocksure was not the impression he should be giving off right now. Did he want to scare her to death? If that was his aim, he might as well just rub his palms together and drool. *Gotcha, darlin'!*

She searched his face as if she hoped he might be joking. Deke was very glad he wasn't, but for her sake, he struggled to keep all trace of smugness out of his expression. Braving it out, she laughed softly, but even as the sound erupted, he detected a note of hysteria in it. "L-Let me reiterate, just to be certain—"

"Re-what?"

"Reiterate." She made an agitated gesture with hands

that were shaking worse than his were. "Repeat what you said. While I was delirious—completely unaware of what was going on—you married me?"

Deke thought that pretty much covered things, but the look in Laura's eyes made him wish he didn't have to own up to it. Circumstances beyond their control had maneuvered her into his grasp; he found reason to rejoice in that, but it wouldn't do for her to feel he was gloating. "Yep. Marrying you, it was all I could think of to do."

Those beautiful eyes of hers started to bulge a little bit, and he noticed that a small vein in her temple was swelling. He couldn't help but stare at it.

"Am I to assume that you proposed to me, and in my addled state, I said yes?"

Deke forced his gaze back to hers. "Laura, honey, I think maybe you oughta calm down a tad before you rupture a vessel."

"I am perfectly calm, and I asked you a question. Did you trick me into saying yes while I was delirious?" Her voice had gone high-pitched and tremulous, not quite a wail, but close.

"What've I ever done to make you think I'd be that sneaky?" Deke tried for the harmless look again. Why, he didn't know. It didn't seem to be working. It had never worked with her.

She pressed a hand over her heart. "By that, can I assume you didn't propose and I didn't say yes?"

"I wouldn't try to trick you into somethin' that way, honey. It was one thing for me to do what needed doin', knowin' you might not be very happy about it. But gettin' you to say yes when you was out of your head? Only a low-down skunk'd pull a stunt like that."

She blinked. Then she blinked again. Deke got the nasty feeling she hoped he might disappear.

Her line of reasoning made no sense at all to him, and he couldn't help but feel mildly offended. "Even if I was that low-down, why would I bother with tricks?" he reasoned. "By Cheyenne law, I didn't need your consent. Granted, it ain't done real often, but bride stealin' happens. The only kicker is if someone objects—someone besides the woman who gets stole, of course, since it usually goes without sayin' that she ain't fond of the idea. You don't even have any relatives here that I gotta worry about."

At that, her face blanched, and her eyes grew rounder. Deke rubbed his nose again. Shit. Why had he said that? He was getting so nervous, he felt like somebody had a fistful of his guts and was giving them a slow twist. He was no good at talking his way out of corners. Never had been, never would be, so why the hell was he trying?

Because if he didn't try, that left only one option, which was to ride roughshod over her.

"Laura." He massaged the back of his neck. "Honey, I never would've done this if there had been another way. You believe that, don't you?"

Hell, no, she didn't believe it. That horrified look in her eyes told him that. The realization made Deke feel even more irritated. True, he was as pleased as a toad with two lily pads about the way this had all turned out, but he hadn't arranged things to happen this way.

"Well, say, hey . . ." He shrugged and tossed in a chuckle for good measure. "Would you listen to me, askin' you such a damned fool question? Of course you believe it. I mean, why"—he lifted his hands to emphasize the sheer stupidity of the question—"would any man in his right mind go through all this folderol to get himself a wife if all he had to do in the first place was grab her by the—"

Deke broke off and teetered there, doing mental handsprings to keep from falling in. He didn't want to say that, for Christ's sake. Sweat began to bead on his forehead.

In need of something to do, he picked up another splinter of firewood and began running his fingers back and forth along its length. When he looked up, he found that Laura was staring at his hands with a panicked expression on her small face. He followed her gaze. It didn't take many brains to figure out what she must be thinking. He immediately stopped stroking the wood.

The low sound of men's laughter drifted in from outside, and voices rang through the night in a language Deke knew Laura couldn't understand. Cheyenne warriors, his friends, some of whom he claimed as kin. He wanted to step to the lodge door and yell at all of them to shut up. The last thing he needed was for her to start thinking about Indians and all the terrible things they did to white women. That would scare her to death.

As if she wasn't halfway there already.

The more that he thought about it, the more her reaction to this marriage started to rankle. It wasn't as if he was so hard put to find a wife that he had to trap one, after all. What had given Laura the idea he even wanted a white wife, anyway? In his experience, white women were usually more fuss and bother than they were worth. This predicament was evidence of that. In ninety-nine cases out of a hundred, a Cheyenne woman would have accepted what her man told her, and that would have been the end of it.

Only he didn't want a Cheyenne woman. He wanted Laura, sassy little piece of baggage that she was. And he had a feeling she would get worse before she got better.

A slight smile touched his mouth, which he quickly squelched. He didn't want her to believe he didn't sympathize with how she felt. He could see her side in this. It was probably more than a little alarming to fall asleep a widow and wake up married. To her way of thinking, they had known each other barely long enough to feel comfortable sharing the same cup of morning coffee. Now he was asking her to share one hell of a lot more. Not in so many words, of course, but a widow with a baby didn't need him to draw her a map. On top of that, he wasn't exactly every lady's heart's desire. In Denver when women saw him coming, they switched sides of the street. Poor Laura had no way to escape his path, and after being married to a bastard like Tristan Cheney, she was probably afraid Deke would walk right over the top of her.

Well, he was who he was. There was no changing it. He couldn't go around keeping his hands hidden or shave a foot off his height or learn fancy Boston parlor talk in five easy lessons.

The look in Laura's eyes told Deke his present tack was getting him nowhere fast. No more playing cat and mouse. Unless he wanted a panicked female on his hands, it was time to toss his rope and get the noose cinched tight so he could exercise some control.

The slender length of firewood Deke was holding suddenly snapped under the pressure of his fingers, jerking both him and Laura back to the moment and the realization that they had been staring at each other. She jumped at the sound.

"Laura, look," he said in as soothing a tone as he could muster. "I think what we need to do here is keep our sights trained on the fix you're in and forget everything else. Do you think you can do that?"

Those eyes. When Deke looked into them, he felt as though he were drowning in bourbon, a hell of a nice way to go, but thought-numbing. The girl had a tongue she could wrap around a post and still have wag to spare. If he meant to stay a step ahead of her, he'd have to keep on his toes.

"No offense intended, Mr. Sheridan, but please understand that this fix I'm in . . . Well, marriage seems a rather drastic step to take. So drastic that it's a little difficult for me to think past it." She touched a hand to her throat. "Please rest assured it's nothing personal. I'd feel that way with anyone, not just you."

"Marriage may be drastic, but it's also the only step to take," he came back. "Do you think I set out on this trip hankerin' to get me a wife and kid? Think again. I wouldn't've done this if there'd been another way."

She steepled her trembling fingertips and brushed them lightly across her lips. "Wh-What if we went to Denver and g-got help? It's only—what—two days away? The immediate threat of Indian attack has probably passed by now. I'm certain the sheriff would enlist the aid of volunteers if we asked. Maybe with a show of strength to back us, Black Stone can be made to listen to reason."

Deke jerked off the headband of cobalt trade beads and swiped at his forehead. "A show of strength. Rifles, you mean? Toted by white men who'd as soon shoot a Cheyenne as look at one? Don't ask me to do that, Laura."

"We could choose the men carefully. Decent, God-fearing men, that's all we'd bring back with us."

"There ain't such a thing as decent white men when it comes to Indians. Especially right now with the hate runnin' so high. There'd be a bloodbath for sure."

"You don't know that. Not every man in Denver is an Indian hater. It's worth a try, surely. Better that than leaping into a marriage both of us will abhor."

Deke wasn't certain what *abhor* meant, but he got her gist. "You're the one that's got a problem with this marriage, darlin', not me. As for a show of force bein' worth a try? It'd be kinda like gamblin' with lives on a throw of the dice, wouldn't it?" He flashed her a humorless smile. "You're askin' me to risk the lives of people I love, to choose between them and you." He dropped the beads into his shirt pocket. "Sorry, but you lose. I won't do it. My way, nobody stands to get hurt."

"Oh, really! And what of me?" she blurted.

By her expression, Deke knew she regretted saying the words. For his part, he was glad they were finally out in the open. "What about you? I reckon maybe this ain't a leg up on your last marriage, but at least it can't be worse." He looked directly into her eyes. "Since the first, you been sayin' there wasn't no price so dear you wouldn't pay it to get that boy back. Now you're shilly-shallyin'. What you gotta ask yourself is, how bad do you really want that baby?"

At that, what little color remained in her face drained away, and the pupils of her eyes became gigantic. "But marriage, Mr. Sheridan? I scarcely know you. We met barely a week ago, and I slept through most of that."

"I was awake. Half of us was gettin' acquainted."

A tiny muscle in her cheek started to twitch. She stared at him for several endless moments as though she had never seen him before. Deke didn't allow his gaze to falter.

If she saw the possessiveness he felt toward her in his eyes, so be it.

"Wh-Why couldn't we simply *pretend* to be married? Just for a few days, until I get Jonathan back and I'm strong enough to leave?"

"Because there ain't no such thing as pretendin' among the People. If you say somethin' is so, it's so. I said we was married. That makes it a fact."

"To your way of thinking."

"Right now, I carry the vote."

Deke could almost see the wheels turning in her mind. He knew she was thinking ahead to when they would leave here, that his vote and heathen beliefs wouldn't count for much in Denver. Well, he had news for her on that score, but he would deliver it later tonight when the moment felt right. For now, he had to herd her little butt over this first rough spot. Before he knew it, Star might come with the baby, and he couldn't risk Laura saying something in front of the squaw that would give them away.

Bracing his elbows on his knees, Deke leaned forward, ignoring the heat against his face that rose from the small fire. "Laura, how's about if I make all of this a little bit simpler for you?"

"I—I would appreciate it," she said thinly.

He doubted that. Hating himself even as he did it, Deke assumed a stern, don't-trifle-with-me expression. "If you're that set against this marriage, I'll go out there right now and tell Black Stone I lied to him—that you ain't my wife and that Jonathan's not my son."

She caught her bottom lip between her teeth and bit down until the flesh turned white. "And if you do that? What will happen?"

"Well, we'll lay over here for a few days until you can travel; then we'll light out for Denver. Without your baby." He lifted his hands. "What you do when you get to Denver is your business. At that point, I'll wash my hands of the whole aggravatin' mess. I'm sure you're right. The sheriff'll round up volunteers to bring you back here."

Hope flared in her eyes.

Quick to dash it, Deke added, "But don't expect Black Stone and his band to be waitin' here for you like lambs for the slaughter. They won't be. And I gotta tell you, honey, the chances of them volunteers findin' a band of Cheyenne Indians when they don't wanna be found is gonna be slim."

"I—I could hire another tracker. You did say there were others in Denver as good as you."

"That's what I said. But I was talkin' about findin' kidnappers when I said it. There's only one man I know in this territory worth his salt at trackin' Indians."

Her eyes implored him. "W-Would you give me that man's name?"

Deke dealt the stunning blow. "You're lookin' at him."

Laura's shoulders sagged, and she squeezed her eyes closed. Her face had gone so white, it frightened him. Afraid he might relent, he fixed his gaze on the fire for a moment. There was no backing out of this. If they did, she'd lose that kid, and he wasn't about to see that happen, not over a handful of silly fears he could chase away if she would only give him half a chance.

"That's your first choice," he added. "The second is acceptin' this marriage. If you do that, you get your baby back. I guess what it all boils down to is how much you really love him."

At that, her eyes flew open. "That is unfair!"

Since first meeting her, one thing Deke had always admired about Laura was that she didn't let her lack of bulk stop her from standing up for herself. "It's the way I call it. If the truth hurts, as the sayin' goes."

"How can you question my love for my baby? It's not a question of that at all. It's . . ." Her mouth thinned with dislike. "This isn't a matter of how much I love my child or how much I'll happily sacrifice for him. It's a matter of principle. I'm being pushed into a marriage against my will. What of my personal freedom? What of my inalienable right to choose the man I wish to marry?"

"I'm givin' you a choice." He glanced around as if they had an audience. "Didn't I give this gal a choice?"

Her eyes flashed at him. "This is not a joking matter."

"It sure as hell ain't. Marryin' a gal who gets the bit between her teeth at every turn ain't exactly high on my list, I'll tell you that, and if that's the way it's gonna be, I wash my hands of it."

Tears began to shimmer in her eyes, but Deke didn't allow himself to pay them any heed.

"You talk about principles, darlin'? What about mine?" He thumped his chest. "I lied for you, goddammit. To people who'd sooner cut out their tongues as lie to me. Not so I could trap you. You're a real pretty little gal, but no woman on earth's that pretty. I done it so you'd get that baby back. Because for some crazy reason, I care about you, and I knew it'd kill you to lose him."

The tears had formed pools and were welling over her lower lashes onto her pale cheeks.

"You wanna throw that back in my teeth? Hey, sweetheart, that's fine by me. Just say the word. I'll go set things straight with Black Stone. It's your baby that'll get took. And the bottom line is, if you don't go along with this, that ain't my problem. I've done what I can to fix this mess, and that's all you or anybody else can expect from me."

"I just want my baby," she said.

"No, you want him with no cost to yourself. Sorry, honey, but that ain't how things work in this old world." Deke held her gaze. "The way I see it, you're damned lucky I even want to marry you. Have you stopped to think of the mess you'd be in if I ran the other way?"

"Why do you? Want to marry me, I mean?" she asked shrilly.

The question stopped Deke dead for a second. Then he decided, given the hurtful things Tristan Cheney had said to her, that telling Laura the naked truth would probably do her more good in the long run than a hundred smooth lies. "You're a beautiful woman, that's why. And I want you. What man in his right mind wouldn't?"

"It takes far more to make a marriage work than that, Mr. Sheridan."

"It sure does. Cooperatin' with each other, for starters. I reckon what you gotta decide is if you can meet me halfway. I ain't real fond of the idea of harnessin' myself into the traces with a woman who's gonna be fightin' me with every step."

"I won't fight you!"

He let that hang between them for a moment. "Does that mean you agree to the marriage?"

Her mouth quivered at the corners as she said, "Yes. I'll give it a try, at least."

"No toe-dippin'," he warned. "If you don't like the looks of the water, don't wade in. I mean that. I can't treat a marriage like I would a boot and take it off if it starts to pinch. If we do this, Laura, it's for life."

As he had a few minutes ago, Deke could see her thoughts racing. The little minx was already planning her getaway, damn her stubborn hide. He'd nix that idea in short order, but first things first.

"Well?" he pressed. "Do I go find Black Stone and tell him the truth? Or do you agree to things as they stand? Make up your mind, Laura. Star'll be here with the baby before long, and once she comes, the time for choices is over."

Laura wrung the cloth of her skirt in her hands, looking at him as if he were trying to shove her off a cliff. "I, um, agree to the marriage," she murmured.

He cocked his head. "I didn't quite catch that."

"I agree to the marriage," she said more firmly.

"For life, with no maybe riding drag?"

"For life, with no maybe riding drag."

Chapter 16

WITH THAT SETTLED, DEKE PUSHED UP FROM the fire and walked slowly toward Laura's pallet. She shrank against the leather wall behind her, regarding his advance with the same wariness as she might have that of a side-winder. He couldn't help but wonder what she expected him to do to her. Considering all she had suffered at Tristan's hands, there was probably no telling.

Hunkering at the edge of the fur, Deke settled a specula-tive gaze on her, knowing as he did that she would be furi-ous if she knew the thoughts going through his head. For all Tristan's browbeating, she still had a goodly measure of tat-tered pride, and she wouldn't appreciate being compared to a horse—not one damned bit.

Deke meant no slight. Since early boyhood, he had been catching, breaking, and training wild horses, most of them terrified from the get-go. Now approaching thirty-two, he had been at it for well over twenty years and had perfected his handling of the difficult animals until it was almost an art. Since it went without saying that he had captured and tamed very few frightened women—none, to be exact—he had no knowledge of them at all. When faced with a prob-lem, it seemed only smart for a man to draw on his own experience, and his was with horses.

More years back than Deke cared to count, he had come into possession of a pretty little mare that had been "rough broke" by a rancher with more rowels on his spurs than he had good sense. While questioning the rancher, Deke learned that in an attempt to cure the mare of spooking when she saw a blanket, he and his men had snubbed her down and flapped one in her face, the result being that she nearly broke her neck rearing, finally snapped the rope, and seriously injured one of the hired hands.

That had been all Deke needed to hear. He saved the mare from being put down by purchasing her, then spent the next five months slowly and gently taming her, *slowly* and *gently* being the key words.

The irony was that, just as the rancher and his men had done, Deke flapped a blanket at the mare, but he started in an adjoining corral where she could see the blanket and get a little nervous, but not feel immediately threatened. After a few days, Deke moved a hair closer, and a few days after that, closer still, until eventually he could flap the blanket right under the mare's nose without spooking her.

Though he knew it would make her mad as blazes if he told her so, Laura reminded Deke a lot of that little mare. From what he had gathered from Laura's ramblings during her delirium, her father and Tristan had given her more than enough reason to fear men and to go a little loco if she felt threatened by one. To Deke's way of thinking, there wasn't a hell of a lot of difference between a snubbed horse being lashed with a quirt and a defenseless woman being laid out by a man's fist. The mare had been locked in a stall and tormented; Laura had been trapped in a nightmarish marriage. At Tristan's hands, Laura had learned to be afraid, and anything that had been taught to her could sure as hell be untaught.

Since it was Deke's feeling that folks and horses reacted to things a lot the same and responded well to similar treatment, he couldn't see the harm in gentling Laura much the same way as he had the frightened mare. Whatever worked— that was his motto. As long as Laura never drew a comparison—which she wouldn't unless she saw him working with horses—she wouldn't realize the insult.

He would have to be constantly on his guard, keep his

mind focused and his temper defused until she began to play out and settle down, which might take days or even weeks.

As Laura saw it, he was the frightening element, and if he meant to confront her fears and prove them groundless, he had to take things slowly and close in on her gradually, blanket flapping with every step.

What she needed right now was some gentle handling. Not too much. Only enough to let her know more was yet to come and that there was nothing to dread. Very gently, Deke framed her face between his hands. At his touch, she jerked and then shuddered. "Easy, darlin'. I ain't about to hurt you."

Her eyes sought his, and her soft mouth quivered as Deke feathered his thumbs along the contours of her cheekbones. He continued the light strokes until he felt some of the tension ease out of her. It was enough, and he released her to drape his arms loosely over his upraised knee.

Striving for just the right pitch to his voice, he said, "I won't ever be heavy-handed with you, Laura. You've got my promise on that."

It was on the tip of Deke's tongue to say more, his aim being to reassure her if he could, but a sound to his left cut him off. He turned on the balls of his feet to see the lodge flap lifting. An instant later, Star peeked inside. Her timing wasn't the best, but it could have been worse. It might do Laura a world of good to see her baby. It couldn't hurt for her to get a taste of the sweetness she might find inside the trap he had sprung around her. It couldn't hurt at all.

He was pleased to note that Star's lovely features were composed and no longer puffy from crying. Giving up the baby now that she had come to love him was no easy thing for her to do. Deke wished he knew of a way to make it easier, but Laura being Laura, he couldn't even promise they'd bring the child back frequently for visits, not that Black Stone, in his present mood, would encourage them to.

Thinking of his brother, Deke looked over Star's shoulder, hoping against hope to see Black Stone behind her. But, no, damn the man's stubborn red hide. He was still sulking and keeping his face hidden from Deke, determined not to relent and accept a white woman into his heart. Eventually he would give in, Deke knew, and probably with a grand gesture, but he would do it in his own sweet time, when he was damned good and ready.

Sugar Girl's pretty little face beamed at Deke over Star's slender shoulder. She waved and grinned, then cast a nervous glance toward Laura, wrinkling her nose. Hostilities being at such a peak between the whites and Cheyenne, Deke could only hope he didn't end up with three females lashing out with their rear hooves inside his mother's lodge.

He nudged Laura. "Look who's here."

Her arms carefully holding a fur-wrapped cradleboard, Star stepped inside. "Me come," she said in English.

Laura's head snapped around and her body went rigid. Smiling at her incredulous expression, Deke moved back to give her a little room. She shot to her knees and held out shaking arms. "My baby! Oh, my baby! Praise God."

Star bobbed her head, blushing with shyness as she came across the lodge. Sugar Girl followed at a safe distance, clearly a little frightened of Laura because she was white and wore such strange-looking clothing. Kneeling on the edge of the furs, Star clung to the cradleboard for a moment before surrendering it.

"Me ain't mother, but got big heart for baby, yep?"

Laura didn't even seem to hear. She snatched the cradleboard from Star's grasp, clutched it to her chest, and started to sob. Star's face fell, and the pain reflected in her big brown eyes nearly broke Deke's heart. She had wanted so badly for Laura to recognize that she had come to love the child and therefore had some claim to him, however slight.

Deke knew Laura didn't mean to be cruel; she was just beside herself. Not that he could blame her. Her baby had been stolen from his cradle, and Laura had suffered through what had probably seemed an endless hell ever since, waiting for this moment.

In a frenzy that was almost frightening, she started tearing at the fur wrapping. Her breath came in animal-like little pants. Her hands shook violently. When at last she got the infant uncovered, a wail erupted from her. Star watched with tears in her eyes as Laura plucked her squirming, kicking child from the confines of the cradleboard, moss trailing, and clamped him to her breasts.

"Oh, God. My Jonathan! It's really you!"

With that, Laura buried her face against sweet infant flesh, began to pitch violently back and forth in a wild parody of rocking, and started to weep. A horrible, chesttearing sound came from her. Deke was afraid she might collapse and unintentionally harm the child, so he rose on his knees behind her to encircle her heaving shoulders with a supporting arm.

Jonathan didn't share in his mother's joy. He screeched and started to wiggle. Laura laughed, albeit a bit hysterically, and brought her head back to feast tear-filled eyes on his red, wrinkled little face. Catching her breath and swallowing a wet sob, she said, "Oh, isn't he the most beautiful baby you've ever seen?"

Truthfully, Deke was used to pretty brown babies with sturdier bodies and thought Jonathan looked sort of pitiful. His tiny face looked like an apple that had shriveled in the sun. Spider veins of a deeper scarlet etched his droopy eyelids and cheeks. His nose was as swollen and red as a town drunk's with funny-looking white spots all over it. His dark hair was thin and stuck straight up in a dull rooster comb over his soft spot. All in all, the best Deke could think of to say was that the baby would probably outgrow it . . . *it* being a sad case of the uglies that no man with eyes could fail to note.

"He's somethin', all right." That much wasn't a lie.

"He's perfect. Just look at him!"

Laura proceeded to do just that, cradling the squalling baby in one arm while she checked him over, counting skinny fingers and toes, touching his mottled skin, cupping his head against her palm and smoothing the shock of hair on top, which promptly sprang back up. Deke thought the poor little guy looked as if he had just gotten the sand scared out of him.

"He's absolutely perfect!" she crooned. "Aren't you, precious boy? Yes, you are."

"I hope he fills out some," Deke said, sincerely concerned now that he was seeing the infant unwrapped. The poor little fellow was made like a frog, all belly, every rib showing, with twig-sized arms and bowed legs. "He's just a shade on the scrawny side, ain't he?"

Accusing amber eyes flashed at Deke.

Instantly realizing his mistake, Deke quickly added, "Of course, he's had a rough haul, ain't he? Poor little thing's been drug from pillar to post. I reckon I'd probably look like I'd been shoved through a small knothole myself. A few more days of feedin' him up should set him right and put some paddin' on his bones."

Now Star and Laura both fixed Deke with accusing gazes. Star proclaimed hotly, "He grow! Big and tall like Flint Eyes."

"He *isn't* scrawny!" Laura cried.

Deke looked up at Sugar Girl, who lifted her hands in a little shrug. She clearly agreed with Deke that the only promising feature the baby had was his noisemaker, which emitted a screech that would put a Cheyenne warrior's battle cry to shame. Deke also read a warning in Sugar Girl's eyes that if they wanted to keep the peace, neither of them should say as much.

Deke was afraid his comments of a few moments ago might have hurt Laura's feelings. He decided this was one time when a white lie was justifiable. "I didn't mean scrawny, exactly," he amended. "Spindly might've been a better word, and hell, he'll outgrow that soon enough. Otherwise, darlin', that is one fine-lookin' boy."

Glancing back up at Sugar Girl, Deke said, "You wanna sit? We got plenty of room here."

He bodily shifted Laura over a hair to provide space. Star followed Laura and the baby as though she were attached to them by invisible string, her hands hovering. When Deke turned back, he found both women still glaring at him. Apparently this was one parley between white and Indian where common ground had been found rather quickly.

Deke's funny bone got tickled at their indignant expressions. "All I said was that he's a little scrawny. I didn't mean nothin' by it. The kid got took from his mama and hauled on horseback for two days, for Christ's sake. He'll fatten up."

Star clucked and shooed Deke away with her hands. Sputtering for a moment because English didn't come easily to her, she finally said, "You shut fuck up, stupid man. Talk bad, you go!" She pointed to the lodge flap. "Go! Me ain't got ears for you."

Laura's whiskey-colored eyes went huge with incredulity at the word Star had used. After a moment, she turned a sparking gaze on Deke. "How could you?"

Deke swallowed. "How could I what?"

She sniffed haughtily. "You taught her that vile word. Don't tell me you didn't."

"I can explain that, though."

"Oh, I'm sure. I'd lie to save face, too, if I were you."

A wise man knew when to retreat. Deke curled a finger under Jonathan's little chin. "Ain't he somethin'? Hey, look, Laura. He's got your dimple. He is without a doubt one handsome boy."

Mollified, she cooed softly and traced loving fingertips over the baby's face. Disturbed from his snooze, Chief lumbered over to see what all the commotion was about. His red, furred jowls hanging in loose folds beneath his bleary eyes, the dog stared with open disgust at the squalling infant. After a moment, he yawned, returned to his napping spot, and flopped back down. Everyone laughed at the canine's woebegone expression.

Star pressed closer to curl a hand over Jonathan's puny chest, taking care not to disturb the shriveled birth cord that protruded from his navel. "He be such pretty baby. Yep."

"You cut that cord a hair short," Deke noted.

Laura and Star both sent him another glare.

"But not that short," he quickly added.

The two women went back to admiring the baby while Deke and Sugar Girl watched.

"He pretty boy."

"He's absolutely perfect. Just look at him."

It went on and on until Deke chuckled. Both women glared at him again. He was starting to feel like he couldn't say shit without getting a mouthful.

"He's hardly lost any weight," Laura gushed. "And here I was so worried!"

Star patted her chest. "Me feed. Baby get fat. Me good mama, yep?"

It finally seemed to dawn on Laura just how much she owed to Star. She stared at the other woman, her eyes filling with tears again. Then she freed a slender arm to hook it around Star's shoulders. "You saved my baby's life. I'll never forget that. Never. Not as long as I live. How shall I ever repay you?"

Star returned the hug, her face aglow. "You, me, be big friends, yep. Me be big friend to baby?"

"Oh, yes," Laura cried. "The best of friends, forever!"

Parting with Jonathan again nearly killed Laura, but she truly wasn't strong enough yet to care for him properly, and according to Deke, his mother warned against her nursing the baby for at least another few days for fear poisons might yet linger in her body. The last thing Laura wanted was to risk making her baby sick.

As she watched Star bundle Jonathan back into the cradleboard, Laura scolded herself for wanting to cry. She was so lucky that someone like Star was caring for her child. Every expression on the pretty little squaw's face conveyed her love for Jonathan, and Laura noted that Star's leather dress had no filthy teeth stitched onto it, only pretty beads. She also looked and smelled clean, her long, shiny black hair neatly bound into plaits, her fingernails short and neatly trimmed, the tips half-mooned with white.

"Hey," Deke said softly as the women left with the baby, "you'll see him again come mornin'. And before you know it, you'll have him with you all the time."

Laura managed a nod. "I know," she said tightly. "It's just difficult."

She felt Deke's hand curl warmly over her shoulder, which jerked her from thoughts of her baby back to contemplating her earlier predicament. He clearly hadn't abandoned his plans to get cozy. A suffocating sensation crawled up her throat as she contemplated what that might mean. If he was bent on asserting his husbandly rights tonight, there was absolutely nothing she could do to stop him, and the ordeal would probably cause her irreparable internal injury.

"Mr. Sheridan?" Her voice came out in a thin squeak that made her want to kick herself.

"Deke," he corrected.

"Deke." Laura glanced over her shoulder to find his silvery gaze was trailing over her hair. Oh, God, what was she going to do? His eyes were as warm as a heated blade, and it didn't take a genius to know what that meant. "I, um, think we need to discuss a few things," she managed to say in a firmer voice.

He lifted his hand from her shoulder to smooth a tendril at her temple with the backs of his knuckles. "Do you, now?"

His voice flowed over her as smoothly as hot honey, so why did it raise gooseflesh on her skin? "I feel I must point out that I recently had a child."

His mouth slanted into a lazy grin. "I'll bear that in mind."

Laura's heart skittered. "Yes, well, as a general rule, women do not engage in . . . in certain, um, intimacies for several weeks after."

"Four, according to my mother," he corrected, "and we've already scratched off one, so you've only got twenty days to go." He was already counting? Laura gulped and, unable to tear her gaze from his, did some quick calculations of her own. A week to regain her strength, two days to reach Denver. That was a total of nine days, which left her an eleven-day grace period in case something went wrong. She relaxed slightly. That gave her plenty of time to get away from this village, where Deke Sheridan's authority over her was absolute. The instant she got her baby safely into Denver, she would extricate herself from this impossible situation.

He trailed his knuckle along the hollow of her cheek. Though her skin shrank from the contact, Laura held herself in check. Until she could get away from this man, she had to play him along. She could do that. He had just agreed to twenty days of abstinence, after all. No harm could come from his touching her face and looking at her.

Except that his gaze was smoldering . . . Laura felt seared by it.

He caught her chin on the edge of his hand. "Honey, I'm not gonna hurt you. Hell, I just spent the better part of a week tryin' to get you mended."

Her pulse slowed slightly. What he said made sense, and she was probably being foolish. It was just—Laura had seen that look in men's eyes before, and it usually boded ill. In addition to that, Deke's eyes gleamed with possessiveness. He truly considered these heathen customs to be binding and felt she belonged to him now. The thought was unsettling, to say the least. Granted, he had treated her kindly thus far, but it was Laura's experience that what went before a marriage seldom followed it. Deke Sheridan had been raised by the Cheyenne, and his attitudes toward white women had most assuredly been molded by them.

Laura tried to moisten her lips, only to find her tongue had gone powder dry. "Then you . . . I can rest assured you have nothing intimate in mind?"

His dark lashes swept low over his eyes. "Nothin' that'll hurt you."

That wasn't what Laura wanted to hear. She wanted a promise that he wouldn't touch her. Not that a man's word could be trusted. "Mr. Sheridan, I scarcely know you."

"Actually, darlin', I was leanin' real heavy toward usin' this next twenty days to get acquainted." His teeth gleamed at her in another slow smile. "You can get that worried look off your face."

"I can?"

He drew his hand from her cheek and sat back against the wall, his shoulders touching the leather at a much higher mark than her own had a little earlier. He patted the expanse of fur in front of him.

"You're lookin' weary, darlin'," he said softly. "Come sit with me and watch the fire for a bit. Since there's no chairs, you can rest against me." His eyes twinkled warmly into hers. "I make a real fine leanin' post."

Laura threw a panicked look at the spot he was indicating she should sit—between his denim-clad legs. Legs that suddenly looked a mile long and thick with muscle at the thigh. She slid her gaze to the empty place beside him. "I, um ... Actually, the lack of chairs doesn't bother me. I'm perfectly comfortable using the wall."

That was a bald-faced lie. Having to sit erect when she felt so weak was exhausting.

"Laura." His voice held a note of indulgent amusement. "I'll make a bargain with you. Try sittin' here for five minutes, and if you hate it, you can move."

A lot could happen in five minutes, and Laura was no fool. "Thank you for offering, but I—"

"Come on," he coaxed in a silky voice. "You got my word I won't go pressin' you for any of them intimacies you're so worried about. This'll be more restful for you." He patted the fur again. "Come on."

When she hesitated, his eyes, still dancing with mischief, settled on hers. "Remember the first night we slept together?"

To her recollection, it had been the first and the last. "Yes, I remember."

"And that little set-to we had?"

"When you behaved like a baboon?"

He nodded. "That there's the time."

"What about it?" she asked, beginning to feel even more nervous.

"Seems to me I made a point that night." The slashes at each corner of his mouth deepened as his mouth settled in another smile. "You recall that point?"

Laura doubted she would ever forget it. "Yes, quite clearly."

"I hate drivin' a point into the ground. Don't you?"

"Meaning I shall sit where you want me to sit, one way or another?" she asked in a voice gone quavery with anger.

"Nope. Meanin' that if I had it in mind to do any of the things you're thinkin' I might, I'd've done started."

Laura swallowed hard. The distance to where he wanted her to sit looked like a hundred miles to her at that moment. If she gave in, he would undoubtedly curl those powerfully roped arms around her. Those same arms could easily subdue her if he wished to touch her where she preferred he not.

Clearly prepared to wait her out, he extended one long leg and dangled a wrist over his upraised knee. Fixing her with that silvery gaze, which always seemed to read far more than she wanted to reveal, he studied her for an endlessly long moment.

"Honey, I know it ain't gonna come easy to you, learnin' to trust me," he said softly. "The way I see it, since it's bound to take a spell, the sooner you set to work on it, the sooner you'll get it licked."

As reluctant as Laura was to comply, she knew she didn't have much choice. There was no mistaking that determined glint in Deke Sheridan's eyes. If she didn't join him on her own steam, he would probably come fetch her.

As she closed the distance between them, Laura recalled Deke's warning not to agree to this marriage unless she was certain of her decision. He had likened it to wading into water over her head. He had been right. She felt as if she were slowly being sucked under as she lowered herself to the furs.

Deke kept his hands resting on his knees as Laura settled herself in front of him. He couldn't help but smile at the care she took to keep a few scant inches between the seam of his jeans and her tailbone, a distance he planned to close as soon as she got her little fanny parked.

When she finally stopped wiggling, he narrowed an eye at her spine. The girl was sitting so straight, she could damned near rule paper. Slowly, so as not to startle her, he slipped an arm around her waist. She jumped as if he had touched her with a hot brand. As he tightened his hold, he heard her breath catch. With a firm pull, he scooted her back on the blanket until her hips pressed against him.

"Go ahead and lean against me, honey."

She allowed her shoulder blades to touch his chest, then jerked erect again as if the touch of him seared her. He pressed his hand against her midriff to draw her closer and bent his head to touch his cheek against her hair. She was shaking, and he knew it wasn't from the cold. "Laura, honey, are you chilly?"

"No," she said faintly.

"What, then?"

"I, um, I'm just feeling a little claustrophobic."

Jesus, that sounded fatal. Deke checked her forehead. She felt cool. "I bite on that bait. What the hell does claus—" He broke off and leaned around to look at her. "I can't even start to tie my tongue around that one. What's it mean?"

"To feel closed in and breathless," she said shakily. "I feel as if I've been stuffed into an envelope and it's made entirely out of hands."

He gave a startled laugh. "Hands? I only got two."

"Yes, I know, but they're rather large."

He took measure of his palm and fingers where they curled over her ribs. He had to admit, there wasn't a lot of woman left for grabs. A suffocating tightness came into his throat. During her illness, she had spent a great deal of time lost in memories and talking out. He knew why closeness like this made her feel as if she couldn't breathe.

Keeping his hands anchored to her ribs, Deke extended his thumbs and wiggled them. "Grab on, darlin'," he whispered huskily.

She glanced down. "Pardon?"

"Grab on to 'em," he repeated. "It's one of the best holds a woman can get on a man. You got it on me that first night, remember? Had my circulation damned near cut off."

She gave a weak laugh. "As if it would do any good."

"As soon as you get some strength back, I'll teach you how to lay a man out if he tries to lay a hand on you."

"You could teach me that?"

Deke chuckled at her dubious expression. "Honey, I could train you up so mean, even I'd be scared of you. And I will. That's a promise. But for tonight"—he wiggled his thumbs at her again—"you gotta settle for cuttin' off my blood flow."

With a hesitance that made his heart catch, she curled her fingers over his thumbs and made tight fists. His entire thumbnail, not to mention the front edge of his knuckle, extended beyond the breadth of her right hand. Seeing that drove home to Deke just how great a physical advantage he had, and how frightened she must feel.

Hunching his shoulders around her, he pressed his jaw against her ear, acutely aware of the silken tendrils of her hair against his skin, so fine and wispy while his was coarse and heavy. He loved the smell of her, which bore traces of the soap he had used to bathe her, but was mainly just female sweetness, a clean, soft smell he couldn't quite name.

"You smell so good, I could spend the whole night just sniffin'."

He turned his lips against the curls at her temple. She was still trembling. Not for the first time, Deke wished Tristan Cheney were still alive so he could shoot the heartless bastard. But wishing didn't make something so. The man was dead, and his legacy to Laura was two years of grief.

Silence, broken only by the snapping of the fire and Chief's snores, settled over them. A thoughtful silence, but not a peaceful one. Deke felt the tension in every line of Laura's body. If his thumbs had been chicken necks, she would have wrung them by now. He smiled against her hair.

"You know what?"

"What?" she asked in a tremulous voice.

"I think it's about time to take another walk. If we don't get it out of the way, you're liable to get droopy-eyed on me." He loosened his arms from around her and gave each of his thumbs a wiggle. "Can you turn me loose, or are we stuck this way?"

She giggled softly, which was compensation enough to Deke for thumbs that had gone to sleep. He moved his hands to his knees and let her scoot to freedom. As she turned to look at him, he detected a bewildered expression in her whiskey-colored eyes. Ah, he had her guessing, did he? At least she was no longer quite so certain she knew what to expect from him.

He sprang to his feet and offered her a hand up. She regarded his outstretched palm for several seconds before she finally crossed it with her slender fingers. Deke hauled her easily to her feet.

"Think you can walk by leaning on my arm, or should I pack you?" he asked.

"Oh, I, um . . ." She wiped her palms on her skirt as if trying to rid herself of his touch. "I think I can manage to walk just fine."

Deke curled a hand over her hip and got a firm grip on her inside elbow. She wasn't weaving as badly now as she had earlier, and he could feel a change in the amount of weight she leaned against him. She wasn't ready to run any footraces yet, but she was strong enough to hash out a couple of fine points about this marriage of theirs that he felt needed to be clarified.

Chapter 17

LAURA MADE HER REPRIEVE IN THE BUSHES last as long as possible. First, she walked at a snail's pace to get there, far more slowly than she truly needed to, and asked Deke to stop more frequently than was actually necessary. Then, once he had delivered her onto the log she had visited earlier and she felt shielded from his gaze by the brush, she took her own sweet time, fussing and fiddling, and just plain dawdling, until she heard him start to pace.

Sitting there alone in the moonlight, she was surprised at the absurd notions that occurred to her. Running away, for instance. Given the sorry condition of her legs and the fact that just walking out here had been difficult enough, she knew she wouldn't get far if she tried such a stunt. Besides, Jonathan was back in the village, and her only way of reclaiming him was to stay and see this through.

Since running away was out of the question, Laura considered feigning illness. For tonight, anyway. But what of tomorrow, and the day after, and the day after that?

It was childish to put off the inevitable. She had agreed to this sham of a marriage, and she would have to accept the consequences until such time as she could get away from the man. That would happen none too soon for Laura. The instant she got her baby safely back to Denver, all Deke Sheridan would see of her was receding dust. She certainly didn't feel obligated to keep promises she had made to him under such deplorable circumstances.

She *wouldn't* surrender herself into another marriage. Once had been nightmare enough. And here, in Colorado? She'd have to be mad. Only a foolish woman counted on some man to take care of her. She either found a way to fend for herself, or she suffered the consequences. In a harsh, cruel land like this, the consequences could be dire indeed.

She was helpless here, utterly helpless, a city woman from the marrow of her bones out. What earthly good was her fluency in French? Who cared if she could walk up and down two flights of stairs while balancing a book on her head? She had to get back to Boston; she simply had to. At least there she could do a halfway commendable job of raising her son into adulthood. Here in this godforsaken place, Jonathan would probably end up dead before his first birthday.

"What're you doin', darlin'? Takin' a snooze?"

Laura leaped at the deep resonance of Deke's voice and pressed a hand to her throat, willing her heart back down into her chest, where it belonged.

"No, just resting for a moment before walking back," she lied.

"You all put back together?"

She checked the buttons on her blouse with quivering fingers. "Yes."

Making no sound to warn of his approach, he emerged out of the gloom into a wash of moonlight. All six feet plus of him. Exhibiting that animal grace she was so quickly coming to resent, he moved slowly forward, his long, denim-covered legs eating up the distance with unnerving ease. Laura stiffened when he straddled the log, sat down, braced his hands in front of him, and leaned toward her.

"A nickel for 'em," he said in a voice pitched to a dangerously low tenor.

"Pardon?"

"I'd offer a penny, but you don't look willin' to sell out cheap. What troublin' thoughts are puttin' all them frown wrinkles on that pretty little forehead of yours?"

"Troubling thoughts?"

In the moonlight, his eyes glittered like chips of ice, and his teeth gleamed blue-white against the dark planes of his harshly cut features. Angled forward as he was, his long hair hung in a shimmery drape over each broad shoulder. "You ever play 'what if' with your troublin' thoughts?"

"No, I can't say as I have. I haven't much time for silly games, least of all when I'm troubled."

"It might be time well spent and save you a peck of heartache, honey."

Laura felt like a fish being maneuvered into a net. "Heartache?"

Those glittering eyes gave her no quarter. "Like say if you was thinkin'—just thinkin' on it, mind you—about runnin' off from me?" He shrugged and finally broke visual contact with her to look at the stars. "It'd be time well spent to play 'what if' before tryin' it. Note I said try, 'cause your chances of succeedin' is slim."

Laura dug her fingernails into the bark of the log. It was very unnerving to have someone introduce one's most guarded thoughts as a topic of conversation. She recalled the times Deke Sheridan had looked into her eyes, the sensation she had had that he read far more than she wished to reveal.

"It's a moot point, isn't it? My baby is here, Mr. Sheridan. Why would I even want to run away?"

"Oh, you wouldn't consider doin' it right now. I meant later." He looked back at her, one winged eyebrow lifted in speculation, his mouth tipped in a smile. "You don't got what it takes to play poker, Laura. Just in case you was thinkin' about lightin' out once you get that baby back," he said evenly, "I think we need to have it understood up front that a Cheyenne man don't take real kindly to his woman runnin' off from him. Fact is, he can get downright ugly about it. I didn't make no bones about my feelin's on this marriage. It's not some temporary measure you can back out of later. I leveled with you about that before you took the leap."

He shifted his weight on the log.

"I don't wanna scare you. That's the last thing I want,

especially right now, with things bein' so hard for you to get used to and all. But you and me, we'd best get us a real clear understandin'."

Laura wanted to avert her face, to break eye contact with him, but she couldn't.

"With me bein' able to track like I can," he went on softly, "you can't rule out what might happen if you try runnin' off and I catch up with you."

"What might happen?" she asked thinly.

"Let's just say I'd be mad enough to hunt cougar with a butter knife, and that's pretty damned mad."

"A-Are you threatening me with physical reprisal, Mr. Sheridan?" Laura jutted her chin. "If so, I shall hasten to inform you that I do not respond well to threats."

He smiled again. "I'll bear it in mind. Meantime, here's another troublin' thought to clutter up that pretty little head of yours. I don't never threaten."

"Oh, really?"

"Nope." He studied her for a moment, then straightened to lift a moccasined foot onto the log and loosely hug his knee. "If I say I'm gonna do somethin', it's a promise you can count on. And I'll flay the hide right off your sassy little butt if you ever try to run from me."

"I beg your pardon?"

"You heard me. There ain't nothin' that'd get me madder quicker, and if you don't believe me, just try it."

He was threatening to take a strap to her backside? Even if he did strip the hide off of her, it was still a punishment one meted out to a child, a humiliating, degrading punishment that an adult should never be subjected to. His saying such a thing was a reflection of his total lack of regard for her, and all her sex.

Rage roiled within Laura, a white-hot, encompassing, overwhelming rage that was born from a sense of utter helplessness. A picture flashed in her mind of Deke Sheridan jerking her out of a stagecoach and bending her over his knee. Knowing him, he would probably add insult to injury and toss up her skirts for good measure. The most awful part was, Laura knew he could probably do it without working up a sweat.

A wise woman would keep her mouth shut. Oh, but knowing it and doing it were two different things. His martial arrogance—that syrupy malevolence—his cocksure attitude that everything would go his way or no way at all. If only she were a man. She'd knock him right off the log.

"Physical violence is no more than I would expect from a man like you," she ground out.

"I'll never be physically violent with you, Laura. Whether you trust in my word or not, you've got it on that."

"Don't make me laugh. You just threatened to flay the hide off my posterior. Or did my ears deceive me?"

"There's a stretch of difference between warmin' your hinder with my strap and knockin' the shit out of you."

Her *hinder*? Laura clenched her teeth and nearly hissed through them. Her *hinder*? She preferred *sassy little butt*. At least that phrase hinted that he saw her as something more than a mindless half-person he now considered to be his property. Next he would pat her on the head. Or maybe check her bite.

"There won't be any *try* to it if I run off," she cried. "Rest assured, if I should ever initiate an escape, and do not take that as an admission that I intend to, it will be well planned. I will also take every precaution to be in the presence of others so my 'sassy little butt' is protected until I am well away from you."

There was a deadly edge to his voice when he replied, "Have a shovel handy, then, 'cause you'll have to bury anybody who makes the mistake of gettin' in my way."

An icy coldness washed over Laura, dousing her anger so quickly, she was rendered speechless. He meant it. Dear God, he truly did.

As if that said it all, Deke returned his attention to the sky again. "Hot damn, but ain't it a pretty night?" All trace of menace was gone from his voice, his tone mellow and almost lazy. "A man could sit out here marvelin' for hours over all them sparkles."

Laura was shaking. Shaking horribly. She wouldn't have to lie now about having a violently upset stomach. What kind of man had she tied up with? A killer. A man whose reputation as a fast gun was almost legend in this territory. Dear Lord, she would never be able to flee. He would come after her—with the same skill at tracking that he had demonstrated while following the comancheros. No matter where she went or who she was with, she would never be free of him, and no one would dare intervene when he found her. "Your eyes sparkle just like them stars do. Did you know that?" he asked gently.

Laura jerked her gaze back to him and saw that he was smiling at her again. Smiling, blast him, as if he hadn't just threatened to peel the hide off her derriére and murder anyone who tried to stop him.

"So pretty. They make me feel the same way them stars do, like I could look at 'em forever." His teeth flashed in a heart-stopping grin. "And maybe get a little loop-legged while I was at it. Yep, them whiskey eyes of yours do pack a powerful wallop."

"After—after saying something so utterly vile, you're trying to woo me, Mr. Sheridan?"

He dropped his foot to the ground, braced his hands on the log between them, and leaned perilously close. "I reckon that is what I'm about. How am I doin'?"

"I can't believe you'd threaten to warm my—my hinder with your strap in one breath, as if I were a child to be punished, and then *dare* to make flowery speeches about my eyes in the next. Do you truly expect a favorable response from me? Am I to gush and fall into your arms?"

"You don't gotta gush."

Laura doubled her hands. Oh, how she longed to smack him sometimes.

"How do you figure me warmin' your fanny a month or two down the road has anything to do with how pretty I think your eyes is tonight?"

"My 'fanny' and my eyes are connected, sirrah."

He chuckled at that. "Now, *there's* a point. And as long as

I can admire them eyes, I reckon your butt'll be where it belongs, too. Don't try runnin' off, and you ain't gonna have a problem with me, Laura. It ain't like I said I'd lay my strap across your backside once a day to keep my lickin' arm in shape, now, is it?"

His *licking arm*? Laura pushed up from the log. "You are, without a single doubt, the most arrogant, brutish boor I have ever had the dubious pleasure of knowing."

With that, she struck off for the village without him, determined to ignore the wobbly, horribly weak feeling in her legs.

"Where you goin'?"

"Leaving you to marvel at the stars by your despicable self."

"The village ain't that way."

Laura spun to an unsteady stop. Finding her way back would be simplicity in itself. She sniffed for the smell of campfires.

"The wind's blowin' wrong," he said with a chuckle.

She was going to murder the man the first chance she got. She truly was. Laura peered through the brush, searching for flickering firelight. Not a glimmer. Then she heard a horse whinny. Hah! He thought he was so smart. She'd show him. With a lift of her skirt, she struck off again.

"Wrong again. Unless you wanna sleep in the horse pasture, of course. I wonder, honey . . . could you find your way out of an upended gunnysack?"

Laura planted her feet and pressed the back of her wrist to her forehead. In a thin, sheerly miserable voice, she said, "You bastard."

He gave a low laugh. "I'll be hornswoggled. Did you say *bastard*? Whew-ee! Talk about a quick learner. Before you know it, sugar, we'll be communicatin' to a fare-thee-well."

He swung his leg over the log and stood up. As he walked toward her, he said, "You gotta get more feelin' into it, though. Cursin' takes a knack and lotsa practice to get it right. If I was you, I'd start off with 'son of a bitch.' Now, there's a dirty name to call me that you can really warm up to.

"It ain't so bad a cussword that a lady couldn't use it, and once you get it down to a gnat's ass, you probably won't need no others. I say it all different ways, and about the time you start thinkin' you got 'em all memorized, I'll probably surprise you with a new one. Like . . ." He frowned slightly. "Say you was just sorta put out with me, you could say it in a plain talkin' voice, like you just did 'bastard.' But when you was a little madder? Oh, hey, the word is a beaut."

Laura stared up at him in speechless amazement. Tristan would have knocked her flat for cursing at him. Deke Sheridan thought it was all a great joke. "I believe I've heard a few of your versions of it, yes."

"Grand, ain't it? You can say it *'son* of a bitch!' or 'son of a *bitch*!' or—when you're so mad you can't see straight—you can really get some satisfaction by draggin' it all out and kickin' things around in between words." His twinkling eyes rested warmly on hers. "Just have a heart and don't kick me."

Perilously close to laughing and wondering if she hadn't taken leave of her senses because she was, Laura looked up at him, a little incredulous at how handsome he was when he grinned like that. She never would have thought it, but Deke Sheridan could, in his own way, literally ooze charm when the mood struck him, and for some reason, she had become a target.

"I think 'son of a bitch' is my favorite cussword even now," he admitted, "and I got me a whole list I use pretty regular-like."

Her pride still stinging from the things he had said earlier, Laura was determined not to be disarmed and strove to keep her face carefully blank. "I'm sure I'll hear all of them sooner or later. If you don't enlighten me, poor Star probably will."

Folding his arms, he said nothing for a long moment. "Me teachin' her that word she said—that was kinda on accident. At the time, I didn't know how filthy a word it was."

Laura also believed in elves and unicorns.

"Truly! You ain't never heard me use it, have you? You gotta understand that in the Cheyenne language, we ain't got bad words folks ain't s'posed to say. So I never thought when I started talkin' English that there was some words I shouldn't oughta learn or teach to my family. Bear in mind, darlin', that I left the Cheyenne and went straight to punchin' cows. The men who taught me English was crude-talkin' cowboys."

He hadn't realized cusswords were bad? A likely story. Not that she blamed him for trying to lie his way out. Teaching Star that horrible word had been absolutely inexcusable.

Laura hugged her waist, pursed her lips, and tried to tap her toe, but her legs were too rubbery to manage it. "Oh, really?" she said sweetly. "Pray tell, Mr. Sheridan, when did you finally become enlightened about the meaning of that word?" Since she seriously doubted he could read, she prodded, "Did someone just up and volunteer the definition one day? Or did you look it up in the dictionary?"

"They got a word like that in the dictionary?"

Now that Laura thought about it, she doubted it. "Well, how did you learn what it meant, then?"

For just an instant, he looked uneasy. Laura watched him, feeling smug, which helped to ease the sting of their last verbal clash, definitely his win. She hoped he got mixed up in his own lies and choked on them. A second later, she had reason to question her vision. If he had felt momentarily uneasy, he certainly recovered quickly.

"Now, *there's* a story," he said, snapping his fingers as his eyes lit up with amusement. "I got my first inklin' of what that word meant at a three-fork supper party."

That was the last thing Laura had expected him to say. "A three what?"

"A three-fork supper party." He graced her with another grin that made her pulse skip and flutter. "You know, one for eatin', one for salad, and one of them itty-bitty, funny-lookin' ones for fishin' around in bowls of red gravy?"

Laura's eyes widened. He had to have seen those tiny forks to be able to tell her about them. "*You* have attended a formal dinner party?"

"Do you think I left the Cheyenne yesterday? It's been fourteen years, darlin'."

Laura was gaping at him again; she couldn't help it. "Please, tell me you didn't say that word at a formal dinner table!"

He chuckled and leveled a finger at her nose. "That's almost *exactly* what my mother-in-law said."

"Your mother-in-law?"

"You sure you wanna hear this story? To tell it right, it gets a little colorful in spots."

Laura was becoming more interested by the second. By this time she had totally forgotten her original reason for asking the question. "Please, Mr. Sheridan, do continue. I'm captivated."

He planted his hands on his hips and took a breath between deep chuckles. "Well, like I said, I was at this three-fork supper party. On top of the fact that I'd never been to one before and found the whole shindig pretty much amazin', I was sittin' next to a great big lady"—he held his hands wide apart—"who was axe-handle-broad across the ass and kept bumpin' my leg with her butt. To make it worse, she was so busty"—he cupped his palms a goodly distance in front of his chest—"that her . . . well, you know them dresses that ain't got no top to speak of? All of us had soup, and it was pipin' hot, and I was real alarmed every time she leaned forward that she was gonna come out of that dress. It ended up I had my eye on her bowl more'n I did my own."

A suffocating sensation rose up the back of Laura's throat.

He put his hands back on his hips. "Anyhow, watchin' her so constant like I was, I couldn't fail to note that she kept fishin' around in that dish of red gravy with her funny-lookin' little fork and bringin' up pink, curly things, which she was eatin' like there wasn't no tomorrow."

"Shrimp?" Laura asked.

He snapped his fingers again. "There you go. Nobody never did get around to tellin' me what they was. That's what started it all, you see, me askin'."

Laura couldn't breathe.

"Anyhow, curiosity plum got the better of me finally, and I said, 'What the'"—he waved a hand to fill in for the missing word—"'is them things?' Well, it went dead quiet. My mother-in-law. she was sittin' to hell and gone down at the end of that long table, but the woman had ears that stretched a mile. And she said"—he raised his voice to a gravelly but feminine-sounding squeak—"'Please tell me you did not say that *filthy* word at my supper table!'"

Almost strangling on swallowed laughter, Laura closed her eyes for an instant. "What happened then?"

He rubbed his nose and sniffed. "Well, I didn't have a clue what filthy word she meant, so I went back over all I'd said, and there was only one word I figured it could be. So I said, real polite-like, 'Fuck, you mean?' And the poor woman fainted."

"Your mother-in-law?" Laura peeped. "Or the fat lady?"

"They was both fat. It was my mother-in-law who fainted, though. Not one of them pretend faints, either, like ladies is so fond of. But a real, flat-out faint. Her head plopped face-down in her soup bowl, and by the time the ruckus was over, she damned near drowned."

Still fighting laughter and losing the battle, Laura clutched Deke's sleeve to stay on her feet. "R-Ruckus? Wh-What kind of ruckus?"

Chuckling himself, he grabbed her arm to hold her up. "It really wasn't funny, you know. There was some real fine-feathered gentlemen there at that table who didn't shine up real good to my language."

"Oh, Deke, wh-what did they do?"

He grinned down at her. "Let's just say it was a night when the red gravy went flyin' and so did I, straight back here to Colorado so's I could ask somebody what the hell 'fuck' meant without gettin' my teeth knocked down my throat."

Laura clamped her free hand over her waist, so weak with the giggles, she could scarcely stand. When her mirth finally began to subside, she moaned. "Oh . . . Mr. Sheridan. What I wouldn't give to turn you loose on my father."

"You don't like him very good, or what?"

That set her to giggling again. "It's just that he's so un-bearably pompous. It would do my heart good to see you upset his applecart—just once."

His silvery gaze cut through the shadows to hold hers. "Send him an invite, darlin', and I'll give it my best shot. I gotta tell you, though. I seem to do my best work when I don't set out to."

Still clinging to his sleeve, Laura inhaled deeply, then slowly exhaled. The fit of laughter had drained what little remaining strength she had.

"Anyhow, now that I explained how I found out what that word means, do you believe I didn't teach it to Black Stone on purpose? It was him who taught it to Star, not me. Not sayin' I ain't to blame, 'cause I taught it to him first."

"Yes," Laura conceded, "I do believe you." With another weak laugh, she added, "No one could make up a story like that. It has to be the truth. I do have one other question, though."

"What's that?"

"You mentioned a mother-in-law. I would presume that means you must have had, and may still have, another wife?"

"God, no. I don't got the energy for two. Delores—that was her name—she sent me dee-vorce papers by pony express."

"When did that occur?"

"Shortly after we come back here to Colorado." His mouth twitched slightly at the corners. "Things wasn't never quite the same between us after I almost drowned her mama in the soup. I think it started to dawn on her that maybe we wasn't what you'd call a matched set."

Laura giggled again, and he grinned.

"She stayed here till the shine wore off—about three weeks, if I recollect it right—then hitched up her fancy skirts and skedaddled back home to San Francisco." He broke off and looked away. "It all happened so long ago, I don't know why I'm talkin' about it."

Before he turned his head, Laura thought she glimpsed shadows in his eyes that hadn't been there a moment earlier. With a sinking sensation, she realized that he had poked fun at himself and made her laugh at his own expense. Those memories still hurt him, deep down inside.

"You met Delores in San Francisco, then? What on earth were you doing there?"

"A cattle-buyin' trip," he replied. "But that's a whole 'nother story."

At a loss for anything else to say, Laura hugged herself against the chill and said, "Well . . ."

He turned his dark head to look at her.

"I really am very weary," she reminded him. "Shall we head back now?"

Apparently Deke Sheridan was nothing if not resilient. A purely mischievous gleam had already replaced the sadness she had glimpsed in his eyes. "You lit out to leave first, honey. So I'll just follow you."

She made an exasperated sound. "You know very well I don't know which way to go."

"Why?"

The thought of kicking him was becoming more tempting by the moment. "Please, Mr. Sheridan, I truly am feeling unaccountably weary. I obviously wasn't paying attention when we walked out here, and it happens to be dark. Aren't those reasons enough?"

"Nope to the last, and as for the first, honey, figurin' out where you are and where you're goin' ain't exactly taxin'." He jabbed a thumb upward. "Get a fix on the sky."

Laura looked up. "I've got a fix," she said, biting back another smile. The man was absolutely impossible. By all rights, she should be furious with him, but somehow he had niggled his way right through her anger. "I suppose you're going to show me how to get my bearings by the moon?"

"The moon? Christ Almighty, darlin', if that's how you try to find your way at night, no wonder you can't find your ass with both hands. What if there ain't a moon? Or what if it came up in the afternoon instead of evenin', and it's sittin' straight overhead or in the west instead of the east?"

"I knew the darned thing wasn't reliable."

He chuckled. "You truly don't know nothin', do you?"

"I know when I'm lost."

"Which is all the time. Find me the North Star."

With her legs still so trembly, Laura had difficulty keeping her balance as she leaned her head back to gaze up at the sky. As he had commented earlier, there were a lot of stars twinkling above them, all of them brilliant. "The North Star is one of the brightest, isn't it?"

"Jesus," he said under his breath.

"Just give me a minute. I'll find it. You can't expect me to locate it as quickly as you. I'm not in practice. And I'll remind you I've been ill. It's taking most of my concentration just to stand up."

He stepped behind her and encircled her waist, taking care to leave her arms free. "Lean against me and let me do the standin' while you do the lookin'."

Preoccupied with her star search, Laura forgot how intimidating she usually found him. In that moment of forgetfulness, she relaxed against him, and as she did, a wonderful warmth flowed over her. The support of his lean body made her feel secure and safe. She knew he had enough strength in that arm to hold her erect even if her knees did fold. He bent to press his cheek against her temple and follow her gaze.

"Darlin', you ain't goin' about this right at all," he whispered huskily. "Let's start at the beginnin', okay? First, find your zenith."

"My zenith? You know a word like *zenith*?"

"Stop tryin' to nettle me and pay attention. Do you even know what the zenith is?"

"The highest point? How can I find that in the sky? It all looks the same height to me."

His chest jerked on a low laugh. "The zenith is the patch of sky right above that pretty little head of yours."

At least he hadn't said *empty*. "My head is not little."

"Average size, then. You got a fix on the sky right above us? Good. Now, goin' out from there and turnin' a slow circle"—he slowly began a revolution, still supporting her weight—"find me *Match-squa-thi' Muga*, the Little Bear."

"The little *what*?"

"The little cup, I think you folks call it."

"You mean the Little Dipper?"

"There you go, the Little Dipper."

Laura pointed triumphantly. "Fooled you. I bet you thought I wouldn't find it."

"I don't think you're blind, darlin', just . . . Never mind. Now, follow the little bugger's tail."

"You were going to say 'ignorant,' weren't you?"

"Nah. Are you followin' the Little Bear's tail?"

"Where shall I follow it to?"

"That bright star at the tip."

"Got it."

"That is the North Star, and it always sits atwixt your zenith and the northern horizon. It's about as straight north as north can get."

"You know a word like *horizon*? I'm amazed."

"If you keep on, I'm gonna paddle your fanny yet." He tightened his hold on her waist to turn her again. "Okay—say there's a cloud over the Little Bear."

"I knew there had to be a hitch."

His chest shook again. "In case you can't see it, you can always look for the Big Bear and use its pointin' stars to find the North Star." He helped her locate the formation and explained which stars pointed north. "Now you got two ways to find the North Star, right?"

"What if both are covered by a cloud?"

"Sit your fanny down until the cloud moves."

"What if I'm trying to run off from you, you're hot on my trail, and I can't afford to sit there waiting?"

"You'll be up the crick without no paddle, that's what."

Laura smiled, enjoying the warmth of him all around her and the ticklish feeling of his breath in her hair. She was losing her mind—that had to be it.

"So . . ." he murmured in a silky voice. "If you're facin' the North Star, which way's north?"

"I am not stupid, Mr. Sheridan. If the star lies to the north, that is north. So whoop-dee-doo. I still don't know where the village is."

"It's southwest. So get your bearin's and point me the right way. Get it on the first try, and I'll carry you back."

Laura closed her eyes. At his impatient grunt, she waved a hand. "Do hush. I've almost got it. Let me see. On a map, west would be—"

"Hold it, hold it, *hold* it!" he interrupted. "Damn if I don't wish Tristan Cheney was here so I could shoot the bastard. Didn't he teach you nothin'? I can see your daddy neglectin' the chore, you livin' in Boston and all. But that husband of yours. What was he thinkin' of, bringin' you into this country and not seein' to it you could find your way around?"

Laura had no answer to that.

Deke took a calming breath. "Okay. Forget tryin' to remember maps and which way everything lays every time you gotta go someplace. At night, alls you need to remind you of your directions is the North Star and your body."

"My body?"

"You're facin' the North Star, so which way are them pretty little breasts of yours pointin'?"

She sputtered and opened her eyes. "Mr. Sheridan!"

"They do point straight ahead."

"You could have said my nose."

"Knowin' you, you'd be ganderin' off at somethin' and follow it. I don't have to worry about you forgettin' where your breasts are. I ain't never seen anybody guard nothin' so close in all my life."

"My *nose* is pointing north," she said with a sniff.

"And that soft little butt?"

She really was going to kick him—the instant he turned her loose. "South," she ground out.

"And your right arm, hangin' down straight to your side?"

"East."

"So which way is southwest, goin' midway atwixt your fanny and left arm?"

Laura pointed the way. Deke chuckled and swept her off her feet. "Now ain't that somethin'?"

"Except that you were here to tell me we needed to go southwest."

"Yeah, well, we'll work on it." He turned suddenly, totally disorienting her. "Now, where is the North Star?"

Laura quickly located her zenith, found the Little Dipper, and pointed.

"And which way's southwest?"

She indicated the way.

"Damn. If I wasn't seein' it with my own eyes, I wouldn't believe it. Boston, you know your directions, with no *ish* stuck on the end."

"I suppose you think I'm incredibly stupid."

He set out walking, carrying her with an ease that was somewhat unsettling. "Not a bit. There's a stretch of difference between bein' stupid and just never bein' taught, honey. Take me, for instance. There's all kinds of things you know that I don't. So many that I bet I could spend the next year just askin' you questions. That don't make me feel stupid, just ignorant."

Still miffed at her own ineptness and convinced that Deke was far more knowledgeable about things that were really useful, at least in this treacherous country, she rolled her eyes and said, "Off the top of your head, name me just one question you're really dying to ask me. And no fair making something up to make me feel better."

"Promise not to laugh?"

"Of course I won't."

"What the hell is a baboon?"

Laura giggled until tears streamed from her eyes.

Chapter 18

LAURA'S LAUGHTER DIED A QUICK DEATH when Deke reached the edge of the village. By the time he shouldered aside the flap to his mother's lodge, she had become downright gloomy. The moment she had been dreading had arrived.

Deke carried her to the bed of furs and gently lowered her onto them. Then he knelt beside her. In the dying firelight, he looked very tall, very dark, and extremely dangerous, not at all the sort of man who would consider giving a woman a reprieve on her wedding night. Laura supposed she should be grateful he was willing to wait to accomplish the full deed until she was recovered from having the baby.

Even so, she had to try. "Mr. Sheridan—"

"Deke."

"Deke." She licked her lips. "I—would you consider—"

"Whatever it is you mean to ask, nope." Bracing one hand on the fur, he leaned over her, the tooth medallion dangling to trail lightly over her right breast. Laura's breath snagged at the riot of sheer sensation that shot through her at the contact. A satisfied glimmer shone in his eyes as he shifted slightly to make another pass. "Know why?"

"Because you're a baboon?"

He chuckled at that and smoothed a tendril of hair from her cheek. "Maybe that, too. But mostly because you gotta learn, sooner or later, that I ain't Tristan Cheney. Tonight is as good a time as any to start. I don't reckon you'll learn much about what kinda man I am if I'm snubbed down by promises."

"You don't even know what I was going to ask."

"Don't need to. Whatever it was, it's got you worried. That's just the way I want you."

"Oh, well, thank you very much. Please, do enjoy my torment."

He chucked her under the chin. "Unless you think the worst of me, darlin', how can I prove you wrong?"

"Wrong? What do you mean?"

"If I told you that, this whole blanket-flappin' lesson would be wasted."

"Blanket what?"

"Never mind."

"In other words, you don't intend to do anything, but you want me to believe you might until the last second so I'll see what a fine fellow you actually are?"

"Now, see there, Boston? You ain't so dumb after all."

"Truly?" she whispered. "You don't intend to do anything?"

He made no reply, simply lowered his hand from her chin to the top button of her blouse.

"What are you doing?"

"As I recollect, you call it two things, undressin' you or removin' your clothing. Take your pick."

"But if you—" Laura grabbed for the buttons he hadn't yet reached. "Why are you removing my clothing if you don't intend to do anything?"

"Did I say that?"

"Yes."

"I didn't. I said I wasn't makin' no promises." He brushed her fingers aside to attack another button. "You was the one who—" He shoved at her fingers again. "I thought I was the one with too many hands?"

Laura felt herself losing the battle as button after button fell away under his fingertips. "Isn't this your mother's lodge?"

"Yep. But not to worry. She's seen lots of undressed

women. Besides, she's stayin' with her sister to give us privacy."

"The *last* thing I want is privacy."

"You want me to holler for company? There's a hundred and fifty people out there. Probably a fair half would come."

That was so preposterous, Laura ignored it. "I—I was thinking of sleeping in my clothes," she put in quickly. "In case I need to take a walk in the middle of the night."

The button midway down her blouse gave way beneath his fingers. "I'll throw a fur around you."

"I could take a chill."

Two more buttons popped free. "I'll make sure that don't happen."

Laura felt her blouse fall open to the waist and closed her eyes. His hand went to the waistband of her skirt, and that, too, fell free. Catching her at the bend of each knee, he drew up her legs to unlace her shoes, then peeled her bloomers, garters, and hose off of her. Her shoes made muffled plops on the dirt as he tossed them away. Next he tugged on her skirt and petticoats. Before Laura could open her eyes and protest, off those came, too.

"Sit up, darlin'." To assist her, he slid a hand under her shoulder blades. "There's a girl."

Laura doubled her hands into tight fists to keep herself from clinging to her blouse. Resistance from her had always made Tristan turn mean, and she had learned the hard way that trying to salvage a bit of her pride at times like this wasn't worth what it had always ended up costing her later in soreness and bruises.

With an incredibly light touch, Deke slid the muslin sleeves down her arms and tugged them off over her hands. A little cry of protest caught in her throat, and she swallowed it down.

"Easy," he whispered. "I ain't gonna hurt you, honey. I swear it."

In Laura's experience, men could forget promises as quickly as they changed moods. Her breath caught when he framed her face between his hands and carefully tipped her back onto the furs. Laura was aware of him in every pore of her skin—of his size, his heat, even that earthen blend of scents that always teased her nostrils when he was near. For hands that were as thick and hard as boards, his rested as lightly against her skin as moth wings. His fingertips feathered lightly over her hair. He bent to touch warm, satiny lips to her forehead. Then he carefully kissed her eyes closed.

Holding her arms rigidly at her sides, Laura waited, fully expecting him to attack the laces on her chemise as he lay down beside her. His chest, bared by his open shirt, pressed hotly against her upper arm, and she felt the coarse, curly triangle of hair on his flat belly tickling the side of her forearm. She didn't move because she was afraid to, didn't speak because she knew pleading was useless, and didn't open her eyes because she was terrified of what she might read in his.

He settled a hand on her tummy, and she gulped. With one upward tug on her chemise, he could strip her bare from the waist down, making her vulnerable to him as no woman ever wants to be with a man she doesn't know well enough to trust. A big man. A man with reserves of strength she probably couldn't imagine.

Laura clenched her teeth, trying not to remember those times when Tristan had come to her, angry, determined to punish her, to make her pay. Nearly a half million dollars, he had always whispered. That was how much she had cheated him of, and he meant to take every cent of it out of her hide. Laura had always felt that her debt to him was paid in full on their wedding night.

Tugging a layer of fur aside, Deke covered them both. As he settled back, he fixed his gaze on Laura's profile. In the feeble firelight, he could see her pulse beat in her throat, see the sheen of cold sweat on her forehead, feel the vibrations of her small body through the fur beneath him.

"G'night, Laura," he whispered, and then tweaked the tip of her small nose.

He watched the expressions that flitted across her face. first stunned amazement, then disbelief, then relief. Be-

neath his hand, he felt the muscles in her belly knot and
then spasm. Her breath caught on a sob that never erupted.
With an audible swallow, she opened her eyes, sought his
gaze, and whispered, "Good night."

Laura awoke the next morning to find herself alone in the
bed of furs. She blinked, momentarily uncertain where she
was. Then her vision cleared and her surroundings came into
focus. Relieved to see only Chief inside the lodge with her,
and he asleep, she sat up and scrambled for her clothes.

No sooner had she finished dressing than the lodge flap
opened. Adjusting her cuffs, Laura turned, fully expecting
to see Deke. The dark masculine face and obsidian black
eyes that stared back at her nearly made her heart stop
beating. She retreated a step as the Cheyenne warrior entered.

He was tall, nearly as tall as Deke, and every bit as broad
at the shoulder. The fact that he was fully dressed in a buckskin shirt and pants did little to ease her mind. The man was
obviously a murderous savage, through and through. He
moved toward her with a pantherlike grace, his long, ebony
hair shifting like silk around his shoulders.

When he came within three feet of her, he raised his
arms as if to address the heavens and said in a booming
voice, "This woman my sister! I have said it!"

Surprised that he knew English, Laura took a moment to
assimilate the meaning of what he had said. "Excuse me?"

Lowering his open arms, he bent slightly at the knees
and came toward her, his posture indicating that he intended to grab her around her hips and pick her up. Laura
inched away from him. "Shoo! You go away! Mr. Sheridan!
Chief!"

The dog raised his head, fixed a disinterested gaze on the
warrior, and yawned.

"Deke!" Laura screamed. "Help me!"

The warrior kept coming. Laura screeched again when
he snaked an arm around her thighs. The next thing she
knew, she was suspended head down over his shoulder, her

posterior pointing skyward. She pummeled his back with her fists.

"Put me down! Oh, my God!"

Across the lodge and out the door he went, Laura bouncing atop his well-muscled shoulder with his every step.

"Mr. Sheridan!" she shrieked. "Mr. Sheridan!"

In her peripheral vision, Laura saw all manner of legs gathering around and following them. Short legs, thin legs, fat legs, long legs, some naked, some covered with buckskin. The man yelled, *"Equiwa neeshematha! Was he kee, she, ke!"*

Voices rose in response, jabbering words she couldn't understand. There was some laughter and a few catcalls. Then, to her vast relief, Laura heard a deep baritone she felt certain belonged to Deke. She couldn't understand a word he said, but he sounded furious. The warrior who carried her yelled the same words he had before and just kept walking. *"Equiwa neeshematha! Was he kee, she, ke!"*

Deke's voice called after them, this time in English, "Laura, it's all right, honey! He won't hurt you."

Twisting at the waist to look frantically around, she tried to find Deke in the crowd of swarming bodies. She couldn't see him. "You make him turn loose of me this *instant*!" she cried. "You brought me here, blast you! It's your duty"— *umph* went her lungs—"to protect me!"

Suddenly the warrior stopped walking and spun about, the motion setting Laura's stomach into a similar revolution. He yelled more gibberish, spun about again, and ducked inside a lodge door. As he bent to set Laura on her feet, he said, "Star, come! Make welcome your sister-in-law."

Staggering to get her balance, her head swimming with dizziness, Laura blinked. Before her vision cleared, the warrior ducked back outside.

"Welcome!" a female voice called out.

Laura turned dumbly to see Star coming toward her, arms spread wide to hug her. While suffering her affectionate embrace, Laura cried, "Who is that awful man?"

Star giggled. "Ah, he Black Stone, you brother, me husband."

"My what? He isn't my brother!"

"He say, and it so."

Star seemed to think this was delightful news indeed. She moved quickly around Laura, patting her arms, squeezing her hands, clearly so excited, she could scarcely contain herself.

"Me be sister-in-law, yep?" She grabbed Laura's hand and led her to a pallet of furs. "Me baby, you baby?" She dropped to her knees by the cradleboard and spread her arms. "We be big happy, yep?"

One look at the cradleboard, and Laura forgot about everything else, including how she had come to be there. Her baby. She sank onto the furs beside Star, gathered her son into her arms, and cried, "Oh, yes, we be big happy."

Arms folded, legs spread, Deke gazed out across the meadow full of milling horses. "*Newabetueke*, forty," he said angrily in Cheyenne.

"*Negotewashe*, sixty, no less," Black Stone shot back. "I will not have my beautiful sister ashamed."

Because there were no swear words in the Cheyenne language, Deke cursed under his breath in English, still scarcely able to believe his brother had pulled such a rotten trick. True, Black Stone had finally relented to accept Laura, and with a grand gesture, just as Deke had suspected he would, but to adopt her and demand Deke marry her according to Cheyenne custom? He was pushing Deke's temper to the very limit.

"A few days ago, my woman was dirt under your feet. Now you start out asking for a hundred head of cattle as a bride price, and you won't come down below sixty?"

"I do not remember the man who said those terrible things about your woman," Black Stone said solemnly. "That man turned my brother's face from me, and I scorn him."

"I am pleased your heart has made room for my woman," Deke replied, striving for patience. "It makes this day one of great gladness for me. But why this game, claiming her as your sister and demanding a bride price? And one so great? Sixty head of prime beef is beyond any woman's worth."

"I would' let my sister go into marriage with nothing? Never."

"I'll go fifty," Deke relented. "But no more than that, Black Stone. It's been a bad year."

Black Stone shrugged. "Plenty of warriors will honor her with better offers."

Beside himself, Deke began mixing cusswords with his Cheyenne, Cheyenne with his English, the blend such a confused mess that even he lost track. "You connivin' son of a bitch! I can't believe you've done this. You know damned well I can give her everything she needs. The only reason you've pulled this is to get revenge against me for turning my back on you the other day."

Black Stone's eyes warmed with laughter, but his expression remained stoic. "My sister will be properly married, and the suitor I accept will honor her with many gifts. If you do not wish to offer sixty cows, I will soon have many offers from others. Perhaps as much as a hundred horses for a woman so beautiful as she. Whiskey hair is very rare in Cheyenne women."

"Accept another offer, Black Stone, and blood will flow. She's *my* woman. I've already taken her to wife, and this stunt you've pulled goes against all tradition, even if she is your sister."

With a lift of his hands, Black Stone shrugged. "You will marry her the Cheyenne way?"

"I don't mind that. But sixty cows? That's a very high price."

"She is a special woman, and she is sister to Black Stone, chief of the horse soldiers. I value her greatly. I will not accept an offer from a stingy man who does not appreciate her."

"I'm in the middle of roundups right now. I may not be able to gather sixty head right away."

"I will give gifts to accompany my sister into marriage in exchange for talking paper. This autumn, all my male relatives and 1 will come to your grazing land with the talking paper to make our choices from your herd."

Deke laughed in spite of himself. Finally relenting, he clapped a hand on his brother's shoulder. "All right, you miserable ass. We have a bargain."

Black Stone smiled. "You will bring the talking paper to my lodge soon?"

Deke pretended to consider that. "Maybe, maybe not. Perhaps I should let you keep your beloved sister at your lodge for a few days. That way, I won't have to hunt to feed her."

At that, Black Stone threw back his head and barked with laughter. "Careful, my brother. Wait too long, and you may find I have accepted the offer of another. Sugar Girl already eats more than I can supply."

Feeling well rested after a long nap, Laura sat in the rear of Black Stone's lodge, cradling her son in her arms. Star and Sugar Girl sat on the furs on each side of her, their graceful hands engaged in the tedious task of stringing tiny beads. It was late afternoon, and the interior of the lodge was filled with golden luminescence from the sun that beat against its west wall.

Filtered sunshine. Laura smiled to herself, perfectly content to remain where she was and pretend Deke Sheridan didn't exist. Except for those times when Star took Jonathan to feed him, Laura was able to hold him, and she couldn't get enough of it. Her baby. There had been times over this last week when she had feared for his life. To have him in her arms, alive and well, filled her with a peace and joy like none she could recall.

The lodge was wonderfully homey. Now that Laura had grown accustomed to it, she thought the arrangement was even more practical than that of a house, compact and simple; every need had been addressed. Even the walls could be rolled up to allow a breeze to flow through. At the moment, they were battened down because it had rained for about an hour, a daily event in the mountains, according to Star. But the squaw had had the flaps up earlier.

In the center of the lodge a small fire crackled gaily, supplemental to a larger fire pit just outside the door where Star did most of her cooking. Black Stone's weapons and shield were kept neatly on a tripod along one wall, as was the paraphernalia needed to operate a household. The small family's clothing was hung on suspended rods or stowed away in leather cases.

Sugar Girl, *Melassa Squithetha* in Cheyenne, who sat on Laura's left, set aside her beadwork to lean close and admire the baby. Over the course of the day, Laura had become better acquainted with both young women, and she liked each immensely, but she sensed there was something special about Sugar Girl. A purity and sweetness, maybe? Laura couldn't pinpoint exactly what it was, but the shy, soft-spoken young woman brought out all her protective instincts. Because Sugar Girl clearly doted on Jonathan and yearned for a baby of her own, Laura couldn't resist asking, "You have no husband, Sugar Girl?"

Toying nervously with the beaded binding on one silken braid, the other young woman blushed and bent her head. "Big years behind me, one almost husband."

Laura deciphered that to mean that several years ago, Sugar Girl had nearly married someone. Since Laura couldn't imagine what might induce a man to call off his wedding to a girl so lovely, her curiosity was stirred. Given the hostilities between whites and Indians, she guessed that a brave's life span might not be very long. "Did your young man die?"

Star, who sat at Laura's right, lowered her beadwork to her lap, her large brown eyes filled with sudden anxiety. She glanced sadly at Sugar Girl, then cupped a hand over her mouth and said in a stage whisper, "Sugar Girl no like almost husband. He terrible mean man to sister, yes? Sugar Girl afraid, no go."

The story struck close to home for Laura. Very close to home. Yet here sat Sugar Girl, unmarried? How on earth had she managed that? That blasted Deke Sheridan! Apparently he had omitted a few very important details about Cheyenne customs.

"What did Sugar Girl do?" Laura asked softly.

Some of the color drained from Star's pretty face. "He make sister free woman. Sugar Girl big afraid, she say no go with him for be wife. Man get big, big angry. Make Sugar Girl free woman, too."

"A free woman?" Oh, Laura would have given her eye-teeth. That man! That impossible man. Why hadn't he told her about this?

"We no say words big years behind us. Make big unhappy." Star placed a hand over her heart. "Big unhappy bad thing, yep? Sugar Girl cry."

"Yes," Laura agreed. Touching Sugar Girl's hand, she softly said, "I'm sorry, Sugar Girl. I didn't mean to say words that would make you sad." With a comforting pat, Laura added conspiratorially, "At least you are a free woman now! Not with that terrible mean man. That should make you very glad."

Sugar Girl gave Laura a horrified look and began to shake her head. "Free woman, bad, bad, bad. Never glad." She gestured with her hands. "No husband want. Free woman big years behind me, free woman big years tomorrow. No babies for Sugar Girl. Never glad. Nope."

Laura could see the girl was becoming very distressed. Evidently, once a free woman, always a free woman, and a girl was no longer eligible for marriage. While that status sounded heavenly to Laura, Sugar Girl and Star clearly didn't share the sentiment.

"Almost husband pass Sugar Girl on prairie, yep?" Star whispered. "Not too good for him no more. Free woman! Spit upon like dirt."

Laura wondered whether there was anything she might do that would make Deke so angry he would pass her by on the prairie, spit upon her, and thereby make a free woman of her. Then she felt bad for making light of something Sugar Girl found so distressing. She looped an arm around the girl's shoulders and gave her a hug. "You're lovely, Sugar Girl. A husband will want you soon. You'll see. And you'll have lots of babies."

Tears swam in the girl's eyes and she shook her head. "Nope. Free woman, no husband want. Never no babies for Sugar Girl."

Laura frowned slightly. Her thoughts drifted to Deke Sheridan and their conversations about marriage. As reluctant as she was to pursue this subject for Sugar Girl's sake, it was far too important to Laura's own future to let it completely drop. "Can anyone be made a free woman?" she asked very gently.

Star blanched and nodded. "Me, you, yep. Husband, almost—husband—he be big mad?" She whooshed air past her lips and threw up her hands. "Make free woman, me, you, anyone, yep."

She looked decidedly apprehensive at the thought. Laura could understand that. After all, the women in this village were completely dependent upon men, even for the food that went into their mouths. To be considered unmarriageable could prove disastrous under these conditions. For Laura, though . . . Her thoughts turned to Boston and the lifestyle that would be available to her as a respected widow and heiress to her father's fortune. The world, as Tristan had once been fond of saying, could be her oyster. Yes, this free-woman business was definitely something Laura meant to investigate.

For the moment, however, Star looked nervous, and Sugar Girl distraught. Hoping to change the subject, Laura curled Jonathan's fingers over one of hers to test his grip. "Just look how strong he is!"

Star giggled. "Nah! Scrawny baby. Little, skinny, sick look, like him stupid father."

Laura burst out laughing, Sugar Girl giggled, and the moment of tension was forgotten.

Chapter 19

WHEN BLACK STONE RETURNED TO HIS LODGE, he didn't speak to Laura or Sugar Girl, nor glance in their direction. Sitting cross-legged at the fire, he leaned forward to stare into the flames. Sugar Girl seemed to take his disregard in stride, but Laura wondered if perhaps she had become invisible.

Not that she was about to complain or try to draw his attention. He was a fierce-looking man with glittering black eyes, chiseled features, and a cruel, humorless mouth. Laura could easily picture him marauding and murdering, and the image made her blood run cold.

Star hurried to prepare the man supper, chattering gaily at him while she mixed and stirred a potful of stew over the low flames in the fire pit. Since Star spoke in Cheyenne, Laura had no idea what she was saying, but when she occasionally laughed, Black Stone's stern expression didn't soften and he seldom looked at her while she talked. All in all, Laura didn't see how the poor girl stood him.

A few minutes after Black Stone had returned to the lodge, a plump little boy of about three came bursting inside. He was dusty and red-cheeked from exertion, his eyes dancing with mischief, his shoulder-length black hair in a stir. He made a beeline for Black Stone and leaped onto the man's crossed legs, jabbering and gesturing with his hands, giggling to punctuate whatever it was he was saying.

"Me baby," Star said proudly, thumping her chest. "He name *Oshasqua*, Muskrat."

Laura fell instantly in love. With those fat, dimpled cheeks, he was the cutest little fellow she had ever seen. His great, shoe-button eyes followed his mother about the lodge. Then he assumed a woebegone expression, asked his father something, and touched his dirty little belly.

"Mah-tah'!" Black Stone growled, and gave a shake of his head, which clued Laura that *mah-tah'* meant no. He said something more, ruffled the little boy's hair, and finished with, *"Oshasqua, psai-wi' skillewaythetha!"*

Star seconded that statement, then, for Laura's benefit, translated. "Muskrat big boy, yes? No baby." She shook her head and smiled.

Muskrat's face puckered, and an instant later, huge tears were making rivulets of mud on his face. He rubbed with a plump fist to make things worse, wailed, and clutched his tummy as though he were in great pain. Black Stone gave him a slight shake. Muskrat cried harder.

Pushing to his feet with the little boy hooked under one arm, the warrior strode to a basket, fished about, and produced an apple, which he moved about under Muskrat's snubbed nose. *"Meshemenake,* eh?"

Muskrat pushed the fruit away. Black Stone glanced at Star, who was happily oblivious to the commotion. He spoke softly to her. She held up a staying hand, shook her head, and said, *"Mah-tah'."*

Muskrat, clearly a great loss to the stage, ceased his screeching for a moment to monitor the exchange between his parents. Fixing his father with tear-filled eyes, he gulped and asked something in a pleading, quavering voice. Black Stone's mouth twitched. Then he shot a measuring glance at his young wife's slender backside where she was bent at the fire. He whispered something to Muskrat, set the child carefully down, and then advanced on Star. She squealed when he pounced and caught her around the waist.

"Mah-tah'!" she cried.

Black Stone growled again, sounding very like an enraged bear. Laura shrank against the leather wall, frightened for Star. Sugar Girl giggled. And Muskrat danced excitedly around, one pudgy hand clamped over his loincloth, as he watched his father sit cross-legged near the fire with Star on his lap.

Star laughed and gave up the battle. Situating herself more comfortably in the cradle of Black Stone's thighs, she opened her arms to Muskrat. The little boy galloped over to her, jumped in her lap, and eagerly began nuzzling as Star unfastened her bodice. Black Stone enfolded both his wife and child in his arms, rested his chin on Star's shoulder, and watched with an indulgent smile as Muskrat settled in for a snack.

Laura was appalled and horribly embarrassed. A child that age? Did they have no sense of decency? Yet for all her judgments, Laura couldn't look away. While Muskrat nursed, both his parents stroked him, every touch of their hands on his chubby little body bespeaking a love that could never be expressed with words.

Watching them made Laura ache inside. She finally bent her head and hugged Jonathan more closely to her, wishing with all her heart that he could have what she had missed and Muskrat took for granted, a father who cared, even about small things, about his child's need to be held close by his mother at the end of a long day, about his hunger, which could never be appeased with an apple or the warmth of his father's arms. Muskrat was far too old to actually need his mother's milk, yet Black Stone understood his son's longing went beyond the physical and saw to it that he had his moment, which Laura was just beginning to realize had been stolen from him by Jonathan's intrusion into their family circle.

Black Stone nuzzled Star's neck and whispered something close to her ear that made her smile and close her eyes. He grinned and tweaked his son's little nose. Muskrat, who obviously wasn't all that hungry, chortled and abandoned his mother's breast to nip at his father's knuckles. Black Stone growled again and began to tickle him. Soon

Muskrat was screeching and flailing, his original reason for seeking Star's lap completely forgotten. Star refastened her dress and joined in the play. Then the three of them settled down for a few moments of quiet, wherein Muskrat's real need, that of physical closeness, was addressed and satisfied.

When Star wiggled free to return to her cooking, Black Stone kept Muskrat on his lap, stroking the child's hair, wiping at the muddy streaks on his chubby face, and whispering to him. Muskrat drifted to sleep, content and smiling.

Laura smiled as well. There was no doubt. Black Stone was a murderous sort, savage through and through.

Deke, apparently invited by Black Stone, showed up for supper, Chief trailing along behind with the ever-present bone clamped between his teeth. As his host had done earlier, Deke sat cross-legged at the fire upon entering the lodge and, after nodding to Laura, virtually ignored her and the other two women present. At mealtime, Star and Sugar Girl served both the men, the child, and the dog large metal bowls of stew accompanied by chunks of bread, after which they dished food for Laura and themselves. The males ate by the fire, the women on the fur pallet, a segregation that suited Laura just fine.

After the meal, Star took Jonathan from Laura to feed him. The instant Laura's arms were empty, Black Stone looked over and said, "Sister, come here."

Laura couldn't miss the twinkle of laughter in Deke's eyes. Well, she had news for him. She was no longer intimidated by Black Stone and wasn't the least frightened by the clipped order. The man might seem as hard as nails at first, but one soon saw what a pussycat he was. A better and more loving father than her own, by far, and a gentle husband. Laura would bet that Black Stone had never threatened to flay the hide off Star's fanny.

Her legs still a bit unsteady from her recent illness, Laura pushed up from the furs and approached the fire. Black Stone motioned for her to sit, which she managed, although with a bit less grace than Star or Sugar Girl because of weakness and the confines of her skirts. But sit, she did, as an Indian might, ankles crossed, her knees bent and raised to support her arms.

"This lazy man wants you for wife," Black Stone informed Laura, his expression not betraying even by so much as a twitch that he might be teasing. "I be good brother, ask you. Does he got favor in your eyes?"

Laura glanced at Deke, completely baffled by this turn of events. The way she had understood it, she and the man were already married. "Black Stone, are you implying that Mr. Sheridan is not yet my husband?" At the note of hope in her voice, Deke's gaze sharpened on hers. "Well? You can't blame me for asking." She looked back at her newly acquired brother. "Am I to understand that you don't consider us to be married, Black Stone?"

Deke intervened and repeated what Laura had said in Cheyenne to be sure Black Stone understood.

"Married white way," Black Stone replied, then pretended to throw something away, his expression filled with disgust, "no good. Whiskey Woman, my sister, marry Cheyenne way."

Laura fastened startled eyes on Deke again. He gave her a sultry look that was filled with promise of reprisal should she prove difficult. Laura chose to ignore him and shifted her gaze back to Black Stone. "What would occur if I didn't wish to marry this man the Cheyenne way?"

Deke coughed, but Laura pretended not to notice. At her question, Black Stone looked mildly surprised. He looked questioningly at Deke, then refocused on Laura. "You no wish marry this man Cheyenne way?"

"Laura," Deke said beneath his breath, "this is nothin' to trifle with."

She kept her attention fixed on Black Stone. She knew she had to be extremely cautious. The last thing she wanted was to jeopardize her claim on Jonathan, after all. But at the same time, if there was a way to keep her son and her freedom, she would be a million times the fool not to take it.

The difficulty would be to learn what she desperately needed to know without burning any of her bridges.

"Not that it's at all the case, Black Stone," she said carefully, "but out of curiosity, I simply must ask. If I didn't wish to marry this man, would I, um, still be your sister?"

His face settling into hard lines that might have been chiseled from granite, Deke turned toward his adopted brother to translate Laura's question.

Black Stone appeared to be offended that she would question the validity or the permanency of her new status. "I say words. Words make Whiskey Woman sister of Black Stone for always." He thumped his chest for emphasis, the blow one of such force that Laura winced. "White man talk?" He pretended to throw something away again. "White man talk, no good. Cheyenne talk? Big good. Never die. Black Stone chief of horse soldiers. Big respect man. Whiskey Woman, sister of Black Stone. Big respect woman."

"I see," Laura said thoughtfully.

"No, goddammit, you don't see," Deke inserted.

Laura sent him a withering look, then turned toward the warrior. "If I am your sister for always, Black Stone, does that mean I can . . ." Laura hesitated. This was a very thin line she was walking. "Well, will I be allowed to go back to the white people for visits? Like Deke—I mean Flint Eyes—does?"

At the question, both men look relieved and chuckled indulgently. Flashing a reassuring smile, Deke said, "Is that what's worryin' you? Honey, just because he's claimed you as his sister, he ain't gonna keep you here. You'll come and go with me. A woman always goes with her husband."

Black Stone slugged himself lightly on the chin and rolled his eyes back. "Black Stone keep Whiskey Woman? Flint Eyes big mad! Whiskey Woman go with her man. Always. Yep."

"No, you misunderstand." Laura made a motion with her hands as if to erase all that had been said. "Not to say it would be my wish, mind you. Please bear that in mind. But what if I weren't married to Flint Eyes? No husband for me? Could Whiskey Woman still come, still go? Like Flint Eyes?"

"Laura, goddammit—"

"Just repeat what I said to him, please," Laura asked sweetly. Deke's gaze turned flat and hard. Signaling with his hands and speaking in a low voice, he did as she asked.

Black Stone looked totally bewildered. "No marry Flint Eyes?"

Careful, she cautioned herself. "I'm just"—she smiled at Deke again—"playing 'what if.' Remember the game you taught me last night, Flint Eyes? How important you said it was for me to look ahead and understand the consequences of my actions?" She pretended to be meek and confused. "Isn't that what you said? I'm just trying to be obedient. I thought you'd be proud of me."

A dangerous glitter entered Deke's eyes. For Black Stone's benefit, he translated. Something he said made his brother laugh. To Laura, he added, "Like most women, give her a choice and she gets plum bogged down tryin' to make up her mind."

Laura leaned around the edge of the fire and, in a whisper she meant only for Deke, said, "And like most men, you conveniently omit details so I'll be certain to make the choice you want me to."

"What the hell does that mean?" he whispered back.

Laura leaned closer. "It means that today certain things came to light, and I want to investigate their possibilities. Does it worry you, my asking questions?" she challenged. "Are you afraid I might discover you neglected to inform me of viable alternatives to marriage?"

His jaw tightened. Gazes locked, their faces mere inches apart, they regarded each other for several tension-packed seconds. Then he rasped, "Hell, no, darlin'. Ask away. Just don't hang yourself with the rope."

Laura's gaze turned contemptuous. Straightening, she smoothed her skirt, taking advantage of the moment to gather her composure. Then she smiled at Black Stone again. "Do you mind my asking questions, Black Stone? I'm not refusing Flint Eyes as a husband, mind you, at least not as matters stand. I'm simply curious about all your delightful Indian customs."

Deke translated, then muttered in English, "Who set your tail on fire?"

Laura ignored the remark. To Black Stone she said, "Now that I am your sister and a Cheyenne woman, I wish to learn all I can so . . ." She moistened her lips. "I want you to feel proud of your new sister, you understand? If I accept Flint Eyes's offer for my hand, I want to accept him as a Cheyenne woman would, with a full understanding of all your ways."

Coming in behind Laura, Deke spoke softly in Cheyenne to clarify all that she had just said. At least Laura hoped that was what he did. As he finished, he leaned toward Laura and whispered, "I ain't never seen the bullshit stacked so deep. Did you bring shovels, or do I gotta wade my way out?"

Laura felt a flush touch her cheeks. "Will my asking foolish woman questions make you angry, Black Stone?"

"First smart thing you said yet. Foolish."

"No make angry," Black Stone replied indulgently. "Whiskey Woman ask, I say answer."

Laura managed to smile again despite her yearning to grab up the coffee can and dump its contents on Deke Sheridan's head. "Well, then . . ." She considered her next query carefully. "What if I chose not to marry Flint Eyes the Cheyenne way? Would you take my child from me?"

"No take baby. Never. Flint Eyes take."

Laura's stomach dropped. "Oh."

Deke's eyes gleamed with satisfaction. "He is my son. In poker, honey, I think the sayin' is, 'I call.'"

After doing some fast mental footwork, Laura said, "I could live with your taking our son."

"You could?"

"But of course. You'll be such a wonderful father. Roping a milk cow so you can feed him every three, maybe four hours. Changing his diapers. Holding him when he cries. When you're busy herding or branding, you can hang him off your pommel. I have every confidence. And at those times when it all just seems too much—why, you could always return him to me so I could care for him."

Deke's dark lashes swept closed, and the corners of his mouth quirked.

Turning back to Black Stone, Laura gave an airy wave of her hand. "So if I chose not to accept Flint Eyes, he would take our son. And what of me? As your sister, would I be permitted—on rare occasion, of course—to return to the white world for visits?"

Deke translated that into Cheyenne. Black Stone smiled at Laura and nodded. "Husband take to white world, you go. Yep. Husband no take, you stay."

"Oh, I see."

Deke chuckled. "You got a hankerin' for one of them handsome braves out there, darlin'?"

Laura shot him a glare. "What if I should never marry?" she asked Black Stone.

Apparently not feeling there was a need for him to translate that, Deke chuckled again and shook his head as he bent forward to refill his coffee cup.

Black Stone grunted. "Whiskey Woman marry. Black Stone no want feed for always."

Since Laura had no intention of hanging around, she didn't see room and board as becoming a problem. Of course, she couldn't tell Black Stone that. "I don't eat very much," she assured the warrior. "Hardly anything at all."

"That's good to hear," Deke murmured. "I don't gotta worry about keepin' much food on the table, then." He took a sip of coffee and winked at her over the rim of his tin cup. "You ever danced to the tune of a razor strap? It takes some real fancy steppin'. Much more of this, and I'm gonna be ready to go hunt that cougar I told you about with a butter knife."

"You're such a charmer."

"I don't need charm, darlin'. You might not know it, but your tit's in a wringer and the washerwoman's crankin' the handle."

Laura had the unholy urge to hit the bottom of his coffee cup. She took a deep breath. Here went nothing. But she had to at least give this her best shot. Returning her gaze to Black Stone, she said, "Is it always necessary for a Cheyenne woman to marry?"

Deke translated. Black Stone considered the question. "Some ugly woman, never no marry. Brother feed for always." He gave Laura an appraising look. "Whiskey Woman no ugly. Many brave like hair. Come with horses. Big want. You marry quick."

"But what if . . ." Laura's pulse escalated. "What if I didn't like any of the braves?"

Black Stone blinked as if he found that thought inconceivable. "No like any?"

"Actually, Black Stone, what I truly, truly want . . ." Laura pressed a fist over her skittering heart to show him how deeply her yearning ran. "What I would really like, above all else, is to be made a free woman, just as Sugar Girl is."

Deke choked and spewed a mouthful of coffee into the fire. Black Stone, who obviously understood what had been said, looked appalled. Star and Sugar Girl, who sat listening to the exchange on the furs, both gasped. Laura smiled at all their stunned expressions.

"I realize it probably strikes all of you as an amazing thing for me to request, but I—"

"Christ!" Deke inserted in a gritty voice. "Amazin' ain't the word. Shut up, Laura. Now."

"Don't tell me to shut up. You deliberately tried to hoodwink me."

Deke tossed the contents of his cup into the fire, dropped the tin container onto the encircling rocks, and shot to his feet. "Black Stone, excuse us for a minute."

"I'm not going anywhere. Let Black Stone address my question. Can I be made a free woman?"

Clearly at a loss, Black Stone turned the matter over to Deke. "You say?"

"I don't got nothin' to say," he snarled. "Tongue That Waggles has said enough for both of us."

Laura sputtered with indignation. "Tongue That Waggles?"

"From mornin' to night without never stoppin'," Deke ground out as he seized her by the arm.

Jerked to her feet and hauled along behind him, Laura had no choice but to follow the man. As he pulled her toward the lodge flap, he grabbed a folded blanket from off a stack along the wall. In Cheyenne, he barked something over his shoulder as he launched Laura out the doorway before him, his grip on her shoulders biting and cruel.

"You're hurting me!"

He gave her a light shove as he released her. With a violent snap of his wrist, he unfolded the blanket and then drew it over his shoulders like a cape. The dying flames of Star's outside cooking fire played across his dark face, washing his features in amber, casting the planes into shadow. His eyes gleamed like burnished silver. Staring up at him, Laura retreated a step.

"You oughta be afraid," he snarled.

"That comes as no surprise. Why do you think I pursued the possibility of becoming a free woman? Because you're such a mellow sort?"

He took a step toward her. "Keep your goddamned voice down. You'll have every man in the village who speaks English standin' in line."

"For what?"

"For a turn at you, you stupid little fool. For once in your life, Laura, tie off that tongue." He advanced another step and said in a raw whisper, "We're smack in the middle of a fuckin' Cheyenne village, in case you ain't looked. That mouth of yours is gonna dig a hole so deep, I won't be able to haul you out. I'm one man against seventy, for Christ's sake."

"Don't use that kind of language in my presence," she whispered back. "How *dare* you?"

He jutted his chin at her. "I'll talk to you any damned way I want, you sassy little piece of baggage, and if you're smart, you'll damned well listen! *Now, shut up!* One more word, and I swear I won't be accountable."

Laura flinched but stood her ground. "For what? Striking me? Go ahead, Mr. Sheridan. I'm no stranger to a man's fists."

He had drawn so close that Laura couldn't fail to notice that his eyes had started to bug. She was so afraid that her legs felt watery. He was a big man. Bigger than Tristan by far. If he struck her using all that strength, he would probably shatter every bone in her face. But better that than letting him walk on every last shred of her dignity. Had he truly believed she was so stupid that she wouldn't find out about the free-woman ceremony?

"Well?" she challenged, wondering even as she did so if she weren't insane. "If you're going to strike me, don't keep me in suspense!"

"I ain't *never* used my fists on a woman in my life!" he shot back. "And I ain't gonna start with a little half jigger of a gal like you."

"Well, there's always that infamous razor strap of yours. I'm surprised you don't wear it looped over your belt."

"I just might start."

"Go ahead. Live up to my worst expectations. Which brings me directly back to this bogus marriage of ours. And don't try to scare me off the subject with dire predictions. I don't see any men lined up out here for a turn with Sugar Girl, and she's a free woman."

His lips drew back over gleaming white teeth. In a low voice so no one else might overhear, he said, "Is that what you want, darlin'? For me to make a free woman of you? For me to pass you on the prairie?"

"It wouldn't hurt my feelings any if you passed me. I think spitting on me is carrying things a little far, but I'm washable, and I'll gladly suffer even that if it's all part of the ceremony to make me free."

"Honey, you got it all wrong. We ain't talkin' about me passin' you by. We're talkin' about you bein' passed from man to man. Usually a whole goddamned soldier society of 'em." He flashed a feral smile. "The Cheyenne call it makin' free with a woman. It's a punishment. The very worst kind.

It's what bastards who need shootin' do when their women make 'em real, real mad. If the woman lives—and that's real rare after forty or fifty men make a feast of her—then the husband or almost-husband who tossed her to 'em spits on her like she's dirt."

Laura's legs buckled.

Deke shot out a hand to grab her by the arm and hold her up. His blanket slipped off one shoulder. "For the rest of that woman's life, she stays dirt. Like Sugar Girl is. A dirty woman no one wants. Not that she minds much. Because after bein' passed, her hunger for that kind of thing has kinda lost its edge. You know what I'm sayin'?

"For the rest of her life, she sticks real close to her own lodge unless someone else is with her. Because she never knows when she might happen upon another son of a bitch who figures there ain't nothin' real wrong with him draggin' a piece of dirt off into the brush and havin' himself a little fun."

Laura closed her eyes, feeling as though she might vomit.

"This ain't Boston, Laura. Folks don't live by the same rules out here. You're walkin' on thin ice during spring thaw. Do you got that?"

She was going to be sick. Horribly, violently sick. A picture of Sugar Girl's sweet face swam through Laura's mind, and bile crawled up her throat.

"You're gonna do what I tell you to do," Deke said in a dangerously smooth voice. "What I tell you, when I tell you. If I snap my fingers and say jump, I wanna see daylight under them feet of yours." He gave her a little shake. "Do you understand me?"

Laura gulped and nodded her head.

"Do you got any more questions? About Cheyenne customs and all? Like maybe what might happen if you make the fool mistake of tellin' Black Stone you don't accept my offer for you?"

"No."

"Look at me, dammit!"

She forced her eyes open and stared up at him through

a blur of tears. Never had she seen him so furious. "No more questions," she managed.

His glittering gaze held hers. "You go back inside now, and in real simple English, you tell Black Stone you've been a stupid woman. That after talkin' to me, my offer makes you real big happy. You got it?" At her nod, he slowly relaxed his grip on her arm. "Then get to it," he bit out. "And when it's done, get your little butt back out here, 'cause I'm not finished with you yet. Not by half."

On legs that threatened to fold with every step, Laura made her way back inside the lodge.

Chapter 20

LAURA'S DISCUSSION WITH BLACK STONE EN-
tailed little more than apologizing and saying how big
happy she was to accept Deke's offer. When she returned to
the lodge, it was to find Sugar Girl badly shaken, which
made Laura feel absolutely horrible. With the girl close to
tears, both Star and Black Stone were otherwise engaged
for a bit of time trying to comfort her. After that, a good
thirty minutes were eaten up while Black Stone, who had
now warmed to the idea of educating Laura to be a proper
Cheyenne woman, more than likely because she had displayed such idiocy, explained the rituals of a wedding. Half
of these she didn't quite understand, either because of the
language barrier, which she was quickly learning could not
be overlooked, or because the customs sounded so barbaric
to her.

None, however, struck her as being quite so barbaric as
the custom of a husband or "almost-husband" being given
free rein over a woman's life, even to the extent that he
could pass her among his acquaintances out on the prairie
to retaliate if she displeased him. Comparatively, her marriage to Tristan was beginning to sound like heaven. At least
social mores had restricted him to merely beating her when
his mood turned foul.

Laura did not look forward to going back outside. If
Deke had ears, he couldn't fail to know how badly she had
upset Sugar Girl, which was bound to make him all the

more angry. He wasn't finished with her yet, he had said. Not by half. What had he meant? Laura couldn't contemplate the possibilities without shaking. Here among these people, it seemed his power over her was even more absolute than Tristan's had been.

The most awful part of it was, Laura couldn't quite blame Deke for being so furious, if for no other reason than the pain she had caused Sugar Girl. And all for what? A last stand for her freedom? Now that she had had time to think about it, she realized how close she had come to landing herself in deep trouble, trouble Deke might not have been able to pull her out of. In view of that, his volatile reaction no longer struck her as being quite so out of line. He was one man against seventy, he had stuck his neck out for her, and she was playing child's games?

Laura felt like crying right along with Sugar Girl. She owed Deke an apology. No two ways about it. At the same time, she knew she probably wouldn't give him one. Saying she was sorry—that came easily if she did so as a mere courtesy. But in serious situations like this, when she had truly messed up, the thought of admitting it terrified her. Tristan had never failed to take any admission of wrongdoing from her as all the more reason to chastise her. To that end, he had played vicious little games, baiting her, trying to make her say the two words he most wanted to hear, damning words that lent all he did from that moment on a certain justification. *I'm sorry.* Laura had learned the hard way never to say those words unless he forced her to, and then only with great reluctance because she knew he would use them against her.

Deke was not Tristan. But the circumstances Laura found herself in tonight were reminiscent of a thousand others that had occurred during her first marriage. Deke was angry, just as Tristan had so often been, rightly or wrongly. She was at Deke's mercy, just as she had once been at Tristan's. A person didn't walk into that kind of a situation asking for it, and in Laura's experience, apologizing, even when she was wrong, was doing just that. Better to be defiant and brazen her way through than to crawl in, asking to be kicked.

When the moment finally came that Laura left Black Stone's lodge and stepped back outside into the darkness, her nerves were twanging like loose guitar strings. Still wearing the army-issue blanket draped over his shoulders, Deke was crouched by the dying fire, one knee elevated, his hands busy at some task she couldn't quite make out.

Because he gave no sign of having heard her come outside and because she was none too anxious for the second segment of their confrontation to occur, Laura hugged herself against the cold and remained frozen in the shadows beyond the firelight. Across the way, other fires crackled cheerily in the darkness, their amber glow illuminating the conical lodges behind them. Occasionally she saw people in silhouette passing to and fro.

Chief lay near Deke's feet, Laura noticed, his bone protected between his spread paws. In an attempt to bolster her courage, she tried to think positively. She had been terrified of Deke Sheridan from the first, and the man hadn't harmed her yet. There was every chance he wouldn't tonight.

Wrong. Those other times he hadn't felt proprietorial. He considered her to be a possession now, and he had given her fair warning of what he'd do if she tried to escape his clutches.

The dog's eyes gleamed when they caught the light and seemed to be fixed on her. If Chief knew she was standing there, Laura guessed Deke probably did as well. She supposed he was ignoring her to drag out the tension, to make her sweat, and she hated him for that. She would take whatever he decided to dish out. She had no choice. But must he torture her?

Well, enough of this. She wasn't a child to stand with her hands cupped protectively over her posterior, sniveling and pleading for clemency. Waiting and dreading what was to come had to be more awful than facing it. If the man was going to beat her, or worse, he could darned well get to his business.

She stepped forward into the shifting circle of anemic light. "I've finished speaking with Black Stone."

He didn't so much as glance up, just kept doing whatever it was he was doing as though he hadn't heard.

"I realize that you're probably angry," she added, determined to brazen it out. "However, in my own defense, I must point out that it was an honest mistake. Given the circumstances, it was natural that I might think you had hoodwinked me, and it hardly seems fair, since I've been coerced into this marriage, that I should be punished for having tried to extricate myself from it."

Laura expected him to begin ranting as Tristan had always done. These dialogues usually began with, "I've had it with you, Laura," and went downhill from there. She steeled herself for the first razorlike slash, fully prepared to argue in her own defense, to lay the blame for everything, including Sugar Girl's distress, at his door rather than her own. But Deke said nothing.

Laura clenched her teeth and peered through the elongated shadows to see. He held a whetstone on his upraised knee and, with light strokes, was working a finer edge onto his knife blade. On the ground in front of him lay a leather strop. From that, Laura surmised he didn't intend to debate the issue and that probably nothing she said would sway him. She stared at the strop for a long moment, then swallowed hard. So be it. He had a surprise coming if he thought she would grovel.

She curled and straightened her fingers. "Do you intend to use that on me?"

He hesitated before completing a pass of steel over stone. After a moment, he said, "I reckon I could do some shavin' on that tongue of yours. If all you could do was grunt and squeak, it might keep you outa trouble." He worked his mouth and spat on the rock, then made circular motions with the blade tip to spread the saliva. "Hell, knowin' you, you'd learn sign language just to spite me, and your hands'd be goin' at full gallop from dawn till dark."

Laura swallowed again. "I wasn't referring to your knife."

He said nothing. She stepped closer. "Well? It appears that you've fetched your strop. I take it that you must intend to use it?"

"That's my knife strop, not my razor strap." He went on sharpening, never looking up.

"Knife strop, razor strap—wherein lies the difference?" Her voice sounded whiny even to her, and she wanted to kick herself.

"A big difference. My knife strop's a little shy on length. A short strop just don't make the right singin' sound. Not satisfyin', if you know what I mean."

"Satisfying?"

"Hell, darlin', if I'm gonna give you a lickin', I wanna have some fun while I'm at it."

Laura gaped at the back of his bent head. Fun? He wanted to have fun? Regathering her courage, which seemed to have scattered momentarily beyond her grasp, she said in a thin voice, "Well?"

"Well what?" He touched the edge of his knife blade to his forearm to see if the steel would shave; then he went back to sharpening. "I'll never cut reeds with my good knife again. Damned if I can work a fine edge back up."

Laura had had enough. "Deke Sheridan, you get up from there this minute."

"What for?"

"To go and get the right strap, damn it! The least you can do is get it over with."

"Don't go tryin' to order me around. I'll beat you when I'm damned good and ready, and not before."

"And when will that be?" she asked shrilly.

"When the mood comes over me." He finally graced her with a glare. "I ain't never seen anybody so all-fired anxious to get a lickin'. You don't got a fever again, do you?"

"I am not anxious. I'm just—" She broke off to glare back at him. "My having to wait for the mood to come over you is an unnecessary torment."

His teeth flashed in a slow grin. "So suffer."

"You are despicable."

"I got that word down. You got a new one you can throw at me?"

Laura took a step toward him, her fists clenched at her sides. "You go and get that miserable strap right this instant!"

"It's clear at the bottom of my saddlebags."

"I don't care where it is. You go get it."

"It's . . ." He peered into the darkness across the way. "Hell, it must be thirty yards over there. Then I'd have to dig around in all that shit lookin' for it, and in the dark, mind you, 'cause there ain't a fire built. Then I'd have to walk clear back here, plus spend a few minutes gettin' my lickin' arm all warmed up. That don't count havin' to catch you. By the time I got all that done, I'd be flat wore out. It don't hardly seem worth the effort. Are you all that bent on it?"

Laura couldn't miss the twinkle that had come into his eyes. He quickly bent his head and went back to sharpening his knife, but not before she saw it and realized, bewilderedly, that he had no intention whatsoever of punishing her, with a strap or otherwise. She felt as though she had been pushing with all her might against a headwind. Her body, braced to go forward, suddenly had nothing to counteract its momentum. She staggered slightly, then regained her balance. A weak, half-hysterical little laugh trailed up her throat.

"Don't push your luck, darlin'," he said gruffly. "I get real out of sorts when people laugh at me."

"I—I'm not laughing. Well, I am, but not—it's just that—I thought surely you'd—" Laura realized she was babbling like an idiot and gave up.

"I got me a real bad habit of sayin' stuff I don't truly mean when I get mad," he admitted in a gruff voice. "I reckon I owe you an apology." He made an abrupt swipe with his knife across the stone and then sighed. "What am I gonna do with you, Boston?"

At the moment Laura was more preoccupied with thoughts of what he wasn't going to do with her, and thanking the Lord.

"I damned near strangled on that last mouthful of coffee,

I hope you know. Bein' around you is so excitin', I feel like I oughta buy tickets. What're you gonna pull next?"

"Nothing," she said weakly. "At least I don't have any immediate plans."

"That's a relief." He glanced up at her. "Can I take that to mean I don't gotta worry about what I'm gonna do with you?"

He wasn't the only one who was relieved. He truly wasn't angry? She felt as though someone had just plucked her off the crumbling edge of a ravine. Scarcely able to believe in her good fortune and hoping to keep him in this benevolent mood, she injected far more lightness into her voice than she might have otherwise. "I would hope. According to these people's customs, it would seem your options are limitless. I'd be just as happy if you didn't consider doing any of them, actually."

He smiled slightly, then tested his knife blade for sharpness on his arm again. "The Cheyenne customs ain't so bad. Not really. In time you'll see that things got a way of workin' out real fair for the womenfolk around here. Maybe even fairer than where you come from."

Still shaken by her narrow escape and feeling none too certain of him yet, Laura knew she should tread with caution. But tonight's revelations so incensed her, she couldn't stop herself from saying, "Fair? What happened to Sugar Girl was fair?"

She no sooner spoke than she regretted it. But to her surprise, Deke looked more amused by her indignation than irritated. He gave her a measuring glance. "No, Laura, what happened to Sugar Girl was far from fair."

"Yet it happened, and it happened among your precious Cheyenne people." After saying that, Laura winced at her own audacity and panned the darkness beyond the fire. For what, she didn't know. A loose bit of cloth to stuff in her mouth, perhaps?

To her amazement, Deke let the slur slide past. "Like anywhere else, there's bad apples and good. Sugar Girl's eldest brother gave her to one who was real rotten."

Laura heartily agreed. "Only an animal would—" She broke off and swallowed the words. As Deke had suggested earlier, for once in her life, she was going to tie off her tongue.

"Go ahead and say it. I can see it's about to choke you," he said with a dry laugh.

"I'm afraid if I do, I'll make you angry."

He raised twinkling eyes to hers. "Honey, you've had my tail tied in a knot ever since I met you. Don't go changin' on me now. I won't know what to think."

"Well, I was just going to say that only an animal would do such a—a monstrous thing to someone so sweet."

"And?" he pressed.

"And that a people who would countenance it . . . Well, I can't help but feel they're equally monstrous."

There. She had said it. Laura watched Deke for his reaction, uncertain what he might do. He didn't even bristle.

"Countenance meanin'?"

"Accept it. Put up with it." Since her saying that much hadn't riled him, Laura couldn't resist adding, "A brother who would allow such a thing to happen to his sister deserves to be shot! And so do all the others who partook in such an atrocity."

He held his arm up to the feeble firelight, blew softly on his skin, then squinted to see if he had shaved off any hair.

Growing more confident by the moment that he wasn't going to get angry, Laura added, "And Black Stone? Star isn't Sugar Girl's sister, is she? That can only mean Black Stone is her brother since she's living with him. Is he the same brother who allowed Sugar Girl and her sister to be betrothed to such a cruel man? Given his greater age, I can only think—"

He ran a thumb and forefinger along the blade's edge. "Black Stone had nothin' to do with nothin'. Get that straight outa your head. He just helped pick up the pieces after the dust got settled. He ain't even blood-related to Sugar Girl. He adopted her. Goin' on five years ago now."

"Adopted her?"

"Yep. Her eldest blood brother, he got killed, and her other blood brothers wasn't much. It was decided, given what happened, that Sugar Girl shouldn't oughta be left there with the mean-hearted bastards."

"Oh." Laura pressed her knees together to steady her stance. "Well, that's something anyway." She glanced uneasily around. "Which lodge do her blood brothers live in?"

"Don't. Sugar Girl came from another band. Black Stone, he's a soldier chief, you see. And his band has a lot of truck with other bands. That's how we come to know Sugar Girl and"—his knife blade grated loudly on the whetstone—"her sister. It's kinda a long story. Just rest assured, things was set right. As right as they could be, anyhow. Some things can't never be undone total, I reckon."

"Set right?"

"If it'll ease your mind any, the sons of bitches who raped Sugar Girl and her sister is all dead. You can't set things much righter than that, now, can you?"

Laura clamped her arms around her waist again. "Black Stone? He avenged her?"

"Nope. His hands was tied. Cheyenne men don't turn against one another with intent to let blood. It's against the law, and Black Stone's a real rule-abidin' sort."

"And what of a law to protect Sugar Girl?" Laura demanded. "Or is there even such a thing?"

"There is. Laws here bein' what they is and not writ down, it's left up to the female relatives of a wronged girl to decide a punishment."

That so surprised Laura that she blinked. "The women here get to sentence the men?" she asked incredulously.

"Not sentence, exactly. And not in all cases. But when a girl is wronged, they decide the punishment and then they carry it out."

"You're kidding."

"I told you things work out real fair around here."

Laura could scarcely believe her ears. Being a Cheyenne woman suddenly didn't sound quite so bad. No white women Laura knew of were granted such authority, not under any circumstances, wronged girl or otherwise.

"You mean Sugar Girl's female relatives killed the men?"

"No. They might've, I reckon, but the cowards hid till the storm blew over. The way our law goes, the avengin' women only get one crack at metin' out a punishment, so if the man or men they're after ain't around, they can't go back later and light into 'em."

She should have known there had to be a catch. "A man must've come up with that twist."

He chuckled. "I reckon. Probably a man who crossed a woman once and found out she still held a grudge fifty years later. There had to be a rule of some kind to protect us fellas."

"Men who wrong young girls don't deserve protecting."

"I'd agree with you there, darlin', but there's wrongin' and then there's wrongin', and sometimes, when the wronged girl is someone well loved, it ain't easy to look at it clearheaded." He bent to pick up his strop, then set his blade to it for a moment. "For instance—here among the Cheyenne, a man's considered guilty of wrongin' a girl if all he does is mess with her knots. Measurin' things in shades, triflin' with her knots is gray, and passin' her on the prairie is black."

"Did you say knots?"

Clearly disgusted with the dullness of his knife, he shook his head, tossed down the strop, and ground his blade against the stone again. "Yeah, knots. Cheyenne girls wear chastity belts made outa rope. No decent girl ever leaves her lodge without her rope, and her mama ties them knots her own secret way so she'll know if anybody touches 'em. There ain't a man in this village, me included, that ain't fiddled with a few knots in his day."

He cast her a lambent glance. "If you'll pardon me for bein' despicable, it'd be a hell of a thing to get killed for fiddlin' when you never got around to doin' nothin' more. That twist in the law you think's so bad gives boys who fiddle a crack to hide in until the mad mamas and aunties work out their anger on things that can be replaced. Boys' lives can't be. If there wasn't no twist, there'd be boys, even if they did no more than feel, who could wind up dead six months later at the hands of angry women who laid in wait to get 'em."

"I see."

"From the way you're frownin', I take it you think dippin' a finger in the honey is a shootin' offense."

Laura's cheeks flamed. Just when she thought she was growing accustomed to Deke's crude language, he shocked her again. "No."

"Then what?"

"I was just trying to picture—oh, never mind."

"What?"

Laura couldn't stand the curiosity. "How on earth can a rope be used as a—a chastity belt?"

"It'd be easier to tie one on you than explain."

"I'll pass."

He laughed at that. "Damn. It might've been kinda fun to fiddle with my own knots." He spat on his whetstone again. "To lasso it quick, darlin', a chastity rope does a real fine job of holdin' a girl's legs together. You start watchin', and you'll see lots of young gals steppin' short as they go about the village. That's cause they're trussed to the knee."

Laura glanced over her shoulder. "Are you serious? What a misery!"

"The biggest misery of my young life, and that's a fact."

"I meant for the poor girls."

"Yeah, for them, too, I reckon. But worse for the boys. All them pretty little gals who can't run, and they don't dare touch 'em after they catch 'em. All they can do is wrap 'em in a blanket and wish." His cheeks creased in a mischievous grin. "Which reminds me why I borrowed this goddamned blanket. It'd be a downright shame not to catch you in my blanket at least once before weddin' you."

Laura threw a startled glance at the blanket. "You, um, were going to tell me what Sugar Girl's female relatives did to avenge her?"

His grin turned wry. "Ah, yes. Since the men went into

hidin', the women had to be content with rippin' hell out of their lodges, breakin' their stuff, and shootin' their horses."

"Someone must not have felt that was enough. The men responsible ended up dead."

"Yep."

"If the women didn't kill them, who did?"

He gave the knife a vicious twist on the whetstone. "A rebel, a man who already walked apart from the People."

Something about the stillness of Deke's expression made Laura's senses go on alert. "Did you know him?"

"I reckon. Sort of, anyhow. He was never an easy man to get a fix on. I never quite understood the things he done, or how come he went about doin' 'em like he did." He shrugged. "Lookin' back, it still don't make real clear sense."

Morbid curiosity had the better of Laura. "What did he do?"

Deke sighed. "I guess it wasn't so much what he did but that he took so long to do it." He glanced up at her. "If he was gonna kill Sugar Girl's brother and all them other bastards, he should've done it the first time, right after they done what they done to her sister. But instead he made a half-assed stab at it, got himself in all kinds of dutch with the People, ended up banished, and didn't come back to finish what he started until years later when it happened again to Sugar Girl."

Laura felt as though a hand were squeezing her heart. Deke Sheridan, a man who loved his people so deeply yet didn't stay with them. Could it be? Or was she imagining the shadows in his eyes? Before he continued, he laughed softly, bitterly.

"By that time, I reckon he must not've figured he had anything to lose, him bein' banished already, and all. The way I saw it, though, he got his guts up a little too late for that girl in there." He jabbed with his knife toward the lodge. "Killin' all the sons of bitches didn't make Sugar Girl's nightmares stop, and it didn't dry her tears. Kinda what us cowboys call bringin' in the hay after it rains."

"Well, at least he did something," Laura said carefully. "Even if he did do it too late. That's better than all the other men who did nothing."

"All told, he killed twenty-two Cheyenne men. Some of 'em he had to track down, and it took him months. When he got around to murderin' those last few, he couldn't even lay it off on bein' crazy mad. Cheyenne folks found that real hard to justify. Like I said, Cheyenne men don't turn on their own. It's a hard and fast rule."

Alert to his every expression, Laura said, "So the rebel was banished because he broke that rule?"

"He could've got back in good standin', I reckon, but he was a stubborn fellow. Wouldn't say he was sorry. Wouldn't make amends with gifts to the dead men's families." He drew his knife from the stone and gazed at the firelight reflecting off it for several seconds. "He knowed what he was doin' when he done it, I guess, and must've figured the punishment fit the crime."

"Did you? Feel the punishment fit the crime, I mean?"

"It's the Cheyenne way."

"That isn't what I asked."

He rubbed at a smudge on the blade. "It wasn't for me to say, Laura. In this world, in any world, it takes bein' sorry to get forgiven, and he wasn't." He took a deep breath and slowly exhaled. "That rebel . . . he was in love with Sugar Girl's sister, you see. Crazy in love, like only young folks can be. She and him made plans to marry the last time he saw her. He was from another band, and while he was away from her tryin' to catch himself enough horses for a bride price, her brother gave her to the other man. The mornin' of the weddin' she tried to—"

He broke off and swore, leaning close to the fire to see where he had nicked himself on the thumb. After a moment, he jiggled his hand and went back to sharpening.

"Anyhow, she tried to run off from her new husband," he finally said, his voice thick and gravelly. "Folks thought she was tryin' to reach the boy she loved. But her husband caught her, and in a rage, he passed her on the prairie."

"Oh, my God." Laura felt sick. "And—the men who raped her—the abusive treatment killed her?"

"No." He gazed into the fire. "After they got done with her, she crawled off and went to a special trystin' spot where her and the boy had been meetin' all that summer. A real pretty spot," he added almost wistfully, "under a big ol' oak tree by a little stream. She hung herself from that tree with her chastity rope." He fell silent. "Without her purity she would've been considered dirt, and I reckon she couldn't bear the shame of that. Couldn't bring herself to face folks."

Laura willed Deke to meet her gaze so she might read the expression in his eyes, but he kept his face carefully averted.

"The boy—he found her. But too late. Too late to tell her he didn't care about her bein' passed, too late to tell her that he loved her anyway and they could make the shame a memory."

Laura couldn't speak. There was nothing to say.

"Anyhow, him bein' young and kinda a hothead, he set out to kill all the bastards that'd done such a terrible thing to her. He wasn't no match for better'n twenty blooded warriors, so he failed and got the beatin' of his young life for his trouble. They damned near killed him."

"And in addition to all that, he was banished?"

"Sort of. Told to make amends with the warriors he tried to kill, anyhow, or he'd have to leave. Somehow he couldn't never find it in his heart to do the first, so he done the second."

"And then came back years later to avenge Sugar Girl?"

Deke smiled slightly. "I reckon you could say he matured out and turned a little meaner than he was at seventeen. On the second try, he made the bastards crawl before they died—like they'd made the girl he loved crawl. After killin' all of 'em, he sure as hell couldn't say he was sorry, not with their blood drippin' from his hands. In the end, I reckon he saw that there was an apartness deep down inside him, that his soul sang a different song than that of his people. He decided he had to walk his own way. He comes back now and again to see his loved ones, but he don't never stay."

Laura studied his dark face, frustrated by the shadows. Was he telling his own story in the third person? Or was she imagining things? "Little wonder he didn't feel sorry. The world is surely a better place without animals like that running around in it. That rebel—why, the way I see it, he should be commended for what he did, not ostracized."

"Ostracized?"

"Banished. Cut off from his people. How horribly unfair. I admire his courage. And I think it's sad his people don't!"

He chuckled. "Well, if I ever happen across his path again, darlin', I'll make sure you get a chance to shake his hand."

"I shall do so, I assure you. And pat him on the back as well." Still trying to read his expression, Laura asked softly, "What were you doing while he avenged Sugar Girl and her sister?"

"Scratchin' my head. He was one puzzlin' fellow."

He sheathed his knife and passed behind her to get some firewood. After positioning the new logs in the flames, he straightened the blanket around his shoulders and turned toward her. "Enough about all that. I brung this blanket out here for a reason, and unless I get to it, the night'll go to waste. Since we're getting' hitched come mornin', it's now or never."

Laura gazed up at him, still uncertain, still wondering. If he had been that boy of long ago, he showed no sign of it now. His eyes twinkled with mischief, and his mouth twitched at the corners as though he were suppressing a smile. Yet so much of the story fitted him. A rebel. Deke Sheridan was definitely considered to be that in both the Cheyenne and white worlds. He was also a man who walked apart. And last, but not least, he could have easily gone gunning for twenty-two men and been successful at killing them.

Last night she remembered him saying he had been away from the Cheyenne for fourteen years. He looked to Laura as though he were about thirty. But he could be thirty-one. If so, he would have been the age of that boy fourteen years ago.

Laura's thoughts were jerked back to the present by his slow approach. She eyed the blanket nervously. "What, exactly, are you planning to do with that blanket?" she asked.

"Court you the Cheyenne way," he said silkily as he continued to advance on her. "You can try to run if you want. Catchin' a woman is all part of the fun."

"I can't run," Laura reminded him, growing uneasy in spite of herself. "My legs are still too weak."

"Really?" His silvery gaze ran the length of her. "You know, Boston? This might prove real interestin'. I ain't never caught a gal in my blanket who wasn't wearin' no rope."

"Perhaps I should go ask Star for one."

"You do, and I'll wring your pretty little neck with it," he said with a chuckle.

Chapter 21

HAVING A MAN COME UP FROM BEHIND AND
envelop her in a blanket seemed highly improper to Laura,
not to mention perilous since he was inside the blanket with
her. Deke clutched the wool in one fist, which left him one
arm free to hug her waist. He drew her close almost instantly, much as he had last night to search for stars, only
this time Laura had nothing to preoccupy her, nothing to
make her forget that large, heavy hand curled so warmly
over her ribs.

For a minute, panic surged through her. She began thinking of all the many things he might do, that no one in the
village would be likely to intervene, that his power over her
was frighteningly absolute.

Then she caught herself and mentally backed up to their
earlier confrontation, she convinced he meant to punish
her, he with no such intention. In that instant of recollection, something happened inside Laura, nothing miraculous,
or momentous, or even so marked she could identify what
it was, but it happened nonetheless. A recession of the
panic, a deliquescence of her fear.

In that moment two things became clear to her: one, that,
come what may, Deke's power over her *was* absolute, and
nothing she did would change it, and two, that he had
proven her wrong at every turn thus far, and because he
had, she owed him an opportunity to prove himself yet
again.

So it was that Laura did not grab frantically for Deke's hand where it rested over her midriff and side. Neither did she hug her breasts. Arms dangling limply at her sides, her body relaxed against his, she simply stood there and waited.

And waited . . .

He only continued to hold her, his hand firmly anchored where he had first placed it, his chin resting atop her head. No subtle or not-so-subtle forays with groping fingers. No rib-crushing hold. No wet, hungry kisses.

Just peacefulness, and a sense that the rest of the world had moved away. There were only the two of them and the hypnotic firelight, the whisper of the night breeze in surrounding cottonwoods, and a sense of security that Laura wasn't at all certain she had experienced with anyone before.

"D-Did you do a lot of this kind of courting when you were young?" she finally asked.

"Enough that you can rest assured you ain't harnessed into the traces with a man who don't know his business under a blanket," was his husky reply.

At his response, Laura smiled slightly and blinked to dispel a searing sensation in her eyes. He knew his business under a blanket? An hour ago, she might have interpreted that as a threat, or at the very least as a startling revelation, but she was quickly coming to realize that what Deke Sheridan said, or how he said it, had little or no relation to the man himself.

Deke put Laura in mind of a gift she had once received as a very young child from her maternal grandmother—a beautiful, jewel-encrusted locket in a tiny velvet-lined box that had been wrapped expressly to frustrate the receiver in layer after layer of lovely paper, each secured with glue and knotted bindings of silk ribbon. It had taken Laura nearly an hour to peel away all the covering to get to her gift.

She wasn't so foolish as to liken Deke to a delicate locket, of course, but in his own way, he was proving to be as surprising a discovery. The only analogical difference was that his wrapping was coarse, his bindings knotted twine. To know him, to truly know him, a person had to peel away his many layers to discover the man underneath. A wonderful man, Laura was coming to suspect. Someone she might trust.

As if he read her thoughts, he chuckled deep in his chest and bent his head around to fasten twinkling eyes on her face. "How much rope you plannin' to play out here?"

Laura fastened a puzzled gaze on his. "Pardon?"

He wiggled his fingers where they rested over her ribs. "How much lead rope?" he repeated. When he saw that she still didn't understand, he added, "After workin' for a spell with a horse, I play it out some slack in the lead rope to see if it'll take its head or behave itself. I got me a real uneasy feelin' you're doin' the same."

Laura gave a startled giggle. "You liken yourself to a horse?"

"I don't know why the hell not," he came back with a grin. "Horses is real fine critters. Well?"

"Well, what?"

"You playin' me out enough slack to hang myself?"

"Yep."

"Shit."

She giggled again, then closed her eyes when she felt him press his face against her hair. His hand, she noticed, remained firmly planted where he had first placed it.

"You ain't no fun at all, girl. Puttin' a man on his honor ain't playin' fair." He wiggled his thumb across the cloth of her blouse. "You sure you don't wanna get a choke hold?"

"And if I did?"

She felt him smile. "Then I could be ornery without feelin' bad."

"I'd prefer you feel bad."

He feathered a touch along the underside of her right breast. "You'd best grab hold."

Laura's breath caught at the tingling sensation. "No, thanks."

"I'm tellin' you, that there is one thumb you'd best not trust."

She raised her lashes slightly. "I shall see."

"It's a downright *dangerous* thumb. Leave it loose to wander around and there ain't no tellin' what might happen."

"I've no doubt it could be dangerous," she said in a voice gone tight with breathlessness. "But it's your thumb, and I have decided you have earned my trust."

"Don't do me no favors, darlin'. What fun can I have if you trust me?"

"I suppose that's up to you."

"Well, hell."

Laura could tell by his tone of voice that he was pleased and trying very hard to hide it under his usual gruffness. No wonder Chief snarled so much; he had learned it from his master.

Instead of taking advantage of her lack of resistance, Deke curled his shoulders around her and began to sway slightly, holding her body firmly to his. The heat of him lulled her, and the hardness of him forced her spine to give. She stared into the leaping flames, her senses alert to his every breath, the thud of his heart against her shoulder, the slight shifts of his fingertips on her ribs. He rubbed his jaw against her hair and sighed, the rise and fall of his chest undulating her body.

The mood that descended was so indescribably tender that Laura nearly wept. Deke chased her melancholy away by suddenly loosening his arm from around her to touch her right hand.

"Which direction?"

"Pardon?"

He laughed softly. "East, west, north, or south? Name me your pointers."

"East," she quickly came back.

"Good girl. And your other arm?"

"West."

He pressed his hard thighs against her fanny.

"South."

Laura's pulse escalated slightly as she recalled the parts

of her body that he had insisted would always point due north if she was facing the North Star. She wondered if he might use this as an opportunity to touch her there.

He surprised her by leaning around to plant a quick kiss on the tip of her nose, his eyes dancing with mischief. "Fooled you."

"North," she said with a relieved smile.

He looped his arm back around her, insisted she locate the North Star, which she did with speed and ease now that he had taught her how to find it.

"Denver's southeast from here," he said. "So which way would you strike out to go there?"

Laura pointed, and he grinned. "Hot damn, girl. Next thing I know, you'll be leadin' me around by the nose."

Laura didn't have such confidence. "Without knowing where towns lie, though, what good will it do me to know my directions?"

"Maps help," he replied. "And you gotta learn to pay attention. Like, say, leavin' out of Denver, you get your bearin's and keep track of which way you're goin'. That way, it's easy to turn back, and it also makes it real easy to figure where you probably are on a map."

"I'll never get the hang of it."

"Yeah, you will, 'cause I'm gonna teach you, and you're a quick learner." He inclined his head toward the vast expanse of darkness beyond the village. "It can be like another Boston out there for you, honey. Street signs, general stores, meat markets. It only seems scary to you 'cause nobody's bothered to teach you."

"Why do you want to be the one who does?" she asked thinly.

He stiffened at the question. "Why in hell wouldn't I?"

Laura swallowed, stricken with a sudden realization that for every layer of wrapping she peeled away from Deke, he was peeling one from her. "It has been my experience that most men enjoy maintaining certain measures of control. If you teach me to be completely self-sufficient, I shall have no need of you."

"Ah." He seemed to consider that for a long moment. "I see what you're sayin'. Hell and naked angels, I wouldn't have no control at all if I taught you how to get along fine without me, would I?"

"Not much," she admitted.

He raised an eyebrow. "A smart man'd keep you dumb and helpless so he could knock the shit out of you once a day whether you needed it or not. Only way to keep a woman in line, right? Teach her too much, and she might start thinkin' for herself. Or even run off if he treated her ornery."

Laura fixed her gaze on the fire, feeling a little sick. He was echoing the sentiments of the other two men who had played major roles in her life, first her father and then Tristan.

Deke straightened and rested his chin atop her head again. She felt the thrust of his jaw and the vibration of his larynx against her scalp when he finally spoke. "I thank you kindly for pointin' all them things out to me. Only a damned fool'd go teachin' you how to run off from him and cover your tracks while you was goin'."

Her mouth felt suddenly cottony. At least a full minute of silence ticked by after he finished speaking, each second measured by the loud beating of her heart.

Deke finally broke the quiet by asking, "If a damned fool like that was to ask you to marry him, what'd be your answer?"

Laura craned her neck to look at him. "I beg your pardon?"

His smile was slow and mischievous. "I think you heard me real clear."

Laura stared up at him for what seemed an endless moment. "You mean you'll teach me all of that?"

"That and more. How to defend yourself against a man twice your size. How to take care of yourself and the baby a thousand miles from nowhere."

She could scarcely believe her ears. "Even though you know I might use the knowledge later to . . ."

"To run off from me?" he filled in.

Laura could see denying it was useless. "Yes."

His lashes made a lazy sweep over his eyes. "Laura, darlin', if a man works his heart out gentlin' a filly like I aim to you, and he still can't turn her loose without knowin' for sure she'll come back when he whistles, she ain't worth keepin'."

Her heart caught at the emotion she saw lurking behind the teasing twinkle in his eyes. "You'd be taking a risk. This may be one filly who values her freedom more than anything else."

"I ain't seen a filly yet that'd head for the hills when she felt free where she was at," was his husky reply. "And I learned a long time ago that packin' plenty of sugar in my pockets works a lot slicker than bein' ornery. A Cheyenne man don't believe in rough breakin'. He's taught from the time he's knee-high that loyalty's gotta be earned. I wanna earn yours."

That he could feel he hadn't already earned her loyalty told Laura more than he could know. She realized she was looking at him through a blur of tears. Was he real, this man? Or was she dreaming him? Deke Sheridan . . . a little uncivilized. What a miscalculation that was. She no longer needed to ask him how old he had been fourteen years ago when he left his people. She knew. Her heart broke a little for the boy he had once been and for the man he had become—both rebels and set apart, both alone and drifting between two worlds, belonging in neither. But what she found most heartbreaking of all was her own blindness. How could she have taken this man's measure by standards that were so completely unfair? How could she have compared him to individuals like Tristan and her father and found him lacking? They weren't fit to breathe the same air he did.

"Hey." He bent his head to catch a trickling tear on her cheek with his jaw. "Don't cry, honey. I didn't mean—"

"Oh, Deke."

Laura wasn't exactly sure how it happened, but somehow she turned within the circle of his arm, and in the next second, she was sobbing and hugging his shoulders.

"Christ," he said under his breath. "Honey, I didn't mean to upset you."

"Oh, God." A jagged rush of air caught in Laura's throat and made a tearing sound. "I'm not upset; I'm . . ."

He didn't understand. He couldn't understand. And she would never be able to explain. How could one stuff the hurts of a lifetime into a few sentences? To even try might make him think she wanted his pity, and she didn't. All she wanted—oh, God, it was madness, but all she wanted was for him to hold her.

As if he sensed that, he somehow managed to gather her close with the arm that held the blanket, then began to thump her on the back with his other hand. It was those thumps, which she knew he meant to be comforting pats, that were her complete undoing. *A hand that could concuss a full-grown bull.* How many times might he have used it against her?

"Aw, honey, don't," he said in a tight voice.

Laura's lungs shuddered at each impact of his hand between her shoulders. In between pats, he rubbed and kneaded her tense muscles. What a wonderful hand it was. A big, callused, clumsy paw of a hand—but she wouldn't have traded it for a thousand more fine-boned and elegant.

"Well, shit." He gave her a few more thumps. "Would it help if I said I'm sorry?"

"F-For what?" she squeaked in between abating sobs.

"I don't know. For whatever in hell it was I said to make you cry."

Laura started to laugh—shrill, wet giggles that she knew bordered on hysteria.

"Jesus Christ."

She laughed harder. A wonderful, cleansing laughter. In between gulps of breath, she managed, "It isn't you. It's me, don't you see? I'm—I'm going crazy."

"Mind if I go along?"

The question sobered Laura because she knew it was

seriously meant. For just an instant, she felt as though she were standing on the edge of a precipice and about to fall. To trust again. To allow herself to need again. For two long years, all she had dreamed about was attaining her freedom, and now Deke was asking her to give it up, to believe in dreams, to make herself vulnerable. To do any of those things would be madness, absolute madness. Hadn't her marriage to Tristan taught her anything? Namely that she could count on no one but herself.

"Oh, Deke, I'm frightened."

She expected him to ask, "Of what?" but instead, he whispered, "I know you are."

The wonder of it was, Laura believed he truly did.

She curled her fingertips into the thick pads of vibrant flesh and muscle over his shoulders, felt the heat of him through his chambray shirt. Strength and solidness, and he was offering them to her as he might a shield.

"What if—" She caught her lip between her teeth. "How can you be sure—I mean—well, what if I don't learn fast? What if you find yourself wishing you'd never gotten yourself saddled with someone like me? Aside from the color of my hair, I'm not a very—"

"Don't," he cut in harshly. "Don't even finish the thought. That's Tristan talkin', and you gotta get all the things he ever told you straight outa your head. What matters now is what I say, and I say you're beautiful and sweet and smart as a whip. You'll make some lucky man a damned fine wife, and I'm first in line askin'." He ran his hand along the curve of her spine.

"I know you're scared, Laura. I ain't askin' you not to be. All I'm askin' is for you to give me a chance. I think I can make you happy, if you'll only let me try."

He made it sound so simple. She wondered fleetingly how he could possibly know what sorts of things Tristan had said to her, but for the moment, the answer to that question seemed rather unimportant when he was demanding an answer to another, far more important one. Laura had no idea why he was even offering her a choice. The situation they were in dictated, didn't it? He had already explained at great length why neither of them had any alternatives. Why press her to acquiesce?

Even as Laura asked herself that, she knew why, and the answer was one of the reasons she was tempted to give him the yes he sought. All practical reasons aside, Deke wanted her to step into his arms only of her own free will. He was as uncomfortable with possessing her against her wishes as she was with being possessed. What appeared to be a sham of a marriage proposal was far, far more. He was trying in the only way he knew to make things right between them, to give her a sense of commitment rather than submission.

It was a sneaky maneuver. It was also very sweet of him to bother. He held all the trumps in this game. It wasn't necessary for him to let her play out her hand. All he need do was lay his cards on the table and scoop up his winnings.

In a quavery voice, Laura came as close to a yes as she possibly could by saying, "I'd like to be happy. It seems like a very long time since I truly was."

He hooked his hand over her shoulder and gave it a gentle squeeze. "Can I take that for a yes?"

Still battling tears, she smiled against his shirt. A yes that actually meant nothing, yet meant the world. Even if it was pretense, she was grateful. It seemed she would be left with her dignity even if he took all else. "Yes," she whispered.

His arm at her waist drew her so close, she could feel his heart pounding. He held her like that for a very long while, not moving, not speaking, the only sounds those of the fire and the wind and their muted breathing.

"I reckon I oughta let you go back inside. Mornin' will come early, and you need the rest. Tomorrow's gonna be a long and tryin' day."

Laura found herself wishing she could collect her baby and go with him now. She slid her hands to his chest and drew back slightly. "Yes, I suppose I should. Star and Black Stone may be waiting for me to come in before they go to bed."

He released her, drew the blanket from around her, and moved away. Laura hugged herself against the sudden chill.

He was grinning as he stepped around the fire to retrieve his strop and whetstone. Then, as though he had second thoughts, he left the stone lying where it was. As he straightened from picking up the strop, he wrapped each end of the leather around his fists, snapping it tight. A mischievous twinkle came into his eyes as he slowly walked back to her. Before Laura realized what he meant to do, he looped his arms over her head, placing the tightly stretched leather across her back to block her escape.

Stepping close, he whispered, "Seems to me like I made you a promise. Just so's you don't get to thinkin' I make a habit of breakin' my word, I'd best lay my strop across your fanny at least once before I leave."

With that, he lowered his arms until the leather was pulled tight across her backside. With a strength that unnerved her, he hauled her toward him. Laura braced her hands on his chest and leaned back to meet his gaze, which had darkened to a smoldering slate gray.

She could see he intended to kiss her, and heaven help her, she couldn't gather the presence of mind to avert her face. Her breath began to come in short, shallow bursts. He bent his head. His hair dipped low to trail over the backs of her fingers, and it felt just as she imagined it might, like the underside of silk, cool and slightly coarse. Beneath her palms, she could feel the muscles in his chest bunch and slacken every time he moved.

His lips touched hers as lightly as a moth wing. Laura wasn't certain what it was she had been expecting, but certainly not this. Heat and a contact that was nearly nonexistent. Expecting him to deepen the kiss at any moment, she braced for it. But it never came. Her lashes lowered over her eyes and her breathing abated while her heart began to slog, each beat a blow against her ribs. She could feel the hard welt of his arousal pressing against her through the layers of their clothing.

His lips still barely touching hers, he executed a silky, hot caress with his mouth, so light, so unassuming, it left her mind reeling. She was accustomed to men who ground their teeth against hers, who clamped their hands under her chin to force her jaws apart so they could gag her with slick, thrusting tongues. Men who demanded and forcefully took.

The whisper-light brush of Deke's mouth didn't even suggest a demand. A kiss? Or her imagination? An actual touch, or the mingled puffs of their breath stirring the air between them? It was madness, but Laura found herself feeling frustrated. Her lips parted slightly. Her lungs grabbed for oxygen. Her skin became electrified. She made fists in the cloth of his shirt and leaned slightly closer, expectant.

She could have sworn he drew back to keep that hairsbreadth of distance between their mouths. Then he completely disarmed her by kissing the tip of her nose, then its bridge, then her eyebrows. For the first time, Laura felt cherished. Her lashes fluttered against her cheeks, and her pent-up breath shuddered softly from her lungs on a wistful sigh. As though he meant to memorize every line, he traced her face with those featherlight lips, at the temple, along her cheek, at her ear, over the curve of her jaw.

Tantalized. It was the only way to describe how he made her feel. A stillness settled within her—a breathless stillness, a sense of waiting and wanting, only she wasn't sure for what. If and when he did kiss her, it would be as it had been dozens of times before, a suffocating rub of saliva-slick mouths and blasts of sour breath that made her feel nauseated.

Only, Deke's breath smelled like steam from coffee—rich and hot, the scent faint but ever so pleasing. And when his lips at last trailed back to hers, his mouth felt more silken than wet. Without conscious thought, Laura placed a quivery hand along his cheek and felt the hard play of muscle along his jaw. Her stomach went fluttery. He felt like heated steel everywhere she touched.

He startled her by nipping gently at her lower lip, the tug of his teeth pulling it into a pout, which he promptly suckled. Laura felt the draw clear to her toes and somehow wound up with her hand in his hair, her fingers clenched into a fist. Her lip still captured by the relentless pull of his mouth, he caught the distended flesh between his teeth and began flicking it lightly with his tongue.

Laura frantically reminded herself that he was toying only with her lip, but the suggestiveness of it made her think of his doing that to her elsewhere. The lady in her was shocked. The woman melted. Heat ... and silk ... steel ... and velvet. And madness. She abandoned her hold on his hair, stepped onto the tops of his moccasined feet to gain some height, and wrapped both arms around his columned neck.

He released her lip only to nip it sharply again with his teeth and soothe away the slight sting with the heat of his mouth. Laura moaned, and he breathed in the sound as he hauled her more snugly against him. His tongue darted past her teeth to engage hers in a flirtatious dance of advance and retreat, each contact so tantalizing that hers soon pressed forward for more. He dragged for the sensitive tissue behind her bottom teeth, teased the thread of flesh there, then trailed his tongue to the insides of her cheeks before flicking his way across her palate.

Laura had never been kissed so thoroughly, never dreamed she could be. In the back of her mind, she knew he would probably make love to her with the same boldness, that he would allow her no reticence, but if he made her feel like this when he did it, would she even be able to think, let alone care where he touched her, or how? She felt as if she had been swept into a swirling vortex where reason didn't dwell.

When he finally drew up for air, Laura felt completely disoriented. He hauled in a ragged breath, then dropped his head back and closed his eyes. She pressed her face into the side of his neck and closed her eyes as well.

"I'll tell you, darlin', you got *Mon'gehela* beat hands down."

Mon'gehela? She felt as if she had stepped into the path

of six galloping horses. Flattened. Yet exhilarated. He continued to hold her until both of them were breathing normally again. Then, very gently, he set her away from him, bent to brush his mouth lightly over hers in farewell, and whispered, "Tomorrow."

With that, he turned and walked away to become an obscure shadow in the firelit darkness. Laura gazed after him in numb disbelief. Tomorrow? She finally fixed her gaze on the flickering firelight, knowing that promise would follow her into the lodge and into sleep to become a whisper in her dreams.

Fifteen miles away in the lee of a deep draw, Francisco Gonzales sat cross-legged and stared sightlessly at the flickering flames of his own fire, his jaw muscle snapping with rage he couldn't vent. In the far reaches of light, disturbed earth and a pile of brush were constant reminders that he had been bested by a gringo and had lost three of his best men in the process. He and his remaining men had been combing the hills for over a week looking for their missing compañeros. Now that they had finally found them, the evidence told its own story of ambush and death.

Gonzales was not a stupid man. He had eventually found the abandoned mine where the Cheney woman and her tracker had holed up. The tracks in that area told him that a large party of Cheyenne warriors had joined the pair there and had escorted them, one via litter, to the safety of the Cheyenne camp in Cougar Flats. Judging by things he had seen inside the mine, Gonzales assumed the woman had fallen ill.

There was only one gringo Gonzales knew of who was so friendly with the Cheyenne that he could signal them for help. Deke Sheridan. Was it any wonder three of Gonzales's best men lay dead? Sheridan was a dangerous man, as skilled at Indian warfare as he was at handling a six-shooter. Ah, yes, dangerous and very deadly.

Gonzales had a score to settle now. In the beginning he had been driven by greed, then a need to protect his identity had strengthened his determination, but now his impetus had become revenge. No one got away with shooting down three of his men. To let such a thing pass would be to invite the same to occur again. In Gonzales's line of work, once a man lost the advantage of fear, he courted death. If he allowed one slight to pass without retaliation, he had to begin watching his back even with his own men. To not strike back, to fail, for any reason, to right a wrong, was considered a sign of weakness.

Deke Sheridan had to die. No matter how long he had to wait, Gonzales knew the time would come when the sneaky bastard wouldn't have the Cheyenne to ride shotgun for him. When that day finally arrived, the gringo was a dead man, and the woman as well if Gonzales couldn't take her alive.

Chapter 22

TOMORROW. THAT HUSKY PROMISE OF DEKE'S
turned out to be one that was not fulfilled, for the following
day turned out to be long and trying, just as he had predicted. Shortly after breakfast, Medicine Woman, Deke's
appointed emissary, arrived at Black Stone's lodge with a
tattered piece of "talking paper" that offered sixty head of
prime cattle as a gift to Black Stone in exchange for his
sister's hand. After the formalities were properly addressed,
Laura was approached to see if she looked upon the marriage with favor. As she had been instructed to do the night
before, Laura meekly turned the matter back over to Black
Stone, the suggestion being that she did indeed wish to
marry the warrior but would bow to her brother's decision.
Black Stone made a great show of deliberation, his black
eyes warm with laughter the entire time, and finally accepted the gift, whereupon he stepped outside to announce
his adopted sister's marriage publicly. After that, the pace
of the day became crazy. Hordes of Indian men gathered
before Black Stone's lodge bearing gifts, all of which Laura
was expected to admire, even if she didn't know what they
were. Cooking utensils, weaponry, foodstuffs, a leather dress
and moccasins, blankets, soap, beads. Two fine-looking
horses were even tethered in front of the lodge. During all
of this, Deke never appeared, and Laura had to muddle her
way through alone, trying to understand and make herself

understood. The experience was trying, to say the least. All she wanted was to grab her baby and find Deke.

Such was not to be the case. When the gift giving ended, a frightening warrior spread a blanket at Laura's feet and gestured for her to sit upon it. When she did so, three other warriors ran up, and each of the four grabbed a corner of the wool, lifting Laura none too smoothly between them. The next thing she knew, she was being carried toward Medicine Woman's lodge with a procession of gift-bearing warriors trailing along behind. When Deke was summoned forth from the lodge, the four warriors began swinging Laura to and fro on the blanket, much to her horror. When she at last went airborne, Deke was there to catch her, but Laura wasn't certain of a safe landing until she was solidly embraced by strong arms.

So it was that she began her marriage with her heart in her throat. She no sooner began to recover from that harrowing experience than Medicine Woman entered the lodge and insisted upon examining Laura to determine whether or not she was well enough to have her child returned to her. The old Indian squaw was not one to suffer shyness, and despite Laura's protests, began peeling away her clothing while Deke looked on. He finally had the good grace to turn his back, which earned him a harsh scolding from his mother. When he refused to cease his foolish behavior, Medicine Woman threw up her arms as if to implore the gods, then tottered over and thumped him sharply on the back of his head with the heel of her hand.

Laura was so surprised, she gave a startled giggle, which earned her a flash of ice blue eyes that sent her diving for cover under the furs. After finishing the examination, Medicine Woman pronounced Laura well enough to care for and nurse Jonathan. Laura spent the remainder of the day getting reaccustomed to the rigors of motherhood and settling into married life, the latter of which included sorting through the multitude of wedding gifts and finding places within the lodge to stack them.

By evening, she was so tired, she could scarcely think, and her weariness was manifested by pallor, which alarmed Deke. He tucked her into bed early, vowing that he would see to it she rested frequently on the morrow.

For Deke, that first night was a torture, in more ways than one. After their kiss the night before, lying beside Laura was a temptation he could scarcely resist, and his body complained at the abstinence in a manner only another man might appreciate. Then, to make matters worse, Jonathan grew hungry shortly after midnight, and Deke had to nudge his exhausted wife awake to feed him. Because the fire had burned low and the lodge was chilly, Deke insisted Laura stay under the furs while he brought the infant to her. Then he lay on his back beside the two, feeling like an outsider, and stared up at the smoke hole where a circle of feeble moonlight glowed.

He heard every suckling sound, every soft murmur, every rustle of cloth. His nose caught the scents peculiar to both mother and infant—a sweet, warm smell that filled him with longing, not for the sensual, but for the closeness and love they shared. He wanted to lie on his side with an arm curled over Laura's waist, the baby snug between them, as he would have if the child were his. He wanted to see the slight smile he knew was probably curving her mouth, and the glow in her eyes, and the tender way she cupped her hand over the baby's silken head. In short, he longed for what he couldn't have, and had to settle for listening.

He was almost grateful when Jonathan suddenly started to whimper. He heard Laura making comforting little sounds, but the baby's cries gained force. A moment later, Jonathan worked a tiny foot free of his wrappings and gave Deke's elbow a healthy kick.

"Something's wrong," Laura cried. "He did this before."

Deke turned onto his side and, after watching the baby churn furiously with his legs for a moment, asked Laura, "You think maybe he needs to be burped?"

In the moonlight, her eyes were shimmering spheres, and there was no mistaking the distress that tightened her small face. Deke pushed up.

"Honey, don't get scared. He can sense it, and it'll just make him cry harder."

He lifted the baby from Laura's arms, laid him over his shoulder, and gave him a couple of light pats. Jonathan let loose with a rolling rumble, then instantly stopped crying and began nuzzling Deke's neck.

"I ain't equipped with a chuck wagon, little fellow," Deke said with a chuckle as he handed the baby back to his mother.

When Deke lay back down, he turned onto his side facing the pair. When Laura threw him a pleading glance, he assured her it was too dark for him to see—the biggest lie he had ever told—and continued to watch. The moment Jonathan began to nurse again, Deke saw what the problem was. The baby would suckle, then nuzzle and squirm. He was clearly not getting a steady flow of nourishment and, in his distress, was sucking air.

Not wishing to embarrass Laura, Deke grasped her hand and placed her fingertips along the side of her breast, showing her how, with a gentle downward stroke, she could start the flow. Jonathan gave a satisfied little *umph* through his nose and settled down, one tiny hand curled over his mother's softness.

Deke had seen some beautiful things in his lifetime, newborn fawns, the streaks across the sky at dawn, eagles in flight. But nothing compared to seeing Laura with her baby. With *his* baby, he decided determinedly. To hell with holding himself apart. Jonathan was his son now, not Tristan Cheney's. And times like this were what created a feeling of family.

Smiling, he trailed his gaze to Laura's lovely face. His guts immediately knotted when he saw streams of silver running down her cheeks. "Laura? What's wrong?"

Clearly humiliated to be caught weeping, she made a choked sound and shook her head, then tried to wipe her cheek on the fur.

"Somethin' must be wrong. Why are you cryin'?"

She curled a trembling hand over Jonathan's head. "I'm

just afraid he's going to get sick again," she squeaked. "It must be me. He never acted like this when he was with Star."

"He's not sick, honey. He just sucked a little air, that's all."

"Why?" she asked shrilly. "He never got air with Star. There must be something wrong with me."

Deke puffed a breath into his cheeks, not at all sure he was the right man for this particular job. Laura was about the most bashful female he had ever known. He thought about having his mother or Star talk to her, but with the language barrier to confuse matters, he was afraid they might do more harm than good.

"There's nothin' wrong with you," he assured her. "You're just nervous and unsure of yourself. Sometimes when a mama gets all nerved up, her milk stops. Touchin' where I just showed you gets it started again. When Jonathan can't get milk, he starts rootin' and sucks a little air. That makes his belly hurt, and he fusses. It won't hurt him none. Pretty soon you'll know when it's happenin'. Until then, just give him a quick burp, get your milk started, and put him back on the—"

Deke broke off and repositioned his arm beneath his head. When he slid a glance Laura's way, he saw that she hadn't noticed the near vulgarity and was touching her breast where he had showed her, her expression intent. What she lacked in knowledge, she made up for with pure-dee-ole worry.

"Laura, he'll start squirmin' and rootin' if he ain't gettin' nothin'. You'll notice straight off."

She lifted luminous eyes to his. "Are you sure? How can you know? You've never had a baby."

Deke chuckled. "Thank God for that." He smoothed a flyaway curl at her temple, knowing that by the gesture she might realize how much he could truly see, yet unable to resist touching her. "I just know, that's all. Things is real different here when it comes to babies and all. We don't think of . . . Well, mamas here don't feel shy. If their little ones get hungry, they feed 'em. I reckon I learned a lot as a boy just by watchin'." At her shocked look, he grinned. "You don't hide to have your supper, do you?"

She wrinkled her nose. "That's quite a different thing."

"To you, maybe, but it ain't to a baby." He gestured at the lodge. "There ain't other rooms to go off and hide in here. If company comes and it's rainin' or cold outside, what're you gonna do, make Jonathan go hungry till everybody leaves? Hell, no. You feed him, and whoever's around don't pay it any mind."

Her eyes widened with apprehension, but at least she no longer looked tearful.

Deke chuckled. "You can throw a blanket over your shoulder or somethin'," he tempered. "Just don't get so worried about bashfulness that you smother my son. I might get a hair testy."

"You actually wouldn't be upset if I—" She broke off and sputtered. "In front of some other man?"

Deke ran a finger down the bridge of her small nose. "If some other man starts lookin' at you like he shouldn't oughta, I'll kill him."

"I thought physical retribution was forbidden here."

"Retri-what?"

"Punishment. Men turning against one another. You said it was forbidden."

Deke's mouth quirked. Laura was quick; he had to give her that. "I'm peculiar about my womenfolk, and I ain't real slick at followin' rules. That's kinda understood around here. But that ain't why things is like they are. It's just the Cheyenne way. A man ignores the women in another man's lodge, pretends like they ain't there. He has truck with his wife, but otherwise, unless he's got important business with another female, he don't pay her no mind. Not even his own sister. He don't talk to her, don't look at her. And if he sees she's gonna feed her baby, he don't even so much as glance her way."

Laura remembered how Black Stone had ignored her existence the afternoon he came into his lodge. "Then how do you know so much about feeding babies, Mr. Sheridan?"

"I used to have me some real excellent side vision."

She gave a startled laugh. "You rascal."

"Boys will be boys. Most got a real keen interest in everything they ain't s'posed to. Some of 'em are so bad for sneakin' looks you get worried their eyes'll stick at the outside corners."

She giggled again. When her mirth subsided, she sighed and touched Jonathan's small hand, smiling when he curled his fingers over hers. "He's very strong," she whispered. "It's amazing how good a grip he has. He can almost lift himself."

"Aw, go on."

"No, really."

He nudged her hand aside to see for himself. When the baby curled his tiny fingers over Deke's, he got a tight feeling in his chest. "He's one fine boy, Laura," he whispered.

And this time Deke sincerely meant that. Looks weren't everything. Deke would see to it that Jonathan grew into such a fine young man that nobody would notice he had a bad case of the homelies.

"I think he's the most beautiful baby I've ever seen," Laura whispered on a sleepy sigh.

Deke saw her eyelashes flutter closed, and smiled to himself. A few minutes later, he started to fall asleep as well, his finger captured in Jonathan's small fist, his knuckles resting lightly against Laura's soft skin, his mind filled with determination.

He wasn't alone anymore. He would never be alone again. He had a family—a beautiful wife and a fine son. Deke's last thought was that he would be the best damned husband and father who had ever walked, or die trying.

During her second day as Deke's wife, Laura learned what an exacting husband he might prove to be. He hovered at her elbow over their morning fire to instruct her on the "proper" way to make cornmeal mush so the mixture wouldn't lump. While he washed the dishes after their meal, he insisted she lie down for a short rest even though she swore she wasn't weary. When the dishes were finished, he slipped his arms through the cradleboard straps, gathered soap, linen, her hairbrush, and the Indian clothing given to her as a wedding gift, then escorted her to a deep pool in the creek for a bath.

As wonderful as a bath sounded, Laura was extremely nervous about disrobing with only a stand of brush between her and Deke to shield her modesty. As a consequence, she gathered up her things from the rock where he had placed them and wandered a bit farther upstream to another still pool. The water was shallower and there was no flat rock handy, but she felt easier about undressing there.

The water proved to be a pleasant surprise, still and shallow enough to be warmed slightly by the sun, the bottom silty with few rocks. Carrying the crudely shaped slab of soap, Laura waded in to midthigh and sat down with a luxurious sigh. The water on her skin felt so good, she couldn't resist lying back and allowing it to buoy her. The loosened tresses of her hair lifted to the surface to float around her. Laura could scarcely wait to scrub her scalp, but first she wanted to enjoy the pleasurable sensation of soaking for a minute.

Ahhhh.

Afraid that Deke might grow impatient and seek her out, Laura soon got down to business, starting at the top of her head and working her way down, abrading her skin with fingertips and nails until it tingled. As she began washing her upper body, she felt a stinging on her fanny, then one on her thigh. She swiped with a hand, then went back to scrubbing.

Wash. Rinse. Wash. Rinse. Soap in her eyes, she bent forward and waggled her face in the water. As she straightened, she felt stings on her breast and belly. She brushed with a hand and felt something soft and—oh, God—slimy stuck to her. She sputtered and tried to see, but soap was still in her eyes. She started to rub her lashes and felt something on her cheek. She blinked and rolled her burning eyes downward. Something brown. Something awful. She squealed and tried to get it off, but it was attached to her skin.

Lunging toward shore, Laura looked down and saw that she had brown things all over her. *Leeches.* Her mind froze on the word, and she began plucking at them and screaming. Oh, God—oh, God. Leeches everywhere.

Laura heard a great splash and saw a blur of buckskin and bronze cutting through the water to reach her. Strong arms snatched her from the pool.

"Son of aaaa *bitch*!"

Deke plopped her fanny on the sandy creek bank and knelt beside her. Laura was too frantic to care that she was naked. "Off me! Get them off me! Oh, God, oh God!" She grabbed and plucked, throwing the disgusting things away, not caring that it hurt to pull them off. "Help me!"

Large hands grabbed her by the shoulders and gave her a shake. "Laura, stop it!" he snarled.

She gulped down a scream and blinked to bring his dark face into focus. A shudder ran the length of her. She gulped again.

"Now, just calm down," he said more gently. "You can't go tearin' the damned things off like that. It makes sores. I either gotta pry 'em off slow with my knife or take you back to the lodge and dab 'em with turpentine."

"The knife!" she squeaked, unable to bear the thought of leaving the vile things on herself a second longer than she had to. "Oh, please, hurry."

Deke drew his knife and bent over her to lightly skim the blade over her skin. Calmer now, Laura realized Jonathan was somewhere nearby and crying. She searched for him and saw that Deke had laid him in the lee of a boulder.

"He's fine," he assured her. "Just scared, probably. You was screechin' to wake the dead." He swore and flung away a leech. "Why the hell did you come upstream? I picked a nice safe spot for you, and what'd ya do but wander off into a bunch of goddamned bloodsuckers."

Laura squeezed her eyes closed. *Bloodsuckers.* Oh, mercy, she was going to throw up. She could feel the awful things all over her, digging in and drawing. She made hard fists and braced them on the dirt, striving to stay calm. Water streamed in rivers from her hair, icy on her skin in the morning breeze.

"Just get them off of me, please," she said thinly, and lifted her lashes. "You can yell at me later."

"I'm tryin' to get 'em off you. As for yellin', I think goin' through this is bad enough." Ice blue eyes arced at her. "Next time, when I stick your little butt someplace, you keep it there, though. Understand? How in hell can I take care of you proper if you wander off?"

Laura had indeed learned her lesson. She had "wandered off" to seek more privacy, afraid that Deke might peek at her through the brush. Well, he was certainly getting an eyeful now. She flinched when his callused fingertips settled on her breast. Morbidly curious, she couldn't resist looking, then wished she hadn't. One of the horrible things had attached itself to her nipple. Her flesh there was pebbled from the cold, and Deke couldn't skim the knife under the leech without cutting her.

"Christ!" He bit out the word.

To Laura's mortification and dismay, he dragged on her shriveled flesh with thumb and forefinger to pull it smooth so he might scrape with the knife. She held her breath until he had pried off the leech and flung it away. Then she waited, half expecting him to either make a lewd comment or let his fingers linger. He did neither and took her completely by surprise by leaving her for a moment to fetch a linen towel, which he draped over her shoulders and tugged closed over her breasts.

Never a look. Never a word to increase her embarrassment. Laura settled an incredulous gaze on his dark face as he bent over her thigh. His light-colored eyes were sharp with concern and never strayed from his task. His hands—those huge, clumsy hands—were so wonderfully warm and gentle and capable.

From behind the black curtains within Laura's mind, vague memories slipped free. Deke's wonderful, magical hands. Soothing away her pain, bathing and filling her with heat. He had touched her like this before, she realized. And she had seen that look in his eyes as well. Worry and tenderness.

Her throat tightened with an emotion she wasn't quite ready to name as she recalled that first night after she awakened from her fever, how he had waggled his thumbs at her and encouraged her to grab hold. To prevent his hands from wandering? Why would he bother, when he had touched her in all those places many times before? No, he had offered her his thumbs for one reason only: to make her feel at ease. She hadn't appreciated the gesture that night.

But she did now. And suddenly she did feel at ease. Or perhaps a better word was *safe*. To say she felt comfortable about having his hands all over her nude body was stretching things a bit far. But as tensely aware of him and embarrassed as she was, she no longer felt frightened.

Deke would never harm her. Or cause her pain if he could avoid it. She was as certain of it in that moment as she was that her name was now Laura Sheridan.

Laura Sheridan. The new name lingered in her mind as she studied her husband. Her life with him would be far different from anything she had known before. This horrendous experience with the leeches drove that point home.

Laura's gaze shifted to Jonathan where he lay quiet now, protected from the sun in the lee of the boulder. Even in his haste to reach her, Deke had thought of the baby's well-being. Now he was caring for her.

It was a very nice feeling, to be cared for. It made her feel safe and secure. It also gave her hope, something she hadn't felt for a very long time.

Looming above the layered foothills, the Rockies reached like giant fingers of granite. Laura fixed her gaze on them, all the while conscious of Deke's light ministrations on her legs. Colorado. For so long she had thought of it as the bane of her existence, a perilous and frightening place, even though it was beautiful. Now she looked forward to pitting herself against it. If any man on earth could teach her how to survive here in this rugged land, it had to be Deke Sheridan.

A flutter of excitement entered Laura's belly. For two endlessly long years, she had yearned for her independence and bridled under the restraints of matrimonial subservience. In all that time she had envisioned freedom as something she could only hope to attain in certain measure, at best to return home to Boston and her father's dominion over her, where she would surely be allowed far more liberties as a divorcée than she had been before her marriage. It had been the most she could expect, for no woman could ever entirely escape the strictures of a male-dominated world.

But Deke was offering her more than that. Under his tutelage, she might learn how to become totally self-sufficient in a wide-open country where social mores could never restrict her. If he was true to his word, he would allow her measures of freedom and independence to exceed any she had ever dreamed possible.

Laura wanted him to begin teaching her immediately. Given her present predicament, the very first thing she wanted to learn was how to choose a bathing spot that was free of leeches.

Chapter 23

"FORWARD ON THE LEFT FOOT," DEKE CALLED. "Not the right, goddammit! Back up and do it correct."

Laura fell back, then swung forward again, this time on her left foot, into three long strides. On the final step she simultaneously spun to the left and, using her right hand, drew the knife Deke had lent her from its scabbard. *One smooth motion,* she reminded herself. *Keep a flick in your wrist.* The knife handle slid easily from her fingers with a sharp snap and sang through the air. Laura watched with a sinking heart as it missed the tree trunk by a miserably wide margin and buried itself in the dirt up to its hilt.

"Blast it!" she cried in frustration. "I'll *never* get it right."

Jonathan in the cradleboard and strapped to his bare back, Deke sauntered slowly forward, the denim of his jeans hugging his long, heavily muscled legs like the peeling on a banana. He eyed the knife with a raised eyebrow. "Hey, darlin', you done fine. Would you just look at that? You finally hit something blade-first."

In a fit of pique, Laura dug dirt with the toe of her moccasin and sent it flying. "It isn't funny."

"And I ain't laughin'. Bringin' a knife out of its spin to hit blade-first is half of the battle." He swung dancing blue eyes toward her. "In another week, you'll be fearsome if you keep on practicin'."

Practicing, practicing. Laura felt as though she had done nothing else in the three days since her marriage. Practicing cooking. Practicing aiming the rifle and Colt. Practicing with the knife. In between sessions, she nursed Jonathan and rested, at Deke's insistence. She was beginning to feel that all she did was practice, feed her baby, eat, and sleep.

"Well, I'm fed up," she said angrily. "I'd rather stick with shooting the rifle." Thus far, Laura had found that taking steady aim with Deke's Colt revolver was nigh unto impossible, and she was as frustrated with trying to master that as she was with knife throwing. "All I care about is being able to defend myself to some degree."

"And if you empty the rifle and don't got time to reload? What then?"

"I'll use it as a club."

Deke chuckled and stepped behind her to massage her aching shoulders. That was yet another thing Laura was growing heartily weary of, being touched so incessantly. He did it deliberately, she knew, and he was very good at it. A continuous sexual parry, pressing his advantage, letting her think this would be the time he might push her for more, making her unbearably nervous in the process, then retreating. There were moments when Laura wanted to grab him by his hair, jerk his handsome face down to within inches of her own, and tell him to either get on with it or leave her alone.

"What if the enemy takes your club away from you?"

"I'll throw dirt in his eyes."

He chuckled again. "And make him mad enough to kill. Better to have a knife as backup."

"Unless I can hit something with it, a knife is useless."

"Not so. With that throwin' style you're developin', you'll scare the holy shit out of somebody."

Laura crossed her arms and stretched her neck, unable to resist the gentle kneading of his strong fingers. He bent his head and feathered his lips along the hairline at her temple. She closed her eyes to enjoy the tingling sensation that prickled over her nape and ribboned down her spine.

"Five more throws," he whispered, "and I'll take you back to the lodge for a nap."

Laura didn't want to throw the knife or take a nap. She wanted to lean against him, just as she was, and feel his lips whispering over her hair.

When she realized what she was thinking, she straightened and moved abruptly away from him. As she went to get the knife, she cast him a wary glance over her shoulder. He stood with his long legs spread, arms akimbo, the crown of Jonathan's dark head nestled on one well-padded shoulder. No shirt. The waistband of his jeans rode low on his hips. Morning sunlight arced off his mahogany hair and accented the unnervingly light color of his eyes.

Eyes that followed her. Eyes that caressed and made her heartbeat accelerate. Eyes that made sensual promises he never carried through on.

Laura jerked the knife from the dirt. As she moved back toward him, the fringe at the bottom of her leather dress tickled the backs of her calves, and she wondered how it might feel if Deke touched her there. Or kissed her there.

What was he doing to her? Laura clenched her fingers around the knife handle. Madness. He was driving her to the brink of madness, and judging by the twinkle in his eyes, he knew it, damn him. Her gaze settled on his lips, the top one defined in a thin, very masculine bow, the bottom full but firm and aglisten with moisture. Her mouth felt suddenly dry. Her pulse thrummed in the back of her throat.

During the journey west, Laura had sometimes visited with other young wives, and they had whispered amongst themselves about the shocking, scandalous things their men demanded of them once the wagon flaps were battened down. At the time, those stories had horrified Laura. She hadn't even been able to conceive people behaving in such a manner. The thought of Tristan taking such liberties had sickened her, and she had been heartily glad he was usually mean drunk when he came to her, rough in the taking but quick to finish.

But Deke ... For reasons beyond her, she found herself wondering sometimes what it might be like to simply lie back and surrender all that she was to him. Hands with a grip like steel but that never left a bruise. Hands that knew a woman's body and how to arouse her. Skilled, silken lips that could coax her into the kind of kiss that carried her beyond reason into a vortex of delicious sensation. A part of Laura yearned to step over that line with him and allow herself to be utterly wanton—just once—to see for herself what those young women on the wagon train had been giggling about.

When she came to stand before him, he gently pried the knife from her fingers and returned it to the scabbard she wore secured at her waist on a rawhide thong. "You look tired," he said softly as he shrugged his shoulders out of the cradleboard straps. Indicating a smooth boulder and a grassy spot beneath a nearby cottonwood, he added, "Let's rest awhile."

Laura followed him to the spot, checked to make sure Jonathan was sleeping soundly after Deke laid him at the base of the tree, then went to lean against the rock with him, her hip a scant inch from his thigh. He stood with his legs slightly extended, ankles crossed, one heel of a moccasin dug into the dirt. His arms were loosely crossed over his flat belly.

Laura watched him from the corner of her eye and recalled his saying he had studied women in the same way as a boy. Surreptitiously, ever curious, mesmerized by the forbidden.

Only, he wasn't forbidden. According to his beliefs, they were married, and it was ridiculously immature to sneak peeks at him. If she wanted to look, why didn't she simply turn her head and let him see her looking? She was fascinated by the sculpted musculature in his arms and shoulders. She yearned to trace a finger along the silken ridge of dark hair that grew along the side of his broad wrist.

But if she looked at him that way, he might look back or take it as an invitation to do more. And she wasn't certain she was ready for that yet. Oh, she wasn't afraid he might carry things too far. Deke was nothing if not solicitous of her well-being, and he would never do anything invasive until her body was completely recovered from childbirth. Laura felt confident of that now.

But, as he had once informed her, there was "more'n one way for a man and woman to parley." Every time Laura thought of his saying that, her imagination ran wild. Deke probably made love to a woman as he did all else, in his own rugged, earthen, elemental way, no holds barred. If she gave him half a chance, he might do all those things to her that the women on the wagon train had whispered about—and possibly more. If he did, she would die of embarrassment.

Laura sneaked another glance at him only to have her gaze collide with his. He was watching her with a secretive, smirky grin as if he knew exactly what she was thinking. Inside her ears, Laura heard her pulse start to go *swi-swish, swi-swish. A* fluttery, hot feeling attacked her stomach.

He crooked a finger, beckoning, his eyes holding hers in a relentless grip. "Come here, darlin'."

Laura swallowed and was about to say no when he reached over and took her hand. Still smiling, he drew her toward him and a fate she wasn't sure she wanted to meet. With his crossed foot, he nudged her ankle until she stepped astraddle his legs, and then he pulled her forward, using his other hand to tug the fringed hem of her dress up so it wouldn't hinder her ascent along his slightly angled thighs.

She wore nothing but the halter he had made for her under the dress, and the skin-warmed denim of his jeans abraded the tender flesh at the apex of her legs.

Due to lack of stature, she could only step so close and keep her feet. A foot and a half of distance remained between their upper bodies, the hem of her skirt riding high, the fringe fanned across the fly of his jeans.

Retaining his grip on her hand, he toyed with her fingertips, tracing her nails with his thumb. His gaze, lambent and sparkling like steel against flint, still held hers captive. Laura wondered how he could do such strange things to her insides by only playing with her fingers.

He lifted his other hand to her hair, smoothed it, tested its texture, teased a tendril into a curl. The contact seemed absurdly intimate. Laura reminded herself of the four nights she had slept beside this man. She had nothing to fear, yet he made her feel imperiled. She sensed that there would be no holding back with Deke. But what truly worried her was that he might weave a spell around her so she had no wish to.

With deft fingertips he untied the thong that secured her single braid, then combed her hair into a heavy curtain over her shoulders. Threading his fingers down its length, he accidentally grazed the sensitized tip of one breast with his knuckles. Or was it an accident? He made another light pass over the same spot. His expression didn't alter, but the heat of his gaze grew searing. Just when she might have protested, he abandoned her hair to rub his thumb over her mouth.

"You are so pretty," he whispered huskily.

Laura parted and relaxed her lips, loving the gentle abrasion of his sandpapery skin tugging on her mouth, then so lightly caressing. Her lashes fluttered low. He made her feel like a candle sitting on a sunny windowsill, warm and pliable, close to melting.

"You're the color of fresh cream," he told her. "With the pink of rose petals here and there, and splashes of whiskey."

Oh, God. Laura made an odd little sound, foreign to her, half moan, half word, and completely nonsensical. This man turned her brain to mush, and the only rational thoughts left to her were deliciously wicked. The kind of thoughts only a sinful, lustful woman would entertain.

"You ever touched your lips with a rose petal?" he asked. Laura was beyond making a reply. "There's nothin' that smells so sweet or feels so soft," he whispered. "That's how your mouth felt the other night when I kissed you— like a rose petal."

She tasted salt and realized she had touched the tip of her tongue to his thumb. She immediately drew it back, shocked at her own forwardness.

"Ahhhh, and whiskey with cream, Laura? You ever tasted that? It's so smooth and rich, you wanna lap it like a cat."

Laura felt his fingers tugging at the leather thongs that held her bodice flap closed. She couldn't move to stop him, didn't want to. The heavy panel of leather fell back like the opened cover of a well-read book. He tugged at the inside thong and drew back the cross panel. Next he reached for the three buttons nestled in her cleavage that held her halter closed.

"Deke," she managed weakly.

"I wanna see them pretty little pink nipples peekin' out at me through that whiskey-colored hair," he insisted huskily. "Don't say no, darlin'. Please."

Warm, leathery fingers scooped her breasts from the tailored cups of chambray, then lifted and rearranged her hair to lie over each shoulder in barely divided drapes.

"Jesus, you're beautiful," he said in a raspy voice. "So damned beautiful. Look and see for yourself. Anybody so pretty shouldn't oughta be bashful. You pleasure me just by standin' there."

Laura looked. She couldn't resist. Her face went hot, but she couldn't avert her gaze as he touched a pale pink crest with the tip of his forefinger. He teased the throbbing bud of flesh with the edge of his nail, coaxing it so erect, it ached. Then he caught the nub between thumb and finger and gave it a sharp roll.

Laura gasped and her knees buckled. The warm saddle of his denim-covered thighs caught her from falling. She wound her fingers over his biceps to hold herself erect. "Deke."

"I'm right here, honey. Don't close them pretty eyes. I wanna look into 'em, and I want you lookin' at me."

"Oh, please." Laura didn't know if she was pleading with him to stop or to do it some more. It was heaven. It was hell. He made her ache with longing in places she hadn't realized she had until now. "Oh, please, Deke."

He bent his dark head and lapped at her nipple. She shuddered and dug her nails into his skin. This was debasing. Immoral. Unladylike. Sinful. So terribly wicked. "Oh, yes," she cried.

He gave a satisfied chuckle, still teasing, still setting her senses into a spin. "You like that, do you?"

The only response Laura was capable of making was a quavery moan. He grabbed her with his teeth. A sharp nip that halted her breath, snapped her spine taut, and made her heart slam to sudden stillness. She abandoned her hold on his arms to sink her hands into his hair, where she made tight fists.

Holding her captured between his teeth, he tortured her with drags of his tongue. She reveled in it, let her head fall back, cried out at the sensations that rocked her. Her pulse resumed, each execution an explosion against her eardrums. He stilled her heart again by suddenly drawing all of her into his mouth. Laura felt the pull clear to her toes and mewled like a fretful child. He switched breasts and treated the other nipple to the same masterful titillation until she felt boneless, mindless, breathless, and totally his.

It was wonderful. It was terrifying. But she was helpless to stop it. Trapped in a dizzying microcosm of feelings, she was vaguely aware that he swung her around to drape her over the smooth boulder. His hands slid like hot brands up her thighs, peeling back her dress, his mouth still at a breast, hungry and demanding as only a man like Deke Sheridan could be. Pressing a hip to the rock, he braced on one elbow and slid his other hand to the nest of curls between her legs. His fingertips slid into her wetness, then sought and found a spot so tender that Laura bucked.

He lifted his head. Startled amber eyes clung to glinting steely blue. "Don't be scared, Boston. I won't hurt you."

Laura made a feeble grab for his wrist, not afraid of him but of the things he was making her feel. Shards of fire leaped from that spot, kindled by each brush of his fingers. She couldn't breathe, couldn't think clearly, couldn't speak. Her body, no longer her own, quivered for him like a plucked bowstring.

And he was watching, his eyes agleam with masculine satisfaction, his hard mouth tipped in a wry grin as he brought his thumb into the play and ground its broad pad in a circular motion over her. She was making a spectacle of herself, he her audience. She wanted him to stop. A wave of embarrassment crashed over her.

"Deke!"

"Let it happen," he urged in a throaty rasp. "Raise your hips and give it to me. There's my girl. Let it happen."

The sensation built. Laura heard herself panting, the sounds growing shorter and quicker. Beneath his thumb, the fiery shards went white-hot and seemed to implode, turning her molten. Her body arched and then jerked, and she cried out.

Afterward, she lay there in stunned disbelief as reality returned to her. Sunshine and man. She was sprawled over the smooth rock like a wanton, her most private places exposed to his searing gaze. She was so ashamed that she wanted to die—until she looked into his eyes. The tenderness there made her forget all else. He dipped his head and kissed her, a sweet, lingering touch of their mouths that soothed her and made her feel like a treasured gift he was carefully rewrapping. By the time he freed her lips, her halter and bodice were put back as they had been, and her skirt had been tugged back down to her knees.

"Ah, Laura, honey," he said with an indulgent smile as he trailed kisses over her blushing cheeks. "Don't feel shy. Not with me. You're the sweetest thing that's ever happened to me. Don't you know that?"

Laura pushed at her hair with a trembling hand. "I just can't quite believe I behaved with such—with such utter abandon."

His eyes had gone all twinkling, a sign that Laura was quickly coming to recognize as dangerous. "Boston, I hate to tell you this, but I was bein' real mannerly that time around."

She blinked. "Mannerly?"

"Hell, yes. I don't want you thinkin' I ain't got couth. When you get over bein' so bashful, I'll show you how that's supposed to be done."

"How, pray?"

He chuckled and grabbed her hands to pull her up off the rock. "Oh, no. Not this boy. I learned a long time ago at a three-fork supper party that there's some things you don't say or talk about to a lady, and that's one of 'em." He chucked her under her chin. "I'll just wait till the time's right and surprise you."

Laura wasn't certain she wanted to be surprised. On the other hand, though, maybe she did.

Chapter 24

SURPRISES. OVER THE NEXT TWO WEEKS, LAURA learned that Deke Sheridan was a man of so many surprises, she could scarcely keep track of them. He not only knew a great deal about babies, but was absolutely wonderful with Jonathan, always willing to hold him, not hesitating to wash and change him, endlessly patient when he grew fussy. There were times when Laura's heart caught at the expression on Deke's face when he looked at her son, sometimes tender, at other times proud, always affectionate. She began to wonder whether Deke didn't truly love the baby as much as he might have if he were his own.

"Look, Laura," he demanded one afternoon. "He's smiling at me!" Another time, after tracing the baby's face with a leathery fingertip, he said, "You know, he might just grow out of it."

"Out of what?" Laura had asked.

An evasive look came into Deke's eyes. "Ah, nothin'," he said, but Laura noticed he continued to study the baby with a pleased smile. Laura began to suspect that perhaps Deke hadn't thought Jonathan to be a very pretty baby when he first saw him.

True to his word, Deke spent hours teaching Laura each day. Under his expert tutelage, she became increasingly proficient with weapons, even learning to throw the knife and hit her target. He also schooled her in the gathering of edible flora, teaching her to recognize a leafy plant he called

Indian lettuce and a white tuber he claimed tasted very much like potatoes, a yellow root that substituted for carrots, wild onions, and watercress.

When Laura was able to gather stew makings without Deke's help, he began teaching her to recognize plants and trees with medicinal properties, which she found particularly fascinating because she knew some of those same plants and trees might have saved her life. No doubting Thomas, she. Not anymore. Medicine Woman clearly knew what she was doing when it came to doctoring, and she had trained her only son well.

The bark from barberry, Laura learned, was a powerful healer that fought inflammation in wounds, cured liver jaundice, diarrhea, dysentery, urinary tract problems, pinkeye, goiters, and female inflammations. It was also believed to keep a person well if consumed regularly.

"If nobody's sick," Deke laughingly added, "its berries can always be used for jams and puddin's, the roots to make yellow dye."

For fever he recommended powdered bayberry bark, and failing to find that, willow bark tea. "I hear tell a woman can dose her man with willow bark tea regular and—" He broke off and shot her a sultry look. "Never mind. I don't want you gettin' ideas."

Intrigued, Laura asked, "What kind of ideas? Come on, Deke, I want to learn all I can. Don't keep things from me."

He shrugged. "Well, too much willow bark tea is s'posed to make a man"—he shot her another look—"less interested in the ladies, if you know what I mean."

Laura giggled. "Oh, really?" She waggled a scolding finger at him. "Watch your step, Mr. Sheridan. Give me too much trouble, and I shall dose you daily!"

He swatted playfully at her, which she easily dodged because he was carrying Jonathan. Laura gained several steps on him, turned, and walked backward. "You'd better be nice to me. I know how to handle you now."

He narrowed one eye. "Come near me with willow bark tea, girl, and I'll flay the hide right off your sassy little butt."

Laura didn't feel the least intimidated, and that felt absolutely wonderful. Eyes stinging with tears of gladness, she stopped retreating and waited for him to come abreast of her. When Deke saw the suspicious shimmer in her eyes, he hooked a hand over the back of her neck and hauled her up against him for a quick hug.

No words, no promises. But Laura was quickly realizing she didn't need them, not with Deke. As for dosing him with willow bark tea? Not on her life. As diligently as he had all else, he had been working very hard to get Laura past her "bashful" stage. Thus far, he hadn't been entirely successful, but Laura was coming to enjoy his efforts more with each passing day.

Denver. When Laura thought of returning there now, she felt indescribably sad. Life among the Cheyenne was idyllic. She loved everything about it, from the new freedom of movement she enjoyed in her Indian clothing to the social activities. Dances by late-night bonfires. Being caught in Deke's blanket and secretly fondled until she nearly went mad trying to keep her expression carefully blank so no one else might guess what he was doing to her. Passing the firelight hours of long summer evenings with Black Stone, Star, and Sugar Girl, playing board games, eating specially made treats, listening to Medicine Woman tell stories of old. So much love, so little pretense. Laura had been accepted by the People, made to feel one with them, and she dreaded the thought of leaving them, perhaps never to see any of them again.

Even so, a great deal of time had passed, and Laura knew Deke had a ranch to run. It began to worry her that he gave no sign of being anxious to leave.

One evening when they were returning to the village from one of their educational walks through the woods, Laura missed Chief, who was usually Deke's constant shadow.

"Where has that mangy, good-for-nothing dog gotten off to?" she asked lightly.

"He's sniffin' out honey, I think."

Laura frowned. "Honey?"

Deke grinned. "A little gal who's in the courtin' mood. Damned mongrel ain't got no loyalty at all when it comes to females. Takes off darned near every time we hit Denver, and I don't see him much till it's time to leave."

"I don't imagine you missed him much. I warn you, Mr. Sheridan, those days are gone forever. Henceforth, no upstairs rooms for you."

Laura happened to glance up and catch him with a wistful expression on his dark face.

"What is it?" she asked softly.

They were near a stream, of which there were many in the foothills, and Deke paused to lean against a cottonwood, his gaze fixed on the rushing water where it eddied and foamed over a fall of rocks. Laura was beginning to think he might not answer her when he suddenly said, "You're strong enough to travel now. The twenty days is up. Twenty-two to be exact. We might oughta be headin' back for Denver shortly."

Though Laura had been acutely aware that they should probably head back for Denver and his ranch soon, she hadn't thought of the passage of time in terms of days, specifically the number they had originally decided she would need to fully recover from childbirth. Yet when she trailed her gaze to Jonathan's round little face where it rested against Deke's back, she could see how greatly he had changed. His skin was creamy now and blushed from sunshine. His dark hair had grown thick and was beginning to curl. His eyelashes were long and silken on his plump cheeks.

"I didn't realize. The time has passed so quickly."

Deke flashed her a meaningful look, but the twinkle she had grown accustomed to seeing in his eyes wasn't there. "It ain't that I've been markin' off the nights or nothin'."

Laura had to smile at that. She no longer dreaded consummating their marriage. Indeed, with so much coaxing from him, she had even begun to anticipate it. She knew that the abstinence hadn't been easy for him. She wondered if, now that the time had arrived, he felt uncertain of how to approach her. A month ago, she would have found it difficult to believe that Deke Sheridan could feel nervous about anything, much less making love to a woman. But now she knew he wasn't nearly as sure of himself as he pretended to be.

"Well." She rubbed her nose. "Goodness, how does one say this?" Wishing she were brazen enough to do much more, she touched his arm. "I'm no longer suffering from a decided lack of enthusiasm."

He chuckled at that and grazed his knuckles along her cheek, his eyes still dark with wistfulness. "It ain't that, Laura. But I thank you kindly for tellin' me." He touched a fingertip to her eyebrows. "Do you know how much I've come to care for you?" he asked in a tight voice. "For you and the baby."

Laura had begun to guess. Sometimes when he looked at her, she saw the love shining in his eyes. At other times, like right now, she not only saw it in his eyes but felt it in the way he touched her. "I think I know, yes."

He dropped his hand, swallowed hard, and returned his gaze to the stream.

"Deke?"

He gestured with a hand to silence her. "I got a load of things I need to say," he finally told her, "and I ain't real sure where to start."

Laura bent her head and scuffed last autumn's mulched cottonwood leaves with the toe of her moccasin. He wasn't the only one who had some things to get off his chest, and she had the most awful feeling his present distress was a direct result of her reticence. An ache filled her, not just in the region of her heart, but an awful, all-encompassing ache that spread to her belly and made her limbs feel strangely numb. Now that she was recovered enough to travel, was he worried about taking her back to Denver? Was he afraid she might still try to leave him if she was given half the chance?

Oh, Deke. Why hadn't she told him before now how much she had come to care for him? How happy she was when she was with him? That she had no intention of running off, not now, not later, no matter where they happened to be?

Deep down, Laura knew the answer to that. She was afraid. Afraid of taking that final and irrevocable step, of making a commitment, of forging ties that could imprison her for a lifetime. This absolutely wonderful man had given her so very much and had been so endlessly patient, trying to impart to her all the knowledge he could to make her feel self-sufficient. But he couldn't give her courage. That had to come from within herself.

To trust again. To allow herself to need again. Those things didn't come easily to her, and to admit them aloud even less so.

Deke suddenly shifted his weight and repositioned his shoulder against the tree, jerking Laura from her thoughts to gaze up at his profile. He looked so very Indian standing there in the dusky light, but she no longer found that intimidating, and she wouldn't have changed a single thing about him. She had come to appreciate this man just as he was, for who he was, rough edges and all.

A muscle along his jaw ticked, which told her just how tense he felt. He scraped the back of his hand across his mouth. "I gotta tell you somethin', Boston, and you ain't gonna be real happy when you hear it."

Laura wondered what dark secret he thought he was hiding, or what horrid thing about himself he meant to reveal. That he had once stood beneath an oak tree, grieving for love that was lost? Or that he had killed twenty-two rapists, perhaps? Or that he had once lived amongst the Cheyenne and ridden into battle against whites with them? She cared about none of those things. Through no fault of his own, Deke Sheridan was different from any other man she had ever met, and to judge him by ordinary standards would be as silly as expecting an apple to look and taste like an orange.

Reaching deep within, Laura found the courage that had eluded her these last several days. "Whatever you're about to tell me, Deke, it doesn't matter."

"Oh, it matters."

Laura willed him to look at her, but he kept his gaze on the stream.

"You see, darlin', I done somethin' real low-down, and I wasn't gonna tell you I done it until . . . well, until it was too late."

"All I care about is what has happened between you and me. Nothing else matters. If you're going to tell me about some horrible thing you once did, forget it. Now that I know you, I probably won't think it was all that horrible, anyway. You can't be blamed for the circumstances you've had to deal with."

"Christ."

Laura touched his arm again. "Deke, I truly mean it. I don't care what you've done or how low-down you think it was."

"I lied to you," he bit out.

Laura drew her hand back and pressed it to her waist. "Oh, I see." After a moment, she smiled. "Well, I suppose I can forgive you for one or two little lies."

"They wasn't little."

Her stomach twisted, and an awful sense of foreboding filled her. Memories. Tristan. For two years he had treated her to a steady diet of treacherous lies. With Deke, she wanted and needed all of that to be behind her, and she couldn't help but feel frightened at the tone in his voice. "What did you lie to me about?"

"Well, you see, that there's just the thing. It was about somethin' real serious." He swiped at his mouth again, then puffed air into his cheeks, a habit he had when he was on the spot. "Before I tell you what the lies was, I'd kinda like to tell why I told 'em so maybe you won't get your tail tied in such a knot over it."

Lies. Plural. She felt as if she might throw up. "Please do."

He shot her a look. "Jesus, you're already gettin' mad, and I ain't even started yet."

He was right, and she knew it. Laura took a deep breath, trying to calm herself. He wasn't Tristan. Maybe he had lied to her, possibly even about something serious, but to immediately believe the worst wasn't fair. "I'm sorry." She waved a hand. "You're right. I, um ... It's just—after Tristan—well, the first things that enter my head are trickery and ..." She gestured again, at a loss for words. "I guess I've never told you about all that, have I?"

"Christ."

That word. Laura's stomach lurched as if he had punched her. He jerked off his headband of cobalt beads to rake his hand through his hair. Then he tucked the beads into his waistband.

"Laura, you gotta hear me out. Will you give me that much?" He finally turned his gaze to her, and the only word to describe the expression she read there was *tormented*. "I think I've earned that, ain't I?"

Looking up at him, Laura realized he had earned that much and more. She was reacting to this irrationally, allowing the past to determine her present. What could Deke have lied to her about that might be so horrible or so treacherous that it would kill her feelings for him or eclipse all the wonderful things he had done?

"Yes, you have earned that," she finally replied.

His gaze clung to hers. There was so much love there. All her life, that was all she had ever really wanted, from her father, then from Tristan, just to be loved, not for her accomplishments or worth, but for herself, regardless of flaws, unconditionally. Now, in the most unlikely circumstances with the most unlikely of men, she had finally found what she most wanted. She would be a fool to turn her back on that.

"From the first second I clapped eyes on you, I—" He broke off and swallowed hard. "Well, not from the first second, I guess, but sometime durin' that first night, every time I looked at you, it scared hell outa me. You're ..." He puffed air into his cheeks again. "Well, to a man like me, Laura, you're a real fine little swatch of calico. Too fine, if you know what I mean. Beautiful ... and fancy-mannered ... and— well, hell, highfalutin says it all, I reckon. Just the kinda woman I learned a long time ago to avoid. Only, you was in a hell of a fix, and I couldn't."

The pain in his eyes wrapped around Laura's heart and wouldn't let go.

"Anyhow," he went on thickly, "I tried real hard not to like you, and for extra measure, just in case bein' myself wasn't despicable enough, I kinda went outa my way there at first to be more despicable so you wouldn't like me none too much neither."

Laura recollected those times all too well. The momentary silence that fell over them was rife with memories.

"I started seein' straight off that you wasn't like most city gals. No offense meant, but the ones I've met aside from you . . . Well, there wasn't much to curry after the ride, if you understand what I mean."

Laura hugged her waist and did her best to smother a smile. Only Deke would say something like that to a woman when he was trying to apologize. She supposed that was one of his most endearing qualities, the way he always managed to stick his foot in his mouth, never realizing he had. To Laura, that made him all the more lovable.

"You wasn't like that," he said softly. "You had guts, for starters. And I never heard you whine even once. And I started to like you whether it was smart to or not. Then the likin' turned to real strong fondness. And you went and got sick. After spendin' a week carin' for you and listenin' to you go on, well, I was bogged down up to my hocks and sinkin' fast. And I had me this feelin'— way deep down—that we was meant to be together, and that all I needed was a chance to make you see it."

Laura took a step toward him. "Deke, I—"

"Now, I know you're probably gonna say that ain't an excuse, that there ain't never no excuse for lyin'. But sometimes, Laura, you just . . ." He lifted his hands in supplication, then slapped his thighs. "You just want somethin' or someone so bad that right and wrong sorta seem to be ridin' double. You know what I mean?"

At the jerk of Deke's shoulders, Jonathan squirmed. Both Laura and Deke grew quiet a moment to be sure he had drifted back to sleep. When he made no further sound, Deke said, "Where was I?"

"About right and wrong riding double," Laura reminded him. "But before you go on, may I get a word in edgewise?"

He sighed. "You said you'd hear me out."

"I know I did. But first, I'd just like to say that no matter what it was that you lied about, it isn't going to alter my feelings. I may be very angry, but—"

"No maybe to it, honey. You're gonna wanna skin me alive and hang my hide on a fence post to dry."

"*That* bad?"

"I tricked you into marryin' me."

For just an instant, Laura felt an awful coldness grabbing her, but she shook it off. Deke was not Tristan. "I *knew* it," she said. "You hoodwinked me. There was a way out of this mess all along, wasn't there?"

Laura meant that in a teasing way, but the instant she said it, she saw her mistake. Deke swung his face aside as though she had slapped him.

"Is that still how you feel?" he asked tautly. "That you're stuck in a mess?" Before she could answer, he turned back to regard her. Even in the dusky light she could see the tears shining in his eyes. "'Cause if it is, there's always dee-vorce. It ain't somethin' Cheyenne women does every day, mind you. But if that's what you want, I reckon I can give you plenty of reason."

Laura was so startled by this revelation that she blinked. "Divorce? Cheyenne women are allowed to divorce their husbands?"

"If there's cause."

"What constitutes a cause?" she asked, still amazed.

"Me diddlin' another woman is one."

"If you dare, divorce will be totally unnecessary because I'll murder you."

It was his turn to blink. When he did, a bit of moisture

slipped onto his cheek, and he made an angry swipe. "Can we back up? I'm gettin' the feelin' we ain't talkin' about the same thing here."

"That's because you've been doing all the talking and won't let me say three little words."

"Laura, when the day comes you can get anything said with only three words, I'll eat my boots."

"You don't own any boots. But I'll settle for watching you eat your moccasins. This is one time three words will do me. I love you, Deke."

He swiped at his cheek again, sniffed, and then closed his eyes. Laura could see he was struggling with everything he had not to lose his control.

"Deke?"

He rubbed at his cheek again, then planted his hands on his hips. After taking a deep, bracing breath, he opened his eyes, looked at her through a suspicious shimmer of wetness, and said, "That's four words, Boston. You lose."

Laura gave a startled giggle. "You, sirrah, are absolutely impossible!"

"I been told that a lot lately."

She laughed again. "I just said I love you. One would think women told you that every day."

His mouth quirked at the corners, then tipped into the lazy grin she had come to love so very much. His eyes still swimming, he said, "Not every day. But a few has said it." His grin broadened. "I just don't make a habit of sayin' it back."

"I see. And in my case?"

"Say it again and see."

Laura's smile vanished, and her own eyes filled with tears. "I love you."

He hooked a hand around the back of her neck and drew her into his arms. Laura could feel him trembling, and in that, she found all the response she needed. She didn't need words. Deke had already told her how much he loved her in a thousand different ways. Twenty-two of those times loomed foremost in her mind, three weeks of abstinence, not that he had been counting.

"Oh, Deke."

"I still ain't told you what I lied to you about."

Taking care not to jostle the cradleboard, Laura hugged his waist. "Do you suppose Star would keep Jonathan for us tonight?"

He pressed his face against her hair. "It was about somethin' real despicable, the kinda thing only a cad and a degenerate and a reprobate would do."

"Thank goodness. You've had my tail tied in a knot ever since I met you. I wouldn't know what to think if you started changing on me now."

He chuckled at that. Then he just held her for a long while, swaying there among the cottonwoods, his arms a safe haven she never wanted to leave. Laura went up on her tiptoes to nestle her face against his neck, loving the smell of him, wind and leather, earth and sunshine, traces of soap scent and saltiness, a blend that was distinctly this man's and only his. What a wonderful thing it was to know that he had wanted her, flaws and all, so badly that he had lied to have her. Considering that she hadn't been able to say *west* without sticking an *ish* on the end, Laura thought that was pretty incredible.

"Oh, Deke, I love you so. I'm glad you lied. If you hadn't, I might not be here with you now."

He made a fist over her braid. "After all the times I said I'd never do you like Tristan done, how can you say that? It wasn't just tellin' you the lie that was bad. I been keepin' it from you all this time and plannin' to make love to you when the twenty days was up so you'd be stuck with me." He took a shuddering breath. "Lies and tricks, just like Tristan. I figured if I made love to you regular, there'd never be a time you could be sure you wasn't with child, and then you wouldn't dare leave me. Your daddy ain't likely to welcome you with open arms if you're pregnant with some uneducated cowboy's brat."

Laura hugged him more tightly. "You're not uneducated, Deke. You've just attended a different hall of learning."

"Are you listenin' to me?"

"Yes. And I'm wondering why you didn't."

"Why I didn't what?"

"When the twenty days were up? Why didn't you make love to me? We've lost two whole days, and now we'll never get them back."

He rubbed a hand up her spine, then curled his fingers over her shoulder and squeezed so hard, it hurt. In a voice gone husky with emotion, he whispered, "If I make love to you, Boston, and then I lose you . . . well, I ain't sure I could stand it. I'll do all I can to be a proper kinda husband for you. I'll get me a haircut and wear regular clothes and I'll try not to curse. I'll even try to talk proper and use big words if you'll teach me. But you gotta promise me in return that you won't hare off the first time the goin' gets rough."

"Oh, Deke. A proper husband? If you touch your hair, I . . ." More tears welled in her eyes. "Well, if you even think about doing such a thing, I'll be mad enough to hunt cougar with a butter knife. And if I wanted a man who dressed differently and didn't curse and used big words, I'd hare off for Boston right now and find me one."

"I ain't no good at three-fork supper parties," he warned.

"If I get me a hankerin' for fancy supper parties, which I seriously doubt, I shan't serve soup."

"If your daddy ever meets me, he'll probably disown you for sure."

"Then he's a fool, and I don't suffer fools gladly."

"You sure?"

There was a wealth of hurt in those two words. Laura turned her face in to the cay of his neck, wishing she knew magic, some words, anything, that might undo all the pain that this man had suffered. Banished by his adopted people, rejected by those of his own race, he had been so terribly, terribly alone. He was so strong in so many ways, yet underneath it all, he was vulnerable as a child might be, still looking for a place where he could love and be loved, for a world that wouldn't turn away from him.

Laura wanted to create that world for him. "I'm very sure," she whispered. "If you have a doubt, sirrah, why don't you try making love to me and find out?"

She felt the tension drain from him. "That's the second time you asked me, you know. One more time, and I might rape you right here under a tree. I'm as randy as a two-peckered goat."

"Mr. Sheridan! That is absolutely despicable!"

"I got that word down, Boston. You got another one you can throw at me?"

"Yes?"

"Now, there's a word I can warm up to."

"Yes," she repeated throatily. "Yes, yes, yes."

He straightened from the tree and drew her into a walk. "First let's see if Star'll keep Jonathan for the night. The first time I make love to you, I don't want no aggravations."

"You're referring to my son as an aggravation?"

"My son," he corrected, "and yeah, he'd be a real aggravation if he was to start squallin' at the wrong time. When a man gets himself a pretty little whiskey-haired gal under his blanket, he wants things nice and peaceful. To enjoy whiskey right, you gotta take it slow and kinda roll the taste over your tongue."

A ribbon of nervousness threaded its way down Laura's spine. But it was a deliciously wicked kind of nervousness. "You will remember, sirrah, that I am a lady."

He hugged her close to his side and bent his dark head to nibble at her ear as they walked, doing crazy things to her insides. "And you taste like a lady," he whispered. "Or maybe more like a jigger of fine brandy warmed by my hand before I touch my tongue to it."

Chapter 25

FIRELIGHT AND DEKE. LAURA FOUND SHE WAS far more nervous about making love with him now that the moment had arrived than she had expected to be. She couldn't help but remember the times with Tristan, not only the pain, but the degradation of being used and of being told she was so ugly that no man would want her if a more comely woman were available. But Jonathan was settled for the night with Star and Black Stone, and there were no other excuses Laura could think of to put off the inevitable.

Deke had built up the fire to ward off the chill of the mountain night, so the inside of the lodge was well illuminated. When he turned to her with that expectant look in his silver eyes, Laura thought she'd never seen a more handsome man. Dressed only in buckskins, with the fire-shine bathing his dark hair, carved features, and powerfully muscled arms and shoulders, he looked as a painting might, wild and sun-burnished, his body a study of supple strength. In comparison, she felt drab and pitifully inadequate.

"Honey, you're shakin'," he whispered as he stepped toward her.

Laura tried to swallow, but her mouth was cottony and the sides of her throat felt paralyzed. She plucked nervously at the bodice flap of her leather dress, knowing he would want her to shed it and dreading the moment when she would have to stand before him with nothing to hide behind. He had seen parts of her, but never all of her at once.

Even that day down at the stream, he had draped her in the towel, and she had been able to hide by hugging herself.

"I, um . . ." It wasn't just vanity. She wanted to please this man. If her body disappointed him, if he told her that, she didn't think she would be able to bear it. "I'm sort of bony," she finally managed.

"Laura, you're beautiful," he told her in a husky voice. "You don't need to worry that I ain't gonna like what I see."

"I don't?" she squeaked.

"No, you don't. I done seen all there is to see, and I can't remember a single spot that ain't pretty."

"My legs are thin, and my knees stick out."

He smiled at that. "You're legs is willowy, and there's cute little dimples in them knees that I been dreamin' about kissin'."

Her eyes widened at that. "My hipbones poke out. Tristan said that they jabbed him and—"

"Tristan was a mean bastard. Don't you know what them hipbones is for?"

Laura blinked. "I . . . well, I suppose . . . No, what are they for?"

"Them there hipbones is love handles."

"Love handles?" she echoed.

He came to a stop before her and placed his hands on his own hips. "I'll show you later. Anything else you're worryin' on?"

Laura spread quivering fingers over her chest. "I'm not very full-figured up top, and my waist has grown thick."

His eyes held hers, agleam with equal parts tender amusement and mischief. "Laura, you're perfect up top, and I bet I can span that waist of yours with my hands."

"I have tear marks, too."

"Say what?"

"Tear marks, on my . . ." She lowered her hand to her waist. "Scars from carrying Jonathan. They're ugly-looking, and—"

"Them I don't remember," he cut in. "Where are they?"

"On my abdomen."

"On your what?"

She giggled, albeit nervously. "On my stomach."

"Them itty-bitty pink lines, you mean?"

"You saw them?"

"All three, and the biggest one ain't as long as my little finger."

"Four, there are four, and the biggest one is much longer than—" He suddenly reached out and tugged a bodice tie loose. "What are you doing?"

"I'm gonna count and measure the goddamned things."

"I'd really rather you—"

"Then I'm gonna kiss every one."

"What?"

He tugged another tie loose, and the top fold of leather fell away. "Laura, you're beautiful, from the tips of your toes, which is the same color of pink as your— Well, never mind. But you're pretty all the way up. And you standin' here worryin' is crazy. Do you think I'm perfect or somethin'?"

"Yes."

He ran a hand behind her neck and drew her close. "Ah, honey."

Laura felt better being held in his arms. "I'm just so afraid you'll think I'm ugly."

He tugged her braid loose and worked his fingers through the interwoven strands. "Ugly? Jesus, Laura. You're the most beautiful woman I've ever clapped eyes on. Do you think I ain't nervous? Well, think again, darlin'. I don't know how to do this like no gentleman from Boston might. I got a knot in my gut the size of a pitch bole, and I'm wonderin' if I shouldn't oughta worry more on bein' polite than makin' you feel nice, for fear I might shock you. Then I get to thinkin' if I'm polite and don't make you feel nice that you might not want me to touch you again. And ... well, hell, I'm in a regular state of befuddlement, and here it is time, and I still ain't made up my—"

"Nice," she interjected and tipped her head back to smile at him.

"What?"

"I—I'd like for you to make me feel nice."

She saw his larynx make a monkey's fist and bob upward. "Nice, huh? You know what you're askin' for?" His eyes held hers. "This is me you're talkin' to, remember, not a—"

"Deke, if I wanted a gentleman from Boston, I'd go there. I want you to make love to me the way you do it."

His eyes heated and his mouth tipped into that lazy, off-centered grin she had come to love so well. "I gotta warn you, no thumb holdin' allowed."

Gathering what little courage she had, Laura drew back to finish unfastening her dress with shaking hands. Deke assisted her by shoving the leather off her shoulders. As he did, the garment's weight came into play and pulled itself down to her waist. With a twist of her hips, Laura sent it plunging to pool around her feet. Deke was already unfastening halter buttons. He peeled the chambray away from her with an urgency that made her breathless, tossed it aside, and then surprised her by retreating two steps so he could get a good look at her.

Laura instinctively hugged her breasts with one arm and angled her other downward to cover the apex of her thighs with a spread hand. Deke shook his head. "Arms down," he whispered.

Laura's skin already burned everywhere his gaze touched, but she forced her arms to her sides, gulping for breath as he perused her from head to toe with unhurried nonchalance. After looking his fill from that angle, he stepped slowly around her, his shadow play dancing upon the walls, eclipsing hers. When he completed the circle, he came to stand before her again, his expression thoughtful.

At last he brought his gaze to hers and smiled. "I stand corrected, Boston. You're worth every cent of a hundred and seventy dollars, plus my services as a tracker in trade. The main trouble with you has been tryin' to collect."

She gave a startled laugh. "You, sirrah, are absolutely unconscionable."

He crooked a finger at her. "Come here and pay up."

The dress at her feet forgotten, Laura started forward and tripped on the puddle of leather. With the same quick reflexes he had displayed the first time she saw him, Deke lunged forward and caught her from falling with arms that felt as hard and hot against her bare skin as molten steel. Laura dragged in a quick breath at the shock, then exhaled into his mouth, for he wasted no time in claiming her lips with his.

At that first silken contact of mouths and tongues, Laura forgot more than just her dress on the floor. Being in Deke's arms made her forget everything but the sensations he evoked within her. He was firelight and shadows, heat and shivers, ecstacy and madness, a man who loved as he did all else, elementally and with a straightforwardness that might indeed have shocked her if she hadn't come to know him so well.

Deke held her clasped so closely to him, though, there wasn't room for a flea to slip between them, let alone shame. Laura surrendered to him as a sapling did the wind, bending to his force and the all-over caress of him on her flesh. He was raw and unpolished. He touched his mouth to places she never dreamed a man might want to kiss or nibble, even the dimples at the small of her back and the sensitive skin on the undersides of her toes. Laura began to feel that her entire body was atingle. Then she was on fire, and he was the bellows that stoked the blaze.

Only when Laura felt him hook her knees over his shoulders did she blink back to momentary reality. She felt the silken heat of his mouth high on the inside of her thigh and jerked with a start. Shoving up on her elbows, she cried, "Deke?"

His mouth slid higher, and he nipped lightly with his teeth. She squeaked, flopped onto her back, and made wild grabs for his hair, shocked to her marrow and fully intending to shove him away.

"Don't!" she cried.

"Why not?" he rasped.

While Laura's benumbed brain tried to sort through the multitude of reasons so she might voice just one, his mouth found her. With one drag of his tongue, all of those inarguable reasons why he shouldn't do this fled her mind. With a sharp pull, he drew the sensitive flange of her between his teeth, then laved the captured flesh.

Sensations, firelight, losing herself in the rugged aura of this man. Laura rode the wave of fire he created within her to its crest, hovered there for a maddening instant, then cried out as he forced her over into a dizzying spiral of amber as searing as the flames that licked the night nearby.

Divested of his buckskins, he rose over her before her senses righted, a broad canopy of rippling bronzed flesh, his dark hair painting her sensitized breasts with silken brushstrokes. Laura felt the hardness of him nudging for entry and realized her knees were still draped over his shoulders. Sudden fear lanced her, and she gasped as he pushed forward, half expecting pain. She fastened frightened eyes on his, then saw the love and concern in his gaze.

"Easy," he whispered in a tight voice. "Stay relaxed, Laura. If it starts to hurt, I'll stop."

But it didn't hurt. He had readied his way, and her body embraced the masculine length of him with wet heat. His face went taut. The expression in his eyes changed, their color awash with the sparks of passion and glazed with need. The tendons along his neck and shoulders stood out in sharp relief, their edges squared-looking and rigid. Laura ran light fingertips along his braced arms, tracing the bulge of veins, feeling each surge of his pulse. For this moment, she surveyed him with lucid apartness, as a woman does when lust momentarily transforms her beloved mate from gentle lover to a male in the clutches of primal urgency.

Deke was beautiful. Beautiful yet frightening. Laura felt a sense of feminine power that was heady. So much strength beneath her fingertips. So much need pressed deep within her. She moved her hips slightly and watched the muscles in his face snap taut over bone, his lips drawing back over gleaming white teeth. Playing with fire . . . But she gloried in the burn. At her encouragement, he thrust forward, no longer gentle, and the fiery shaft of him ignited all it claimed. Her lashes fell low, and she arched to meet and welcome the invasion.

Deke ... She clutched his strong arms and let him carry her upward on another wave of sensation that was far more glorious than anything she ever imagined. Deke ... She melded with his wildness, became one with him in a rush to completion. Then she lay in the safe fold of his arms, too spent to move or think, not caring if the world ended as long as he held her, stroked her hair, and filled her with the pounding of his heartbeat.

When awareness completely returned, Laura studiously avoided lifting her gaze to his face, embarrassed now when she thought of all the things that had passed between them. As if he understood that, Deke pressed kisses to her forehead, drew the furs over her nakedness and his, then spoke softly to her of other, ordinary things. Whether or not Jonathan would sleep through the night. That it sounded as if it might be sprinkling rain outside. Inconsequential murmurs that soothed Laura and allowed her some distance, which she needed more than she could say.

When at last he ran out of things to mention, Deke fell silent for a long while. Then she felt his mouth curve in a smile against her hair. "You're stuck with me now, Boston. I can take you home without worryin' about losin' you."

"That will never be a worry," she whispered softly. "When will we go?"

Just the thought filled Laura with sadness. She didn't want to lose all her new friends. Friends were a commodity that had been sorely lacking in her life until now.

"Tomorrow?" he suggested.

"So soon?" Laura asked shrilly. "We can't possibly be ready so fast."

"What's to get ready? We'll be leavin' the weddin' gifts until another trip. I don't want anything cumbersome loadin' us down, not on this haul."

"Then we'll come back?"

He kissed her hair. "Would you like to?"

"Oh, yes."

He sighed as though that answer pleased him beyond measure. "I was kinda fearful you might not like it here."

"I love it here, and I'm going to miss Star and Sugar Girl."

"Well, then." He sighed again and hugged her close. "Ah, Laura, I love you."

"You finally got around to saying it?"

He chuckled. "I've thought it a hundred times. But it's best to keep the ladies wantin', you know."

She slugged him playfully in the ribs; they tussled a moment, then grew pensive again. "Deke?"

"Hm?"

"The comancheros. Will they be a worry when we leave here?"

"I already asked Black Stone if he would arrange for an escort when we got around to leavin'." He rolled up onto an elbow to look down at her in the shifting amber light. "They'll stay with us until we get close to Denver."

Laura was relieved to hear that. "And you really want to leave tomorrow?"

"I got cattle to worry about. I been gone a long time already. My cows is what puts food on the table." He caught her chin on the edge of his hand. "We'll come back this winter and stay a month or so."

She brightened. "Oh, I'd like that."

He bent his head, letting his mouth barely graze hers. "Laura?"

She breathed in the taste of him and smiled. "What, Mr. Sheridan?"

"You feelin' achy from overuse?"

"Not yet."

He growled low in his throat and lightly bit her lip. "I better relick my calf, then."

Laura nipped him back and slipped her arms around his neck. "Yes, I think you'd better," was her murmured reply.

*   *   *

Good-byes had never come easily to Laura, and those she had to say the next morning came doubly hard. She wept when Star held her son close for a final embrace before slipping him snugly into his cradleboard. She sobbed when she felt wetness on Sugar Girl's cheek when they hugged in farewell. Her whole body trembled when she looked into Medicine Woman's craggy face for the last time and then went to her horse. *What if?* Those two words preceded a hundred thoughts in her mind, making her ache. What if Medicine Woman didn't live until winter? She was so frail now and bent with age. What if Black Stone's band was attacked by whites? What if some of the familiar faces she had come to hold so dear were no longer here when they returned next winter?

Laura knew that for every ache inside her, Deke was lashed with a deeper pain. She could see it in his eyes as he helped her mount her horse, see it in his body movements as he swung into the saddle. Even though Black Stone and nearly twenty other warriors rode with them from the village, Laura felt lonely as she never had.

On a rise at the edge of the flats, Deke wheeled his stallion to look back, and Laura saw tears in his eyes. She drew her horse up by his and gazed at the village with him, her heart breaking for him and for herself and for all those they left behind. Lodges and smoke ribboning toward the sky. People in buckskin moving through the weave of a lifestyle Laura knew was soon to be destroyed. She wanted to raise her fist at the sky and scold God. She wanted to go back to Denver and plead with the people there to leave these people alone. Why, oh, why did there have to be so much ignorance in the world? Why was hatred instinctive between those of different skin colors?

"Deke?"

His jaw muscle tightened as he dragged his gaze from the village to look at her.

"Are you all right?" she asked.

He took a deep breath and slowly exhaled, glancing over his shoulder to see how much distance the other warriors had gained on them. When his eyes once again met Laura's, he managed an anemic smile. "I'm just feelin' a little sadder about leavin' than usual. That's all."

"Is it . . . because of me? Would you have visited with your mother more if I hadn't been here?"

His smile deepened. "Laura, I saw her near every night. It ain't that." He looked down at the village again. "It's just silliness, I reckon. A sad feelin' in my bones. Probably because she's gettin' so old and I know her winters are numbered." He shrugged. "I just got a bad feelin', that's all. It don't mean nothin'."

"A bad feeling? That you might not see Medicine Woman again, you mean?"

He shivered suddenly, as if with cold, only Laura felt no breeze. Her heart twisted at the expression on his face. "No," he said in such a low whisper, she almost couldn't catch the words. "It ain't a bad feelin' just about her. It's for all of 'em. I just have this idea in my head this might be the last time I see some of 'em."

Laura had thought the same herself. "We'll see them again," she said, injecting cheerfulness into her voice. "It's only a few months until winter."

He flexed his shoulders and neck, then reached for his hat where it perched in the vee of his legs atop his saddle horn. With a forward dip of his head, he settled the Stetson over his hair and cocked the brim to just the right angle over his eyes. Laura's gaze touched on the cobalt beads that encircled the crown again and the feather that peeked so jauntily over the tan crown. He was dressed as he had been the first time she saw him, in the sleeveless blue shirt, opened partway down his chest to reveal his medallions, tight denim jeans, and high, fringed moccasins. His gun belt once again rode comfortably at his hips, the holster tied at the thigh.

Uncivilized and dangerous? Perhaps. But after last night, Laura thought he looked good enough to eat. He flashed her a teasing glance. "You ready to ride, Boston? We got a lot of miles to cover."

"Indeed I am, Mr. Sheridan."

Chapter 26

NOW THAT LAURA HAD HER BABY BACK, DEKE half expected her to balk at the long hours in the saddle and sleeping on the cold ground. But as she had from the first, Laura surprised him, pushing ever forward without complaint, always game to go an extra mile if that was what he asked of her. By the middle of the second day of their trip, Deke was so proud of his wife, he was afraid his seams might bust. City gal or no, she was one hell of a woman, no mistake about that.

She constantly quizzed him as they traveled. *Is that west?* she would ask, and point a finger. Nine times out of ten, she was dead-on. She also asked how to tell her directions when the sun was at high noon, which was a damned good question, so Deke showed her how to lay a rock in a sunny spot and check it from all sides to see which way it threw a shadow. The other warriors drew up and waited, not seeming to mind that Flint Eyes had delayed their progress to instruct his whiskey-haired woman.

"What if the rock throws no shadow?" she queried.

"That ain't likely. Most times when it seems like the sun's dead center in the sky, it's a hair off and'll throw shadow of some kind. If it don't, park your butt and wait a few minutes till it does."

"It seems to me we've covered this ground once before," she retorted with a saucy smile. "What if I'm trying to escape an angry husband?"

Deke gave her a lambent look. "Let him catch up and take your medicine."

"And what might that be?"

"When we get to the hotel in Denver, I'll show you."

"That is a dose of medicine I shall look forward to," Laura said softly.

Though Deke refrained from telling Laura because he could see no point in worrying her, he and Black Stone spotted the tracks of a large group of riders late that second day, the sign fairly fresh. It worried both men. Comancheros? There had been shod and unshod horses in the group, a bad indication. Had the bastards been holing up all this time, waiting Deke out? He could scarcely believe it. One of the reasons he had tarried with the Cheyenne for so long was to let the trouble die down.

"It can't be comancheros," he said to Black Stone in Cheyenne. "No one, not even a low-life Mexican with a passion for blondes, could want a woman that badly."

Black Stone glanced toward Laura. "No, not even for hair the color of whiskey." He seemed to ponder the question further; then his brow cleared. "Perhaps you are who they want now, eh?"

"Me?"

"You killed three of Gonzales's men. Vengeance can drive a man to do crazy things."

Making no reply, Deke wheeled his horse and rode back to Laura and the baby. But what Black Stone had said stayed on his mind. Revenge? Deke prayed that wasn't the case, for if it was, he and Laura would be in danger even after they reached his ranch. A group of renegades knew no boundaries. Through Black Stone, Deke had learned that Francisco Gonzales was the comanchero leader and one mean hombre if the stories the Cheyenne had heard about him were true. Until meeting Laura, Deke had never heard Gonzales's name, but he knew the kind, and in his experience, most were the sort who lived by no code whatsoever and gave a new definition to the word *cruel*. To even think of a man such as Gonzales getting his hands on Laura or the baby made Deke's blood go cold.

Later that day, Deke spoke with Black Stone once again. "What should I do, my brother? If it is comancheros, that could mean they're following us."

Scowling at the question, Black Stone grabbed a handful of his pinto's mane to steer it around a rock. Deke circled his horse in the opposite direction. When the two animals resumed their former pace abreast of each other, Black Stone said, "You might return with us to the village and stay with us until Gonzales gives up."

Deke considered that. "I've already been gone from my ranch for way over a month, not to mention that I would be putting my wife and child through four days of hard riding for nothing. We're so close to Denver now. It'd be crazy to turn back. Sooner or later, and it's got to be sooner if I expect to have a ranch when I get back, we'll have to make this trip. If I go back with you and wait for a few more days, there's nothing to say the situation will have changed."

Black Stone had clearly thought all the same things, and he nodded. "We will ride with you for as far as we can. As long as we are with you, you will be safe."

"If you're right and Gonzales is out to get revenge, I'll have to watch my back long after this journey is over."

"Yes," Black Stone agreed. "Until the man is dead."

"What if I get Laura safely home, and Gonzales comes to the ranch when I'm not there? Now that I've got a family, I won't take many long trips, but there will be times when I'll have no choice. Even if I leave men behind to watch after Laura, they wouldn't stand a chance against that many fast guns."

"No." Black Stone squinted into the slanting sunlight, then spat to clear his mouth of the dust raised by the many horses in front of them. "It is a problem, Flint Eyes. One for which I see no answer. You can only hope they make a move now while you are among friends."

Deke snorted. "Every comanchero I ever met was a coward. They'll wait and jump me when I'm alone."

"We would ride the entire way to Denver with you if we could."

"I know you would, Black Stone. But right now, with so much trouble brewing, you'd probably get shot for your trouble. I can't ask you to stay with us for much longer. It's too risky."

This time it was Black Stone who rode away without making a reply.

The worry began to mushroom in Deke's mind. He imagined what might happen to Laura if Gonzales got his hands on her, and the pictures that went through his head made him feel sick. So many times he had told Laura she had nothing to fear while she was with him, that he would always protect her. Now he began to see what a foolish promise that had been. This country could be vicious. One man, no matter how fast with a gun, no matter how true to his woman, could be alive one moment and dead the next, with only buzzards to note his passing. If that happened to Deke, Laura would be left to fend for herself and the baby.

After having lived so many years alone, Deke was accustomed to worrying about nobody but himself. To suddenly have the responsibility of a wife and child seemed a frightening burden. As much as he had taught Laura, she still had much to learn. She would be next to helpless if anything happened to him. Looking over at her, Deke traced the features of her sweet face with concerned eyes. Had he found the one woman he was fated to spend his life with? Or had he made a selfish decision that could end up costing Laura untold suffering? To even ask himself that question nearly broke Deke's heart. But he loved Laura and the baby too much to ignore the doubts that nagged him. Given time, he could train her well, and eventually she would be able to make her own way, evading pursuers, living off the land, until she could reach a town and help. But what if fate intervened and there was no time?

Even though it was too late now to change things, guilt became an ache within Deke. He thought of when he first met Laura, how quickly he had begun to care for her. She was so beautiful and sweet and fine, the kind of woman a man like him could rarely hope to have. Yet Laura had fallen into his hands. And selfish bastard that he was, he had made the most of the circumstances, railroading her into a relationship she had abhorred. Now, even though she had accepted things and Deke felt sure she loved him, he still couldn't guarantee her the things a woman should be able to take for granted, security at the top of the list.

Where had his head been? Deke asked himself. Up his butt, he guessed. For a woman who had lived through all that Laura had, security was vitally important. One husband had already abandoned her. She trusted Deke to be there for her when she needed him. He had sworn he always would be. Now, when he looked at the harsh realities, he realized it was a promise he might not be able to keep.

He tried to absolve himself. He hadn't started any of this, after all. And even if he hadn't married Laura, they would still have been faced with the same dangers, namely trying to make it safely back to Denver. Ah, but it was after they reached Denver that he had to think about. Her father might have answered her wire, and there could be money waiting for her there. If Deke hadn't married her, he could have used that money to put her and the baby on a stage for Boston. As unhappy as Laura might have been back East, as unhappy as she might continue to be if she were to return there, at least she and the baby would be safe. Deke couldn't guarantee the same if they stayed with him in Colorado.

Stop it! he told himself. *What's done is done. You love her; she loves you. This is how it was meant to be. Somehow, someway, things will work out.*

As they rode ever closer to Denver, Deke clung to that hope. Things had to work out. He couldn't even contemplate Laura and the baby ending up in the hands of a bastard like Francisco Gonzales.

At first light the next morning, Black Stone and his warriors prepared to take their leave and head back into the foothills. The farewell between him and Deke was emotional, for neither knew when they might next embrace, if ever. Both battled tears, then lost the fight.

"You know the song in my heart," Black Stone said in a tight voice.

Deke stepped back and crossed his extended arms so they might clasp each other's wrists, symbolic of eternal unity. His Cheyenne brother did likewise. As each applied a grip, strength surged between them and seemed to bolster each of them.

Seeing the worry in his brother's eyes, Deke said, "You've come with us too far as it is, Black Stone. I doubt we're more than three hours out of Denver right now. If I can't hold my own for that short a distance, I'm a pitiful excuse for a man."

"Ah, yes." Black Stone's eyes danced with laughter. "Very pitiful, that is you."

"Besides, we might come across whites over the next rise. You know it, and I know it. The time has come for us to go our separate ways."

"Always, the time seems to come."

Tears slipped onto sunbaked cheeks to be chased away by the dew-kissed morning breeze, leaving only salt trails to tell the tale. Deke felt no shame. This man walked within him in secret places no other would ever journey, not even Laura. He and Black Stone shared memories, some joyful, many sad, some that still rankled to this day. In that moment, both recalled their first parting, which had begun with a fistfight and ended with bitter farewells. A foolish thing, to have lashed out at each other so violently. But the rift between them had cut deep, making them both bleed, and the loyalty of a lifetime had not been easily severed. It had taken anger to cut those ties, and love to mend the wounds. Now, years later, they were parting yet again, wiser and less judgmental, accepting each other's differences, loving each other in spite of them. It was as it should be. But it was also heartbreaking.

"You know where my soul walks," Deke told him softly.

Releasing Black Stone's wrists, he pressed a fist over his heart. "I am one with the People."

"And I am one with you."

With that, Black Stone leaped onto his pinto. He hesitated there for a moment, tall and regal on his mount, his black hair drifting across his chest to touch the self-inflicted scars from his Sun Dance. He looked to Laura, his obsidian eyes expressionless. During the journey, he had not spoken a word to her. He did so now, and with a simple eloquence that brought a lump to Deke's throat.

"Wife of my brother, sister of my heart, I honor you." With that, he raised a fist skyward. "My heart will sing words of you, always. My children will be told of the whiskey-haired woman who is my sister, and they will pass those words on to their children. A hundred winters from now, the People will speak of you, and say only good things. I am Black Stone, your brother, and forever your loyal friend."

He wheeled his horse, raising a funnel of dust that concealed his departure. By the time the air began to clear, he and the other warriors had diminished to toy figures, their cries floating back to Deke and Laura on the wind.

"What did he say to me?" Laura asked.

"That he loves you," Deke whispered shakily.

Before embarking on the final leg of their journey into Denver, Deke strapped Tristan Cheney's gun belt around Laura's hips and gave her his extra Colt revolver, fully loaded. Clearly unaware of the danger they might yet face, Laura grinned and patted the gun.

"Think I can hit anything with it?"

Deke didn't force a smile. The time had come for Laura to fully understand what they might be up against. "At very close range, yes. And that's all that matters." He held her gaze for an endless moment. "Just in case there's trouble, Laura, I want you to save two slugs."

Her smile faltered. "For what?"

Deke swallowed. "If something happens to me—" He

broke off and looked away. "A temple shot is quick. There's no pain. Take care of the baby first. Then yourself." He dragged his gaze back to her. "It's a terrible thing to even think about, I know. But I want your promise you'll do it before you let the comancheros take you."

The blood dropped from her face. "The comancheros?" She glanced uneasily around. "They aren't still a threat? Not after all this time."

"Probably not. But we did spot tracks yesterday, and they looked fairly fresh. Shod and unshod horses traveling together."

He could see by her expression that she remembered what that meant. "Do you think it could be the same group? That they might attack us? And if they do, you're asking me to shoot my baby?"

"I'm not sayin' it'll even happen, honey. I'm just preparin' you for the worst. A bullet in the temple'd be a mercy." He swallowed and searched for words he wished he didn't have to say. "Remember the day I left you and said I was gonna lead them three Mexes off our scent?" At her nod, he added, "Well, I didn't. I killed 'em."

Her pupils dilated, but otherwise she showed no reaction.

"Anyhow, it could be that Gonzales—accordin' to Black Stone, he's their leader—it could be he wants revenge, and when his kind takes revenge, he lashes out at whoever's handy. You and Jonathan . . . well, you'd be his whippin' posts if somethin' happened to me, the only ones left for him to take out his anger on. And it'd be bad, Laura, real bad. Worse than just bein' used hard and sold, like they mighta done before. You understand?"

At last she nodded.

"The two cartridges? They're just for in case—if somethin' goes wrong, that's all." Deke tried to smile. "I don't mean to scare you." He bent to give her a quick kiss, then touched a hand to Jonathan's dark head where it rested on her slender shoulder. "You ready to ride?"

Making a visible attempt to regain her composure, she

said brightly, "I'm ready for a bath, that's what. In a great huge tub of hot water. With scented soap!"

Deke's heart caught at her show of bravado. By her pallor, he knew she comprehended the possible danger and that she was now as worried as he was. As he walked toward his horse, he couldn't help but wonder if she didn't secretly wish she could slip into silk after that bath. Her world in Boston had not been rife with danger at every turn, and she wouldn't be human if she wasn't thinking about that right now, if not for her own sake, for Jonathan's. As he swung onto his horse, he asked, "You miss them hot baths, do you?"

She lifted an elegant amber eyebrow as she settled herself into the saddle and reached for her horse's reins. "You aren't about to tell me I won't be able to indulge in hot baths at your ranch, are you?"

"No. Water's cheap."

She dimpled a cheek at him. "Then yes, I miss hot baths."

"There anything else you miss?"

"A real bed?"

Deke relaxed and chased away his doubts. "I can promise you one of them, too." After a moment, he managed a genuine smile. "Quick as I can, I'll build you a house—like them you see in the city. We'll even have us one of them rooms folks don't never use, a parlor, I think it's called. And a room just for eatin' with one of them mile-long tables."

She giggled at that. "If you're hoping to drown your new mother-in-law in her soup, you're in for a disappointment. My mother passed away years ago."

"I can live without fat ladies drownin' in their soup if you can live without three-fork supper parties."

"I always detested three-fork suppers, sirrah, so I shall be a very happy lady."

"Sounds to me like you've come down in the world, Boston."

She leaned back and took a deep breath of the morning air, as if to savor its taste. "By whose measuring stick? Just look at this glorious morning!"

*   *   *

Two hours later, despite the warmth of the summer morning, Deke felt a chill slither over his skin. Death hung on the breeze, waiting, circling like a vulture. He couldn't say how he knew that. He only knew it was so. When he breathed in the air, it filmed his nostrils and tasted of metal at the back of his tongue. All the hair on his body prickled with dread.

The chilling sensation had begun to drift around him about thirty minutes ago, vague and almost unnoticeable. But Deke had experienced the feeling too many times to ignore it. Soon the electrical heaviness in the air seemed so thick, he could scarcely breathe. He slowed his horse to ride abreast of Laura, watching for any movement on the surrounding hillsides, alert for any warnings from Chief, who padded along at right flank, his bristles already standing, his bone abandoned someplace behind them on the trail. Deke knew the dog would never drop his bone without reason, and by its absence, he guessed Chief felt death in the air, too.

Animal instinct? Deke guessed maybe so. Or a trait that had been trained into him by the Cheyenne. Either way, it was a sixth sense most folks didn't have, one that some people would say wasn't quite human. Inhuman or not, Deke was glad he had it. Instinct had saved his life more than once, and now he had two lives far more precious than his own to worry about. He began to watch for someplace to hole up, natural cover to guard his back so he might outwait the enemy, whoever it was, and force them to come at him head-on.

No such luck. When the first rifle shot rang out, the closest thing Deke saw that would provide cover of any kind was a large boulder. He felt the bullet whiz past his face a split second before the sound ripped through the air. Laura's horse reared in reaction. Deke's, trained to ignore noise, flinched but remained steady. All in one movement, Deke grabbed Laura's gelding's bridle and dropped to the ground between their mounts, jerking Laura down with him as he went. Caught off guard, she stumbled and fell. For a horrible moment, Deke was afraid she or the baby might be injured by her horse's flashing hooves. More shots rang out, which only increased the animal's panic.

While trying to hold both horses steady, Deke helped her to gain her feet. "Stay between the horses! Grab a stirrup strap in each hand."

While she did so, Deke positioned himself at the animals' heads so he could guide them. He hoped to make it to the boulder, using the breadth of the horses to shield Laura and the baby from rifle fire. To do that, he had to keep the animals broadside to the snipers. Deke's own body was an open target, but he couldn't think about that, not now.

"Keep your head down, Laura!" he barked.

She ducked and fastened gigantic amber eyes on his. "Oh, God, Deke!"

The boulder. To Deke it looked as if it were a hundred miles away. He slogged backward toward it, glancing over his shoulder to gauge the distance, feeling as though his feet were mired in mud. Another shot rang out, and Deke's stallion screamed as it lunged forward onto its knees.

From that moment on, things seemed to happen before Deke could move. His black, propelled by the force of the slug, fell toward Laura, throwing her and the baby into the other horse. Another rifle shot rang out. Deke sprang between the huge animals and heaved sideways with his shoulder, using all his strength to keep his fatally injured mount from rolling. At the last instant, Laura regained her balance and scrambled out of harm's way, shoving frantically against her own horse in her panic.

To Deke it seemed they made it through one narrow escape only to confront another. With his horse down, Laura and the baby were completely unprotected. Releasing her mount, he hooked an arm around her waist and dove for the dirt, doing his best to protect Jonathan from harm as they landed. Then, going up on one elbow and knee, he crab-walked toward the rock, dragging Laura and Jonathan along beneath him. Reality shrank to a deafening cacophony, the gutshot horse screaming, the infant squalling, Laura sobbing, Chief adding to the din with snarls and barks. Another shot rang out. Deke's lungs whined for breath. A few more feet. He only had to pull them a few more feet.

Another report split the air, and dirt geysered only inches in front of their heads. Deke hunched his shoulders around Laura, tightened his hold on her waist, and heaved forward with all his might. Three more feet. He could feel Laura digging in with her elbows and toes, trying her best to propel her own weight. Two more feet. Lead peppered the ground all around them. Deke knew their luck couldn't hold. With a strength he hadn't realized he possessed, he made a final, desperate lunge for safety. Chief scrambled for cover behind the rock with them, whining and sniffing each of them. Deke shoved him away and pushed up to peer over the rock.

His rifle. His goddamned rifle! It was still in the saddle boot, his cartridges and spare cylinders for the Colts in the saddlebags. The injured horse was throwing its head and trying futilely to get to its feet. Its screams were horrible. Deke drew his Colt and took careful aim, praying a well-placed head shot would put the thick-skulled animal out of its misery. The report of a rifle and a spray of granite sent Deke diving for cover again before he could pull the trigger.

"You miserable sons of bitches! If you won't let me shoot him, you do it!"

"We will send you to hell with him, my gringo friend," a voice called back. "Simply show yourself again, eh?"

"Gonzales!" Laura cried. "I'd recognize that voice anywhere."

The poor horse let out another piercing shriek. Hearing it in such pain, knowing it was gutshot, Deke cursed under his breath. Gonzales didn't have an axe to grind with the stallion. Yet he was happy to let it die a slow, agonizing death to exact some small measure of revenge. That was exactly why Deke had cautioned Laura to save back two rounds in the Colt, because men of Gonzales's ilk had no mercy. He would be just as senselessly vicious with a woman and child.

Deke inched his head back up to peer over the boulder again. The rifle. He stared at its varnished stock, aware of his blood rushing in his ears. He had to reach his Henry. Without it, he couldn't hold off the comancheros, and Laura and the baby would die. Or worse. He started forward. Laura grabbed his arm.

"No! If you go out there, you'll be shot!"

"Cover me!"

"C-Cover you?"

Deke rolled out from behind the rock. "With the revolver!" he called back, yelling to be heard above the injured horse's screams. "Keep the bastards busy."

Deke really didn't expect much help from Laura's quarter, and he was more than a little surprised when he heard the Colt bark. He dove into some brush, then glanced back, his surprise turning to amazement. She was returning the comancheros' fire, and doing a damned fine job of keeping herself protected while she was at it. He had known grown men to piss their pants when up against far better odds. Yet there was Laura, inching her head up, taking careful aim. The Colt barked again.

Despite his sense of urgency, Deke felt a swell of pride. Hot damn, she was something. Though why he should feel proud, he didn't know. Her grit wasn't his doing. Boston, born and bred, maybe. But the steel in that girl's spine was pure Coloradan.

The Colt's effective range was only fifty yards, but at least Laura's fire would keep the renegades' heads down for a few minutes. That was all the time Deke needed. Parting the foliage, he focused on his Henry again. At a distance of six to seven hundred yards, an ordinary marksman could put two out of three balls inside a ring two feet across with that Henry. The rifle was also capable of putting out five accurate rounds in as many seconds. If Deke had a brag, it was that he was no ordinary marksman. The Henry wouldn't turn him into a one-man army, but more than a few of those comancheros would eat lead if he could get his hands on it.

There was no way around it. To reach the Henry, he had to cross that open area to the stallion.

"Two bullets!" he called back to Laura. "Save the last two. Promise me!"

"Just get the rifle, Deke! Let me worry about me, for heaven's sake!"

Her return fire ceased for a moment, and Deke knew she was pulling cartridges from her gun belt to reload. Bless her heart. Rifle fire began to pepper the ground in front of the rock. Deke waited to leave the brush until he heard the Colt's report again. Then he sprang forward into a run. Three scrambling steps, a dive for the horse. The Colt barked each time his feet hit the dirt. He couldn't have asked for better backup. The poor horse grunted and whinnied when Deke's body slammed into it. He hooked an arm around the saddle to grab the Henry's stock. With a mighty jerk, he dislodged the rifle from its boot, jacked the lever, pressed the barrel against the back of the stallion's skull, and pulled the trigger. To hell, Deke might very well go, but one of the sins he burned for would not be allowing a helpless animal to suffer. The loss of one rimfire cartridge wouldn't mean a difference between life and death for Laura and the baby.

The bastards.

Laying the rifle aside, Deke drew his knife, took a bracing breath, and then raised himself to slash wildly at the saddle-bag strap. He couldn't waste time trying to dislodge the bag that was pinned under the dead horse. Luckily, the bag on top was the one holding his cartridges. *Luckily?* Deke nearly laughed. At himself for thinking the word. At life because it was such a bitch. At long last, he had someone to love. Two someones to love. Something to live for. And those miserable excuses for men out there were trying their damnedest to snatch it all away from him.

He rolled onto his back, thankful that a bullet hadn't found him while he was partially exposed. The sky stretched above him, and around him loomed a sudden, eerie silence.

Laura must be reloading. Please, God, let her be reloading! Jonathan wasn't crying now. Chief had stopped barking.

Fear clutched Deke. He scanned the bushy hillside behind the boulder. What if some of the comancheros had circled around and come in on them from behind? What if, at this very moment, Laura and the baby were dead?

Deke shoved up on an elbow. "Laura!"

In answer, her Colt spat lead. Relief shot through him. Doing a belly crawl, he slithered back toward the brush, the Henry and saddlebag tucked under one arm so he might use his other hand to haul himself over the ground. When he reached the protective shelter of the boulder again, it was to find Laura crouched over the cradleboard, gun in hand. Deke wanted to tell her right then what a hell of a woman he thought she was, but there was no time. He tossed the saddlebag in her direction and took up a firing position. "While I'm emptyin' one weapon, you reload the other," he said through clenched teeth. "That way, we can keep up a steady return fire. Get all the spare Colt cylinders out and handy."

"Are you all right?"

Deke jacked a cartridge into the Henry. "I'm fine. Just reload!"

With that, he pushed up, sighted in along the sweeping barrel, and fired at the first man he saw.

One comanchero, on his way to hell.

Deke whipped back down behind the rock, jacked a cartridge in, and sprang onto his knees again to shoot. Ah, the beautiful sound of his Henry. A leg wound this time. Deke wasn't proud. Down to operate the lever action. Back up. The odds were pitiful. He knew it. But he'd fight with all he had. For Laura. For the life they might have made together.

Seeing Deke in action filled Laura with awe. Oh, she had always known he had a dangerous, deadly side. But never, not in her wildest imaginings, had she envisioned him like this, every movement measured and precise, his eyes glittering with murderous intent, the muscles in his face drawn taut. He and the Henry worked together as if they were one.

Where she had fired wildly, Deke did not. At such a distance, he didn't hit his mark with every bullet, but he always came close.

Laura worked feverishly to keep him supplied with weaponry, and soon she forgot everything but the lethal rhythm. Reloading the Henry, slapping it into his capable hands. Reloading the Colt, holding it at the ready. He scarcely spared her a glance. When he wasn't shooting, he was scanning the hillside behind them. Laura realized that he feared the comancheros would circle around behind them. If that happened, not even Deke would be able to hold them off.

As frightened as she was for Deke and herself, Laura's biggest fear was for Jonathan. Her baby, her sweet, precious baby. For the first time in weeks, she wondered what in heaven's name she was doing in this godforsaken land where death was as commonplace as breathing. It was no place to raise a child.

Please, God. Protect my baby. Please, God, don't let him die. Get us out of this. Please, get us out of this. The prayer became a litany in Laura's mind. With numb determination, she tried to do her part to save her son, reloading Deke's weapons with mechanical precision, not allowing herself to think beyond that.

"Son of a bitch!"

Laura followed Deke's gaze and saw two men zigzagging down the opposite hillside. They hit the draw and rolled. Deke fired at one and hit him. With amazing speed, he pumped the lever action again and got off another shot. Then he cursed furiously under his breath. She knew why. The second man had gotten across the clearing. Now the enemy could come at them from both front and rear. Fear filled her. A horrible, cold, crawling fear. Her gaze shifted to Jonathan. Bundled into his cradleboard, all he could move was his head and little fists. He was crying, but Laura couldn't hear him. It was as if everything around her had been reduced to one element: terror.

She saw Deke look at the Colt on her hip, and she knew

what he was thinking. If the comanchero took cover on the hillside above them, which he'd surely do at any moment, he would be able to pick Deke off. She and the baby would be left alone.

A wild urge to run struck Laura. But there was nowhere to go, no escape from this madness that had become her and Deke's reality. The look in his eyes nearly broke her heart. He glanced at the hillside again, then dragged his gaze back to the baby. She guessed that he was afraid she might not have the courage to take her child's life, and he wanted to spare her the horror of having to do it if he could.

"No!" she cried. "Not until you're dead, and they're right on top of me! I'll do it if it comes to that! I swear I will. But not until there's no hope."

His ice blue eyes held hers and searched deep. For an awful moment, Laura feared he didn't believe she had the necessary mettle to carry through, that he would see it finished himself rather than risk Gonzales's getting his hands on her and Jonathan.

Tears filled her eyes. She spread a hand on her chest and leaned toward him. "Damn you, Deke! For a month you've been teaching me how to use these guns! Preaching at me day and night to stand up for myself. Telling me I could do it! Now you want me to take the coward's way out?"

For a heartbeat longer, he held her gaze. Then he slapped the Henry into her hands, grabbed the freshly reloaded Colt, spun to take up his firing stance, and said, "Reload!"

Laura gave a sob that was equal parts relief and hysterical laughter. One word. *Reload!* But it meant everything to her. More than his whispering how much he loved her. More than his saying she was beautiful. It meant— Laura bent over the Henry, her hands moving feverishly. Tears nearly blinded her. Deke believed in her. But what really meant the world to Laura was that he had taught her to believe in herself.

She was no longer Sterling Van Hauessen's daughter, an elegantly trimmed ornament who spoke French and glided along stairwells, elated because she could balance a thick tome on her head. She was no longer Tristan Cheney's wife, a spiritless servant to his every whim, afraid of his shadow and her own as well.

She was Laura Sheridan. Not just Deke's wife, which was something to be proud of, but his partner. They were fighting for their lives. And her contribution could mean the difference between winning or losing. She didn't kid herself. The odds were stacked against them. But if she had to die today, she would take something with her that had been denied her in life. Her pride. It was Deke's gift to her, and no one, not Francisco Gonzales or anyone else, was going to cheat her out of it.

"Reload!"

In response, Laura slapped the reloaded rifle into Deke's hand. As he handed her the empty Colt, their gazes locked. Only for an instant. Just long enough for him to flash her a quick grin. She knew it was absolute madness, insane beyond comprehension, but she smiled back.

Perhaps it was nothing more than a rush of false courage, some sort of numbness peculiar to shock, but Laura no longer quivered with terror. She suddenly felt invincible, and it seemed to her in those next few moments that there were worse fates than dying.

"Pick up the pace, Boston," he yelled at her. "You gotta start guardin' my back. We'll have company comin' in from the rear any second."

Laura wasn't sure she could work any faster than she already was. But she gave it her best, laid the reloaded Colt near Deke's leg, and drew hers from the holster to train it on the hillside.

"Think you can kill a man?" he asked in a lull between shots. "Wingin' him ain't good enough. You gotta make one shot count, and it's gotta keep him down."

Laura brushed hair from her eyes, her gaze still pinned on the hillside. Movement. She dropped to her butt, tucked a foot under her thigh, and braced her extended arms over an upraised knee to steady her aim. *Seventy yards.* It was a long shot, the kind only an expert marksman could take with any success. Sunlight glinted off the comanchero's rifle, a rifle she knew had four to five times the accurate reach of her weapon. Everything Deke had ever said to her went whispering through her mind. *Windage and elevation. Not a man, a target. Total concentration. Don't shoot until you got a steady bead.* She clenched her teeth. Took a deep breath and exhaled, blocking out the sounds of gunfire. When her lungs were totally emptied, when absolute stillness settled within her body, she locked her muscles and smoothly pulled the trigger. The blast of the weapon imploded against her eardrums, seeming far louder and more deadly than it ever had.

Deke had the answer to his question. Her stomach lurched as her target rolled down the hillside, suddenly looking very like a human being.

"Don't think about it. You got him before he got one of us. Real simple, Boston." He cracked off another shot. Then his hand curled warmly over her shoulder to give it a quick squeeze. "You got a job to do, Laura, and I'm countin' on you. Reload!"

He laid the Henry next to her and picked up the Colt.

Chapter 27

LAURA HAD NEVER LOOKED DEATH IN THE eye before, and when the moment finally arrived, she felt chilled and emptied. The ironic thing was, she and Deke might have held the comancheros off indefinitely if not for running low on ammunition. She had just loaded the Henry with the last of the rimfire cartridges, and Deke was firing those now. They had only one spare cylinder left for the Colt revolvers. Six cartridges, four of which had to be saved, one for each of them, counting Chief.

Hollow-eyed, Laura looked first at her baby, then at Deke. To take her child's life? Laura wasn't at all sure she could do something so monstrous. Yet she couldn't bear the thought of those horrible men getting their hands on him. There would be no trade made to the Indians this time. Laura knew Deke was right about that. Gonzales would be so enraged, he would take out his anger on anything that breathed when this battle was finished.

Laura curled her hand around the Colt revolver's smooth stock. Her baby. Oh, God, if there were only a way she might die first so she wouldn't have to live through this nightmare.

Deke's hand covered hers. She looked up and saw that the Henry lay empty beside him. Because of the comanchero gunfire all around them, she hadn't noticed the sudden cessation of shooting from behind the boulder. Deke. His eyes held hers, and Laura knew what he was about to do. How insane that she should feel relieved. But she did. Relieved and grateful because he had the strength to do what she feared she couldn't.

The ache in his gaze made her want to scream, to rail at God. He loved her and Jonathan so much. If ever she had doubted that, his selfless actions this morning, shielding them with his own body, had dispelled the notion. It wasn't fair that he should be forced to do something so utterly against nature. Not this man. Oh, how she wished she had the courage to put the Colt to her temple and pull the trigger herself. If she weren't such a coward, she would spare him that much, at least. It was enough that he had Jonathan and Chief to think about before himself.

"Deke. You don't have to—I can do it if you'll just— Jonathan, I can't—"

He wrested the gun from her numb fingers and hooked an arm around her waist. How odd that she found sanctuary there in his embrace, just as she had so many other times. How insane that she should feel safe and loved and protected when she knew what he was about to do. He pressed his lips to her forehead—warm, wonderful lips. Laura closed her eyes and concentrated on the heat of him, the solidity of him. Something cold pressed against her temple. She blocked the sensation out, shoved away the flash of terror that tried to clutch her. She wouldn't make this harder for him. She wouldn't.

"I love you, Deke," she managed to say, praying the sound of gunfire all around them hadn't drowned out her words.

She felt his chest jerk and knew he had heard, that he was sobbing. Making fists in his shirt, she clung to him, praying for courage, not for herself but for him. If he couldn't do this thing, then she would have to, and she wasn't at all sure she could. She felt him tense, heard the hammer click back, and she braced herself for the explosion of sound. It never came.

Suddenly Deke released her. Laura fell back and fastened questioning eyes on his dark face. A look of sheer incredulity swept across his features. The next instant, he brandished the Colt in the air and let loose with a high-pitched cry that turned her skin icy. That cry seemed to echo and reecho in the rolling hills around them. Laura blinked and cocked her head, not trusting her ears. But the sound kept repeating itself.

Cheyenne war cries.

"Black Stone!" he cried. Then he drew her back into his arms for a hug that nearly crushed her ribs. "Laura, we're safe! It's Black Stone! He must've heard the shooting!"

Laura remembered Deke telling her how a single shot in these mountains could echo for miles, but even so, she could scarcely comprehend their reprieve. So close. Oh, God, they had come so close. She had heard Deke draw back the hammer of the Colt. In another second, he might have— She shoved the thought away.

They scrambled to peer over the rock. Cheyenne warriors. Laura had never seen such a beautiful sight. They rode low along the backs of their ponies, shooting their rifles one-handed with terrifying accuracy. Panicked comancheros wriggled out from under brush and overhanging rocks. Laura realized she was screaming, with relief or terror, she didn't know, and clamped a hand over her mouth.

Seconds, minutes, hours. Time became meaningless, death the only measure. The comancheros, caught off guard and away from their horses, had no chance to flee. Black Stone and his horse soldiers cut them down, one after another, until their war cries drifted away to silence and the rifle fire became a memory in her stunned mind. When the warriors sprang from their horses to count coup, Laura turned away, feeling as though she might retch. She was acutely conscious that Deke sprang out from behind the rock to run down and greet his friends.

Friends who were peeling scalps from human heads as casually as she might the skin from an apple.

She heard her husband's voice, his words incomprehensible, his tone unmistakably jubilant. A moment later, she heard him give a victory yell and wondered if he had joined in the butchery. *No, not Deke.* Yet even as she assured herself of that, she knew she was kidding herself. As wonderful a man as Deke was, he was also very much a Cheyenne in his thinking, and to him, counting coup might be as much a part of battle as the actual fighting.

Frantically Laura tried to push away her revulsion and recall the village. Star and Sugar Girl. Medicine Woman and Muskrat. The cheerful fires that warmed the mountain night air. Good people, wonderful people. Their customs were simply different from her own.

In her attempt to block out the sickening pictures that formed in her mind every time she heard a victory cry ringing from the draw, Laura straightened her shoulders and took deep, cleansing breaths. As she did so, her gaze fell on the hillside behind the boulder, on the comanchero she had killed. Not a target, but a man. She stared at his outstretched arm, then at his hand. Blood stained his fingers.

Laura didn't have time to seek privacy in the bushes. Her stomach turned inside out with no warning, and she emptied its contents right there, kneeling beside her child. Her living child. A child who had nearly died. She should be elated. Thanking God. Thanking Black Stone. As Deke had said, he must have heard the shooting, and at great risk to himself and his men, he had come to their aid. She should be out there with them right now, expressing her gratitude, rejoicing with them.

Instead, she retched and retched until there was nothing more to come up. Death. It seemed to be all around her. When she finally lifted her head, she saw the man she had killed again and was stricken with dry heaves.

This wasn't real. None of it could be real because human beings didn't do things like this to one another. Only animals did, and she wasn't an animal. Yet she had taken another's life with scarcely a pause, her only thought at the time to place her bullet in a fatal spot. And, oh, God forgive her, she had done so.

After her nausea passed, Laura braced her hands on her knees and straightened, feeling oddly separate from reality.

Shock? There was no other explanation for the numbness, for the feeling that nothing around her had substance. She braced her back against the boulder and drew the cradleboard across her lap.

Her baby was alive. That was all she must think about. A bad dream. That was all this was, and if she sat here long enough, the ugliness would slip away, just as it did when she awoke from nightmares.

The instant Deke returned to the boulder, he recognized Laura's symptoms and gently took the baby from her. Her fixed gaze was blank. Her face was deathly pale. A short distance away, he saw evidence that she had been violently ill. He wanted to kick himself for not staying here with her. He of all people knew how a person felt after that first battle, that there was little glory in it and a whole lot of regret. For someone of Laura's refined sensibilities, Deke guessed the horror would be doubled. To know she had taken a life. To see a number of other human beings killed. It was little wonder she stared at nothing now, apart from him and the ugliness that surrounded her.

Shrugging his shoulders into the cradleboard straps, Deke went to his horse and wrested his other saddlebag from under the dead animal. The instant he dived his hand into the pack, he felt dampness and knew his jug of liquor had been shattered. *Christ.* Laura needed a belt of whiskey to snap her out of it. Black Stone and his men had already made short work of a burial detail and were fleeing back into the foothills to put as much distance between themselves and Denver as they could before darkness fell.

The baby began to cry. Deke took him to Laura and was more relieved than he could say when she responded, albeit haltingly, to the child's wails. He left her to feed the baby while he stripped his dead horse and hid the riding gear under some brush. Next he caught Laura's gelding and made ready to ride. It wasn't far to Denver now. Not far at all.

Deke paused a moment to gaze eastward and remembered a time when he, like Laura, had emptied his belly after a battle. Nowadays he only got cold sweats, and he wasn't entirely sure that was a good thing. The years had turned him hard. The kill-or-be-killed existence here had somehow separated him from his own humanity, teaching him to rationalize and justify.

He took a deep breath and wiped his moist palms on his jeans. Cold sweats. Icy trickles running down his spine. It made him feel empty to remember the boy he had once been, because he bore no resemblance to him now.

Before dark, he would have Laura and the baby settled into a Denver hotel room for the night. She would feel safe there, embraced by a world that was familiar to her, a world where Deke had never been welcomed. Laura's world, not his.

The ache within him intensified. For as long as he lived, he would never forget that awful moment when he had pressed the barrel of the Colt to Laura's temple and drawn the hammer back. If Black Stone had arrived one second later, just one miserable second, Deke might have pulled that trigger. Every time he thought about it, his legs felt as if they turned to water.

Was this the kind of life he wanted for Laura? Recalling the blank look in her eyes, he knew the answer to that question. Loving a woman and possessing her, that was the easy part. Loving her enough to let her go. That took a little more doing.

Riding through miles of cotton. Entering Denver. People reeling to a stop on the boardwalks to stare at her Indian clothing. Laura was aware of it all, yet not. Deke, so patient and gentle, helping her off the horse, holding her close to his side as he entered the hotel and rented a room. Deke, carrying her up a long flight of stairs, peeling back the bedclothes, laying her on a wonderfully soft mattress covered with crisp sheets, drawing a blanket over her, stroking her hair. Deke, filling her mouth with whiskey, ordering her to swallow. Deke, gently putting the sleeping baby in her arms and whispering that he had errands to run.

He would be back soon, he said. Laura drifted to sleep, clutching her child and his promise close to her heart, too numb and exhausted to ask questions. All she wanted was to be unaware for a while, to let the awfulness of the day move away from her so she could awaken refreshed and begin to put it in perspective.

She would, she assured herself as she drifted into blessed slumber. Tomorrow she would be strong. Tomorrow she would look back on today and be able to make sense of it all. Tomorrow. But not right now.

Carrying a bundle of warm sandwiches under one arm and clothing for Laura and the baby under his other, Deke strode quickly along the boardwalk, anxious to get back to the hotel. When the dangling clapboard sign came into view, he quickened his pace. He knew Laura was probably sleeping peacefully, just as she had been when he left her, and that she would awaken if Jonathan began to cry. If anyone tried to disturb her, Deke had left Chief in the room to stand guard. But even so, he couldn't shake the feeling that he should hurry back to her. Because of that, he had bypassed the telegraph office. He would check to see if there had been any dispatches received from her father in the morning.

As he stepped into the dimly lit hotel lobby, Deke saw two well-dressed, gray-haired gentlemen rise from the horsehair sofa at the opposite side of the room, but he didn't pay much attention until the more slender of the two stepped into his path, blocking his way to the stairs.

"Pardon me. Are you Deke Sheridan, by any chance?"

Deke focused on the man's face. After taking a long, hard look into a pair of amber-colored eyes that were uncannily familiar, he swallowed hard and said, "Yep, that's my name. What can I do for you?"

Deke knew. Oh, yes, he knew. And he felt as if his heart were lying on the floor at his feet. The man was dressed in an expensive charcoal suit with a matching silk vest that boasted a gold watch chain held just so by a diamond stickpin. A diamond, for Christ's sake.

"I understand that you were hired as a tracker by a woman named Laura Cheney?"

"That's right."

"I'm her father, Sterling Van Hauessen."

Laura's father, here in Denver. It was a sign, surely. Not just money in response to her wire, which she could have accepted or sent back, but her father, in the flesh. He had obviously come all this way for only one reason: to take his daughter and grandson back with him to Boston. Good old Boston, where the chairs were covered in finest velvet, where the ladies wore silk dresses and fluttered perfumed lace handkerchiefs in front of their noses when men like Deke walked past them on the street.

Still so Indian in his thinking, Deke was a believer in signs, lightning to herald the birth of a great warrior, the daytime sightings of owls to portend death. His head was chock-full of superstitions. Laura's father, answering her wire in person. It was a sign Deke couldn't ignore, a portent of death for him, but of life for Laura and Jonathan.

For two days he had tortured himself with the question. Should I send her back home? Sterling Van Hauessen's appearance in Denver answered that question.

Loving someone as deeply as he loved Laura wasn't always enough, Deke realized. Sometimes things weren't meant to be, no matter how right they seemed.

In a split second that seemed to Deke an eternity, all his hopes and dreams turned to dust, and he accepted that this was the end. Laura . . . being with her. He likened their time together to a flower in springtime, glorious while in bloom, but destined to wither. None of the truly beautiful things in his life seemed to last long.

"Mr. Van Hauessen," he replied solemnly. Looking into those amber eyes, Deke noted a marked difference from Laura's. Van Hauessen's eyes were cold. Cold and calculating. The eyes of a man who had lost his heart. Deke knew he couldn't allow himself to think about that. For Laura's sake, he had to accept this with whatever grace he could muster. She would never leave him, otherwise. No matter how cold a man Van Hauessen was, he could give Laura things Deke couldn't.

Shifting his packages, Deke extended his hand in greeting. "Pleased to meet ya." He turned an expectant gaze to the other gentleman who approached from his right, a short, round man with a crescent of gray hair that extended from ear to ear around an otherwise bald head.

"Sheldon Becker," the man introduced himself coolly. "An old friend of the family, and soon to be Mrs. Cheney's intended, I hope."

Sheldon Becker. Deke's guts clenched, and he resisted the impulse to say, "Old is right. Old enough to be her father." He ran his gaze over the man's elegant black frock coat and cutaway suit. Money. Both men reeked of it. In Boston, Laura and Jonathan would have luxuries Deke could never even dream of giving them. He wouldn't allow himself to picture Laura suffering Becker's touch. His beautiful Laura, buried under all that fat. The thought made Deke feel physically sick. But if that ended up being Laura's choice, it was not Deke's place to stand in her way.

Keeping his voice carefully friendly, Deke gestured toward the adjoining bar. "I think we need to talk, Mr. Van Hauessen. There's some things you need to know before you see your daughter."

And so it was that Deke led the way into the watering hole, familiar territory to him, yet oddly strange, possibly because the two men accompanying him made him feel like a dirty sock. He wanted to hide his scarred hands. En route to a table, he found himself wishing that he had stopped someplace for a wash and shave, maybe even for a haircut and respectable clothes. But he had done none of those things, and even if he had, he doubted it would make a difference. He was who he was, and fancy trimming would never change that.

As they approached an empty table, Deke yelled for a jug and three glasses. Taking one of the four chairs for himself, Deke placed his packages on another, then motioned for each of his companions to grab a seat. After the barkeep served them, Deke uncorked the bottle with his teeth and sloshed a measure of whiskey into each tumbler. With his every movement, he was aware that Van Hauessen and Becker watched him with appalled expressions on their faces.

Deke slid them each a glass and lifted his own. "Here's lookin' at ya." He tossed the whiskey down in one gulp, said, "Ahhhh," and bared his clenched teeth as the burn spread to his guts. "Not bad stuff," he said with a whistle.

The two Bostonians regarded him with their eyebrows raised and took precise little sips of their liquor, pinkies extended, diamonds flashing on their fingers, Van Hauessen's slender, Becker's pudgy. Deke decided he didn't feel quite so out of place as he had at the three-fork supper party, but close.

How to tell Sterling Van Hauessen that he had married his daughter, that was the question. And it didn't seem to Deke there was an easy answer. No matter how gently he tried to put it, Laura's father was not going to react calmly to the news. Deke knew that just by looking into the man's eyes. He was already about to choke just at the thought of Laura being in Deke's company for five weeks. When he learned she had also shared Deke's bed, things were bound to get ugly.

In the end, Deke chose to be direct and to the point. "Mr. Van Hauessen, you ain't gonna like this none too good, but I can't think of a easy way to say it. While Laura and me was in the foothills with the Cheyenne, we got married."

Silence. Van Hauessen simply stared. Becker frowned, as if he had heard but couldn't quite credit his ears.

"I beg your pardon?" Van Hauessen finally said.

"We got married," Deke repeated.

Becker flung himself back in his chair and barked with laughter. "You? You and Laura?" He pressed a hand over his jiggling belly. "Oh, Lord, that is rich." Glancing at Van Hauessen, he said, "He's lying through his teeth. Whom could they have found to witness the vows? They were out in the middle of nowhere!"

Deke didn't appreciate being called a liar. But he struggled to stay calm. For Laura. Because she would be the only one hurt if this turned ugly. "We was married the Cheyenne way," he explained.

Again Becker laughed. "The Cheyenne way? Please, do enlighten us. Did you jump over a rope together? Or cut your thumbs and mix your blood?" His fat face suddenly went hard and contorted. "Or do Cheyenne warriors just drag a girl off somewhere and rape her, then call it a marriage?"

Deke looked at Van Hauessen. In a low-pitched, expressionless voice, he said, "I think you'd best invite your friend to leave."

Becker didn't take the hint. His jowls aquiver with outrage, he leaned forward and planted a fist on the table. "You dare to sit there and tell us that Laura agreed to marry you? You? My God. I've never heard anything quite so absurd."

Deke felt his guts tightening and knew he couldn't take much more of this without losing his temper. "That's what I'm tellin' you."

Becker snorted. "And did you remove that monstrous hat during the ceremony? Where did you get that feather? From the ass of a molting eagle?"

That cut it. For Laura's sake, Deke had tried to be civil, but men like these would keep pushing until he pushed back. He fixed Becker with a hard, flat gaze. With slow, deliberate movements, he removed his Stetson and placed it on the table. "I only take off my hat when I'm fixin' to stomp somebody's ass," he said with biting clarity.

Becker immediately sobered. Van Hauessen sniffed and gave his glass a slow turn. When he lifted his gaze to Deke again, he said, "There is no need for this conversation to become unpleasant."

"I agree," Deke replied. "Like I suggested a second ago, maybe you and me oughta finish talkin' alone. It don't seem to me that Mr. Becker's got any business hearin' what's gonna be said anyhow."

Van Hauessen's gray mustache twitched. "As Mr. Becker

said, he has every hope of becoming Laura's intended. That gives him a certain interest in matters."

Deke bit down hard on his back teeth. Laura was right; her father was unbearably pompous. "Yeah, well, Mr. Becker here is liable to change his mind about wantin' to be her intended if he finds out later that she's got a loaf of my bread bakin' in her oven."

Van Hauessen's hollowed cheeks turned an alarming shade of red. He took a moment to smooth his silver hair before saying, "I beg your pardon?"

"Bread in her oven," Deke repeated, and tossed down his second whiskey. He glanced toward Becker. "1 hope that don't throw a hitch in your fancy get-along, Sheldon, old man. It was just an Injun weddin', a simple enough thing to pretend didn't happen, but if she's carryin' my child, things might get a little sticky. Don't you think?"

Becker, who had just taken a sip of whiskey, strangled as he tried to swallow. Liquid trickled from his nostrils, tears began to stream from his eyes, and he fished frantically for a neatly pressed linen handkerchief to dab his face. Mildly fascinated, Deke watched the man blow his nose with dainty little huffs, one flared nostril at a time. Van Hauessen sat so erect on his chair, he looked as if someone might have shoved a corncob up his ass.

"Dear God," he finally managed to say. "You and my daughter? My Laura? I want to see her. Immediately."

"Nope."

"What do you mean, no?" Van Hauessen braced an arm on the table and leaned forward. "Now, see here, Mr. Sheridan! Correct me if I'm wrong, but an Indian marriage does not give you legal rights, conjugal or otherwise."

"What kinda rights?"

"Conjugal!" The man blinked furiously. "Marital, if you prefer. If you have laid a hand on my daughter, I'll see you hang."

Deke completely forgot his vow to keep his temper. "Where the hell was you when Tristan Cheney was layin' his hands on her, you miserable sack of shit? Where was you when she wired you for help from Independence? And a few weeks later, from I can't remember where? Why wasn't you oozin' concern then?" It was Deke's turn to lean forward, and when he did so, he swept the whiskey bottle and glasses out of his way. "All it took was you learnin' Cheney was dead. That makes Laura worth somethin' again, don't it? And here you come with your highest bidder ridin' drag, his tongue hangin' clear to the goddamned floor just at the thought of gettin' his slimy hands on her."

"I don't have to take these insults!" Becker said huffily.

"You sure as hell don't. Consider it an engraved invite to leave."

"How dare you!" Van Hauessen sputtered.

"How dare I what? Call the cards the way I see 'em? Seems to me like you're the one steppin' over the line, Van Hauessen. What kinda man sells his daughter? And don't tell me that ain't what you got in mind." He shot another meaningful look at Becker.

"The very insinuation that I would sell my daughter for any amount of money is absolutely outlandish. I'm a wealthy man in my own right. I have no need of Becker's money, I assure you."

"No, but you'd sure as hell'd like a piece of his shipping business, wouldn't you? What'd Laura call it? A merger? Between Van Hauessen Exports and Becker Fleets? A nice little deal between the two of you with Laura in the middle, your daughter, his wife, and hopefully the mama of a few Van Hauessen and Becker brats to keep the ties strong?"

"That is a despicable accusation."

"But the truth. I got it straight from your daughter." Remembering all the feelings and emotions Laura had divulged to him during her illness, Deke hooked a thumb toward Becker. "Look at him, for Christ's sake. Can you blame her for jumpin' at the chance to marry Cheney? Mr. Becker is as old as you are. What kinda husband would he make for a girl Laura's age?"

"A better choice than she's capable of making on her own, obviously," Van Hauessen retorted icily. "First Tristan

Cheney, and now you? Laura is clearly incapable of judging character."

"I've had enough of this." With a disdainful snort, Becker hauled himself up, using the table to raise his considerable bulk. "Sterling, I'm off to find Laura. Money talks. This time that miserable little clerk will tell us what room she's in, or I shall know the reason why."

"Don't count on it," Deke inserted. "I told that clerk I didn't want nobody gettin' that room number. He knows if he gives it out, I'll tack his hide to the wall and use it for target practice."

Becker huffed. "Your audacity is absolutely astounding."

Deke wasn't sure what *audacity* meant. "Buy tickets. You ain't seen nothin' yet."

Becker tugged on his vest, which had rolled up over his stomach. "I'm off to find her, Sterling."

Deke sat back in his chair and grinned. "On second thought," he said just loudly enough for Van Hauessen's ears, "I hope the clerk gives him that room number. I got a dog standin' guard in our room that could save Laura a lot of grief. He's got a real bad habit of gettin' a man by the crotch and not turnin' loose till I tell him to."

Van Hauessen regarded Deke with undisguised distaste. "You know, Mr. Sheridan, I have a feeling that you are doing your level best to shock me."

Still wearing the grin, Deke replied, "Shockin' folks, that's what I do best." He kicked his chair back on its hind legs and plopped a moccasin on the table's edge. "You wanna know how I figure it, Mr. Van Hauessen? You ain't gonna like me, no matter what I do, so I might as well go for grass."

Laura's father tugged on his shirt cuffs, positioning them a precise inch below the edge of his jacket sleeves. Then he folded his arms and rested them on the table. He gazed into the depths of his glass, then smiled slightly. A smile that was as calculated and precise as his adjustment of his shirtsleeves.

"You may be wrong about that. I think I do like you, though I can't imagine why."

Deke had played too much poker to fall for that. "I don't give a shit if you like me, Mr. Van Hauessen. That ain't my aim, and it ain't my game."

"What is your game? To come out of this with my daughter as your wife? Surely you must realize that Laura could never be happy here. She was raised in affluent social circles with every advantage. What could you possibly offer her? And what of my grandson? What sort of education would he receive here? Laura wouldn't countenance her son wearing moccasins and a dirty Stetson with a bedraggled feather stuck in the hatband." He glanced at the hatband in question. "What is it made of, by the way? Cobalt trade beads of some sort? Very quaint."

Deke nudged his hat with the side of his foot. "Yep. That hatband's one of a kind, all right. My Cheyenne mother strung them beads for me years ago when I killed my first white man. I was thirteen, if I remember correct."

"Am I supposed to feel intimidated, Sheridan?"

"Nope. You asked. I told you."

"Shall we stick to the subject of my daughter?"

"You changed the subject—I didn't."

"We were discussing your aim. If it is your hope to somehow lay claim to my daughter, surely you realize how absurd an idea that is. Laura would be miserably unhappy here."

Deke drew his foot from the table and rocked forward in his chair, bringing the front legs to the floor with a sharp report. "She was miserable in Boston, too."

"There were compensations."

"So you don't deny it?"

"My daughter is a headstrong young woman. Controlling her and keeping her happy didn't always go hand in hand."

Deke flashed another smile. "Well, now, I reckon that's my aim, to see to it you work real hard at keepin' her happy. If I let her go back with you, that is."

"Let her?"

"That's right. She won't go unless I talk her into it. Trust me on that."

Van Hauessen smirked. "So why would you convince her to leave?"

"Because I'm afraid you're right, and she'll be miserable here if she stays. I'd rather she was away from me and happy."

"I see."

"No, you don't see," Deke said softly, "and that's the cryin' shame of it all. But the way I see it, that don't matter. With a few rules laid down for you, I think you can give Laura the kind of life she deserves, and I aim to see you do just that."

"Rules?"

"Yep. My terms, Mr. Van Hauessen, which you'll accept if you want your daughter and grandson to live with you in Boston. My picture of things ain't exactly what you had in mind, no mergers with Becker Fleets and all that—unless Laura decides that's what she wants. But you'll have the boy to carry on for you in the family business. That's somethin', at least."

"Your arrogance knows no bounds."

"When a man can shoot like I can, he don't gotta have bounds, Mr. Van Hauessen, just guts. I know you're thinkin' that I'd be tossed in jail if I went to Boston wavin' a gun around, and you're probably right."

"It's good to know you realize that."

"Yep, I realize lots of things. Like, for instance, I realize I ain't gonna get thrown in jail until I'm seen, and I'm real handy at keepin' my head low, even in places like Boston. With my Henry and my naked eye, I can pick an acorn off a tree with one shot at two hundred yards. A man makes a lot bigger target. If Laura was to write me that her daddy was makin' her real unhappy, I don't reckon I'd travel all the way to Boston just to shoot at acorns. Do you?"

Van Hauessen's face flushed. Then the color faded.

"Are you threatening me?"

"I sure as hell am. You still think you like me?" Deke asked in a low voice.

"Less and less, by the moment."

"Then I think we're startin' to understand each other, ain't we?"

"What are your terms, Mr. Sheridan?"

Deke poured himself another serving of whiskey and began to list them.

Laura heard Deke whispering her name long before she reached wakefulness, and she moved through the blackness toward him, becoming aware of him, measure by measure. His hand on her hair, his hip pressed against her side, the hardness of his arm braced on the mattress at her back. Something awful hovered at the edges of her mind, but in her drowsiness, she was able to shove it away and not face it now. Deke. He was all she wanted or needed to think about. She opened her eyes and blinked to bring his dark features into focus. His mahogany hair fell forward, forming a curtain around their faces. She looked into those incredibly light blue eyes of his and smiled slightly.

He grinned back and lifted a steaming mug of coffee from the bedside table. "A cup of wake-up, fresh from the restaurant down the street."

Laura glanced bewilderedly around and spied Jonathan where Deke had moved him onto the bed beside her. She pushed up on an elbow, feeling oddly disoriented, her limbs leaden. Deke fluffed a pillow and put it at her back. When she was sitting comfortably, he cupped her hands around the warm mug.

"Take a sip," he said. "We gotta talk, darlin', and I want you awake."

Laura blinked again and took a careful mouthful of the hot brew. The shot of caffeine and his serious tone brought her more awake, and she remembered the day's events with a jolt. So much ugliness to be faced. She wasn't sure she could deal with it yet and sincerely hoped that wasn't what he wished to discuss. "Talk? About what?"

He smoothed a stray curl from her cheek. "About us."

Laura's gaze shot to his. "Us?" The sad expression in his eyes made her heart catch. "What do you mean, about us?"

"Don't go gettin' upset. I just been doin' a lot of thinkin'." He looked deeply into her eyes. "How much do you love me, Laura?"

"What kind of question is that? With all my heart, of course."

He nudged the brim of his hat back and flashed her a slow smile. "Enough that nothin' could make you stop?"

"Nothing," she assured him, and as she said those words, she knew them to be absolutely true. One of the things she had come to love the most about Deke was his ability to sense how she felt. Tonight, however, his intuitiveness unnerved her. Sometimes one needed time to circle feelings before trying to deal with them. "And you? How much do you love me?"

"More than I can say." He traced the bridge of her nose. Then he took a deep breath and sighed. "Things has happened real quick for us, ain't they, Boston? We started out from here just a hair over five weeks ago, me hatin' you, you hatin' me, and now here we are, married."

Laura had a bad feeling about this conversation, a very bad feeling. But she was so groggy, it was difficult for her to concentrate on it and decipher exactly why. "Yes, things happened rather quickly. But we were thrust into extraordinary circumstances."

"A month ago, all you wanted was to hightail it home for Boston and never clap eyes on Colorado again. Remember that?"

"Of course."

"What changed your mind?"

"Loving you," she replied, perhaps a little too quickly. *Don't do this, Deke,* she wanted to cry. *Not yet. Let me put some distance between myself and this morning first. Please?* But she could see he had no intention of allowing her to do that. "Loving you. That's what changed my mind."

"Ah, but Colorado's just the same. What happened this mornin' proved that. It's hard country, Laura. You lovin' me don't change that. It don't make men like Gonzales not exist." He let his gaze slide around the dimly lit room. Then he studied the lantern for a long moment. "I think we both gotta think about what almost happened today. I think we gotta think about it real hard."

Laura shivered. "I'd rather not. Maybe tomorrow. Right now I'd rather pretend it didn't happen."

"We can't pretend that." He measured off a scant distance between thumb and forefinger. "I came just that close to puttin' a bullet in your brain, for God's sake. If Black Stone had showed up one minute later, you would've been dead, and Jonathan, too. Maybe you can pretend that didn't happen, but I can't. I was the one who damned near pulled the trigger."

Laura squeezed her eyes closed. "Oh, Deke, don't. Please don't. Not tonight."

"How do you think it made me feel, knowin' I might get shot and that you'd be left to face them bastards all alone?"

Laura knew how it had made him feel. Desperate. Desperate enough to take her life and Jonathan's rather than let it happen. "Oh, Deke, what is the point? It happened. It's over. Let's try to put it behind us."

"It's part of daily life here, darlin'. We can't put it behind us." He caught her chin on the edge of his hand. "You got a son to think about, Laura. I gotta think about him, too. This can be a dangerous place. If you and the boy stay here, I gotta know, deep down in my heart, that it's the right thing for both of you."

"It is the right thing!" she cried shrilly.

"Who you tryin' to convince, Laura? Me or yourself?"

Laura couldn't answer that. She cupped a trembling hand over her eyes, unable to speak, not wishing to try, for fear of what she might say. The horror of this morning was still too fresh, the memory of how terrified she had been for Jonathan still too close.

"Laura." He cursed under his breath. "If it was just me and you, maybe I'd see things different. But it ain't. We got Jonathan to think about. If you and him stay here, I gotta know it's what you truly think is best. That you've thought it through real careful and made your decision with your head and not your heart."

"Deke, there are risks everywhere."

"Yeah, but every day in this country can be a gamble. I never realized just how big a gamble until today. Always before, it was only me, and close brushes never scared me as bad. I could think, 'Well, it just wasn't my time,' and go on from there. It's different when it could've been you or Jonathan. Can you understand that?"

"You protected us," she whispered fiercely. "With your own body, you protected us. That's all I want to remember."

He drew in a ragged breath. "I've told you a few times that I'd always take care of you, that I'd never light out when you was countin' on me. I realize now that I was makin' a promise I can't keep. A man don't decide when he's gonna die."

"Don't," she cried.

"Don't what? Make you look at the truth?"

"Deke, I love you."

"I know you do. But how you and me feel ain't all that's important here. Almost from the first, I finagled to have you." His eyes crinkled at the corners in a sad smile. "Remember me tellin' you how sometimes a man forelegs himself a filly, and the fall can break her neck? I throwed you some loops there at the start, and if somethin' should happen to you or Jonathan because I did, I—" He broke off and shook his head. "I couldn't live with the guilt, Laura. I'd never forgive myself."

Laura's heart twisted at the look in his eyes. He meant it. He truly meant it. He was thinking about sending them away. "What are you saying?"

"That I need some time to think, and you do, too. I want us both to be damned sure a life here with me is what's best for you and the baby."

"I don't need time to think."

"Don't you?" He rubbed his thumb lightly over her mouth. "Laura, love, can you say you didn't look at Jonathan this mornin' and wish the two of you was anyplace but there with me? Tell me you didn't, and I'll never bring any of this up again."

Laura couldn't tell him that because it would be a lie.

"Tell me it don't scare the sand out of you to think about bein' left alone. You know I'd never choose for it to happen, that I'd never leave you willingly, but it could happen, just the same."

It was an undeniable truth, and for the life of her, Laura could think of absolutely nothing she might say to change it. She shifted her gaze to Jonathan. Deke was right. They both had to think of the baby, of what might be best for him. Jonathan's life had nearly been ended that morning. The same might happen again. Such a thing would probably never occur in Boston.

"I reckon I've made my point," he said softly.

A panicky feeling welled within Laura, very like the one she had felt this morning when the barrel of Deke's Colt pressed against her temple. She looked up, silently pleading. "I don't know if I can leave you."

He lifted her face, his gaze trailing slowly over her features. His mouth quivered slightly at the corners, and he caught his bottom lip between his teeth. After a moment, he swallowed and managed to grin, but a suspicious sheen had gathered at the corners of his eyes.

"You can do whatever you got to," he said with certainty. "You lovin' Jonathan like you do, puttin' him before yourself, that's one of the things I've always admired about you. I ain't got a question in my mind that you'll do what's best for him now."

"Oh, Deke, that isn't fair."

"Life ain't fair, honey. And in some places, it's rougher than in others. Colorado's one of 'em." He took his hat off and pinched the creases in its crown, his expression thoughtful. "If I could see where life here would be better—for you and the baby . . ." He flexed his shoulders and sighed. "If I could even weigh things out and see that Colorado could come close, I'd hogtie you and never let you leave. You gotta know that. But the fact is that Boston's got a heap more to offer, safety and security at the top of the list. I don't even know if Jonathan could get proper schoolin' here." He glanced up, his eyes twinkling yet unmistakably sad. "It'd be a hell of a note if he growed up to be like me. In Boston he can learn to be a real fancy gentleman. He'll have a home like I could never give him. Nice clothes. The best schools. You and me both have gotta think about all them things and feel certain sure raisin' him here, where he won't have 'em, is what's right for him."

"Yes," Laura said thinly. That one word was so difficult to push up her throat that she felt exhausted after uttering it and rested her head against the pillow, weary in a way she had never been, drained in a way she hadn't thought possible.

"I ain't sayin' I want you to go to Boston and never look back," he told her huskily. "I think there's things here in Colorado that's real fine, too. Fancy clothes ain't everything. Growin' up here can be a real fun time for a boy, and I think I could do real good by Jonathan in lots of ways. But not in the ways you growed up thinkin' was important." He paused for a moment. "I guess what I'm askin' is for you to take a good, hard look inside yourself, Laura. Not at how you feel or how you think I feel, but at what you want for your baby."

"That's a tall order."

"Yep."

"You don't know my father. Once I'm back under his thumb, I may not be allowed a choice, let alone a chance to contact you if I want to come back here."

Deke smiled at that. "Now, that there's a problem I think I took care of. Your daddy and me just had us a real long talk, and he understands real clear that you're gonna be doin' your own decidin' from here on out."

"My father? Here?" she asked incredulously.

After her initial amazement had passed, Deke filled her in on all that had transpired while she slept.

"Anyhow," he finished, "he's agreed to my terms. If you go back with him, he won't be arrangin' no marriage with Becker. He'll be content just to have you and his grandson with him, and that's how it should be. He's also agreed that he won't give you trouble if you decide to come back here to Colorado. If he does, all you gotta do is send me a telegraph or a letter, and I'll hightail it to Boston."

"You dictated terms to my father?" she whispered. "How on earth did you—"

"I just told him a story I know about acorns," Deke said with a chuckle. "After that, he was real accommodatin'."

Laura couldn't share his confidence. "Deke, you have to understand that my father isn't a man who always keeps his word. What he agrees to now and what he does later may be two different things. He might not allow me to contact you once we're safely away from here."

"He understands that I'm gonna expect letters from you real regular. If I don't get 'em, I'll know somethin' is wrong."

"He might stand over me while I write to you."

At that, he chuckled again. "I thought of that. The way I see it, we need us a trick up our sleeves to make sure you can let me know if somethin' has gone wrong. I was thinkin' on a special word—one just you and me know about. In every letter, you can be sure to use that word at least once to let me know things is all okay. If you write me a letter and don't use that word, I'll know things has gone sour."

Laura grinned. "I think maybe you understand my father better than I gave you credit for. What special word would we use?"

"Your favorite one," he said silkily. "Despicable. I promise to start learnin' how to spell it tomorrow."

Laura giggled. Then she grew serious. It was one thing to discuss leaving him. It would be quite another to actually do it. They gazed into each other's eyes for several endless seconds, communicating in a way only lovers can. Laura knew this was as difficult for him as it was for her.

"For Jonathan," he whispered.

She finally nodded. "And how long a time must I think things over?"

He smoothed her hair, then curled his hand over her nape, his fingertips lightly caressing. "Until the dust settles," he replied. "However long that takes." His eyes warmed on hers. "If you decide halfway home that you're absolutely sure Colorado is where you wanna raise that boy, stop wherever you are and wire me for money. I'll come into town real regular and check at the telegraph office."

Laura shifted her attention to Jonathan. She studied his precious profile for a moment, feeling overwhelmed by the decisions Deke was asking her to make. Her son's future, everything he might one day be, rested entirely in her hands, and no matter how she might try to rationalize it, she feared that, in the end, the advantages Boston had to offer would far outweigh those in Colorado.

"Hey."

She glanced up to find Deke smiling at her. Smiling through tears. Upon seeing them, she threw herself into his arms and clung to him with all her might, not at all sure she would be able to let him go.

"Oh, Deke. I can't do this!"

He pressed his face against the curve of her neck and began to rub her back, comforting her, as he had always done. Laura sobbed when he started to pat her. Those wonderful thumps from his big hands. How would she live without them?

"We got somethin' special, you and me," he whispered shakily. "The kind of feelin' some folks never find. If it turns out that you stay in Boston, if it turns out that you and me can't never see each other again, we'll always have that feelin'. You know what I'm sayin'?"

Laura did know, and that was the heartbreak of it. To love him so much, and to know he loved her as well. Their time together had been so short, and now he was saying it might have to last them a lifetime.

When he finally drew away, Laura let him go. As if by mutual consent, they both turned their gazes to Jonathan. Deke braced a hand on the bed to lean over him and press a farewell kiss to his forehead.

"He's turnin' out to be a real fine-lookin' boy," he said softly.

Laura agreed with a murmur. As Deke straightened, she whispered, "You're not leaving right now, are you?"

He pushed up from the bed and picked up his hat. "I still got some things to do before I call it a night." He snapped his fingers at Chief. "And you and your daddy got a lot of catchin' up to do."

Because he avoided looking into her eyes, Laura sensed he didn't intend to come back. She felt as if a cold metal band were tightening around her chest. "Is this it? Good-bye, just like that?"

"I ain't never gonna tell you good-bye, Boston. Sayin' the words would break my heart. So I just ain't gonna say 'em."

"I don't even know where your ranch is. You can't just—"

"Hell, it's easy to find." He hooked a thumb toward the window. "Head north about five miles till you hit a wagon road. Cut left onto it and go westish until your wadin' ankle-deep in cow shit." His eyes took on a mischievous glint. "If you hit the Rockies, you'll know you've gone too far."

Because she was perilously close to tears, Laura took her cue from him and said lightly, "Westish? Can you name me a direction without an *ish* stuck on the end, Mr. Sheridan?"

He strode to the door. As he opened it, he paused to look back at her. "Hell, Boston, with directions like that, how lost can you possibly get?"

With that, he and Chief stepped out of the room. And out of her life. Laura sat there, staring at the closed door, for a very long while, feeling as though he had ripped the very heart out of her.

"Pretty damned lost," she whispered.

And then she wept.

Chapter 28

THE REMAINDER OF THAT NIGHT AND THE FOL-
lowing day became a blur in Laura's mind. With his usual
assertiveness, her father took control, ordering her and
Jonathan traveling wardrobes from the local dressmaker's,
purchasing trunks and all the necessities to fill them, toilet-
ries, brushes, and wardrobe accessories. Money was no ob-
ject. Laura had forgotten how it felt to name anything she
wanted or needed and have it be hers.

Things. So many things that she had once taken for
granted. Eating at the nicest restaurant in town. Expensive
perfume. Silk against her skin. Not having to do any sort of
work, and knowing she would never have to again. It was a
seductive thought.

Toward late afternoon, she stood at the hotel room window, gazing down at the Denver street below. She watched
people as they passed by, mothers with children, married
couples. It seemed to her they were all conversing with one
another. Seeing those people made her feel incredibly
lonely. During all the rush to prepare for the return trip to
Boston, her father had said very little to her. *Hello, darling.*
Empty words, coming from him, and she had yearned to
hear Deke say "darlin'" in that lazy way he had. *It's good to
see you again.* Was her father truly glad to see her? Laura
wasn't certain, and that made her feel empty.

Not that she had expected anything more. How else was
she to feel without Deke? He had become the most impor-

tant person in her world. And now he was gone. It was amazing how attached one could grow to another person in five short weeks. She knew the feeling was mutual. *If I make love to you, Boston, and then I lose you—well, I ain't sure I could stand it.* The evening he had said that to her, things had seemed so simple. She had been so certain that their future was decided.

The click of a revolver hammer had changed all that.

Don't think about him, she ordered herself. Her feelings weren't what she had to consider. If that were the case, she wouldn't be here now, for she knew where she wanted to be. What she had to think of was Jonathan's welfare, not just about the sort of life her father could provide for him, but his safety and well-being. Wherever she decided to raise Jonathan, she had to know it was the very best place. Deke had to know that as well.

Pressing her hand against her waist, Laura was acutely conscious of the fine fabric of her new dress against her palm. Turning from the window, she settled her gaze on Jonathan. He looked adorable in the little suit her father had bought him. Checkered wool in ocher tones, with buff-colored gaiters and tiny little high-top shoes. A far cry from animal hides and moss. He looked like a wizened little old man.

Moving toward him, Laura managed a smile. He was awake and pumping his hands and feet, his dark blue eyes fastened curiously on the ceiling. Laura looked up and saw nothing fascinating. But, then, everything was new to Jonathan. Deke claimed the nicest thing about babies was that they made adults look at the world through their eyes.

"Hello, there," she said softly, and sat beside her son on the mattress. "Jonathan? What do you see up there?"

At the sound of her voice, he turned to look at her and smiled. At just that moment, the hotel room door opened, and her father stepped in. Laura threw him an excited grin. "Daddy, he just smiled at me!"

"Hm." Her father stepped to the dresser and sifted through some papers he had laid there, not so much as glancing at the baby.

"Daddy, didn't you hear me? Jonathan smiled. He's never done that before. Not a real smile, anyway. Oh, I wish Deke could have seen him. He was always calling me over to look, convinced he was smiling, but—"

Laura broke off as her father whirled to look at her. "Deke, Deke, Deke!" he snapped. "I am heartily sick of hearing that man's name, and if you would refrain from saying it, I would be much appreciative."

Laura swallowed. "He's a very nice man, Daddy."

"Nice? Nice! He is, without question, the most uncouth individual I've ever had the misfortune of meeting."

"Daddy, if not for Deke, Jonathan and I might be dead."

"Yes, well." He sighed and fluttered the paper. "For that, I'm grateful to him. But gratitude doesn't blind me to the sort of man he is, Laura. Definitely not a proper father for Jonathan, that's for certain, and I believe you've made a very wise decision, returning to Boston. God forbid that my grandson should have grown up patterning himself after that fellow. The mere thought makes me shudder."

Not a proper father? Deke had said almost the same thing last night, that it would be a terrible thing if Jonathan grew up to be like him. Her throat tightened, and tears burned under her eyelids. As she recalled, she had been so upset, she hadn't argued with him on that point, and she should have. If Jonathan grew up to be half the man Deke Sheridan was, Laura would be pleased.

In her mind's eye, she pictured Deke. His twinkling gaze, his lopsided grin, the way he threw his dark head back when he laughed. Then she remembered other things, his tenderness, his big, clumsy hands, the way it felt when he held her, the expression that always softened his features when he looked at Jonathan. Deke. He had shielded her and the baby with his own body. Laura wasn't certain her father would have done the same.

She studied her father now, comparing him to Deke, finding him lacking. He could give Jonathan so many things. But could he give him the right things? Would he listen when her son needed to talk? Would he hug him when he needed affection? Would he spend time with him, or would he always be too busy and distracted, as he was now?

"Daddy ..." Laura stood and walked slowly across the room. "Daddy?"

He was studying the paper again. "I do believe I've found an error here," he muttered.

Laura sighed. "Must we dine with Sheldon tonight?"

"I don't know, dear. We'll see."

We'll see. His pat answer. A safe answer. No matter what she might ask, he could safely make that reply without paying attention. Daddy, may I jump out the attic window? We'll see. Laura couldn't count the times he had said that to her over the years. We'll see ...

Feeling frustrated, she took a calming breath. Deke wanted her to take this time, to weigh things carefully, to make her decision with her head instead of her heart. If she constantly found fault with her father, she wouldn't be giving Boston and a life there with him a very fair chance.

She decided to try again.

"Daddy, I thought it might be nice if just the three of us spent some time together. Just you and me, with Jonathan. Wouldn't that be pleasant? We've had so little time today. I'd enjoy getting a chance to talk with you."

He graced her with a glance. "Oh? What about?"

"I, um ..." Laura shrugged. "I don't know. About things. The last two years with Tristan. About my ... I'm feeling kind of lonely, Daddy. And a little scared."

He looked up again, studying her over the rims of his spectacles. "Scared?"

"Yes. I want to be certain I'm doing the right thing."

He looked irritated at that. "Don't be a goose, Laura. Of course you are. And how can you be lonely? I'm here. Jonathan's here." Even as he finished speaking, his voice was trailing off, as was his attention.

"But, Daddy, you don't talk to me."

He quirked an eyebrow. "I'm talking to you right now."

He called this talking? Laura looked deeply into his eyes. It was frightening, the coldness she saw there. Certainly no love. It was as though her father looked through her instead of at her. She imagined Jonathan, ten years from now, looking into those cold eyes, seeing no love. Laura knew how that felt. As a child, it had been her sole endeavor to please her father, to make him proud of her. She had never succeeded in doing either.

Deke was proud of her. His voice echoed in her mind. *Reload!* She wanted to weep at the memory. To be shoulder to shoulder with a man like Deke Sheridan, to know he trusted her to do her part. It had been the greatest of compliments, and she would carry that prideful feeling inside her always. Her father didn't understand that. The people in his life were part of the fancy trappings, possessions he took for granted.

Was that what she truly wanted for Jonathan?

Stop it, Laura. Make the best of this. "Wouldn't you like to hear about what's happened to me these last two years, Daddy?"

"Actually, darling, I believe the less we speak of Tristan, the better." He flashed her one of those quick smiles that never warmed his expression. "Why don't you play with the baby for a few more minutes? Let me finish up here, and then we'll talk for a bit, if you'd like."

Resigned, Laura returned to the bed. Upon seeing her, Jonathan dimpled his cheek again. "Daddy, he did it again. Looked right at me and smiled, I swear. Come and see. Hurry, before he starts fussing because he's hungry."

Her father didn't glance up. "Hm." He scratched his head and sniffed. "I wonder if that silly woman can spell her own name, let alone add a column of figures."

"Daddy? Are you listening?"

"Yes, of course. In a minute, dear. I didn't realize you were hungry. We'll leave shortly. Sheldon found a nice place to eat, he said."

"Trust Sheldon to do so," Laura said. She straightened and fixed her father with a thoughtful gaze. "Daddy?"

"Hm?"

In a bright voice, she said, "Daddy, have you held Jonathan yet?"

He flicked a disinterested glance toward the bed. "Not right now, darling. I haven't time." He frowned over his papers again. "I do believe that dressmaker tallied this column of figures incorrectly."

Echoes from the past. Laura tipped her head and thought back over everything that had been said since her father had entered the room. One word kept repeating itself. *Daddy.* And suddenly the present seemed blended with a thousand yesterdays, and she heard herself, clamoring for her father's attention, saying that same word, over and over. *Daddy. Daddy! Daddy?* A rather desperate note laced it each time. A plea. What she was actually saying was, "Look at me. Pay attention to me." But he never had.

Laura gave a little laugh. "Oh, dear. Will the error bankrupt us?"

He glanced up, still scowling. "Of course not. I simply don't wish to overpay."

"Heaven forbid." Laura gave Jonathan a jiggle and bent to kiss his cheek. "You're right. That's far more important than holding your grandson."

"Hm." Apparently oblivious, he readjusted his spectacles on his nose. "There *is* a discrepancy. Of five dollars, if I've figured correctly."

Laura jiggled the bed again and watched her son's eyes widen. An ache filled her as she thought of Deke. She had never had to ask him to hold Jonathan; he always volunteered. And he had been as excited as she whenever the baby did something new.

A first smile . . . To her father, it meant nothing. To Deke, it would have meant the world, and he had missed seeing it.

That evening just before dusk, Deke went out to sit on his front stoop and gazed at the low hill across the creek where he had always planned to build a house one day. A big one with five bedrooms for a passel of kids. Pine and cottonwood grew over there. The grass was brilliant green. The view of the Rockies was fantastic.

Beckoned by dreams, he pushed up and strolled that way, Chief plodding happily along beside him. Deke's hired hands had butchered a steer day before yesterday, so the dog had a new bone clamped between his teeth.

When he reached the creek, Deke picked his way across on stepping-stones, then leaped to the bank. He imagined how it might be if Laura were with him now. Her first question would probably be, "Are there leeches in that water?" He smiled at the thought as he walked among the trees. The breeze whispered softly in the cottonwood leaves and creaked the pine boughs. It seemed to him the whispers said her name, over and over. *Laura . . .*

He knew she was probably gone by now. Deke didn't peg Sterling Van Hauessen as a man who would let any grass grow under his feet. He had probably booked passage on the first eastbound stage. Deke wasn't familiar with the route. He wondered where Laura and Jonathan would stay tonight. Then he shoved the question aside. They were out of his life now. He had to stop thinking about them every waking moment.

Lengthening his stride to measure a yard, Deke paced off the spot where he wanted to build his foundation for the house. After all, Laura might come back to Colorado, and if she did, he wanted everything to be ready for her.

Fool. She'll never come back here, and you damned well know it. Deke broke his pace and gazed at his cabin. One miserable room, and none too clean at that. He was crazy for hoping a woman like Laura might want to spend the rest of her life here. Five weeks ago, she had detested everything about this country, including him. Once she was settled back in Boston and got another taste of the good life, she'd be thanking her lucky stars she wasn't here.

Leaning against a tree, Deke fixed his gaze on the mountains and imagined that all his hopes and dreams were being carried away by the whispering gusts of the Colorado wind. It was over, and he had to accept that. Somehow he had to get on with his life.

Time lost substance. Deke wasn't sure how long he stood there, staring at those mountains through a shimmer of tears. The dusk deepened to that pinkish twilight that comes just before full darkness. An eerie time of day, he thought. Full of shadows. And loneliness. Time for an evening fire, but there wasn't much point in building one when he had no one to share it with.

"Deee-eeke?"

He blinked and cocked his head to glance at Chief. The dog just lay there, his breaths coming in slow huffs that would soon be snores.

"Deee-eeke? Yoo-hoooo!"

Deke straightened and peered through the trees toward the cabin. A figure stood in the shadows of the stoop overhang. He didn't recognize the horse. He moved slowly forward, his right hand hanging loose at his side, his fingers flexing. In this country, a man never knew when trouble might come knocking at his door.

As he strode out of the trees, the figure on his stoop came down the step. A woman. In a leather dress. He froze and stared at her, not quite able to believe his eyes. Amber hair. Even in the poor light, the braid that encircled her crown gleamed like whiskey held up to firelight. On her back, she wore a cradleboard.

It couldn't be . . . She was gone.

Putting her hands on her hips, she walked around the side of the house and peered out across the grassland. Deke's gaze fell to the seductive sway of her walk, to the graceful curve of leg where it met slender ankle. He quickened his pace.

"Laura?"

At the sound of his voice, she whirled. Then she broke into a run. He did as well. They met at the creek, each drawing up on an opposite bank, their gazes routing through the shadows, clinging. She seemed to be waiting for him to speak. Deke wanted to ask her a dozen questions, most important if she was there to stay. But he was afraid to hear her answer.

The seconds ticked past, measured by his heartbeats. She began to look uneasy. Then she tipped her head, her expression questioning. "Have you seen Deke Sheridan around here anywhere?"

That was a damned fool question if ever he had heard one. Before he could tell her so, she said, "I've been wading ankle-deep through cow manure for the last ten miles. My son is exhausted. I'm exhausted. Isn't that just like a man, never where he says he'll be when his wife needs him?"

Deke swallowed hard. "What're you doin' here, Boston? I thought we agreed you was gonna—"

"Jonathan smiled today, and you missed it," she cut in.

"What?"

She stepped a little closer to the water's edge. "He smiled, Deke. His first real smile."

"He did?" Deke glanced at the dark head resting on her shoulder. "Well, I'll be."

"Daddy was too busy to even come look."

"Well, he hasn't been around Jonathan much. Maybe he don't realize what a big deal his first smile is."

"Smiles aren't important to him," she said softly. Catching her lower lip between her teeth, she just stood there for a moment, her expression wistful. "Smiles are something I can't live without. Does that make any sense at all?"

Deke gazed across the creek at her, at her sweet face, into her pleading eyes. It was crazy, absolutely crazy. What woman in her right mind would give up everything that her father had to offer in exchange for a smile? But knowing Laura as he did, knowing what he did about her life, he understood what she couldn't seem to put into words.

"Laura, darlin', I don't even got a house. Just a one-room cabin, and it ain't too clean."

She glanced over her shoulder. "I can clean it up. And I don't care how many rooms it has as long as Jonathan and I can live there with you."

"I ain't got water plumbed in."

"You can help me haul it in buckets."

"It needs to be caulked. The wind whistles through the cracks, and unless I get a house built, it'll be colder than a witch's tit in there come winter."

"We'll spoon to keep warm."

"Spoon?"

She gave him a quavery smile. "You don't mean to tell me you ain't never spooned? What does folks do here in Colorado for excitement?"

With four long strides, Deke lunged across the creek and gained the opposite bank. Dripping wet, he scooped Laura into his arms. "Jesus, honey, are you sure?"

She clung to his neck. Deke pressed his face against her hair. His jaw rested on Jonathan's silken head. He closed his eyes, inhaling the scents he had thought never to smell again. Laura and Jonathan. To Deke, they had become as necessary as breathing.

"I'm sure," she whispered. "I have to tell you, though, that I made the decision with my heart and not my head. In all my life, there has been only one person who stood by me through everything, only one person who loved me just because I'm me. I know you'll love my son just as unconditionally."

"Just as what?"

She hugged him more tightly and started to laugh. "Oh, Deke, I love you. Unconditionally. It means no matter what. And that's how you love us. All day long I kept thinking of all the *things* Daddy could give Jonathan. Everything money can buy. But don't you see? Things aren't important. It's who you share them with. It's hugs and teasing and laughter. It's talking to one another and listening. It's caring about feelings. In Boston, neither of us would have you, and without you, our lives would be empty." She leaned back to search his gaze. "Do you understand what I'm saying? You don't come with any guarantees, but what in life does? All we can do is take the very best life has to offer today and take our chances on tomorrow. If I've got to take risks, I want everything that matters to me riding on you."

Taking chances. Deke supposed she was right. Life was one big gamble, no matter where you were, Colorado or Boston or points in between. On the other hand, though, every good poker player knew that luck, good or bad, usually came in runs. Up to this moment in his life, he had been dealt some pretty lousy hands. He was long overdue for a winning streak.

He leaned around to look at Jonathan. "You say he smiled?"

"Twice. And just as big as you please!"

Deke rocked back to see her face. Amber hair and amber eyes. Behind her rose the Rockies, majestic black crags that were already reaching into the night. He had set her free, and she had come back to him. Not for money. Not for all the fine things he might give her. But for a smile, of all things. It just happened that he had plenty of those on hand to give her.

In Cheyenne he whispered, *"Was he kee, she, ke."*

"What?" she asked softly.

"It is a very fine day," he translated. "It's what the Cheyenne say when good things begin. *Was he kee, she, ke.*"

"Was he kee, she, ke," she repeated.

As they gazed into each other's eyes, both knew that this was more than just the beginning of something good. It was the beginning of something beautiful.

For the three of them.

Read on for an excerpt from
Catherine Anderson's

PERFECT TIMING

Available now from Signet

QUINCY HARRIGAN'S RIDING BOOTS OFFERED poor traction on the patches of ice-encrusted snow, which in the faint light of predawn looked bluish white on his scraggly front lawn. Carefully holding a mug of coffee in one hand, he picked his way between two muddy ranch vehicles, wondering when his dooryard had become a parking lot for pickups, the tractor, and two dented ATVs. Walking with his head bent, he realized his hair had gotten so long that it dangled in a dark brown hank over his left eye. *Damn.* He'd been out of town and missed his appointment with the barber. Rescheduling was out of the question. From one day to the next, he didn't know when he'd have to leave again, and while he was here, he was far too busy to drive clear into town for a walk-in visit. It was a wonder he even managed to grab a few hours of sleep. This morning, he felt the exhaustion in every muscle of his body, and he seriously doubted the freshly brewed French roast would give him the jolt of energy he needed.

No matter. Compared to his sister-in-law Loni, he had little reason to complain. At least he wasn't fighting for his life. The thought made his heart twist, and the lump that seemed to have taken up permanent residence at the base of his throat throbbed like a toothache. He stopped to gaze across his ranch, taking in the huge taupe-colored arena that loomed over all the smaller buildings. Twenty years ago, this had been an empty piece of land, signed over to him by his father. Now, just having turned forty, Quincy saw the story of his adult life in every structure, fence post, and nail. This ranch had been his dream since childhood, but now that he'd accomplished everything he'd planned, all he felt was empty.

Why Loni? The question had haunted his every waking moment for the past month—ever since the doctor here in Crystal Falls, Oregon, had first uttered the word *leukemia* and referred Loni to specialists at the Knight Cancer Institute in Portland. How was it fair that Loni had been the one stricken with such a serious illness? Quincy's brother Clint worshiped the ground she walked on. She had two children who needed her. By comparison, no one really depended on him.

Quincy blinked away tears and forced his feet to move again. Loni wasn't going to die, damn it. She was young, and up until two months ago, when she'd sickened with what everyone thought was the flu, she'd been the picture of health. There were surely treatments available for whatever kind of leukemia she had. Nearly every day, people were either cured or put into remission. It was silly of him to be thinking such gloomy thoughts. And he sure as hell didn't have time for them. Everyone else in the family except his sister Sam, who had volunteered to care for Clint and Loni's kids, was in Portland to lend their support, and while it was Quincy's turn to stay here, looking after all six ranches, he had to make sure everything ran smoothly. It was a hell of a job for one man, but both Parker and Zach had been trading off with him, and he hadn't yet heard either of them complain. He wouldn't, either.

Halfway to the arena, Quincy stopped to take a swig of coffee, hoping the hot slide of liquid would lessen the ache in his chest. Fat chance. He couldn't think of Loni without struggling to breathe. When had he come to love her like a sister? At first, just being around her had given him the willies. A bona fide clairvoyant who worked closely with the FBI to locate missing children, Loni could get flashes of a person's past, present, or future by a mere touch of hands.

Like most men, Quincy had a private life, and there were certain aspects of it that he preferred not to share with anyone. It had bothered him to think that Loni might see him with a woman in an X-rated moment.

Now, after coming to know Loni, Quincy realized that whatever she saw when they made physical contact was immediately buried deep within her. She had no desire to inflict harm or embarrassment with her gift of second sight. Over time, Quincy had stopped worrying about that. If Loni had ever seen him during an intensely private moment, she'd never let on, and he'd finally come to trust that she would never breathe a word of it to anyone, not even to Clint. After that, growing to love her hadn't been a big jump for him.

Now it was a done deal. He could almost see her, big blue eyes dominating a heart-shaped face framed by a wealth of dark, glossy hair. *Pretty*. But, more important, she was every bit as sweet and dear as she appeared to be. No wonder Clint suddenly looked as if he'd been run over by a semi truck, his burnished face tinted with undertones of gray, his brown eyes, so like Quincy's own, filled with inexpressible worry and pain. Clint adored his children, but it was Loni who was the true center of his life. Without her, how would he go on? Just thinking about it made Quincy's stomach roil.

Though March had finally arrived, the air was so cold it burned Quincy's lungs when he drew a deep breath. He wished he'd thought to grab his lined Levi's jacket before leaving the house. Icy fingers curled over his shirt collar and sent a chill crawling down his spine. From the holding sheds, he heard equines neighing and grunting, their way of calling for breakfast. The sound helped to center him and clear his head. He had animals counting on him, and he'd best kick it into high gear.

Just as Quincy reached the berm of snow that had collected over the winter under the eaves of the arena, his cell phone emitted the sound of a horse whinnying, a tone reserved only for members of his family. As he jerked the device from his belt, he half expected to see his dad's name on the screen. Frank had rented a hotel suite near the cancer institute, and he and his wife had been at Clint's side ever since Loni had been admitted there. Always an early riser, Frank often buzzed Quincy to give him an update before the sun came up.

Quincy's pulse stuttered when he saw that the caller was Clint. "Hey, Clint," he said. "How is she?"

Silence. Then Clint's voice came over the air, wobbly and hoarse. "It's bad, Quincy. Real bad. I just talked with the team of specialists taking care of Loni."

Quincy had never heard Clint sound so shaken. "At this hour?" It was all Quincy could think to say—a futile attempt to sound normal when his brother's world might be tipping off its axis. "I thought only ranchers were crazy enough to start work this early."

"They're busy men, and a lot of lives are in their hands." Clint swallowed. The sound came through to Quincy, a hollow plunk that painted a picture he didn't want to see. "Loni has acute myelogenous leukemia, a very aggressive strain that's often unresponsive to treatment. The doctors say they told me the name of it a while back, but apparently it went in one ear and out the other."

Quincy wanted to ask Clint more questions, but he sensed that his brother needed to get this said without interruption.

"Now they've finally determined her AML subtype. I guess they had a devil of a time doing that—something about the AML morphology under a microscope not matching up quite right with any other cancers they've seen."

"What're you saying, Clint—that she's got one-of-a-kind leukemia?"

"Something like that. By now the doctors would be willing to settle for a close match just to begin treatment. Problem is, she's so far gone it's way too late for remission induction therapy. Her platelet counts are too low for her to undergo chemo or a bone marrow transplant."

"Whoa." Quincy stepped over the pile of snow to lean a

shoulder against the eastern exterior wall of the arena. Quelling rising panic, he managed, "If she's too sick for either of those, what kind of treatment can they give her?"

Quincy's blood ran as cold as the crystallized air when he heard Clint sob. He could not recall ever having seen or heard his oldest brother cry as an adult. "Nothing," Clint said brokenly. "There's . . . nothing . . . they . . . can do. At best, they give her . . . a week or two . . . but it'll be a miracle if she holds on that long."

The mug of coffee slipped from Quincy's hand. He flinched as hot liquid slopped onto his pant leg. His brain told him to pull the drenched denim away from his skin, but he couldn't get the message to his hands. He stared stupidly at the spray of brown on the snow. None of this was happening. It couldn't be. Fury at what he was unable to control shot through him in a painful rush. Words blasted out of him.

"Then we need to get her to another center! The Mayo Clinic, maybe. Samantha's brother-in-law, Rafe Kendrick, is standing by to fly her anyplace you name. In his jet, she'll have all the comforts of home. We can't just let her—" Quincy couldn't finish the sentence. "There are all kinds of treatments. Somebody, somewhere, can do something! A really good team of doctors can put her into remission. I know it."

"She already has a really good team of doctors, some of the best." For several seconds, Clint rasped for breath. The sound reminded Quincy of the story he'd once read to his little sister, Sam, about a tiny train that huffed and puffed to get up a steep grade. "It's not their fault she has some weird subtype they've never seen! And it's . . . too . . . late to take her somewhere else. She . . . could . . . die during a long flight. This is my . . . fault, Quincy, all mine. I screwed around, thinking she had a bad case of flu. Jesus, help me. I . . . should . . . have realized! If I'd gotten her up here sooner, they might have been . . . able . . . to . . . save her. Now all they can do is give her transfusions . . . and . . . IV fluids. That helps, but it's a short-term fix, and now she's getting so dehydrated, they have to poke her and poke her to . . . even . . . find . . . a vein."

Quincy hauled in a ragged breath and squeezed his eyes shut. *Focus,* he ordered himself. His brother needed him to say all the right things, and his mind had gone as blank as a crashed computer screen. "Clint, no matter what happens, this isn't your fault. You took her in to see competent doctors here. They just didn't realize what they were dealing with at first, and we lost precious time. If you're sure she's in the best hands available, then we just have to trust in the team up there and pray like crazy that she takes a sudden turn for the good."

"I'm fresh out of prayers." Clint sniffed, and Quincy heard a muffled sound like cloth brushing the cell phone. He could almost see his brother wiping his nose with his shirtsleeve. "The worst part is that she's begging to go home."

To die, was Quincy's first thought.

Clint blew that theory all to hell by saying, "She's convinced she isn't dying. She says she had a vision and saw our third child, a little boy we'll name Francis Wayne after Dad. I can tell she believes it, clear to the bottom of her heart. She thinks she's going to get well and have another child." A brief moment of quiet came over the air. Then Clint added, "You know how, when I first met Loni, I discounted her visions as a bunch of hocus-pocus crap, but she made a believer out of me? I've never doubted her visions since— until now."

Quincy felt tears trickling down his cheeks and turning to ice where they gathered at the corners of his mouth. "What she sees in her visions is never wrong. Hell, even the FBI acts as if everything she tells them comes straight from the Holy Grail."

"Exactly," Clint said, his voice pitched barely above a whisper, "and now I'm doubting what she tells me. Five specialists out in the hall, telling me she's dying. Her looking like a corpse already and spinning dreams I know can't happen—" He broke off. "She's dying, Quincy. I see the signs. No matter what she saw in her vision, I'm going . . . to . . . lose her. And God help me, I don't know how I'll survive it."

Quincy tried to gather his wits. This was new ground for him. As the oldest, Clint had always been the one who held everything together, the one who spoke while everyone else listened. Quincy knew Loni's divinations hadn't been wrong yet, but there could always be a first time. Loni had never been able to see her own future, only those of others. Wasn't it possible that she had indeed seen a third child, named after their father, Frank, but the little boy wouldn't be born to Loni? Maybe in the future, Clint would start over with a second wife, and she would be the one to present him with another son.

The very thought of Clint with some other woman made Quincy want to puke. *No.* It just couldn't happen. Clint was loyal to the bone. He'd never love anyone but Loni.

"You wanna hear the worst part?" Clint asked. "She's clinging to life by a thread, and that vision of a third child is her only hope. What if she looks into my eyes and sees I'm not convinced, that I believe the doctors and not her?"

Quincy had no clue how to respond. His mind kicked into autopilot. *Get there.* He had to help his brother. "I'll book a charter flight. I can be there with you in three hours."

"No. As great as it'd be to see you, I'm honoring Loni's wishes and taking her home this morning. We'll be there by late afternoon. Dad and Dee Dee flew out last night and are at their place now, probably sleeping off the red-eye flight. Parker and Rainie just left for the airport. Zach and Mandy are staying with me to provide moral support, and they'll fly back with me and Loni on the charter jet."

"But, Clint, you need me right now."

"What I need is for you to be *there* looking after my place. If I come home to a disaster in my stable, I'll lose it, I swear to God. I'm counting on you."

Quincy nodded. "You got it, bro. Everything at your ranch is running like clockwork, and I'll see that it stays that way. If need be, I'll call Dad for help."

"Good. I'll see you tonight?"

"Yeah, I'll mosey over when I wrap it up for the day."

Quincy ended the call and stared blankly at his iPhone, a recent purchase that did everything but tap-dance. Too bad it couldn't also perform a miracle and save the life of his sister-in-law. As he slowly became aware of his surroundings again, he realized that making his feet move took a gargantuan effort. With only determination fueling him, he strode toward the north end of the arena to enter by the personnel door.

If anything on earth soothed Quincy, it was being in the arena-cum-stable at the break of dawn before any of his employees arrived to disturb the quiet. He loved the smells that were synonymous with horses—freshly turned straw, molasses-coated grain, hay waiting to be forked, and manure. The fabulous aroma of frying bacon from his forewoman Pauline's upstairs viewing-room apartment added to the bouquet. Though Quincy no longer ate bacon, he still appreciated the scent.

As was his habit, he made his rounds, visiting every mare and stallion to make sure all was well before ending his tour at Beethoven's stall. The stud was Quincy's special baby, and for reasons he'd never clearly defined, he always lingered with him the longest, finding a sense of peace that seemed to elude him everywhere else. Beethoven, a gorgeous black, nickered in greeting and stepped over for his morning ration of petting. The horse was such a love bug that Quincy often joked that Beethoven would morph into a lapdog if he could. The huge beast laid his massive head on Quincy's shoulder, chuffing and rubbing cheeks, a show of affection that always dislodged Quincy's black Stetson. Prepared, Quincy caught the hat before it hit the ground.

"Hey, buddy," he whispered around the logjam in his throat. "I hope your morning is off to a better start than mine."

Beethoven grunted, a contented sound that told Quincy the horse was as happy as a mouse in a cheese factory. He smiled and scanned the stall, checking to make sure all was as it should be. His gaze slid over the far left corner and then jerked back to a lump of green that didn't belong there. He stared for a moment at what appeared to be a woman asleep in the straw. *What the hell?* Surely it was only a trick of the light. His ranch was armed to the teeth with high-tech security, and that was especially true in the arena, with every door, window, skylight, and paddock gate wired to an alarm. If anyone entered without punching in the pass code, which was changed frequently, a siren went off loudly enough to burst eardrums. Quincy had heard nothing.

And yet—well, shit—there *was* a woman curled up in the corner. She wore a getup that reminded Quincy of something he might see at a Renaissance fair. Wrapped around her head was a thick multilayered band of antique linen that was then secured over the crown by a see-through scarf of the same color. The linen band appeared to be of high quality and looked to Quincy like the oil filter on his truck. The transparent scarf shimmered like spun gold and was somehow pleated at the crown and looped loosely beneath the woman's chin. Her hair, a bright, fiery red, followed the slender bend of her back and was surely long enough to reach well below her knees when she was standing. Her silk gown, a deep green and floor-length, judging by the way the skirt billowed around her, sported voluminous sleeves and a plunging, square neckline, which revealed a modest white underdress laced to the waist.

As if she sensed his gaze on her, she jerked awake and, hampered by the long dress, struggled to her feet. To Quincy's amazement, Beethoven merely whickered and circled away. Normally the stallion grew nervous when he was approached by anyone except Quincy.

"God's teeth!" As round as dimes and as clear blue as a Caribbean lagoon on a hot summer day, her eyes flashed with irritation. "Ye scared the bee-Jesus out of me."

Quincy recognized an Irish brogue when he heard one. His dad's mother, Mariah Eileen O'Grady, had been born in the old country. But as Quincy recalled, she'd never said *bejesus* as two separate words or used the expression *God's teeth.* "How did you get in here?" he demanded, doing his best not to notice those expressive eyes or the delicate perfection of her oval face. "The whole place is wired."

Bewilderment creased her brow. She cast a wary glance around the stall. "Where might it be?"

"What?"

"The wire," she expounded. "I see none."

Quincy clenched his teeth. If not for the weird getup, she might have been quite a looker, with that bright red hair, creamy skin, and stunning blue eyes, but Quincy was in no mood to appreciate a woman's feminine attributes. Well, scratch that. Truly beautiful women were difficult for any man to ignore, but he meant to give it his best shot.

"I asked you a question. Answer me." The perimeters of Quincy's ranch could be breached by deer or elk that sailed over the fences, but the warning alarms went off if the cameras detected large body masses that lingered near the property lines, the idea being that any human would take at least a few seconds to scale a five-foot barrier. Voice strained with anger, not to mention worry over his sister-in-law, he repeated the question. "How did you get in my arena?"

"Is that what ye call it, an arena?" Her frown deepened. She swatted at the straw on her wrinkled skirts. As she bent forward, Quincy's gaze shot to the slender nip of her waist and the temptingly round flare of her hips. When he realized where he was staring, he forced himself to look up, only to find his attention riveted to her silk bodice, which showcased small but perfectly shaped breasts. "'Tis so different here."

Losing patience, Quincy raised his voice. "I'll ask you one more time before I call the police. How did you get in here?"

"The police? 'Tis a word I've never heard."

Quincy had an unholy urge to vault over the stall gate and shake her until her teeth rattled. "Listen, lady, you're in serious trouble. Committing a B and E is a felony offense in

Oregon, with a sentence of five to twenty. Start talking, and fast, or you'll be cooling your jets in a cell until you have gray hair."

She paled and lifted her chin, which sported a deep cleft that mirrored the dimple that flashed in her right cheek when she spoke. "I do not understand all yer strange words. Me name is Ceara O'Ceallaigh. I seek audience with a man named Quincy O'Hourigan, sir. I shall speak with him, and only him. 'Tis not a tale for the ears of another."

"You have the first name right, but my last name isn't O'Hourigan."

She winced, flapped her wrist, and muttered something in what sounded like Gaelic. Her quaint mannerisms drove home to Quincy that she was not only beautiful, but also as cute as a button. "Harrigan, I mean. 'Tis forgetful I am. Me whole long life, I've heard naught but the name O'Hourigan and learned of the change to Harrigan only a short while ago. When your ancestors sailed to this land in the eighteen hundreds, they changed the family surname." Her brilliant blue gaze sought his. "So you are Sir Quincy?"

"No *sir* attached."

Quincy pressed the phone icon on his cell. His favorites popped up on the screen, and he was about to tap 911 when she said, "Ye asked how I got in here. My reply may ring strange to yer ears. 'Tis simply where I landed. I can tell ye no more. I prayed to the Blessed Ones to bring me to a place where I might encounter ye, and here I am."

Quincy froze with his finger poised over the button he'd entered as a speed dial on his phone for 911. "You prayed to . . . Say what?"

She studied him as if he were an incredibly dense five-year-old. Damn, but those big blue eyes did pack a wallop. What man could look into them without struggling to break visual contact? "'Struth, sir. No lie has passed my lips. 'Tis where the Blessed Ones dropped me." She trailed her gaze over his face. "I suspected you were Sir Quincy. You bear a striking resemblance to the man I saw in me mum's crystal ball."

Quincy cocked his head, certain that he must have misheard her. "Come again?"

"Please, sir, do not ask that of me. 'Twas a difficult journey, and I've no yearning to endure it twice." She smiled slightly, and with the gentle curve of her lips, her entire face seemed to glow. "Traveling forward in time is taxing."